PRISCILLA

Carlton C. Clarke

RoseDog Books
PITTSBURGH, PENNSYLVANIA 15238

RoseDog Books
585 Alpha Drive, Suite 103
Pittsburgh, PA 15238
Visit our website at *www.rosedogbookstore.com*

ISBN: 978-1-6442-6832-2
eISBN: 978-1-6442-6855-1

CHAPTER ONE

There is that almost audible silence that exists when the work stops and the last person has left for the day. With eye glasses resting on open files, e-mails, and other correspondence waiting to be read and the blinking green eyes of monitors sleeping, the Operations Department, like most any other department, in most any other company, in most any other city adopts the appearance of a ghost town. To Case, this time is akin to a second shift. Now, after everyone has gone, he can relax in his world. He can expand his mind and concentrate on his own matters without distraction. When your world is your work, this is the time that you seek. Then she walked past his office.

Priscilla. The name did not suit her. Try as he might, he could not get used to calling her Priscilla. He thought her name should be Simone, or Nicole, or Natasha. Yeah, Natasha would be a good name for her. An aristocratic Russian. It seemed to fit. Case pictured her in a matching coat and hat made of black sable, standing in the middle of Red Square in Moscow waiting for him; her thick, gray hair against the dark, luxurious fur. Natasha. In his mind, that would certainly be better than Priscilla.

It has been six weeks since she started working for the bank. From the first day he saw her, he was intrigued. At first, he thought it might be the hair. Thick, full, shoulder length, gray hair. In its own way, it was stunning. She seemed to be too young to have her hair turn completely gray. But after a while, he dismissed that thought. The color suited her, but that was not it. There was more to this woman than her hair color.

He became aware of her a few days after she was assigned to his department. He watched her as she performed one of the more mundane tasks that are usually given to the temp. There was a light in her eye when the task was assigned. She seemed to take the task more as a challenge. Priscilla didn't just do the job, she owned the job. And when it was done, it was more than right. It was perfect. Case wondered was she like that with everything? What was she like when she was not working, when she was doing something fun? What was she like in bed? Who owned who then?

Secure in his office, John "Jack" Case allowed himself to think like one of the guys. He spoke loudly inside his head and then let the questions bounce off the walls and come back to him. In his mind, that was okay as long as he kept those thoughts to himself. As much as he would have liked to have the answers to those questions (actually, the real treat was the process of getting to the answers), Case kept his distance. He had been down that road before, and experience is a hard and very effective teacher.

He held the sight of her in his mind long after she was out of view. That someone other than him was in the office surprised him. That the person was her pleased him. He held the image of her in his mind because he wanted it to be there. What was she doing there? Would she pass by again? Maybe I should go out and speak with her? Maybe not. Supposed she wants me to? Even the most disciplined can be tempted as common sense fought against a spontaneous thrill. Case turned his back to the door, stared at the ceiling, and became so lost in his thoughts that he did not notice her approach. Her image reflected in the window drew his attention. He turned to see her framed by the doorway.

"Welcome back. May I come in?" Without waiting for an answer, she stepped into his office and sat down in the armchair directly in front of him. She leaned back in the chair, crossed her legs, and looked directly at him. Her posture could have been construed as either inviting or daring. The expression on her face left little doubt that how you construed it is up to you. A confident woman is very attractive to most men. Case was no exception.

Priscilla was dressed in a black silk blouse, which was the perfect canvas for her hair, and a compliment to her oxford gray wool skirt. Both the skirt and the blouse seemed to amplify all of the curves of her well-proportioned body without looking tight. To Case's eye, that was the sign of custom-made clothes. The stockings that she wore had a slight sheen to them. This only enhanced the shapeliness of her legs and gave an exotic look to a rather conservative outfit. Her shoes were simple, heeled, black pumps with red soles. While there was no way to tell, one could safely assume that her shoes were as expensive as the rest of her clothes. Priscilla stared him straight in the eye.

"What were you thinking about?"

"You're working late tonight. While we do need the help, I do not see the need for you to put in overtime." Case was being insincere, and he did not like it. That was the part of being a manager that he had trouble with. It did not suit his temperament to be a phony. He was glad she was working late. He was glad to have her in his office, alone, after everyone had gone. He wished he could have just said that, but he knew the reasons why he could not, and he did not.

Priscilla crossed her hands in her lap as her lips formed an enigmatic smile.

"Actually, I am here on my own time. I signed out at five, so there is no need to worry about my hours. But I really do not think my overtime was on your mind when I passed by."

"Why do you say that?"

"Because I have been watching you in the same way that you have been watching me." Priscilla arched an eyebrow.

"And please don't deny it. I have been aware of you ever since my first day here."

Case smiled back at her. He found her candor to be refreshing.

"Are you always this direct?"

Her gaze was as direct as her answer.

"Yes."

Instead of leaning back in his chair as most men would do in this situation (a sign of a puffed up ego), Case leaned forward, resting his elbows on his desk. Her candor was addictive and refreshing. Her response touched a part of him

3

that Case did not know could still be touched. The spontaneous thrill won out. Case decided to meet her candor with some of his own.

"I was wondering two things about you."

His body English was not lost on Priscilla. She made a note of it to herself but did not move.

"Really? What are they?" Her sly smile was challenging.

"Your name, I do not think it suits you."

"I get that a lot. Tell me, what would you change it to?" She shifted in the chair and leaned forward attentively.

It struck Case that it would not be hard to imagine what she might look like first thing in the morning.

"My choice would be Natasha." Her ease put him at ease. With that secret thought now out in the open, Case relaxed.

She laughed with her eyes.

"Natasha? I like that. I am glad you didn't say Simone or Nicole. Those are the names that most guys pick for me. I do not particularly like either one of them." Silently, Case thanked his good fortune.

"Now what was the second thing?" Her stare became more intense.

"Direct again?"

"Life is too short."

Case fidgeted with a paper clip as he considered the ground he was about to walk on. He could have shut this down, but he didn't. Now he can't. Was the thrill of taking a chance with this woman worth the downside risk of where this might go? What was on his mind would be dangerous to reveal. If he took the dare and said what he was thinking, what would she do? Would she report him to Human Resources? Or would she blab this encounter all over the office? There was this look in her eye, a mischievous look that was goading him. He did not know her. Was it worth taking the dare? In a flash, common sense kicked in with a thought that allowed Case a safe exit.

"I was thinking that your style of dress does not match the name Priscilla. A woman with that name wears sensible shoes and clothes that do not appear to be as expensive as yours. You do not fit that image."

"You forgot one thing." There was a twinkle in her eye that Case found infectious.

"What would that be?" Case saw his exit being blocked.

"It's my experience that most men think that a woman named Priscilla wears what they call grannie panties." The smile on her face could only be described as toxic.

Case dropped the corners of his mouth.

"I suppose." This was going too far and Case knew it.

"Well, the shoe part is fairly obvious. And as far as my style of dress is concerned, I'm not like everyone else, so why should I dress like everyone else? But aren't you just a little bit curious about the last part?"

Case felt like he was in the ring and being boxed into a corner. The only option would be to throw a punch and dance out.

"I'd be lying if I said I wasn't, but this conversation has gone a bit too far already."

"I disagree." Priscilla arched her left eyebrow, rose to her feet, unzipped her skirt, and let it fall to the floor. She then slowly turned and then gave him a full 360-degree view of her black silk lingerie.

Case maintained a neutral expression, although inwardly he enjoyed the sight that was presented to him. He knew he was walking a fine line. He was not so much concerned about someone walking in on them as he was about where this would eventually lead.

Priscilla placed her hands on her hips.

"I like this game. But I think there is something else that you are wondering about. It is something all men are interested in but are either too scared or too gentlemanly to ask about." Priscilla pondered the man before her and made a judgement. I don't think you are afraid of much, so my guess is that you are too much of a gentleman to ask. So, let me take one little bit of mystery out of your life."

As she moved the papers on his desk, Case was mesmerized by this woman who, so confidently, walked into his office and presented herself to him. All of his senses told him that he was dealing with someone who was determined to have her way, so let it play out. But the questions were exploding in his mind. Did he give her some sign, some indication that this is what he wanted? How far would this go? How far would he let this go? The questions were entertaining. The thought of making love to her right here, right now, popped into his mind. And just as quickly, he dismissed the thought and the questions. There is that old saying, "That when something is too easy, it is never good." He had been down that road as well and it did not end well.

She turned her back to him and spoke to him over her shoulder.

"Close your eyes."

Case was too old for kid games and kept his eyes open.

In one motion, she removed the thin panty, revealing a completely bare vagina. She slid onto the desk and spread her legs wide, resting the soles of her shoes on the arms of his chair. He could smell the scent of her as it lured him in. But he held fast. Discipline. He knew exactly where he would be without it.

"Thanks for clearing that up, but it was never a question in my mind." Again, he kept his expression neutral.

"Really?" It was his lack of a reaction more than his response that shocked her.

"Yes."

Priscilla looked upon him as one would a worthy adversary.

"It appears what they say about you is true." He watched her bend effortlessly to get dressed. Just as she zipped up her skirt, the Mexican cleaning crew entered the floor.

"And just what is it that has been said?" He already knew some of the things that had been said about him, but with her, he was curious.

Priscilla's laugh was light.

"Silly, I can't tell you that. They would never speak to me again. Besides, I think you already know." Instead of standing by the desk or heading for the door, Priscilla reclaimed her seat and crossed her gorgeous legs once again.

"So, where do we go from here?"

Case stared at her for a long minute to give the impression that he was actually thinking about what she said. He had taken this thing further than he should have. That nothing happened and neither of them had cause to be embarrassed or feel humiliated was a sign that it had gone far enough. Case exhaled a small sigh of relief.

"Well, I'm leaving." He straightened the papers on his desk back into their neat piles, then went through the log off motions while she remained seated. She did not rise from her seat until he turned off the light in the office. Holding the door for her, he spoke in a tone that was soft but authoritative.

"I will see you tomorrow."

In the darkness, Priscilla thought about being the aggressor. It would not have been the first time. But instead she let the thought pass and stepped out of the office before him, giving him a sly, over the shoulder, look.

"Oh, I think you will see me sooner than that." She walked away with a slow, smooth motion that has been the buzz of the office ever since she was hired. Case waited for the elevator to close on her and then he took the stairs.

In her car, Priscilla gripped the wheel and let the excitement of the encounter wash over her. She took a moment to reflect on what she had accomplished. She fired the first salvo, and while she did not score a hit, she got a pretty good look at his defenses.

"Impressive." It seemed like he might be the exception to the rule, the one out of ten, the man who did not follow convention. But she needed to know more. Priscilla smiled and welcomed the excitement that she felt in the pit of her stomach.

Case chastised himself during the ride from the office. Why did he go there? What was the purpose of that? Surely you know better, Case. What are you trying to prove? He peppered himself with all of the right reasons why he should not have given in to some baser instincts. But then there was the satisfaction of taking her to the limit. Calling her bluff. He had not felt that in quite a while. And then there were her last words.

"You will see me sooner than that." She did not seem like the type to say something just for the hell of it. Would there be a note on his car tomorrow or an e-mail with pictures attached? Would this happen again? He stopped himself before his imagination got the better of him. But the thought still nagged at him. What did she mean by, "…you will see me sooner than that?" Case started his car and made a smooth turn out of the parking lot. He was again intrigued. And that seemed to explain it all.

•   •   •   •   •

Monday night was work out night. The gym was its usual two-hour affair of grunting and groaning, lifting and pulling, breathing and sweating. Case went through his routine with practiced efficiency. This is where he left the office and all of the problems that came with it. That included attractive and aggressive temps who seemed to have appetites bigger than their common sense. Case showered, dressed, and left the gym only to find the infamous head of grey hair, along with her gorgeous legs and the rest of her body, leaning against his car smoking a cigarette. The light from the lamps in the parking lot seemed to give her hair a particular glow.

Priscilla took a long drag, then looked at him with the same expression that she had in his office.

"You never did answer my question."

"That's because I didn't know that you and I were a we. How did you find me?" There was no anger in his voice, although he was not pleased at the thought that that she probably followed him.

Priscilla took one last drag, then crushed the butt under her shoe. Case found the motion of her foot erotic.

"I told you earlier. You interest me." She moved closer to him.

"I knew this is where you went after work long before today. Besides, I know a few more things about you. Some good, some are… well, let's not say what they are. Does that scare you?" The sly smile returned as she placed the palm of her hand on his chest.

"Um, nice."

He looked at her hand on his chest, then into her eyes.

"No, it does not scare me. Is it supposed to?"

She read his look and removed her hand.

"You know, most men are afraid of me. I find that boring. I am glad that you are not. Oh, and I know that you are not afraid. If you were and just lying about it, I would know. I could feel it."

Priscilla backed away from him. She had gone as far as she cared to go for now.

"Now it's my turn to say, 'I will see you tomorrow.' And if I see you sooner than that, believe me, I will make it worth your while." She touched his face with her right hand and walked away. He stood there to see where she was parked, then watched as she peeled out of the parking lot. After what seemed to be a very long time, Case nodded his head and took a different way home.

With the top down on her Corvette, Priscilla let the night air wash over her as she sped home. She made her move, and now the game, her game, her favorite past time, is on. Smiling, she felt the rush of excitement that always came with the chase. How would he react when she decided it was time to close the trap? Would he be like the rest and take her? Or would she have to take him? How long would it take? What would she have to do? Priscilla laughed out loud at the last question. That's what made it fun. What would she do if she were he? What would he make her do? She had done quite a few things in her life. Some were a hell of lot worse than others. And the worst of the lot was pretty bad. There is not much that she would not do. But he didn't know that. Or did he? That thought brought a smile to her face.

Darkness was just settling in on Mt. Airy Road. Priscilla took a left on Beekman Lane, slowing down as she passed the Judge's house. Twice he complained to the local police about the sound of her car. As a show of his clout, for the next few nights after each of the complaints, there was an officer stationed just inside the block to clock her speed. It had crossed her mind to purposely push the issue and take the matter up in court as harassment, but instead, she decided to be the only homeowner in the private community not to contribute to the local PBA fund.

Up the driveway, push a button, into the garage. Automatic sensors turned on the lights as she went from room to room. Five thousand square feet is more house than one person will ever need, but if anyone cared about it, that was their business. She certainly did not.

Priscilla was excited from both encounters. She could not wait to get undressed and left a trail of clothes from the garage to the bedroom. With the rush still fresh in the pit of her stomach, she wanted to be naked. She stood bare before the mirror and relived the moment in the office. Priscilla looked at the area between her legs and laughed to her self.

"So, it was never a question, Mr. Case? I don't believe you. I think you were holding back." In her mind, she was back in the office, seated on his desk with her legs spread, inviting him in. She saw his eyes on her. She felt his strength. Priscilla was glad he did not take her there. In fact, she would have been surprised at him if he did. He did not seem like that type, which is the reason why she chose him.

"So now we will see, Mr. Case, who you really are."

CHAPTER TWO

The morning light shining on his black 1997 Porsche 911 Carrera Turbo brought back memories of the night before. Case half expected to find her there when he walked out the door of his apartment building. During the ride home last night, Case dismissed what had happened as the actions of someone looking for one last thrill. A woman who is old enough to know exactly what she wants and young enough to go for it. And, in the process, not really giving a damn what anyone thinks because she is long past worrying about that. But given all of that, Case was still concerned by the chance that she took. But he was content with himself at how he handled it.

Last night, he felt pretty good about his show of discipline, but he could not help but wonder what it would have been like to have her, just once. What would he do if there was a repeat performance? Suppose she did not take no for an answer? Case pushed the thoughts out of his mind. There would be no encores. Last night was one of a kind. He was intrigued, and what happened last night heightened that sense, but it was best to leave it there. She started it. He ended it. Discipline. Keep everything in its proper place.

Case started his car and listened to the engine note. He liked the sound that it made. Case watched the pictures flash in his mind. It had been a long time for him. Longer than Case cared to admit. Sitting still in his car, listening to the engine purr, was like going back in time. He bought Porsche while stationed in Europe. It was a present to himself with the bonus that he received for completing a particularly difficult assignment. On the day that Case took delivery of the car, he met... Case stopped himself. The episode with Priscilla opened a box that he preferred remain shut. Case put the car in gear and went to work.

Franklin Valley Savings & Loan is one of many regional banks located in New Jersey. With slightly over one billion dollars in total assets, it is positioned just about in the middle of the regional banking community. It's main branch and corporate offices are located in an office park just off of Route One in West Windsor, New Jersey. The modern, glass dominated construction of the structure allowed it to blend seamlessly with the trees and well-maintained grass in the surrounding area. At four stories, it is one of the tallest buildings in the area. Adding to the sense of calm was a man-made lake that attracted more than its share of geese and ducks.

Case pulled into the spot marked Operations V.P., secured his car, and then out of habit more than anything else, checked his perimeter and the roofline of the building. Satisfied that all appeared to be as it should be, he entered the building.

The Operations Department is one of four departments that comprise Franklin Valley Savings & Loan. Operations is responsible for bank security, physical plant, and any hard copy records that need to be maintained. With a total of ten employees, it is not the biggest of the bank's functional sections, but it is just as important.

Case did not start out as the manager of the department. Hired as a supervisor in the security unit, Case outlasted a number of managers who took particular exception to his independent ways and his unwillingness to kiss rings, asses, and anything else that required kissing in order to get ahead. When he was promoted to Vice President, Case gave a nod to the rare occasion where competence and integrity trumped politics and nepotism.

When he arrived at his department on the third floor, Case found himself looking for Priscilla. He stopped, froze, and focused on his own office door. He could not allow her into his life. When he walked past her desk and did not see her there, he relaxed. He took her absence as good fortune. Seated at his desk, he could not prevent himself from revisiting the scene from the night before. He sat back in his chair, steepled his fingers, and saw her before him, naked between her waist and her knees. Case stopped his train of thought in the middle of what might have happened. Again, he reminded himself to keep everything in its place. Now was not the time or the place. Perhaps later he might revisit those thoughts but not now. There was work to do.

Not long into the day, Skip Hunter (his first name really was Skip), the Manager of the Commercial Banking Division, made his presence known on the floor.

A good bit over six feet, and tennis trim, most of the birthday pools placed Skip in his mid to late 30's. He never challenged them. Skip's long suit is looks and charm. He parlayed a Rutger's MBA into a management position at the bank. Despite his education, Skip did not waste a lot of time on technical issues. His theory is that he would always be able to get someone else to take up that slack. That someone else would invariably be a woman or some hapless junior nobody who believed his bullshit. In Skip's world, there was no need to do the heavy lifting when there was someone else to do it.

A wife and three kids notwithstanding, any woman, all women were fair game as far as Skip was concerned. When the harassment claims were made, his looks and his charm usually got him off the hook. And when that didn't work, he relied on his secondary skills of negotiating a cash settlement with his accuser, using the banks money, of course.

But the creation of Skip Hunter did not come into existence on its own. There were many a woman who were drawn to him like moths to a flame. For any one of a number of reasons, they thought they would be different with him, that it would be different with him. They thought that they would be the one to change him or that he would not be that way with them. Even though they knew what to expect, they still went. Willingly. And just like the many that came before them, and as night follows day, they got hurt.

Skip called out names as he made his way through the maze of cubicles and file cabinets. No female was immune. None were overlooked. Touching, smiling, it was as if he was the incumbent Mayor of Women Town, up for reelection. There were some who took his attention as a sign of some sort of intimacy between him and her. They reveled in it, exchanging knowing looks with one another, then returning to their duties but hardly thinking about what it was they were supposed to be doing. Then there were the others who tried to make a show of not being impressed, and yet would have been angry had they been overlooked.

Case heard his arrival on the floor before he actually saw him. He knew that Skip would eventually make his way to his office, and Case was not looking forward to it. For some reason, Skip wanted the world to believe that they were close friends. Case would have been happy in letting the world continue to believe the truth, that they were simply employees of the bank. He did not particularly want to hear about Skip's latest conquest or current target. Nor did he want to hear about what was happening on the other floors (half of the bank knew that Skip was a notorious gossip, so most of what he was told was disinformation anyway). But Case was a survivor. And the politics of survival sometimes dictate the allegiances that one makes. Skip was connected and on the fast track. There was value there and Case knew it. So, he would endure Skip Hunter and whatever it was he had to say. At least for a little while.

Skip paused at the doorway before stepping inside.

"Lena, lunch, Thursday? Great! You're buying." She thought he was joking. He knew he wasn't. Skip then stepped into Case's office, closing the door behind him.

"Hey, big guy, how do you stand it?!"

Case clearly did not know what Skip was talking about. He leveled Skip with the flat, expressionless look that he was known and hated for. It is a look that says in very plain, blunt terms, "I could not care less about what it is you are trying to tell me." More than once, Case's facial expressions were the subject of negative comments in his fitness reports. More than once, he refused to sign them.

"Her?! Grey hair. Nice body. Great legs. Don't tell me you don't know who I'm talking about!" Skip flopped down in the armchair, exhausted from making his rounds and being frustrated.

"Is she in? I have not seen her all day." After making a less than half-hearted attempt to see Priscilla's desk from behind his own, Case turned back to the computer screen. "She's out there. I'm in here. She does her work and I do mine. Pretty simple. Works fine." The only part of his body that moved was his lips.

Skip got up, looked out onto the floor, then sat back down.

"Man. I tell you, if I ever got the chance to nail that, I would not stop. They would have to shoot me or something, but I am telling you, I would not stop." Skip flashed his famous smile for effect, but the effort was wasted.

Case pictured Skip humping wildly while Priscilla was smoking a cigarette and reading the latest issue of Cosmo. With a huge amount of effort, he stifled a smile. Case countered with a question that he knew would annoy his colleague.

"When are you having lunch with her?"

Skip threw up his hands, jumped out of the seat, and started pacing the office like an expectant father.

"That's the point. I can't get to first base with her. And that name, Priscilla. I hate that name. Her name should be Nicole. Yeah, Nicole. That would be better. What do you think?" Skip was clearly pleased with his own ingenuity.

"I think you should go over there and tell her that." Even though Case could barely contain himself, again, all that moved were his lips.

"It would be a great way to break the ice."

Skip thought about the suggestion for a moment before responding with the smile.

"Not a bad idea, buddy. Turn the name into a conversation piece. Use it to get my foot in the door. I'll give it some thought. Thanks." Skip got up, put his hand on the doorknob, then froze.

"By the way, you heard about the meeting this afternoon, didn't you?"

The comment struck a nerve with Case. The meeting was mandatory, and Skip acted like the option of not attending existed.

"Yes. I'll be there."

Skip opened the door to the office, framing himself in the doorway.

"Great. Let's grab coffee afterwards."

Case saw the play before the ball was snapped. Skip found out what was on the agenda and that there was going to be an issue discussed that he did not understand. Case's job would be to explain it to him.

"Sure. I'll meet you in the dining room right after the meeting." There, show one defense then switch to another. If Skip would be able to find him after the meeting, he would be truly deserving of the name Hunter.

The conference room on the fourth floor of the Savings & Loan building was one of the few places where cost was not a consideration in decorating. The table and matching credenza are highly polished and hand-crafted pieces of furniture made of pecan wood. The chairs are Italian leather and have been known to put many a man to sleep. On the walls are original oils and sculptures rested on pedestals in the corners. Present are all of the pre-requisite electronic wizardry that are standard equipment in this world of instant communication and then there are the hidden tape recorders in the sculpture pedestals. Form and function.

Bill Sharp, Senior Vice President of Franklin Valley Savings & Loan, never gave advance notice of his managers meetings. It was his theory that spur of the moment meetings were the best way to see who was on top of their unit. If you did not have a vacation planned or some business reason for missing a called meeting, you were doomed.

Case stepped off the elevator, greeted the other managers and senior supervisors, then masterfully hid his surprise and anger when he saw Priscilla seated in the corner of the conference room. He did not acknowledge her, nor did he pretend not to see her. He simply took his seat and waited to see how this would play out.

Senior Vice Presidents of banks are not known for their patience. Bill Sharp was no exception. As a former European Station Manager for the Central Intelligence Agency, Bill Sharp did not like surprises. He took notice of the unknown female seated in the corner as he entered the room and made no attempt to hide his displeasure. Before taking his seat, he addressed Priscilla in a tone used by fathers when addressing a petulant child. "Miss, this is to be a closed-door session for managers and senior supervisors only. I believe you are in the wrong meeting."

Pricilla did not flinch.

"No, I think this is the right meeting, Fourth floor conference room, two o'clock?" She met him eye to eye and did not blink.

Clearly annoyed (time is money, and this woman is wasting both), the edge of his tone became keener.

"Miss, I will ask you only one more time to leave. If you do not, I will have security not only remove you, but have you arrested." To punctuate his last point, he moved from the door to the credenza, resting his hand on the phone.

Everyone in the room was on edge as they waited for this one woman to determine the outcome of this action. Priscilla waited for a two count, then slowly rose from her seat.

"Perhaps maybe I am in the wrong meeting." She cast a glance toward Case, who looked back at her with no emotion, save anger. Skip Hunter flashed his signature smile, hoping that she would look his way before she left. She didn't.

Sharp stared at the door for 30 seconds after it was closed.

"Does anyone know that woman?" There was more amazement in the question than anger.

It is Case's belief that the obvious should never be avoided.

"She works for me. I do not know how she found out about the meeting. I did not invite her."

The fact that she worked for Case seemed to diffuse the situation. Sharp relaxed.

"Jack, we'll have a word after this." Case nodded his assent.

"Now, let's get started…"

The formal meeting lasted exactly one hour. The private one afterwards was quite a bit shorter. Bill Sharp recruited Case to work for the bank when Jack's position with the Agency was compromised. Bill Sharp needed someone to watch the things that he could not see. That someone was Jack Case.

"Jack, that woman is trouble. Get rid of her."

Case saw no need to apologize, so he didn't.

"I do not know how she found out about the meeting, Bill. She's just a temp. I'll let her go this afternoon." Case held the door open for his boss as they walked out of the conference room.

At the elevator, Sharp took on a look of regret and second thought.

"Best looking piece of ass we've had here in quite some time." He held the door of the lift open with his foot.

"Listen, no harm, no foul. If you need her, keep her on for a while, but keep an eye on her, Jack." He let the door close as he reached over to push the button for his floor.

Case had seen this 180 pivot by Bill Sharp before, so it did not come as a surprise. Nor was he surprised when he found Priscilla sitting in his office, her mouth formed a thin smile across her face.

"So, am I fired?"

Case did not say a word as he studied the woman seated in his office. What kind of woman pulls a stunt like that. And she has the nerve to sit there smiling at me. As was his practiced habit, Case refrained from saying the first thing that came into his mind. He just took a seat behind his desk and calmed the emotion that was building up inside of him.

Priscilla shifted in her seat and crossed her legs. Normally, there would be yelling and screaming or just a terse, two-word statement like, "Get out." But with this man, there was nothing. He was angry. Of that there was no doubt. She could feel it. And then it struck her that she was about to lose the prize that she worked so hard to capture. This was her game, but she was about to lose it. There did not appear to be any way out of this and that was the vacuum that created the limb that Priscilla was currently sitting on. With a lot less confidence and her smile fading, Priscilla asked her question again.

"Am I fired?"

Case spoke in a soft voice.

"No, but you should be. What the hell was that stunt all about? Who told you about the meeting and what were you doing there?" Case kept his tone even, but he could not hide the anger in his eyes. Had his boss been anyone other than Bill Sharp, it would have been his ass, not hers.

"Your buddy, Skip, told me about the meeting. I thought it would be fun to see you in action. Besides, the grapevine has it that you and Bill are pretty tight, so I didn't think sitting in on the meeting would get you in trouble."

Case, again, thought before he spoke.

"Listen, we need you, and good people are hard to find. If you pull a stunt like that again, you will be fired. Am I clear on that?"

"Yes, Jack. Very clear." Priscilla stood and gave Case a wry smile.

"Well, since I'm still employed, I guess I'll get back to work." Case watched her with a wary eye as she walked out of his office.

Again, he admonished himself.

"I should have fired her anyway. Why didn't I?" Case sat down behind his desk and pondered the thought that Priscilla knew he would not fire her. Case asked himself a question that he knew he could not answer.

Back at her desk, Priscilla felt a rush that was almost too much to bear. In the conference room, she was on her own. Exposed. He did not move to protect her. In the office, there was anger so strong, she could taste it, but there was also control. What would he be like if he were to let go? How far would he go with her? What was he capable of? The questions stoked the flame that was already burning inside her. It would be a good while before she would be able to type, file, or do anything else.

Peggy Finn waited for Priscilla to leave at the end of the day before coming into Case's office.

"We have a problem, boss." Case gave her his patented "What now?" look.

"Carmen called and said that there are complications with her pregnancy, and she will not be coming back. With the new bank card coming out in a few weeks, we are going to need some help."

Franklin Valley Savings & Loan is sponsoring a new special edition debit card. The logistics of actually getting the card to account holders, the security of the card, and coordinating the validation of the card all fell to the Operations Department. As the Vice President in charge of Operations, the buck for all of this stopped with Jack Case.

Case anticipated the next question.

"So, you would like to hire Priscilla to a permanent slot?"

Peggy liked the fact that Case did not waste a lot of time with bullshit. She had worked for a lot of managers, both men and women, who could not order lunch, much less make business decisions. Case was not like that. It was either yes or no, go or stop. Very seldom was there anything in between. It made life simple. But there was one other reason why she was devoted to Case. The other managers that she worked for got rid of her for one petty reason or another. Later, she would find out that they could not contend with her size. Case was the only manager who did not let her 300 pound girth become an issue. And because he accepted her as she was, Peggy now found the strength to change. She has already lost 25 pounds in three weeks.

"You know temps. They come and go as they please. She's a damn good worker and probably over qualified for what we need her to do. On the other hand, I heard about the incident in the conference room, so if you want to let her go, I'll understand."

It never ceased to amaze Case at how fast news travels between floors. Case took about ten seconds to weigh the needs of the many against his own personal issues.

"Contact H.R., let them know what we're doing, then make her an offer at Carmen's salary. I have already spoken with her about the conference room thing. One thing though, document everything that she does, good and bad. If she steps out of line one time, she's history. Clear?"

"Yes, sir." Case watched the massive woman squeeze through the door, dismissing the idea that she looked somewhat slimmer as some sort of clothing illusion. His other more immediate thought was that, like it or not, Priscilla Whittington was no longer a temporary problem.

CHAPTER THREE

Bank security was one of Case's responsibilities. He did not usually order background checks on hourly employees, but Priscilla had proven that she was not the usual clerical. At some point, he would have to document the expense, but for now, he justified the cost within himself that there was a need to have this done. The package that he got from his investigator made for interesting reading.

"Priscilla Marie Whittington. Birth name Weiss; Born October 25th, 1978 in Portland, Oregon. Finished high school in Los Angeles. Attended and graduated from Highpoint College in Northern California with a degree in history. Married twice; First husband, Richard Stone. Second husband, William Whittington. There are no children from either union. Both husbands died violently. Subject was held for questioning in both deaths, but never charged or arrested. Both cases were closed administratively. No children, no family, no dependants.

During the time between college and her first marriage, the Subject travelled throughout Europe. Social media checks are inconclusive with no remarkable posts or notations. Subject has a house with a current appraised value of $900,000. There is no recorded mortgage on the property. There are no liens attached to the property. Subject's credit rating is A plus. Up to date on all payments with none in arrears. Net worth appears to be several million dollars. There are two cars registered to the subject. One is a black Chevrolet Corvette bearing New Jersey license number LQZ 9646; the other vehicle is a red Volvo bearing New Jersey license number TVQ2309. Neither vehicle has any warrants outstanding, nor have there been any liens attached. There is no record of any traffic violations, and there are no loss payees shown. End of report." Case thumbed through the information with interest.

Included in the package were photographs of Priscilla, her house, both of the cars registered to her, copies of her driver's license, car registrations, the deed to her house, a report from TRW, and her college transcript. There was also a profile giving her approximate height and weight, hair color, social security number, credit card numbers, bank account numbers, and telephone numbers. Case spent a lot of time with the photographs of Priscilla. One was a head shot; the other was a full body shot. Both were very flattering. What was interesting was that while she did not seem to be aware of the camera, she did not seem to be unaware of it. In the headshot, her face was turned one way, but her eyes were looking in the opposite direction. It was as if she knew she was being watched.

From his own surveillance days, Case recognized this trait. It is common to entertainers and other "show business" people. They expect to be watched, so they act like they are being watched. It is not paranoia but a different type of vanity. Case looked at the photo from different angles. There was something in the look on her face. Case highlighted the caption reference to the deaths of her husbands, and that she was questioned but not charged, before he returned all of the documents to their envelope. He would want to know more about this. With the exception of the "head shot," he locked the package in the safe in his office. Case continued to study the shot and the subject.

"Interesting." Two husbands. Two unsolved murders. Now a wealthy widow who, for some reason, has me in her sights.

"What is she, some kind of black widow?" Case kept the question to himself. He continued to stare at the photo, half expecting it to answer him. With no answer forthcoming, Case put the photo in his desk drawer.

Priscilla hesitated before accepting the permanent position. She had not been a regular employee anywhere for years. In the end, she realized that it did not change matters much. The job was secondary. She could leave whenever she wanted to. Right now, Case was still the man she wanted. Nothing was going to interfere with that.

She watched him as he walked about the office. Head up, chest out, Priscilla figured Case to be ex-military. Probably an officer, but then again, maybe not. She pictured him in a number of different uniforms (laughing out loud at the sight of him in a sailor's cap and bell-bottom pants) and opted for the Army. She saw him easily as a career soldier, leading men. She watched him in their department staff meetings, organized, prepared, leaving no doubt as to who was in charge, but yet inviting comments and the opinions of the rest of his staff. Always under control.

"How do I get to you, Mr. Case? What will it take to break through that shell?" Priscilla let the thoughts echo in her mind as she watched him walk past her desk and into his office.

The questions were still fresh in Priscilla's mind as she turned into her driveway that night. Once inside the house, she followed her nose to the kitchen where Estrella, her friend and housekeeper, was putting the finishing touches on dinner.

"Huele esta bien. ¿Arroz con pollo?"

"Yes. How was your day?" It was a game that they played. Priscilla would speak to Estrella in Spanish. Estrella would answer in English. It helped them both perfect skills they were trying to master.

Priscilla poured herself a glass of Chardonnay, then went through the day's mail.

"Esta bien."

"How was our Mr. Case today?" There were no secrets between these two women.

Priscilla switched to English.

"He is going to be tough one, Estrella. It's been two months now and no matter what I do, I cannot get through that shell." Not seeing anything of importance in the mail, Priscilla switched her attention to the newspaper lying on the counter. A small article about a third murder victim in as many months caught her attention.

"Did you see this story about the woman they found with her throat cut?"

Estrella ignored the question and took on her friend's burden.

"You look good. You dress nice. You speak good. Maybe he no like women?" Estrella poured some of the wine into the dish cooking on the stove, then began to make the salad.

Priscilla laughed at the thought of Jack Case being gay.

"No, not this one. I am positive of that. Besides, remember the guy from the computer company." They both laughed at the openly homosexual coworker who begged Priscilla to "straighten him out" and would not take no for an answer. When she finally relented and invited him over, he could not perform. The three of them ended up talking the night away and finishing two bottles of wine.

Estrella laughed at the memory.

"Si, I remember him. Maybe Mr. Case is married?"

Priscilla was tired and not in the mood for a question and answer session. She picked up the paper, the mail, and her glass of wine, scanning the article of the vicious murder.

"No, he is not married. I doubt if he ever was. But that would not have anything to do with it anyway. I'm going to change. I'll be down in a bit." Estrella watched her friend leave the kitchen and wondered if she would ever tire of this very dangerous game that she chose to play.

Estrella Bonita Ortega had first-hand knowledge of what can happen when you toy with the wrong man. American or Mexican, it did not matter. A man is a man. In her homeland, she met such a man who she had to have. Looking back, all of the signs were there to stay away from him. But she was young and foolish and unknowing. Had it not been for her friend, she probably would be dead by now from the beatings. But she is not, thanks to her friend, her savior, Priscilla Whittington.

Estrella set the table, opened the wine, then as she lit the candles, said a silent prayer that it would go well for her friend. She would do anything for this woman who saved her from the Devil himself. But the truth is that there was little else that she could do but pray for Priscilla so, at least she did that much.

Priscilla only half listened during dinner as Estrella began to recount the current story line from her favorite tele-novella, as well as all of the things that she was able to accomplish during the day. When she noticed that her employer was no longer listening, Estrella stopped speaking. She was not hurt, as she had seen this before in her friend. When she wanted something or someone, that was all that she could think about.

Case was upper most in Priscilla's thoughts. She found herself wondering where he was, what he was doing, and who he might be with. She went through all of the women in the office who he might be secretly seeing but could not make a match. Priscilla tried to conjure up the type of woman he would like, but then decided that she did not know enough about him to paint that picture.

"What was it that she did know?"

Priscilla went back in time. Two and half months ago, she was bored. Her last conquest was too easily had. The chase left her unfulfilled, and the sex was mediocre. She quit the job soon after she started. It was only after Priscilla threatened to expose the affair to the man's wife did he stop calling her. Frustrated, she began to troll the various office parks in search of a new target.

It was a simple matter for Priscilla to sit in her car and watch the various office workers as they made their way from the parking lot to the building. She concentrated on the men who appeared to be in charge in one way or another. Some were obvious because they parked in spots labeled President or Vice President. For others, she would have to make an assumption by the way they walked or the style of brief case that they carried. But once she identified a man as the one she wanted, Priscilla used what means she could to get close to him.

Her favorite method is to get hired by the company that he worked for. Since most firms hire third party vendors to do their cleaning work, there was no job within the firm that was beneath her. The opinions of her co-workers mattered little to Priscilla. They could think what they want. She was there for a purpose, and whatever they thought of her simply did not matter.

On this particular day, Priscilla was attracted first to the car. Men were her specialty. She knew their likes and dislikes, what they took pride in, and the things that they could not care less about. When Priscilla saw the black Porsche and the pristine condition that it was in, she had a picture of the driver before he stepped out of the car. When Jack Case emerged, Priscilla was convinced that she had found the next prize in the game that she played.

Later that day, she went to the Human Resources department and asked if there were any openings. Priscilla was told that there were no openings available and was referred to the bank's web site. During the conversation, Priscilla noted the name of a temp agency on a desk calendar. Her next stop was to file with the agency. During the application process, Priscilla said that she was referred to the agency by Franklin Valley S&L. She was told by the agency that they would get back to her.

Priscilla used the time to study Jack Case. She followed him to and from work, as well as to the other places he frequented. She studied where he went for lunch, when he did take lunch, and what he ate. From a distance, Priscilla studied the life of John "Jack" Case for the sole purpose of one day having him all to herself.

Priscilla came back to the present. Frustrated, she left her food half-eaten and began to pace the floor. Since that night in his office, he acted like she did not exist. What she did should have been enough. It was with the others but not with him. Priscilla stopped pacing and felt the tension build within her. Then, realizing she would not rest this night, Priscilla picked up her car keys and her bag and left. It was time to make something happen.

The night was overcast. Rain was in the air. A cool fall wind was blowing, creating an eerie, spooky feeling. Priscilla put the top on the Corvette and pulled on a baseball cap that she kept in the pocket behind the passenger seat. She drove with a purpose but kept her speed low. This was not the time to get pulled over by some bored town cop with nothing else to do.

The route to Case's apartment was not new to her. She has been there more than once. Watching to see who came and who went, hoping to see what he did and what he did not do. But tonight would be different. It was time for her to fire another shot. This one would be for effect.

The last traffic light just before the entrance to his complex seemed to take forever to change. When it did, Priscilla felt her heart rate quicken. The thrill of the hunt. A half a mile, then left into the complex, a quarter mile, turn left, take that road to the end. She turned into the last set of apartments, killing her lights before she came to a stop. The black car disappeared in the darkness. In her dark blue sweat suit and black baseball cap, Priscilla looked more like a thief than a widow twice over worth several million dollars. She got out of her car and blended into the shadows created by the trees that separated the buildings. When she got to his building, she stood in the darkness and stared at his windows on the second floor. Just as she was about to make her move, the door opened. Priscilla froze.

It had been one of those "Corporate America" days. Staff conflicts. Professional conflicts. Corporate conflicts. Fault and blame were thrown around in the office like a cafeteria food fight, with some of each landing on everyone. Case went from being a referee, to a target, to an instigator, on any one of number of issues. The day did not come to an end. Jack Case just decided that he had enough and left.

By the time that Case arrived at his apartment, he was edgy. The thought of staying in did not appeal to him, neither did the thought of going to the gym. He needed something that he could not get at home. Something to take his mind off of the problems of today and what he might be faced with tomorrow. He thought about Priscilla, and just as quickly, dismissed that thought. She was more of a problem than a solution and that was not what he needed right now. As he stepped out into the night, out of the corner of his eye, he noticed something in the shadows that did not belong there. Case kept his motion normal, not giving any indication that he noticed whoever it was who was hiding in the shadows.

Priscilla held her breath as she watched him walk to his car. He did not notice her. She exhaled, then cursed her bad luck as he started his car, switched on the headlights, and backed out of the space. She thought of trying to get to her own car to catch up with him, but dressed as she was, if she were caught running, there would be a lot of explaining to do. Besides, if she did catch up to him, what would she say? She would be on the defensive with no advantage. Luck was not with her tonight. She took a wild shot and missed badly.

Case knew what the area around his apartment looked like at any time of the day or night and under any kind of condition, so the only explanation for what he saw was that there was someone standing there. Case thought about turning around to investigate who might have been waiting in the shadows. On the off chance that it just might be Priscilla, he kept going. Case was just not in the mood for a confrontation. Not tonight. If it was not her, then someone was either going to or leaving someplace that they should not have been. To Case's way of thinking, that would classify as none of his business. He started his car, dropped it into gear, headed towards the industrial section of town.

The only change Case made to the Porsche was to upgrade the sound system. The original factory system had a cassette deck and did not have hands free phone capability. Instead of a cheaper aftermarket unit, Case had the dealer install the latest Porsche sound system that came complete with all the bells and whistles. Case kept it simple, slipped a C.D. into the drive, and let Stanley Turrentine's "Don't Mess with Mr. T" begin to take the edge off, but the tension was still there. Tonight, there was something basic that was driving Jack Case. Something that was brought to the surface by the stress of the day and forces he had no control over. It would only be satisfied by forces he did control. Case needed to blow off some steam and he knew just where to go to do that. He paused at the stop sign that guarded the entrance to the complex and then made a smooth right turn into another part of the world.

The music created a mood which caused Case's mind to wander. In another life, he would have come home and his house would have been wrapped in this song. "She" would have greeted him with a kiss and a scotch and his favorite meal. Whatever happened during the day would have been left outside with the rest of the trash. And then, as if someone's cell phone went off at the most exciting part of the movie, Case came back to the present.

"This is not Europe. She is not here or anywhere else for that matter. And you need to move on!" Case pressed the throttle, hoping that the increased speed would force the admonishments into his head.

Priscilla banged her fist on the steering wheel of her car and sat staring at the door to Case's apartment. Her frustration was well beyond tolerable. She was right there, and then just like that, he was gone. She thought about trying to catch up him but quickly dismissed that thought. There were too many things that could go wrong and she would not be any closer to him than she is now. Priscilla scowled as she made a U-turn and headed to the entrance to the complex. She was accustomed to having her way, to getting what she wanted. This was her game and it was not going the way that she wanted it to go. Then, at just that moment, a thought entered her head that changed her scowl to a smile.

"Perhaps I might just have my way after all."

By the time he got to the railroad tracks, the stress of the day was beginning to fade. The music had gone from Stanley Turrentine to Milt Jackson, and now, Lee Morgan. Case took pride in this C.D. Whenever he was tense, it never failed to relax him. He took the turn faster than he normally would. The skid coming just at the apex of the trumpet solo gave him a short rush. Case smiled at the feeling. He was glad he came out.

Two miles down the road that ran parallel to the railroad tracks was McCoy's. At some time in the distant past, the frame structure was a family style restaurant and a haven to the immigrant Hungarians who worked in the warehouses along the rail route. Now food is no longer served, and it has become a haven to a different clientele.

Sometime in the not too distant past, the place was bought by a collection of legal and illegal interests. The exterior was redesigned and modernized. The adjacent property was also purchased with the intent to increase the parking lot. The hidden agenda was to provide a wider view of anyone, legal or illegal, who might want to interfere with the business inside.

Case let the final bars of "Capra Black" play out before he killed the engine. Outside the car, he stretched and took a deep breath of the night air.

And, as is his habit, Case scanned the perimeter for anything that seemed out of the ordinary. The amount of cars in the lot told him that there would be plenty of space to sit in peace. That was all he wanted. To sit in peace. To drink in peace. To be someplace where he could relax, unwind, and leave the problems of the day at the door.

The interior of McCoy's had been updated in a mixture of greys and reds. On the first floor, there were booths against three of the walls and tables between the bar and the booths. The bar was against the longest of the walls. Instead of stools, there are comfortable leather-like chairs to sit in, not on. However, after that, McCoy's was just like any other gentlemen's club. The sound of loud music mixed with cheap perfume and cigarette smoke was the atmosphere. The stage was in the middle of the room with seating around the perimeter. There are the requisite flashing lights, brass poles, and mirrors. If you were not interested in the dancers, there are television monitors and a giant projection unit showing every sporting event going on in the world at that time. And then there was the part of McCoy's that wasn't like any other joint. The second floor was an invitation only casino. Poker, Black Jack, Craps, and other games of chance were enjoyed by those in the know. As with any self-respecting gentlemen's club, there were the private rooms for the private things that people did at private parties.

Case was known and trusted by management to be admitted to the second floor. There had been more than a few nights when Case had been both lucky and just as many when he had been unlucky. Tonight, Case just wanted to relax, take the edge off, and have his beer served to him by a woman wearing as little as possible.

Case drank slowly. He was in no hurry. He had the night to himself. There was no crowd to speak of, so he picked a table away from the stage that gave him an unobstructed view of the T.V. monitors and the women dancing. He was alone, and it was his choice to decide who or what to look at. The office was a train that had long since left the station. It was time to sit back and unwind.

The service in McCoy's is efficient to a fault. Case was served a beer within three minutes of taking a seat. He told the waitress to leave his tab open, closed his eyes, and let himself imagine he was in a different time and a different place. When he felt the hand on his shoulder, he thought it was one of the dancers coming over to hustle him for a drink. This time there was a noticeable reaction when he looked into the grey hair and blue eyes of Priscilla.

"Hi, sailor. New in town?" Priscilla signaled for the waitress, then took a seat beside Case.

"Buy you a drink?"

"I do not like being followed, Priscilla. Nor do I like anyone forcing themselves into my life." Without thinking, Jack Case produced a book of matches as Priscilla brought the cigarette to her lips. After lighting her cigarette, Case returned his attention to the stage. Perhaps on a different night at a different time, say maybe a few years ago, her showing up might have been interesting. Even, perhaps, welcomed. But this was now, and tonight was not a good night.

The waitress responded quickly and flipped a napkin in front of Priscilla.

"Absolute on the rocks and another for my friend."

"No need to get mad, Jack. You're a good man, and good men are hard to find. Besides, why should I wait for you to make the first move? You may never make it, and then where would I be?" Priscilla punctuated her statement with a smile. In another time and another place with another man, it would have worked.

"Listen, Priscilla, what happened in the office was a mistake. It never should have happened, and quite frankly, I am sorry that it did."

Priscilla smiled and crossed her legs.

"But it did happen and now here we are."

Case maintained a flat expression on his face and turned his attention to one of the monitors at the end of the bar. The waitress returned with the drinks, setting them down on the table while trying to read the situation before. Priscilla handed her a 20 dollar bill and motioned that she should keep the change.

Priscilla picked up her drink.

"Salud." Case responded by motioning in her direction but made it clear that he would not touch her glass. Priscilla leaned close, resting her elbows on her knees.

"Come on, Case, don't you like the attention. When was the last time a woman threw herself at you?"

The remark hit a nerve, but Case managed to maintain control. He leaned back in his seat and crossed his legs.

"Women do not throw themselves at me. And if a woman were to throw herself at me, then I would get suspicious. Whether I like this attention or not is hardly the point. You may find this hard to believe, but the tricks that work on most men will not work with me." Case drained what was left of his beer, glanced at the fresh beer on the table, then looked away.

"Listen, don't play this game with me."

Doubt was slowly creeping into Priscilla's mind. She did not like brick walls, and Jack Case was starting to look like pure cinder block. All she was looking for was a crease or a wrinkle. Something to tell her that she was on the right track. There was nothing. Priscilla was running out of options. And she knew it.

A song came on that happened to be one of her favorites. Interested to see what the dancer would do with the song, Priscilla turned and was surprised to see an empty stage. Without a second thought, she knocked down what was left of her drink, kicked off her shoes, and in three steps was on the stage.

Jack was about to order his own beer when his hand froze in mid-air. He watched as Priscilla stepped through the opening in the bar and leapt onto the stage. So surprised was he that he had to look to his left to make sure that it was really Priscilla who was on the stage and not someone who looked like her.

The rule in McCoy's is that there are no rules. The club is what is known as a Protected Venue, meaning that the dancers are free to show as much or as little as they care to. Priscilla picked up on that in a hurry. Halfway through the song, she was out of the top of her sweat suit. By the end of the song, her bra was off and her pants were down to her knees. When the second song started, Priscilla was in her thong, barefoot, working the pole and the men seated at the edge of the stage. Now she was in her own world.

Priscilla went back in time. She recalled the days right after college when she was backpacking around Europe. For two months, she danced in a strip club in Paris. The idea was to keep from starving to death. That rationale lasted only one day. Not only was she good at it, she loved it. And the men loved her. During the time that she danced, Priscilla made more money than in any of her part-time jobs while in school. In addition to the money that she made, Priscilla also learned more about men than she ever thought she would know. That knowledge, in time, proved to be more valuable than all of the money that she made.

On the stage in McCoy's, she felt the music more than heard it. It had been a long time. Soon, she was mesmerized by the images of herself in the mirrors that surrounded the stage and the faces of the men beneath her. Priscilla's moves were pure eroticism. She spread her legs, licked her lips, and rubbed her crotch so suggestively that no one in the club was immune. She was in her own world, and everyone there was on the outside looking in.

Pricilla looked down into the faces of the hungry men that wanted her. So obvious were their thoughts that it seemed like she was the only woman left on Earth. She saw the money that they threw and more that was being offered. That they would pay a price, any price, only took her higher. Soon there was a third song and a fourth song and there were bills of all denominations all over the stage. By the fifth song, the manager held out his hand from the edge of the stage.

"Okay, lady, your dates gone. Time to let the professionals earn their keep." There was wild applause from the men and evil stares from the dancers as Priscilla climbed down from the stage. Suddenly, the words from the manager kicked in, and Priscilla looked over at the table where they had been sitting. Case was gone. Another wild shot. Another wild miss.

CHAPTER FOUR

The tension pain that had so easily left him just a short while ago returned, but this time, it was more intense than before. Jack looked around the club and it suddenly felt like a very strange place. Jack dropped a 20 dollar bill on the table and left McCoy's before anyone could make the connection that she was the same woman who was sitting with him.

Outside, the night was raw, and it matched his mood. A cold wind blew hard, cold rain in several directions at once. There was no turning away from it, so Jack took the rain on. Face to face. Man to man. The rain won. Inside his car, Jack was relieved to be out of the cold. But then that thought reminded him of why he was there in the first place and that led to what drove him from the bar.

Jack started his car, recklessly backed out of the space, then turned into traffic, nearly catching the business end of an 18-wheeler. He was furious. Mad at himself for a display of weakness that has led to the unwanted attention of a lunatic woman. Convinced that he would not have this problem had it not been for that encounter in his office, he took his anger out on the car and the road. Ahead of him was a Taurus. Jack down shifted, stomped on the throttle, and sped around the slow-moving vehicle, again, barely missing another on-coming truck.

Jack's mind began to work.

"The person in the shadows had to have been her. She knows where I live. She knows where I go. What is this all about? What does she want?" Jack continued to mull the questions around in his brain. He needed to go somewhere safe. Somewhere he could not be found. If he went home, how did he know she would not follow him there? He did not need to see her again tonight. No, he needed a place that he was sure she did not know about. There was a place. He had not been there in a very long time. Case actually could not remember the last time he had been there. He checked his mirror, turned left at the light, and then disappeared into a moonless, rain swept night.

Priscilla put her clothes back on and then returned to their table. He was gone. At that point, she could have had any man in the bar. Right then and there, they would have done anything for her, but the one that she wanted was gone. She collected her purse, refused the money that she earned from dancing, and went out into the cold, wet night, thinking that no amount of rain could make her feel any worse than she did right now.

Despite the short walk across the parking lot, Priscilla was soaked to the bone. She fell into the seat of the Corvette, not feeling a thing.

"That was a pretty dumb stunt. What were you thinking? That you were the same little hot bitch that you were in college?" Priscilla flipped down the sun visor and checked herself out in the mirror. It was a big mistake.

The harsh light from inside the car only accentuated her rain matted hair. The lines in her face seemed more pronounced. The fatigue in her eyes was obvious. Priscilla looked worn out. With the look came a feeling that she had not felt before. Old. Priscilla flipped up the visor, only to be met by her reflection in the windshield in front of her and in the glass around her. Her first thought was to leave the car. Get out and get away from the reflections of the things inside of her that she did not want to see. To go back into that bar, pick up the first man she laid her eyes on, and make him take her. Make him give her back her youth. The reflection in the door glass told her what her mind would not. "Don't." Priscilla hesitated for two seconds, then started her car and headed home.

"Well, well, stranger. We haven't seen you in here in a dog's age. How ya been, Jack?" The salutation was quiet enough so that only Jack heard it. He was thankful for that. Stella could be loud and boisterous, but fortunately for both of them, she saved that side of herself for the other patrons who needed it. Tonight, Jack Case was not in the mood for it.

"What brings you out on a night like this?"

The two friends traded kisses on the cheek and then stared at each other for what seemed like a very long time. Jack slid onto the barstool as Stella reached for a bottle of bourbon without looking for it. She poured a drink for him and one for herself. With no need for a verbal acknowledgement, they touched the bottoms of their glasses and smiled at one another. Their presence together was toast enough.

Estelle Hart had once been a lounge singer and not half bad at it. For the stage, she changed her name to Stella Heart. She met Case in Europe in a jazz club that was not usually frequented by Americans. They formed a friendship out of their love of the music. They formed a bond based on the shared pain of love lost.

Had Stella not been several years older than Case, they might have saved each other. But that was not to be. After one night, they both realized that they would be better friends than lovers. Stella left to go back on the road with the first band that would have her. Case stood on the platform and watched her leave.

When the road got old, she took the earnings that she had been smart enough to save and began looking for a place where she could sing what she wanted, when she wanted, and would not have to leave. She found it in The Winepress in the little suburban town of Kingston, New Jersey. Stella bought in as a partner, and after a year, she bought the place outright. Basically a local hangout, the Press, as it is known in town, is popular for its good food and generous drinks. Stella made sure she carried on that tradition when she took over.

From time to time, Some of Stella's musician friends would stop by and get into impromptu jam sessions. On those occasions, the night never ended without Stella taking the mic for a song or two. Her bar had the comfortable feel of a place where you could come and take a load off, share a confidence with a friend, and leave in far better shape than when you came in. It was not too long before the two friends renewed a relationship that they both had feared was lost forever.

Jack thought for a minute, then took a sip of the bourbon that was poured for him.

"It has been a long time. Been workin' hard, Stella. I had not realized it. I guess the time sort of got away from me." Jack took another sip and felt the tension pain start to ease. He wished he had come here instead of trying to satisfy a more basic need, but that was water under the bridge.

"How have you been?"

Stella smiled and took a sip of her own drink.

"You're lyin', Jack, but that's okay. You'd tell a lie in a minute if you thought the truth would hurt. I've been good. Payin' my bills and even makin' a buck or two here and there despite what you see." The dining room was empty, and there were only a few people in the bar area.

"Glad to hear somebody is making money." He nodded in the direction of the piano on the stage.

"Mind if I play a little?"

Stella smiled a knowing smile.

"No one has touched that thing since the last time you played it. Everything is electric now. Needs a little tuning, but if that don't bother you, then go ahead. Whoever don't like it can leave." Before he left, Stella topped him off and gave him a smile.

Jack flipped open the keyboard cover, then slid up and down the scale to loosen his fingers. From the third run of the scales, he went into Ellington's "Sophisticated Lady." When Stella brought him a second drink, she joined him on the piano bench, with her own drink in her hand. Jack acknowledged the gentle applause from two of the three people at the bar.

"There's two things I know about you, Jack." He looked at her suspiciously as he took a sip from his glass.

"One of them is that if you had put your mind to it earlier in life, you would have made a pretty fair musician." Stella took a sip of her drink, then began to hum "Sophisticated Lady" to herself while he played it in the abstract.

"So, what's the other thing?" Jack continued to play as he looked her in the eye.

"You only play the piano when you have woman troubles. Especially when you start off with 'Sophisticated Lady'". Stella rose to her feet.

"I hope it works out better than the last time. Don't be a stranger, Jack." Stella kissed him softly on the lips and then returned to the bar, leaving Jack to the thoughts that he chose to express on the keyboard.

After a few more bars, Jack closed the cover to the keyboard, finished his drink, and left the stage. Playing an out of tune piano in a bar while trying to figure out what to do about a woman made him feel like a cliché from a 1940's B-movie. He was no closer to figuring out a solution to his problem, but at least the pain in his head was gone. Jack placed two 20s on the bar. Stella took one and gave him back the other.

"You get the musician's discount tonight."

Jack smiled.

"Thanks, Stella." He took a look around before turning up the collar to his jacket.

"It's always good to have someplace to come to." Jack again took the rain on, but this time, the match ended in a tie.

Priscilla drove faster than she should have. More than once, she almost lost control of her car. Only the trio of God's grace, dumb luck, and GM engineering kept her from going into a ditch or sliding into a guardrail. She skidded to a stop in her garage, shut off the engine, and then sat in the car, reliving the nights events.

Priscilla cursed Jack Case. How could he refuse her? She threw herself at him, performed for him, and then he walked out on her. A voice inside of her told Priscilla that he wasn't worth it, that he did not deserve her, that she should quit this round of the game and walk away. Leave him high and dry. She did not need him, the job, or the money. Find someone else. Surely there were others out there just waiting for her. But another voice told her that is what he wanted, that she would be giving in to him, that he would have beaten her at her own game. She said the words aloud. She repeated the phase again, "that he would have beaten her at her own game." It still had force. This is her game. She is supposed to win. But right now, she was losing. A new resolve came over Pricilla Whittington. And with that resolve came a new voice.

"Isn't this what you want? Isn't he the one you've been looking for? Isn't this the challenge you have been looking for? Make him want you, make him crazy for you. Take what you want and then leave him." With her hair dry now and the light of the garage more subdued than the light in the car, her features softened. Priscilla was back on an even keel. She softly closed the car door, then went directly to her bedroom to give some more thought to how she would win at her own game.

CHAPTER FIVE

Detective Blair Collins walked with a purpose as she made her way from the parking lot to Somerset County police headquarters in Somerville, New Jersey. Blair had been in Somerville for the past three weeks. And for what seemed like the 100th time, she marveled at the good fortune that got her to this point.

At five foot four and 110 pounds, she fit the image of an upwardly mobile corporate executive. A short, black female, neatly dressed in a grey business suit, carrying a briefcase, pocket book, and wearing sensible two inch pumps. The .38 caliber Smith & Wesson in a shoulder rig and her badge neatly clipped to her slacks were the only proof of her actual occupation.

Blair thought back to a point in time ten months past. Seated at her cubicle, she was looking for an angle on a credit card fraud ring when the Chief of Detectives for the New Jersey State Police suddenly appeared in her office. With a look on his face that most perpetrators would not like to see on any cop's face, he proceeded directly into her Captain's office. Everyone on the floor, detectives and civilian workers, were accustomed to his normal habit of stopping to chit chat with the troops before meeting with the brass. Something today was very wrong.

After ten minutes of the Chief talking, the Captain listening, the Chief pointing, and the Captain nodding, the Chief left the office, pausing to briefly look in Blair's direction before heading through the door. Five minutes after that, Blair was called into the office of her Captain.

41

"The Chief wants you for a TDY."

Blair was not pleased. The last temp duty that she had was driving around some politician who wanted to show diversity on the police force.

"Yes. What is it?" She masterfully hid the irritation in her voice.

Blair's Captain was a career cop. While he did not have anything specific against women, he did come up in the force during the time when racial profiling was the standing order. For that reason, he was uncomfortable around her and every other black person under his command. The Captain took up a defensive position in the chair behind his desk.

"There's a series of murders of young women that Trenton is in a snit about. The cases are high priority and high profile. Because of all of the different municipalities in this state, no one town can be in charge of the investigation. Trenton wants us to handle it with an assist from the locals."

Blair was confused and did not try to hide it.

"How come homicide is not taking the point on this?"

The Captain took off his glasses and rubbed his eyes.

"They are, but Trenton wants a female detective on this, and right now, you are the only one that's available."

Blair's mood brightened considerable, but this time, she hid it well.

"Wow! Okay. Great."

The Captain made a face.

"Listen, Blair, this is a homicide case with heavy heat under it. It's not spring break. You are to meet up with a Lieutenant Maxine Stout in Somerville. You will work under her direction, but you are to keep us informed. It will be up to the local P.D. to determine if you are assigned a partner or not. Stout will be informed to give you every possible assistance. Do not talk to the press or any of the local politicians. You will use your own car and log the miles on your expense account. Any questions?"

Blair was still processing the information. The only word she could utter was no.

"Good. Transfer what you're working on to me and I will see that it is reassigned." The Captain paused for a minute and then spoke.

"Blair, cases like this can take a bad turn. Be careful and do not stick your neck out. You are still new at this, so don't be a hero. Am I understood?"

"Yes, sir."

"Dismissed."

That day, Blair collected and printed all that could be found on the three murders. She also found out that there were three other detectives assigned to the case. The thought is that each detective would be assigned to a local municipality rather than work out of a single office. In that manner, with an assist from the locals, manpower and experience could be maximized. Also, if there was any screw up, it could be blamed on the locals and not the State Police.

By-passing the lift, Blair took the stairs up to the detective squad located on the second floor. She stepped through the door barely breathing hard. Compared to the six-mile run that she did almost every morning, the two flights of stairs were nothing.

The office was a carbon copy of most any other municipal agency. The carpeting, desks, walls, and filing cabinets were all gun metal gray. Every computer was a Dell laptop and all phones were black. In fact, the only colorful items in the entire office both happened to be at her corner desk. One was the wall map with the multi-colored pins stuck in it. The other was Lieutenant Maxine Stout.

"Morning, Max. Make yourself comfortable." Blair felt like putting on her sunglasses at the sight of the bright yellow suit and red blouse sitting in her chair with her feet on her desk. Max allowed herself the luxury of completing her review of the collection of newspaper clippings pinned next to the map before swinging her feet off of the desk. At five foot, nine inches, she was already taller than the average woman. The red four-inch heels that she wore placed her well over six feet in height.

Maxine became a police officer as soon as the job was open to women. She took every exam, distinguished herself with some rather unique busts, and along the way, made it known to anyone and everyone that she would not be denied. In short order, she made detective, and soon after that, she was in command of the squad.

There is a train of thought among women in law enforcement that you should not call attention to the fact that you are a woman. To Max's (as she prefers to be called) way of thinking, that concept was stupid. She was one of a handful of women in the department. The thought that she should try to blend did not make any sense to her. Hence the brightly colored clothes, the high heels, and the manicured nails with the airbrush designs. That was her official line.

Lt. Stout ignored the sarcasm.

"Good morning to you. This is an interesting collection of articles. Is there anything new on this case?" Blair felt like a midget next to her superior.

"Another woman was found just outside of Philly yesterday." Blair made a mental note to take the clippings down and lock them in her desk.

"I have an appointment to talk to the investigating officer today."

Max glanced at the wall map before walking away.

"Good. Keep me posted on your progress."

Blair did not relax until the door to Max's office closed. She would have preferred a different sight first thing in the morning but accepted the fact that one cannot always have what one wants. Russ Matson intercepted her in route to the break room.

"Morning, Blair. Can I buy you a cup of coffee?"

"Morning, Russ. How goes it in the world of almost-retired police officers?" Blair smiled warmly. She honestly liked Russ despite the stale cigarette smell that was as much a part of him as his easy-going personality.

"Just counting the days, Blair. Just counting the days." The aging cop poured her cup first, then his own. He motioned to a table in the corner.

"Can I talk to you for a minute?"

"Sure, Russ. What's on your mind?" Blair took pride in the fact that she was one of the few people in the office that had the patience for Russ. While he did tend to ramble, he had the experience of 45 years on the job. It was Blair's belief that there was always something to learn from anyone who lasted that long in this line of work.

"Two things actually. The first is that case that you are working on. The murders? Have you considered the depth of the incision? That would give you an indication of the strength of the person who made the cut, which would add to your suspect profile."

Blair rolled her eyes in her mind. This was the third time that Russ had reminded her of the depth of the incision.

"Thanks, Russ. I've got that covered. What was the other thing?"

"Well, it's about Max. Now I hate to be a prude about this, and I know times have changed for you gals, but could you ask Max not to sit with her feet on the desk when she has a dress on. Some of us guys are uncomfortable when we can see right up to her skivvies." Russ's cheeks flushed as he put on his best grandfatherly smile.

Blair wondered when that was going to come. She had heard about some of Max's habits. The fact that she was the only other woman in the office made her the only option in terms of dealing with it. Blair was not surprised that it was Russ who took on the task of approaching her about it.

"I think it would be more effective if the request came from you, Russ."

"I know, and I agree. But you know I'm two months away from retirement. I can't afford to have any kind of discrimination business in my file. Could you handle this one for me please?"

The kindly face and the oppressive smell of the unfiltered cigarettes that the elderly detective chain smoked blocked the thought of any further discussion in Blair's mind. The only out left was a bold face lie.

"I will have a word with her this afternoon."

Relieved, Russ got up from the table, dumping the rest of his coffee in the sink.

"Thanks, Blair. Listen, don't forget about the depth of the incision, O.K.?"

"Sure, Russ. I won't forget." As he walked away, Blair went in the opposite direction so that she could take in a few deep breaths of fresh air.

Blair prepped for the meeting with the Philadelphia P.D. by reading over the latest news account of the murder. Half way through it, she stopped. The facts in this article were so similar to the ten others hanging on her wall, they all could have been written by the same person. Disgusted, she updated her computer file on what she knew, then left for her meet.

Blair opted not to draw a car from the motor pool and made the drive to Philly in her beat-up Corolla. Not having to put up with stale cigarette smoke in a pool car meant more to her than the wear and tear on her POV. Since she had time on her hands, Blair skipped the highways and took the local routes. The changing of the leaves is something that does not happen in California, so she used the drive to witness one of the miracles of nature.

The varying shades of orange and brown brought to her mind images of beauty. Unfortunately, the logical progression of the thought led to the reason for the drive. They had all been beautiful women. And now they were dead. Dead at the hand of some maniacal assailant. It was her job to catch him. Going into her fourth week on the case, she was no closer to this madman now than at the beginning of assignment.

The thought did not depress her as much as it gave purpose to her actions. Blair cleared her mind of thoughts of beauty and re-focused on the questions she would ask the P.P.D. Detective. She remembered one of the things that Russ had told her.

"Always keep an open mind. You never know when you will find that one clue that will break the case wide open." With that, Blair reviewed the facts that she knew about this case.

This was the fourth murder. The only common denominator was that all of the victims were woman. True, they were all pretty, but what woman isn't pretty in her own way. They were all between 30 and 40 years of age, of various builds (one was rail thin, one was 180 pounds), and various ethnicities. All died from a cut across the throat after they had been sexually assaulted. There were no other wounds on the bodies, and they were all found along a road, having been brought there after they had been killed. Although her colleagues disagreed, it seemed to Blair that the killer wanted the bodies to be found. That is her explanation for why they were left at the side of the road and not hidden somewhere. There was nothing in the background of the women to indicate that they had known each other or shared any common experience. For all intents and purposes, it would seem as if these victims had been picked at random.

Blair did not buy the "random" theory. Her gut told her that there was a connection. She just could not put her finger on it. Yet. After checking with the F.B.I. and calling around across the country, she was able to learn that there were groups of murders of women in four other states. They all had similar aspects, though they were not exactly the same. There was no distinct pattern. Blair mapped the locations of the past murders as well as the most recent in the hopes of determining a trail. There did not appear to be a readily apparent pattern. Blair felt the window closing rapidly.

Blair turned onto Market Street, then proceeded to Fourth Street East. The third precinct was on the corner. She parked across the street in the municipal lot, dodged the traffic, and took the steps two at a time into the building. The desk Sergeant was a low rent version of Russ Matson.

"So, you're State Police, huh." He took a long time with her business card and badge. "Kinda short, ain't ya? Well, no matter, I'm going to have to ask you to secure your piece. Since 9/11, only P.P.D. carry guns on the premises. Everyone else has to check theirs, even you state troopers." His broad smile confirmed that he enjoyed being a bully.

Blair let the insults go in one ear and out the other. She had been down this road before and knew that there would be an opening where she would get a lick in. She opened her jacket, removed and unloaded the S&W .38 Special with a two-inch barrel, placing the shells in a paper cup. She then handed the empty weapon and the cup to the Sergeant.

"Hey guys! Get a load of this antique." The Sergeant held up the pistol. No one took notice of it.

Blair pinned on her visitors pass, then took advantage of the opening.

"You know, Sarge, I would bet that the barrel on that antique is bigger than the one in your pants and shoots a hellava lot straighter. Make sure it's there when I get back." The effect of the remark could not have been more apparent than if Blair had taken a piece of wood and smacked the aging officer between the eyes. Feeling pretty good about herself, Blair took the stairs up to the Detective Bureau, leaving the Sergeant to deal with the ridicule from his colleagues on the desk.

Once she completed her meeting with the detective assigned to the case, Blair took a trip to the morgue to view the body. She then went to the crime scene and spent time examining where the body was found and the surrounding area. By the time she finished making her notes, it was after six in the evening when Blair returned to the office. County detectives do not usually work night tours, so the office was deserted when Blair arrived. Blair took in the quiet willingly. She had learned a few things today and was hoping for some peace and quiet to collect her thoughts. She was surprised to see a light still on in Max's office. On the theory that it is better to tell than be asked, Blair decided to brief her superior tonight to avoid having to do it tomorrow.

Blair paused in the doorway. Max had her feet on the desk and was reading the latest issue of a women's body building magazine. The crotch of her panties was clearly visible to anyone who would care to look. It reminded her of the conversation she had earlier with Russ Matson. With some effort, Blair pushed that conversation out of her mind and re-focused her attention. She knocked once on the door, then entered the office.

"You're here late."

Max looked up, smiled, and put the magazine down on the desk with the cover up. Blair made the mental note that anyone trying to hide something would have put the magazine in a drawer.

"Hey, Blair, come in."

Blair took a seat, making sure that she was not in line with the view of her boss's panties. "I thought I would catch you up on the Philly trip. I met with…"

Max waved her off.

"We can go over that in the morning. Listen, I hear that you're a runner. You know if you strengthen your upper body, it will help your running. You and I should get together in the gym one of these days. I could show you some things." Max swung her legs off the desk and stood up in what appeared to be one motion.

"Do you have any plans tonight? How about dinner?"

The question caught Blair totally off guard.

"Well, thanks, but I, uh, planned to get my notes in the system tonight." Although she was starving, there was something about Maxine Stout that made her uncomfortable.

Max slipped on her jacket after placing her service weapon and shoulder holster in her tan Coach pocket book.

"I've heard good things about you from a few folks, Blair. You know Russ will be retiring in a couple of months. Perhaps you could think about transferring here permanently. I would really like to have you on my team."

There was something in Max's tone that crossed the line of business. Blair heeded the voice inside her that told her it was time to go.

"I've known about Russ's plans and have in fact thought about a transfer. I will give it some serious thought and get back to you shortly. I am sorry about dinner." Blair stood as she spoke, hoping to exit on the last word. Max cut her off.

Standing very close, Max used both hands to adjust the lapels on Blair's jacket. During the course of the act, she let her hands casually brush against Blair's breasts.

"Nice suit. Take as long as you like to make up your mind. And don't worry about dinner. I am sure we will get together soon." Max stepped away from Blair, picked up her purse, and then left the office.

"Don't stay too late."

Blair stood in the middle of the office, wondering if the East Coast moved just a bit too fast.

CHAPTER SIX

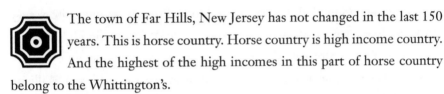 The town of Far Hills, New Jersey has not changed in the last 150 years. This is horse country. Horse country is high income country. And the highest of the high incomes in this part of horse country belong to the Whittington's.

The Whittington Stables (don't ever call it a ranch or a farm) are located five miles off of State Route 202 (It is an open secret in town that the horses seen on the property are merely for show). Four and half miles of the only road that leads to the main house are private. Security is a serious matter here. Unless you have business at the house, you don't belong on that road. Sensors and C.C.D. cameras will alert the guard long before you will ever see the house. If your license plate is not on the list, you will be arrested for trespassing without debate.

The Whittington family was one of the first to settle in this area. Liam Whittington was a Welsh farmer who came to America with the clothes on his back, a keen mind, and nothing else. He met his wife on the passage over. The young couple set up a small mercantile business in New York City, which soon expanded from selling dry goods to buying and selling real estate. They ventured into New Jersey when everyone else was moving to Long Island. Soon, they were acquiring parcel upon parcel of farm land. It is speculated that the Whittington Stables now sits on 500 acres of land.

During prohibition, Liam Whittington leased warehouse space to the rumrunners and bootleggers. Even though he did not engage in the buying and selling of illegal alcohol, Liam enjoyed the protection and the company of organized crime. From then until well into the 1950's, the Whittington family walked side by side with organized crime and just ahead of the law.

In the mid-1950's, Preston Whittington (Liam's only son) decided to clean up the family's name. He married a pretty socialite from a well-established family named Victoria, liquidated the family's questionable assets, save the property in Far Hills and some real estate holdings in New York, and bought a seat on the Stock Exchange for what seemed, at that time, to be the princely sum of $10,000. Preston's son, William, was ten-years-old at the time. With those moves and his marriage to Victoria, Preston brought instant respectability to the Whittington name.

With the trading skills that ran in his blood, Preston became quite a savvy stock and bond broker. Within a very short time, Whittington Holdings became one of the most successful, privately owned, brokerage houses on Wall Street. When the time was right, Preston passed the baton to his son, William, who took it and not only ran with it, but increased the pace.

Where the father was good, the son was better. Year-end double-digit returns became the norm. For every loser, there were two to three winners. William Whittington (Do not even think of calling him "Bill") became one of the leading voices on Wall Street. His moves were watched and matched. Companies were made and destroyed simply by whom he was seen having lunch with. It seemed like the House of Whittington could do no wrong. And then the 80's hit.

Preston died of a heart attack in 1986, the same month that William's wife filed for divorce. The stock market crashed the next year, and it seemed like the rocket ship that flew so well for so long was now in a tailspin heading back to earth. Instead of walking away from the controls and wallowing in self-pity like so many of his friends had done, William attacked in the style of his father and his grandfather. He leveraged his equity, found a partner, and rebuilt his families fortune. At the direction of his mother, William divested a good portion of the family's wealth into a trust and managed it solely for the account of himself, his mother, and his sister. The other portion of the Whittington portfolio provided the income for the Trust, which benefited certain philanthropic causes. In due course, William married a woman 12 years his junior. Her name was Priscilla.

Trap Martin knew the story of the Whittington family better than he knew his own family history. There was no need to review it, but going over the Whittington story before his meeting put him in the proper frame of mind. And one had to be in the proper frame of mind to deal with Victoria Whittington. Trap looked at his watch. He would get to the Far Hills Inn ahead of his client. Good. Anyone who ever kept Victoria Whittington waiting never worked for her again.

The Far Hills Inn is a landmark. It is the former home of the first settlers in the area. The last family member, Edith Scott, turned the house into a bed and breakfast inn and later cultivated the dining room into a five-star restaurant. No expense was spared in either the decoration of the interior or the quality of the fare. It was a wise investment. The Inn, as it is known locally, is now regarded as one of the finest dining experiences within 100 miles and the only place outside of her estate where the imperious Victoria Whittington can be seen.

Trap parked his hunter green Jaguar at the far end of the parking lot. One would have a hard time placing him with this car if he was not seen getting out of it. His plaid sports coat, stripped shirt, and paisley tie clashed so violently, you could almost feel the conflict. The color of his slacks seemed to have some correlation to one of the colors in his tie, but it was a stretch. His only pair of shoes had never been polished in the six years that he has owned them. Standing at the main entrance and under the guise of admiring a perfect day, Trap sneered at his surroundings and the people who lived within them. "Here I am, walking on your turf, breathing your air, and about to eat your food. Ready or not, here I come." Trap Martin did not try to suppress the smile on his face.

On each one of his quarterly visits here, Trap saw the image of his high school football coach looking up at him. His face was as battered as the desk, and his voice was an audible manifestation of years of unfulfilled dreams.

"Martin, I see you applied to all of these high-end, blue blood schools, but let me tell you something, boy. You might be hot shit on the football field, but inside, you ain't nothing but a peckerwood piece of white trailer trash. I'm bettin' you'll last one year, maybe two before your dick gets you in trouble and they throw your ass out."

Trap recalled the anger that flashed and the urge to throw a punch. He wanted to hit the old man just one time and end it all. But he didn't. Some force within him held him back. In the end, his bitter, old football coach signed the application, attested to his stats, and then ate crow as Trap Martin played four years of football for Yale. Trap always wondered what his coach did with the blown-up picture he sent him of receiving his diploma while shaking the hand of the president of Yale University. Trap's guess was that he ripped it up into about a million pieces. He was the kind of guy that hated to be proven wrong.

Martin Security Associates is a wholly owned subsidiary of the Whittington Trust. As a private trust, there is no obligation to disclose the functions of its subsidiary properties or the employees of those properties. Therefore no one, other than the clients of Martin Associates, knows that Trap Martin and the people who work for him are the private security force of the Whittington family.

Trap was standing in front of the Far Hills Inn when the Whittington limousine appeared. His hulking body, dressed in clothes that challenged every fashion rule, while standing in front of a high-end establishment was almost comical. Trap motioned to the driver to stay in the car as he opened the door and assisted his employer out of the restored Bentley.

"Thank you, Mr. Martin. How perfectly splendid you look today." As the President and C.E.O. of the Whittington Trust took his hand and alit from the car, it never ceased to amaze Trap how strong she was for a woman whose age exceeded her weight.

Victoria Whittington relaxed her grip only after she regained her balance and her poise. Any movement she made in public was measured and calculated. She considered herself to be the last bastion of old, secure money. In her world, it is the responsibility of her station to project the image of security lest anyone think that the family's fortune is at risk. Victoria took this responsibility quite seriously.

The cost of styling her hair for the short period that she was out would feed a family of four for a month. Shoes, dress, hose, and undergarments were purchased just for this trip, then donated to a local charity. That way it will be impossible for her to be seen in the same dress twice. The walker and cane that she used at home would be left at the door when the car is brought around. To be escorted is one thing, but absolutely no one outside of the estate will ever see Victoria Whittington with the slightest appearance of being feeble.

"Thank you, Mrs. Whittington. May I say that you look especially fit yourself." Trap flashed the smile that opened more doors than the bottom of his shoe while he made sure he kept a firm grip on his employer. In the interim between the vehicle and the stairs, another woman emerged carrying a brief-case and an attitude.

"Hello, Doris."

With a nod, Doris uttered one word.

"Trap." Her expression, like her voice, was cold and detached.

Martin helped the elder Whittington up the stairs, then held the door open as they stepped through. Doris tried to take over the escort duties, but the elder Whittington would have none of that.

"Mr. Martin, if you please..." Trap extended his arm, showing his trophy to her table while Doris fumed and brought up the rear.

Doris Whittington did not like what her mother turned into around Trap Martin. There were the compliments back and forth, the touching between them, the subtle acquiescence and deference on her mother's part, and the equally subtle assertiveness and patronage from him. For 89 days of each quarter, Doris was the steady right hand of the last remaining matriarch. The indispensable Chief of Staff that made all things happen. But on this one day, Doris Whittington reverted to being just the daughter. Dressed in her gray business suit, white bow blouse, flesh colored hose, and moderate pumps with moderate heels, Doris felt drab in the glow of her mother's bright floral print dress and stunning silver blue hair. As she watched them saunter through the entrance, she felt like the little sister tagging along on a date.

At 2:30 in the afternoon, only the idle rich are present in the main dining room of the Far Hills Inn. Their wealth, which was almost on the same level as the Whittington fortune, made the sighting of Victoria Whittington a non-event. Still, there was a pause in the conversations and respectful nods as she walked by.

The three guests were shown to a private room off to the side of the main dining area that offered a peaceful view of a small brook that ran across the property. There was only one table in the room, and it was set for three. Along the walls were the extra chairs for the room and an antique server with a silver tea service. In keeping with the rest of the establishment, the fabric on the seats matched the wallpaper on the walls, which coordinated perfectly with the carpet and the trim. The flat ware and the table service were also coordi-nated to match the colors both inside the room and out. The goal of this at-tention to detail was to provide as harmonious a setting as possible. As Trap helped adjust the chair of the most powerful woman he knew, both Doris and the maitre'd blanched at the one detail that was about to destroy the harmony that the decorator tried so expensively to attain.

Such was the power of Victoria Whittington that her beverage and lunch order were taken in advance. It would not do to have anyone see her fumbling over what to drink or have to eat, nor did she feel that she should wait like everyone else to be served. Placed to the right of her seat in a wine stand was a silver decanter with a vodka martini chilling on ice. In front of her service was a crystal martini glass with a perfectly sliced zest of lemon resting peace-fully at the bottom of the glass. With a swiftness that one would not expect from someone who is twice the age of the youngest person in the room, Vic-toria Whittington took the back of her hand and slapped the glass off the table. It hit the wall and shattered into a dozen pieces. She then sat back in her chair and fixed the maitre'd with a deadly stare.

"Young man. If I had wanted lemons in my drink, I would have ordered lemonade. My instructions are quite specific. If you or your staff cannot follow them, then I will be forced to find accommodations elsewhere that can and will."

What made the admonishment even more intimidating was the presence of a hulking Trap Martin, who appeared ready to mete out whatever punishment Victoria Whittington deemed necessary. A bus boy appeared instantly to clean up the glass shards. The maitre'd was about to exit the room when Doris cleared her throat. The sound froze him in place. Doris glanced at the martini set in the wine stand and was pleased to know that the young man could at least take a hint. He picked up the entire wine stand and hustled out of the room. In what seemed to be no less than ten seconds, the crystal glass was replaced with an exact replica. In the glass were three Spanish olives. In less than ten seconds after that, the wine stand was replaced and inside of it was a freshly made vodka martini. The maitre'd poured the drink, then stood ramrod straight, waiting for a reaction.

Victoria swirled the olives in the liquid and then slowly raised the glass to her lips.

"This will do. You may now serve my guests." Both Trap and Doris ordered ice tea. Their drinks arrived with equal speed. After the departure of the maitre'd, Trap thought he heard the words, "You're fired" come from somewhere in the restaurant, but he let it go as something that was none of his business, either professionally or personally.

Trap eyed the menu that was on his plate, instantaneously decided on the breast of duck, and then turned his attention to Doris.

"You are looking well, Doris. How are things with you?" Trap's warm smile was met with cold, blue eyes.

"Mr. Martin, I believe the purpose of this meeting is to talk about you, not me." Doris returned the menu to her plate and then turned to her mother.

"I am ready, Mother."

Using the buzzer on the arm of her chair, Victoria signaled for the maitre'd at the same time that she drained her glass. He seemed to appear in less than a second. Accompanying him was a female bartender with a freshly made martini and a fresh glass filled with olives. While the bartender refreshed Victoria's drink, Trap used the time to do what he did best.

It was his estimation that the bartender was between 22 and 25, about 130 pounds, and wore a 34C bra. From the tight fit of her tuxedo pants around her hips, Trap surmised that her underwear of choice was a thong. He further thought that she would not screw you on the first date, but if you got a second date, you were in. The curve of her full lips gave that last bit away. As he made a mental note to come back to test his theory, Trap found Doris staring at him.

Doris did not take her eyes off of Trap as she ordered.

"I'll have the roast pork with apples."

"Very good. And for you, sir?"

"I'll have the duck." As soon as the word "duck" was said, menus were scooped up, and the maitre'd was a blur out of the room. The closing of the doors to the room was left to a waiter stationed just for that purpose.

Victoria took a discrete sip of her second drink, smiled, and let the liquid take effect. She then placed her hand on top of Trap's.

"Mr. Martin, thank you for taking the time to meet with us today." One of the rules of old money is to compliment the help and never pull rank unless you have to.

Trap launched a 100 mega-watt smile that made Victoria blush.

"The pleasure is mine, Mrs. Whittington. I thank you for seeing me." Trap folded his hands on the edge of the table. He looked like the new kid in school on the first day of class.

Victoria returned the smile with one of her own, then turned to her daughter.

"Doris, if you would start us off please?"

Having had just about enough of this show of patronage, the Chief of Staff welcomed the opportunity to cut through the bullshit.

"Trap, through the third quarter, you continue to operate profitably. The affairs of your private investigation department, along with the sub-contracted security assignments, continue to off-set the cost of domestic security. There have not been any lost time incidents, nor have there been any complaints from clients regarding service. Services fees are paid in a timely fashion, and personal expenses are all properly accounted for. We did notice that there were several high value equipment purchases, and we would like an explanation of these costs. Also, it was reported to our office that a brutality suit was brought against you. Our corporate counsel has reviewed the matter and sent it to the insurance company for handling. However, we will need your explanation for our file should the Trust become involved." Doris's lips seemed to disappear when she finished her report. Trap found this habit of hers comical but stifled a laugh.

"Regarding the expenses, there was an operation that called for sophisticated equipment and weaponry. I did not see the need to use the clandestine market to make the purchase, as the equipment was readily available legally. I used my personal credit card so as to not subject the trust to any undo scrutiny." Trap had anticipated the question and was proud that he took the time to formulate an answer.

"Would you care for a description of the purchase?"

Before Doris could speak, Victoria raised her hand.

"That will not be necessary, Mr. Martin. That purchase was made for the Jennings matter, was it not?" Victoria took another sip of her martini, then balanced her elbows on the arms of the chair. Trap nodded his head in assent.

"I received a call from Edith Jennings at the conclusion of that very sordid business. She was most complementary of your discretion in the handling of the matter. Edith is an old friend. I am glad it went well. Thank you, Mr. Martin."

While it never ceased to amaze Trap how knowledgeable Victoria was of his affairs, it was an irritation to Doris of how little she knew. Looking at the combination of the jacket and tie, Doris had trouble imagining Trap being discrete.

"I'm sorry. I saw no listing of a Jennings in your client roster. Will someone please tell me what this is all about?" Trap entertained himself with the disappearing act of Doris's lips.

"Doris, Mr. Martin is bound by ethical guidelines not to divulge a client's circumstances.

As the person who referred Edith to Mr. Martin, I can tell you that her youngest daughter found herself in a compromising position with some very unsavory individuals. Mr. Martin and his associates were able to resolve the situation in a manner that was favorable to the Jennings family." Victoria drained her glass, signaling that this part of the discussion was over.

There were a dozen questions that Doris wanted to ask, but she knew better. There are people in this world who do not like to be questioned. Victoria Whittington is one of them. Frustrated, Doris sat back in her chair and finished what remained of her ice tea.

"And the brutality suit? May I have some sort of an explanation about that?" Doris was fully aware of the edge to her tone. Victoria raised an eyebrow but chose not to respond.

Trap acknowledged his boss, and then smiling, engaged Doris.

"That is also related to the Jennings case. However, I can tell you that the action will be dropped. There is no need to retain separate counsel or even send it to the insurance company. If you want, I will write that down for your file." Trap tried to make his lips disappear like Doris's.

Trap went back in time to that night on the side of the hill. They were able to recover both the girl and the money, but things got a little out of control when one of the players got smart. Two of Trap's men had to pull him off of the guy. Trap was able to get the County Prosecutor to throw out the attempted murder charge and drop the whole thing down to simple assault. Given the criminal record of the man Trap almost beat to death, the prosecutor was able to convince the man to drop his civil suit. The prosecutor then dropped the charges against Trap.

"Thank you, Mr. Martin. We would welcome your statement. Our analysis projects that at the end of the fourth quarter, Martin & Associates will end the year profitably and will qualify for the usual profit sharing consideration. That concludes my report, Mother."

"Thank you, Doris." Victoria looked to the door, and it seemed to open on the force of her gaze. The maitre'd stood to the side as three waiters brought in the three meals. They were followed by the bartender, who placed a fresh martini mix in the wine stand. The plates were precisely placed before them, with the waiters retiring without a sound. Trap watched the bartender as she walked out. He would definitely be back to check her out.

The maitre'd stood at the server until Victoria took her first bite.

"This is fine. Thank you." With a nod of his head, the maitre'd backed out of the room, closed the door, and then ran to the bar for the drink that was waiting for him.

Out of the corner of his eye, Trap watched as Victoria cut her fish into small pieces. He wondered to himself how many men and women she had cut up like that in one way or another. Part of him wanted to know the answer, but there was a part of him that is perfectly satisfied in not ever knowing the answer to that question.

Victoria was half way through her meal when she rested her knife and fork. Trap knew what was coming and was not looking forward to it. Doris tried to appear impassive. Trap knew she wasn't.

"Mr. Martin, do you have any further information on that murderous adulterer who is responsible for the death of my son?"

A glass full of Spanish olives was left on the server by the bartender. Trap rose from his seat, placed three of the olives in Victoria's glass, then refreshed her drink. Doris cursed herself for not being faster.

"As you know, we have been keeping her under surveillance. She is now working in the operations section of Franklin Valley Savings & Loan. She appears to be involved or trying to get involved with the head of the operations section. That would be a John Case. We have not been able to get anything on him. As a matter of fact, his records appear to be too clean. In any event, we will continue to monitor her."

Doris cocked her head to the side and cast a suspicious glance.

"How can someone's record be 'too clean?'"

Trap was enjoying the duck and fought hard with himself not to take a dinner roll and sop up the gravy.

"There is a certain profile that matches a person's economic position, social position, and professional position. In this guy's case, there should be some missed credit card payments, a traffic ticket or two, or some other kind of glitches that will say, 'this is a regular guy that has hit a few bumps in the road.' There is nothing like that on Case. If I were working him, I would say that his record is almost fabricated." Trap looked at the plate and wished there was more.

Victoria Whittington could not have been more disinterested.

"Mr. Martin, the focus of this investigation, and what you are being paid more than adequately to do, is to apprehend Priscilla." She looked straight at Doris in order to make the point to both of them.

"I do not care one whit about this Case fellow. If it is his misfortune to become involved with that woman, then that is his affair. Not ours. Is that clear?" Doris and Trap nodded their assent as the reprimand hit home.

"I do not want you to wait for something to happen. I want you to make something happen. I want you to do whatever it is you need to do to make that woman pay for the death of my son. Have I made myself understood?" Victoria's eyes were ablaze with hatred.

Trap suddenly became uncomfortable. He fought back the image of his high school coach that was struggling to be seen.

"Yes, Mrs. Whittington. That is very clear."

"Good. Now let's see what they have here for dessert."

CHAPTER SEVEN

Trap and Doris lay together on the king-size bed of the Wayfarer Motel. Trap was naked, except for his socks, which were a hideous shade of beige. Doris remained dressed in her suit, with the skirt bunched around her waist. She played with the hairs on his chest while two glasses of champagne sat on the nightstand adjacent to the bed.

"Why do you keep your socks on?"

Trap reached for a glass of champagne.

"You don't give me time to take them off." He took a sip, then passed her the glass.

Doris took a sip from the glass, handed it back, then rolled off the bed. She stood up, smoothed her skirt, and to Trap's eye, looked somewhat sexy in the conservative gray suit with her white blouse open and revealing her large breasts.

"Do you know why I keep my clothes on when you fuck me?" The question seemed ridiculous to Trap as he watched take her clothes off. He sat up in the bed, refilled the glass, and shook his head.

"No."

"She makes me wear this suit or something like it whenever we meet with you. She wants me to look dumpy so she can play Miss Dress-Up in her silk print dresses. So, I keep this suit on just to get back at her. God, if she knew I was fucking you..." Trap let her ramble. She underestimated her mother, but that was her mistake, not his.

Trap noticed the care that she took in hanging the garments in the closet. It seemed to contradict what she just said. If she hated the suit, then why take the time to hang it up? Why not just throw it on the chair and then come back and suck my dick? Trap smiled to himself with that last statement. She did come by that particular talent honestly.

With her back to him, Trap gauged her ample ass and the fold of fat at her waist. She was a big woman but not sloppy. There was just enough of a shape left to imply that years ago Doris Whittington might have been somewhat of an athlete. Trap took another sip of champagne, then crossed his legs.

"Old man Whittington must have been a big boy. I bet old Doris was a bitch on the lacrosse field," he thought to himself.

As she hung up her suit and removed her blouse, Doris spoke with her back to Trap.

"Do you know why I ordered the roast pork for lunch?" Trap made a disinterested face. "It was because you were such a pig when that bartender walked into the room." Trap took another sip of his drink and made another disinterested face.

"I was sitting right there and you undressed her right in front of me. You would fuck anything, wouldn't you?"

Trap looked up at Doris, took a sip, then placed his arm behind his head.

"She's a woman, isn't she? Why not?" For an instant, Trap saw an image from long ago replayed in his mind. He smiled involuntarily.

It was not what he said but the smile that came afterwards. That was the slight that she needed. Doris threw the rest of her champagne in Trap's face. Faster than one would expect from a man of his size, Trap leapt from the bed and knocked the glass from her hand. He held both of her wrists in one hand as he dragged her back to the bed. With absolutely no concern as to how it might feel, Trap threw her like a rag doll across the bed.

Trap slapped her ass several times and then mounted her from the rear. To him, she was nothing more than an object conveniently placed here for his pleasure. A perk that came with the job. A hired hand doing what was expected of him.

Doris cried out again as she felt the full force of him. But she pushed into him as well. "More, you bastard. Give me more!" The sounds of flesh meeting flesh filled the room. As did the scent of sex mixed with sweat and uncontrolled lust. Soon, they were breathing as one, moving as one, and when the crescendo was upon them, they cried out as one.

"Why did it have to be him? He was not what she wanted. He was a tool to her, but what was she to him? Did it matter?" Doris let the questions bounce around in her head as she looked out the window.

"No, it did not matter. I'm getting what I want without having to work too hard for it." Doris allowed herself to take a deep breath and relax.

Day turned to night in the world outside of the Wayfarer Motel. Inside, the room and the people in it were bathed in a golden glow. They were into their second bottle of champagne as the sun set below the horizon. Doris glanced at their image in the mirror on the ceiling. Not liking what she saw, she turned away.

"Trap, tell me about the Jennings case."

"I can't."

Doris sat up, becoming animated.

"You can. I am an admitted attorney and 'Of Counsel' to the Trust. What you tell me is protected by privilege. Now tell me about the case."

Trap reached for the champagne bottle, and instead of using a glass, brought the bottle to his lips.

He muttered to himself, "Whatever…"

"Jennings youngest, Amber, is a little freak and a druggie. She got caught up with some guys who took porn photos of her with all sorts of playmates, doing all sorts of nasty things. Unbeknownst to little precious, they tried to blackmail her folks. The demand was three million dollars. They threatened to go public with the photos. If the police were called, they said that they would kill Amber. That's when I was called."

"What did you do?"

"I put a team together. I picked up night scopes and silencers for the weapons and a GPS tracker that could only be picked up on my frequency.

We delivered the money, then tailed the pick-up. When they were all together, we got the money and Amber."

"What did you do to them, Trap? Give me all of the details." There was excitement in her eyes as she stroked his penis.

Trap took another pull from the bottle.

"Let's just say they won't be taking anymore photos of anyone and leave it at that."

Doris was breathing hard, biting her lip and fondling her breast.

"Did you have to shoot any of them?"

Trap looked at her warily.

"We took care of them. That is all you need to know."

Doris closed her eyes, continued to rub herself against Trap's body, and then fell over on her back beside him.

"You beat them bad, didn't you?" Doris bit her lower lip and placed her hands between her legs.

"I know you beat them badly. God, I wish I could have been there. I would have wanted to see that."

Trap looked at the woman in bed with him, not believing what he was hearing.

"How do you know that?"

"Because I know you, Trap." Doris let the feeling wash over her.

"There's a brutality suit against you, remember? Um, I bet you beat them with your fists. Yeah, I think that's what you did. You beat each one of them. And when you were finished, there was blood all over the place." She took his hand in hers and examined his knuckles. Then she took the hand to her mouth and began to lick the cracked and bruised skin.

"Am I right, Trap? Is that what you did?" She examined the hand as if it were a portal into the past.

Trap frowned inside. She was closer to the truth than he would ever admit to, but that was not what bothered him. She knew a bit too much about him to get that close.

"You wanted to know the story, so I told you. How it ended is not important."

Doris knew she was right. But she also knew when to back off. Trap was a dangerous man, and who she is would not matter if he was pushed too far.

"Trap, do you think you will ever get anything on Priscilla?"

Trap knew that if he told her what he really thought, she would go back to her mother with it and that would be the end of his gravy train.

"Yes, eventually we will get something on her." Pausing for a minute, he decided that he had better embellish the point to show that he had been paying attention.

"And if not, we will get enough information to make something stick. All we need is right combination of opportunity and timing."

Doris touched him the way she knew he liked it. There was something that she needed to know, and she wanted him to give her an answer. Hesitantly, and in a small voice, she asked the question.

"Would you really fuck my mother?"

Trap gave her a long look, thought for a minute, then took a sip from his glass.

"About four years ago, just after I started working for your mother, she called me into her office. She told the secretary to hold all calls and then she locked the door. You were away on a trip.

Victoria told me that she was very pleased with my work and that the acquisition of my company was turning out to be quite profitable for her. I thanked her for her comments, but she waved them off. She told me that I was entitled to a bonus for all of my efforts, but before she would tell me what my bonus would be, there was one thing that she wanted me to do."

Doris was now intrigued. For the last seven years, she had been the second in command within the Trust organization, and her mother's only advisor and confidant. She had never known her mother to be alone with any man, for any reason, after her father died, much less to close and lock the door to her office.

"What was it that she asked you to do?"

Trap sat up in the bed.

"She sat on the sofa in her office and said 'Mr. Martin, come here please.' I went over to her, not having a clue as to what it was she wanted. Then she reached inside my pants and began to work on me. When I was at the point that she wanted, she lay back on the sofa, lifted her dress, and said, 'If you please...'. I took that to mean only one thing, so I did as I was asked. When we were done, she gave me the keys to my first Jaguar. In the glove box was a bonus check for $50,000. Would I fuck your mother? I already have."

Doris was incredulous.

"Why, the old bitch! The old, prudish bitch! You mean to tell me...?" Doris let out a coarse laugh.

"I can't even imagine her doing that. I have new respect for her now. Did you ever do her again?"

"That's none of your business."

Doris was now convinced that Trap Martin was nothing more than a tool. A tool to be used by both her and her mother. Did this make her more like her mother? She did not know. What she did know is that it excited her. She bit her lower lip and looked at Trap with hooded eyes.

"Give it to me again, Trap. Hard and rough. Make it hurt. Just like before." Trap Martin studied the woman beside him, then reached for his pants and removed his belt.

CHAPTER EIGHT

Jack Case sat in his office pondering the sea of trees outside his window. He had made a decision to stay well away from Priscilla and it soured him. To avoid her would imply that he is afraid of her and he just could not allow that. He had to do something. He could not let her get away with invading his life. He let that happen once during his tour in Europe. He would not let that happen again. Jack took out the surveillance photo and began to study it, yet again. He felt his body relax as an idea formed in his head. She started this. He would finish it. Case left his office that evening with a mission in mind.

Estrella Ortega moved through the huge Wegmann's Supermarket at a slow, easy pace. She liked to listen to the conversations of the people around her. Not for the information but to pick up the different ways of speaking. She loved it here in America. She loved seeing the different types of people and the way they lived among each other. In her village, everyone was the same, with the same dream and the same slim chances of that dream ever coming true. Here, everyone's life is a dream. They may not know it, but she did. Estrella could not help but be amazed at the difference.

With her shopping done, she stepped out of the store into a crisp clear day. Estrella loaded the groceries into the trunk of her 1995 Volvo sedan. Pricilla had wanted to buy her a later model car, but she would not hear of it.

This would do fine. Estrella closed the trunk lid, oblivious to the eyes that followed her until her pale blue car melded into traffic.

In between rolling homemade cigarettes, The Eyes assessed the traffic in and out of the store. Only the women were of interest. To The Eyes, the parking lot was like a pond on a grassy plain, teeming with different types of game. The Eyes were looking for a particular type of game. One that was elusive and hard to spot. The Eyes would be patient. He knew how to wait. It would not take much effort to catch what you wanted if you knew what to look for and were prepared to wait for it. The Eyes knew that.

The Pathfinder blended in with the other SUV's parked in the lot. The perfect camouflage for the type of game he was after. It did not take long before The Eyes spotted the female of the species that he was after. He raised the Canon digital camera, focused, and fired. There. Now he would track her.

Doris sat at her desk, staring out the window at the morning scene, sore from the events of the prior day. The pain that she felt was like a souvenir from a recent vacation. She bit her lower lip at the thought of how she came to have her souvenir and who gave it to her.

Was Trap telling her the truth? Would he ever get something on Priscilla and avenge her brother's death? No, she did not think so. But she wouldn't tell her mother that. Not only would the old biddy not believe her, but why should she compromise the only man who gave her what she wanted, the way she wanted it? Doris smiled at that thought. Well, perhaps he wasn't the only man or woman for that matter, but he was the latest and the best so far. Doris let that thought hang in the air as she returned to the night before. Then she gave in to the urge, closed her eyes, and let her right-hand fall between her legs.

Blair picked up the photos of the fourth dead woman and studied the image for the tenth time. There were no footprints or tire tracks. No fingerprints or other forensic evidence to point her in some kind of direction. But still, there was this nagging itch about the photograph.

"What is it? Where is it?" Blair uttered the question out loud just as Russ Matson was passing by.

"Did you say something, Blair?" The grandfatherly expression on his face was so kind, Blair wondered how he could have ever arrested anyone.

"No, Russ. I was just thinking out loud."

"Well, there's no harm in that I guess." As the soon-to-be-retired cop walked away, a light bulb lit up in Blair's head. She quickly made some notes, grabbed her bag, and ran out of the office.

To anyone who cared to look, Priscilla was sorting forms. The fact of the matter is that only her hands were sorting the forms. Her mind was sorting out the puzzle that bore the name of Jack Case. There had to be a way to get to him. She thought about all the others and the things that she had done to have her way with them. Some were easy and hardly worth the effort and then there were others that were more difficult. But in the end, she always won. She made them want her, and when they could not help themselves, it was her decision whether or not they would have her. That was the point of it. It was with that very thought that the answer hit her. There was nothing about Jack Case that was like any of the others. He was like a smooth surface that you could not get a grip on. There was confidence but no ego. There was caution but no fear. Fast and loose one minute, under complete control the next.

Priscilla paused for a moment and then let a smile crease her face. Control. No man could resist her when she made it known that she wanted him. No man, except Case. He wanted her. She felt it. She knew it. She saw it in his eyes and heard it in his voice. But he held himself back. He was in control, not her. That was the difference. That's what set him apart. Priscilla re-focused both on her work and her play. This was her game. There is no way he would be better at it than her.

It was after ten before Case arrived at his office. He had spent most of the night working on the problem named Priscilla. Before he came to work, Jack took some time to put the finishing touches on what he hoped to be the solution to his problem. Proud of his work, he slipped the disc into the computer, prepared the remaining parts of his plan, and then left for the day.

The scream was heard throughout the office. It was a piercing, bloodcurdling scream that is usually heard in horror movies or during back ally rapes.

Peggy Finn was the first to arrive at the cubicle. Growing up amongst the troubles in the North of Ireland, there was very little that she had not seen and even less that she was afraid of.

Priscilla was standing outside of her cubicle shaking. On her computer screen is an image of herself, old and disheveled. Her hair is a mess, her clothes ragged and torn, her skin sagging and fallow. She is standing barefoot on a street corner, with a shopping bag by her side and her hand outstretched begging for money. Garbage and filth surrounded her. So lifelike, it appeared to be a recent photograph and not a computer-generated image. Pricilla looked at the image again, became frightened anew, and turned away, covering her face with her hands.

Peggy powered off the computer, then placing a comforting arm around the frightened woman, led her away from the other clerks who made no attempt to suppress their laughter.

"Come on, let's go outside for a while."

The cool fall air felt good. It seemed to wash away most of the image that she saw. The only thing that remained was the look of utter despair and hopelessness on the face of the woman on the screen. On her. It would be a long time before she would come to grips with that look.

Priscilla suddenly became very much aware of herself. She felt naked, that every inch of her was exposed for all the world to see. The Scorpio within her lived on the edge. She was not afraid of anything but that. Priscilla suddenly looked around for some place to hide, but there was no place to go, nowhere to run. She was losing control.

Peggy put both hands on her shoulders.

"Priscilla, it's ok. Someone is playing a joke on you, that's all. Don't worry. I'll get I.T. to remove it when we get back. Just calm down." Peggy's words sounded far away. "Come on, we'll have you work at another station for the day."

Priscilla looked at her supervisor with pleading eyes.

"Peggy, what I saw today was my worst nightmare. I would kill myself before I let that happen to me." The expression on Priscilla's face was begging for understanding.

Peggy had seen pure fear before and recognized it in this woman.

"I know, Priscilla. We'll make it go away." It was only after those words were said that Priscilla was able to reenter the building.

Peggy Finn never quite believed the cockiness of this woman that everyone else bought into. Perhaps it was because no one ever gave *her* the benefit of the doubt that she refused to accept the obvious. As Peggy looked at their reflection in the entrance door, she had to laugh to herself. Here she was obese, dumpy, dressed for comfort rather than style, consoling this trim, chic, look of perfection. How crazy is this? Before she could give it another thought, Peggy laughed involuntarily. Priscilla focused on the reflection and laughed as well. Then she turned to her newfound friend.

"Thank you, Peggy. Thanks for being there."

She paused for a minute, then added, "Congratulations." Peggy eyed her suspiciously. "On your weight loss. It looks like you must have lost about 30 pounds."

Peggy smiled sheepishly, "I did not think anyone had noticed."

"I did not know how you would take it if it was called to your attention, so I thought that I would wait until the right time to mention it. But yes, I did notice."

"Thank you. I am working very hard at it." Peggy felt a new pride grow within her.

"Well, keep up the good work." The reflection disappeared as they re-entered the building. In its place was the forming of a bond that would be much more permanent.

CHAPTER NINE

Priscilla's thoughts centered around the one person responsible for the image on her computer. Jack Case. All she had to go on was her intuition, but that was enough for her. She was convinced that he was responsible. But what next? Was there more to this? Priscilla had never encountered this before. In her game, the men she went after either succumbed to her wishes, or if she determined them not to be worthy of her, she sent them packing, left to wonder what might have been. No man had ever fought back. She was always the hunter, the aggressor. She was the one who did the scaring. Now the tables have been turned. Her mark had actually changed the rules to her game. Where would this lead? She had no clue. Priscilla was out on a limb again, only this time, instead of excitement, for the first time in her life, she felt a fear that she had never experienced before.

The Eyes moved confidently. His quarry was unaware of his presence. He found what he needed. But before he could use it, he had to know the nature of the beast. He had to be with her in her element. He had to get close to her. The Eyes rolled another cigarette and watched.

Blair Collins left the coroner's office, and suddenly, the day seemed brighter, the air seemed fresher, and her car did not look so beat up. She had a lead. Not a great lead. Not a solid lead. But a lead. Something that could turn into evidence given a little bit of luck and the right answers to the right questions. Yes, the day did in deed seem brighter.

Priscilla could not concentrate. She was angry. She wanted revenge. She had a taste for blood that would not go away. Yet, Priscilla was also self-conscience. Her panic attack was out of character for her. It seemed to her that every laugh in the office was directed at her; that she was the subject of every conversation or comment. Priscilla was off balance. It was a feeling that she was not accustomed to.

"Peggy, if you do not mind, I would like to leave early today. I'm sorry, but I am still rattled from this morning." This was an admission that Priscilla was clearly having trouble with and it showed.

"Not a problem. Go home." Peggy's smile was warm and understanding.

"Take a hot bath and forget about today. It's in the past."

Priscilla stood in the entrance to the building and turned her collar up to the cool afternoon breeze. She was glad to be out of the office. Had Case been in, she would have confronted him. The fact that he was not made him all the more suspect. Priscilla felt empowered at the thought of confronting Case. No one gets away with humiliating her.

"I will see you tomorrow, Mr. Case."

On the passenger seat of her black Corvette was an envelope. Priscilla knew she had not left it there. The only explanation is that someone got into her car and placed it there. One thought and a thousand feelings ran through Priscilla's body. Priscilla looked around knowing that she would not see anyone, but she felt the need to check nonetheless. A voice from inside told her to rip the envelope up and not view the contents.

"Just tear it into a million pieces, throw them out the window, and then drive away." There was no name. No postmark. The envelope was not sealed. With her hands protected by expensive kid leather driving gloves, Priscilla lifted the flap and withdrew the contents inside. One look and she wished she hadn't.

Inside the envelope was an eight by ten enlargement of the lower third of the computer image from this morning. It showed her dirty bare feet and the lower portion of her dirty tattered garment standing next to an overflowing garbage can in greater detail. The upper portion of her body, along with the rest of the scene, was edited from the picture. While the effect was not as frightening as this morning, the photo rekindled the feelings and her fear. Once again, a scream came forth. Only this time, it was a scream of anger. Priscilla violently ripped the photo, the envelope, and the thoughts that she had of the game to be played with Jack Case into 100 pieces and threw them all out of the window of her car. She vented her rage on the transmission of her car as she slammed it into reverse and sped out of the parking lot. She did not know what she would do, but he would pay. That much she knew. Jack Case was going to pay.

As soon as Blair got back to the office, she pulled up all the information she could find on knives. It was not too long before she hit pay dirt. She then started working the phones, calling the F.B.I., A.T.F., and the Defense Department. Blair then faxed requests for autopsy reports from the other murder cases. She was on to something, and she knew it. She was in the middle of dialing a number when Russ Matson ambled by.

"Still talking to yourself?" With a newspaper under his arm and his tie undone, it was clear that Russ was done for the day. Blair's response was a big smile and a kiss on the cheek of the face of the man who just might have helped break her case. Russ touched his cheek as he watched her walk away.

"I'll take that as a no."

Priscilla's rage and fear subsided by the time she reached her home. Defiantly, she waited until the door was down and locked before she entered the house. No one was going to sneak in and plant anything else in her car if she could help it.

Estee was at her usual place by the stove. The smells of food being prepared did little to blunt the edge to Priscilla's tone. She bypassed Spanish and spoke English.

"Was there any mail today?"

Estrella could tell from the way Priscilla entered the room that her day had not gone well. Rather than feel the wrath of her friend, she gestured with her wooden spoon and responded with the same degree of courtesy that was shown to her.

"The mail, it is there on the counter, where it always is."

The chill in the response was just enough to bring Priscilla back to reality. She stopped in her tracks and sheepishly smiled at her one and only friend.

"I'm sorry, Estee. I had a bad day today. I did not mean to take it out on you." As an indication of her sincerity, Priscilla hugged Estrella, letting her head rest on her shoulder.

Estrella touched her hand.

"I know the day is bad for you. I can tell. You are home early. The dinner is no ready yet. You need to do the exercise. Go now to the basement. I will call you when the dinner it is ready."

Flipping through the days mail and not finding any strange envelopes further lightened the mood. Her friend was right. A good workout always made her feel better.

"Thanks, Estee." After stopping at the hall closet to hang up her coat, Priscilla went to her bedroom, changed into a leotard, tights, and sneakers, then went to the basement exercise area to begin her workout. She froze in her tracks when she saw the envelope taped to the data display of the treadmill.

Pricilla froze in her tracks.

"ESTEE!" She backed away from the treadmill and yelled up the stair case.

"ESTEE!" Estrella found her friend at the bottom of the stairs, consumed in anger.

"Que pasa, hermana? Que es esto?" Estrella had never seen Priscilla so angry.

Pricilla pointed to the treadmill.

"How did that get there?"

Estrella glanced at the exercise machine.

"I do not know. I did not put it there."

"Someone was in here, Estrella. How did they get in here?" The look in her eyes was anger, but the tone of her voice was fear.

"Yo no se. I don't know. I was out for a little while at the shopping place, but I did not go for long. The house, it was locked, and I set the alarm just like you showed me. I do not know." Estrella's eyes began to fill with tears.

She was afraid. And the first thought that a scarred illegal immigrant has is that they will be sent back to the one place that they never want to return to.

"Please, hermana, I do not know how the thing it got there."

Perhaps it was the tears in her eyes or maybe it was the sound in Estrella's voice. Whatever it was, it brought Priscilla back from the brink of hysteria. Someone had to be strong here. It was just the two of them. In a few seconds, Priscilla was able to regain her composure or at least fake it.

"It's okay, Estrella. I believe you." Instinctively, she did believe her friend. But she also knew that someone got into her house and planted that envelope. That issue would have to be dealt with.

Again, a voice in Priscilla's head told her to rip the envelope up without opening it. But then there was another voice, a much stronger voice, telling her to face whatever it was that was in that envelope.

"Look it in the eye and stare it down. Open it."

Estrella looked at the envelope. There was something here that frightened her friend who had no fear. Common sense is universal and exists in any language. If her friend is afraid of this envelope, if there is something in it that would make her this mad and so afraid, then she should be afraid of it as well. Estrella did not move.

"Estrella, please, open the envelope." Priscilla stood with her arms folded and her body evenly balanced. The soft, affirmative tone of Priscilla's voice was what was needed to change the feeling in the air. This was the woman that Estrella knew. This was the woman that she would do anything for. Estrella did not know who the other woman was, but for this woman, she would open the envelope and face whatever was in there.

What she found was a photo. An eight by ten replica of the portrait shot taken for the background check. Estrella exhaled audibly.

"It is a photograph, hermana. It is a very nice picture of you." With childlike innocence, Estrella brought the photo to Priscilla.

Priscilla examined the photo as if she did not recognize the face looking back at her. "Thanks, Estrella. I am sorry if I frightened you." Priscilla suddenly felt very tired. Her thoughts had one theme.

"Someone was in here, but how did they get in?" She began to doubt herself. The reports of the recent murders of women came alive in her head.

"Maybe it wasn't Case? Maybe it was someone else? But who?" She was about to relax when another, more frightening thought entered her mind.

"Could whoever it is still be in here?"

"It is okay, hermana. The dinner is almost ready." Estrella placed a gentle hand on Priscilla's shoulder, then started to leave to put the finishing touches on the meal.

Priscilla put a firm hand on her friend's shoulder.

"Estrella, wait. Stay with me." Priscilla led her friend back up to the kitchen. She went to her desk and removed the .32 caliber automatic that was in the lower left-hand drawer. It was one of two guns in the house; the second, a .38 caliber revolver, was located in the nightstand by her bed. Priscilla loaded the weapon, chambered a round, then took Estrella by the hand.

"Stay behind me." Frightened beyond measure, all the woman could do was nod her head.

Priscilla led the way through the house. All doors were opened. Every place where someone could hide was searched. It was only when she was convinced that there was no one in the house did she relax.

"Hermana, why you no call the police?" Estrella was visibly drained.

Priscilla replaced the pistol in the drawer but did not unload it.

"The house was not broken into. Nothing was taken. I did not want them to think that I was just some crazy woman imaging things. Besides, I handle my own problems." Estrella did not understand the last part but made no effort to question it. With shaky hands, she returned to putting the finishing touches on dinner as Priscilla headed upstairs. Now they both had had bad days.

By the time Priscilla came back downstairs, the table was set, the wine was poured, and Estrella was seated, waiting for her. The meal was a fish dish in a tomato-based sauce. It was accompanied by the obligatory rice, as well as sautéed mixed vegetables and fresh baked bread for dipping. The aroma washed away the last traces of fear from the day. By the end of dinner, both women were laughing at themselves.

While Estrella cleared the table, Priscilla read more about the fourth woman found murdered in the area. There was nothing to indicate that any of the murders occurred indoors or that the murderer knew his victims. This seemed to relieve her fears that the envelopes could be related to these gruesome events. She had just gotten to the end of the article when Estrella walked into the room. Suddenly feeling the value of her friendship with this woman, Priscilla rose from her chair and hugged her friend.

"Estrella, please be careful when you are out. You are the only friend I have, and I do not want to lose you."

Estrella smiled a smile that was meant to be reassuring.

"Si, hermana. I will be careful." She returned the hug of her friend and employer, then retired to her room to study English and pray for a safe night.

It was seven o'clock by the time Blair left the office, but she was happy with the progress that she made with her one slim lead. It would be 24 hours before anyone could get back to her, so the only thing left to do is to get some rest and a good night's sleep. On the way home, Blair picked up a take-out order of Peking duck and the latest issue of the Atlantic Monthly. It would be a good night.

Priscilla surfed all 88 channels on the 60 inch T.V. three times and then called it a night. Before going upstairs, she checked all of the doors and windows on the first floor. Priscilla then called the alarm company prior to entering the alarm code. It was not that she did not trust the alarm. She had more than her share of false alarms to know that it worked. It was just that on this night, Priscilla needed to know that there was a live person on the other end of the line. Only with that reassurance was she able to climb the stairs to her bedroom.

To the extent that Priscilla could avoid the most mundane matters, she did. Motion detectors controlled most of the lights in her house. That way she did not have to worry about turning a light off when she left a room, nor did she have to look for a light switch when she entered a room. To Priscilla's way of thinking, if she could afford to have this level of comfort, then why not?

The monitor in the hall signaled to the bedroom that she was coming. Priscilla walked into a well-lit room, which further allayed her fears, although she did pause in the doorway for a second and scanned the room. She shed her clothes without a second thought, spent the required time in the bathroom, then, dressed only in her underwear, she approached the satin sheets of her bed. The white paper peeking out from beneath the pillow was almost invisible against the pale pink sheets.

Priscilla almost laughed at the pang of panic that flashed through her body. Certain that whatever was inside the envelope was harmless, she sat on the edge of the bed, opened the flap, and pulled out the contents. What was inside was the upper two-thirds of the computer image from this morning. Once again, she was face to face with her worst nightmare. Priscilla dropped the envelope, covering her face with her hands. She tried to scream, but the sound seemed to be stuck deep in her throat. Without warning, the light in the bathroom went out. Then the hall light turned itself off. Priscilla felt like she did not have any control over what was happening around her. She wrapped her arms around her knees as she sat frozen in terror on the king-size bed. One last glance at the picture on the floor did it. Priscilla decided that she had had enough.

CHAPTER TEN

Case called in, checked his messages, and then had his call transferred to Peggy Finn. She told him what happened to Priscilla and that she allowed her to leave the office early. "She was really spooked, boss. Whoever sent her that photo knew exactly how to get to her." Case signed off by telling Peggy that he agreed with her decision, and he would look into the matter with I.T.

Case thought for a long minute after he turned off his cell phone and before he started his car. He was not proud of what he had done, but it was something that needed to be done. That sentence seemed to sum up his very existence and anything of substance that he ever did.

"It was nothing to be proud of but something that had to be done." Jack Case started his car, turned into the traffic, and drove off.

The Eyes tracked the beast to her lair. Invisible in the shadows, he kept a vigil as day turned into night. If she came out, he would track her. Only when all of the lights in the lair went out did he leave.

The Eyes downloaded the pictures from the camera into his computer and then printed the images. He had what he needed. Looking at the pictures ignited the flame within him that drove him on his quest. He was close to the end. He was almost done. He only needed three more. The thought saddened him. He rolled a cigarette, licked the paper to seal it, then lit the match. The Eyes studied the look on the beast. Then he took out his scissors and began to crop the printed image, saving the parts he wanted, and disregarding the rest. He could have done this on the computer, but he liked the feel of the scissors cutting. He liked the thought of being in control. He liked seeing the beast disfigured and then remade into the shape that he adored. Yes, this is what he liked.

The occupant, as well as the car, were nearly invisible on the quiet, tree-lined street. From this vantage point, three quarters of Priscilla's house was in view. The part-time private detective thought this assignment to be almost like charity. Tail the subject from the time she leaves her place of employment until she reaches her home. Follow her until she retires for the night and then log off.

Priscilla stopped shaking. Her eyes, her face, her entire body became as cold and as hard as ice. She picked up the envelope and carried it and the photo, into the bathroom. There, she slowly ripped them into eight equal pieces and then flushed them down the toilet. She was wounded. Somehow, some way, he found the nerve that she kept well hidden. He found it and plucked it again and again and again. Pricilla took the revolver from the nightstand, checked that it was fully loaded, and without stopping to put on any other clothing, went to the garage. If it were not for the coat that was hanging by the door, she would have driven into the night dressed only in her underwear.

• • • • •

As the lights inside the house went out in sequence, one of the associates of "Martin Security Associates" recorded the time in his notebook. He shook his head at the waste of time he made looking at his watch.

"This bitch is like clockwork. Same time every night." Waiting the required hour after the last light went out, he was just about to leave when the garage door opened. The signature sound of the Corvette exhaust was unmistakable as it backed out onto the street. Without coming to a full stop, Priscilla shifted the car into first and sped off into the night. Without turning on the headlights of his own car, the P.I. slowly followed her. He was happy for the extra time on the clock, but this meant that his wife would be asleep by the time he got home.

"Oh well, no sex for you tonight, buddy."

Priscilla tightened her grip on the steering wheel and drove without thinking. Priscilla pressed the throttle further. No one does this to her. No one. Then, forced to stop at a traffic light, all she saw was an image. The image of her standing in front of him in her underwear. She is pointing her gun at him and he is just looking back at her. Totally relaxed. Just looking at her. Again, he is in control. Again, she loses.

The moonlighting officer watched as the Corvette pulled over to the side of the road. He started to stop and check her out, using the excuse that he was wondering if she needed any help, but he decided against it. Instead he kept his speed even and passed right by her. Out of the corner of his eye, he could swear that she was not wearing anything under her coat.

Pricilla pulled over as her mind finally caught up to her emotions. She took a deep breath and rested her head on the steering wheel. What was she doing out here, more naked than dressed, with a loaded gun on the passenger seat of her car? What did she think she was going to do? She was a lot of things in the minds of a lot of different people, and sometimes even in her own mind, but she was not a murderer. That fact had been proven in a court of law. So, what was she going to do, scare him? Jack Case? That was laughable. No wonder he just looked back at her. Feeling like a virgin who is trying to be a seductress and failing badly at the moment of truth, Priscilla buttoned her coat, turned her car around, and returned home.

The Eyes rarely slept. Only when fatigue became unbearable did the eyes close. But they did not stay closed for long. There was much to be done. She was out there and the portrait had to be completed. He was close. It would not take very much longer now.

Blair Collins very seldom slept passed 5:30. This day was no exception. After a morning stretch, 50 push-ups and 100 sit-ups, she was out the door for a six-mile run. Thirty-five minutes later, she would be back. This was her favorite time of the day. At the end of her run, with the sun coming up, she felt alive.

In middle of putting on the slacks to her dark blue, Ellen Tracey suit, Blair caught sight of her framed law degree out of the corner of her eye. She smiled (she did not know why), took a sip of her tea, then thought about her father, McFarland Collins, a prominent black southern California attorney.

He made his name before affirmative action and empowerment programs, which is to say he made his name the hard way. He wanted to be an attorney and he did. He wanted to become rich and he did. He wanted to become powerful and he did. He wanted his first born to be a son and that is where he began to pay for all his other wants. Blair McFarland Collins was born (The name Blair, representing the one concession her father would ever make to his wife who worked two jobs, while pregnant, to support him through law school).

Instead of her father, Blair idolized her uncle, who was a New York City detective. Despite the efforts of McFarland Collins (at one point, he banned his brother from his house), the nephew and niece remained close. When Blair announced at a very early age that she would join law enforcement so that she could be just like her Uncle Mason, her father took steps against that thought. McFarland Collins destined that his first born would follow him into practice. She would excel in civil litigation and discrimination law and build on his legacy. If she expanded the firm and made a lot of money doing it, then that would be a bonus. There was no way she would become a cheap flat foot, who he had come to despise.

In preparation for the possibility that the child would have other thoughts and to keep her focused on her grades, McFarland Collins created a trust fund. The deal was simple, go to law school and graduate at a decent level in your class and the money is yours. Do not go, or worse yet, waste my money by graduating at the bottom of your class and you do not receive one red cent.

Blair was 14-years-old when she demanded that he put his terms in writing. To this day, she still finds the look on his face amusing. However, to humor the child, he did, and that is when he paid the second price for his success.

After graduating from the University of California at Davis in the upper third of her class and then graduating from Stanford Law School (her father's alma mater) in the upper five percent, Blair then passed the California Bar exam with minimal study. At that point, Blair felt that she had satisfied the terms of her contract and could now pursue the career that she wanted instead of joining her father's firm. When Blair announced that she was pursuing a career in law enforcement, her father flew into a rage. Despite the threats from her father and the pleading of her mother, she refused to change her mind. Even her beloved uncle tried to persuade Blair to change her mind. She would not think of it. Finally, McFarland Collins acted in the only manner he could. He cut Blair out of her trust fund. Blair Collins reacted in the only manner that she could. She sued her father.

The contract that she had with her father was the only evidence she had or needed. She argued that the consideration needed to make the contract formal was the monetary value of the time she spent in law school as represented by the salary that she could have made as a police officer. This point was enhanced by the fact that she was prohibited, by contract, from doing anything else. By cancelling the trust fund, Blair argued that her father changed the terms of the contract unilaterally and that was a violation of the terms.

While there was no real case law exactly on point, Blair did find some relevant citations regarding the restrictions of exclusive contracts. Blair argued her case objectively, caught her father flat footed, and won her Summary Judgment motion with a ruling from the judge that she clearly satisfied the terms of the contract. After the verdict was rendered, the judge admonished McFarland Collins for forcing his daughter to bring this matter before him.

The novel trial made the local papers. For a period of time, McFarland Collins was the butt of jokes and comments whenever he was seen in public. That this most feared of trial attorneys was defeated by his own daughter was much too noteworthy to let go. His only sanctuary was his office, where he still ruled with an iron fist, but even there he knew that the staff was talking about him behind his back. Collins hated to lose and briefly entertained an appeal, but with the closing words of the judge still ringing in his ears, he quickly abandoned that thought. If he lost the appeal, he would not be able to show his face in State Court again.

McFarland Collins satisfied the judgment against him by releasing the trust fund claimed by the Plaintiff and paying her legal fees. Then he formally disowned his one and only child. Despite the attempts on her part (which included an offer to return the money or make a joint donation to charity), the pleadings of her mother, and the efforts of the other members of their family, there was no reconciliation. McFarland Collins made it clear that he would not be caught dead in the same room with "the person who used to be my daughter." Further should he find out that anyone in his family has been communicating with "that woman," they will be cut out of his will and forever be his enemy.

Seeing no future in remaining in California, Blair decided to move as far away from her father as possible. She packed her belongings in her car and headed east.

The one person that defied her father was her beloved uncle. The day that she graduated from the New Jersey State Police academy, he was the only family member to attend. Divorced and childless, he could not have been prouder. For Blair, his presence was all that mattered. However, the following day, Detective Sergeant Mason Collins was shot to death answering a hold up call at a local liquor store in the East New York section of Brooklyn. Blair received the flag from the coffin as the only family member in attendance.

When Blair last checked, her fund account stood at roughly $1.2 million, gaining four percent interest annually. As stubborn as her father, Blair vowed never to spend one cent of the money unless she absolutely had to. At one time, she considered giving it all away. Blair quickly came to her senses and decided to only use a portion of the interest earned, most of which she donated to charity.

However, there is no charitable donation that will take the place of not having been to a wedding, funeral, or spent Thanksgiving or Christmas with a blood relative in over ten years. Any contact with her mother is through a clandestine phone call or e-mail from a remote location. There are no birthday cards received or sent, nor is there any one to call when she is sick. Her work became her sole focus. Her cop friends replaced whatever family she might have had. Relationships came and went after Blair made it clear that marriage, or anything serious for that matter, was not in her future. All daughters worship their fathers. McFarland Collins left a scar on Blair that time would never heal. Blair washed away the rest of the emptiness of her personal thoughts with the remains of her tea. There was a case to be solved and it was time to get to it.

Martin Security Associates is one of four tenants in a two-story building along Route 1. Trap turned into the driveway, drove around to the rear of the building, and parked in the reserved space with his name on it. Only one time did someone else dare park in his space. When they returned to their car, they found a .22 caliber bullet hole in each one of the tires. No one has parked in his space again.

Resplendent in a worn gray suit, a dingy white shirt, and a blue tie highlighted with a coffee stain or two, all made of some form of blended fabric, Trap was the picture of success in his mind. Before entering the building, he took a moment to survey the parking lot. He saw the one car in the lot that mattered to him. Today was starting off well.

Gineen Walker, as far as the Whittington Trust was concerned, was Trap's secretary and a full-time employee. As with everything else in life, there was much more to her role than answering phones. Reports, invoices, and expense accounts were not Trap's strong suit and that is where Gineen's role started. The other things she did to contribute to the successful operation of his business is where her true value lied.

Trap's office was in the corner of the building with windows on two sides. To the rear of the building was a golf course and to the left was a farm. There was no way for anyone to see into his office without him seeing them. Aside from the gray metal desk that he salvaged from a building on the brink of destruction and some furniture that was purchased from a hotel going out of business, there was nothing else in the huge space.

The furniture reflected his personal taste in just about everything material.

"Why buy new, when used will do?" The walls were bare, despite the state requirement that his license be prominently displayed at all times and in need of paint. The carpet on the floor was as institutional as the desk. The only items in the office that were up to date, and as such, out of place, were a full array of electronic communications gear and the IBM "Think Pad" lap top computer that was sitting on a table to the left of his desk. At the far end of the office was a microwave and coffee maker sitting atop what used to be a dresser.

Gineen was in the midst of pouring his coffee when he came up behind her. Pulling her close, Trap kissed her on the neck and squeezed her breast, then sat down to go through the day's paperwork. Gineen served him his coffee (two sugars, not too much creamer), hung up his suit jacket, then took a seat on the sofa with pad and pen in hand.

Trap looked up and was about to speak when he caught a full view of his secretary. The split in her leather skirt revealed almost the entire length of her beautiful legs. The shear blouse that she wore would be too revealing for normal office attire but was right in line with the expectations of her employer. The package was rounded out with ample make-up and lipstick and hair that needed only minimum attention. Trap put the file down and leaned back in his chair. Taking the signal, Gineen got up, closed, and locked the door to the office as she unbuttoned her blouse and then positioned herself on her boss's lap. With one thing leading to another, it was not too long before both were spent and satisfied.

Gineen had no problem with this part of her job. In fact, to her, it was the best part. Having sex was what she liked to do, and here, she had the best of both worlds. An ex-street princess, Gineen hit hooker lotto three years ago. Trap needed some help on a matrimonial that he was working. His client wanted out of her marriage because her husband was boring. The husband wouldn't hear of it. Trap needed to pin something on him, but as boring guys go, this one was world class. Time and expense money were running out. He had to make up some dirt on the guy, and he had to do it fast.

Trap went down to Sixth Street, just off Park Place in Newark. He was well familiar with this corner and the women who worked it, having tailed more than one John Doe there before. There was one woman in the group that always made him take a second look. Dark skinned with almond shaped eyes, she was of average height, weight, and build. But there was something about Gineen that set her apart from the other hookers on the corner. She was not the best-looking woman in the bunch, but she seemed to have the most class. For what he had in mind, she was what he needed.

When the Jaguar pulled over to the curb, all the girls flocked to it. Gineen had been out on the street long enough to know that the driver was not necessarily as nice as the car. Rich guys have their issues. She was not in the mood to barter, or at the very worst, get slapped around by some guy just because he drove a nice car. Besides, she was one date away from making her night. She could afford to be choosy. It was only when her co-worker came over to her with the 100 dollar bill that she gave the car a second look.

"Um, girl, I don't know what it is you got, but he gimme me this 50 just to give you this c-note. You might want to check this one out." There was no jealousy in the woman's tone. Fifty bucks just to deliver a message is as good as a date.

Gineen took the bill and 'ho strolled past her colleague.

"Shit, girl, I've seen big bills before." Gineen leaned in the open window, giving the big spender a free look at her breasts.

"I heard you wanted to see me."

"Get in." Trap was not in the mood to waste a lot of time.

"Are you as big as this bill?" Gineen wanted to show that she was not impressed with the money.

"Cut the bullshit. I've got a job for you." Trap reached over to open the door. Gineen did not move.

"Not so fast, honey. This here just got my attention. Tell me what you want and how much you gonna pay. Then I get in the car." Gineen had been busted enough times to know most of the cop tricks. The law was clear, and if you knew it, you stayed out of jail.

The response was unexpected. Trap studied the woman, and it was only then that he noticed the ugly scar on the side of her face.

"I can't talk here. Get in."

Gineen was hungry, her feet hurt, and she was in no mood herself to play games.

"Look, see that black Jeep over there. There're two guys in it. They see me get in this car, I go on the clock. If I ain't back in 20 minutes, then I got a price to pay. I paid it once, I ain't payin' it again."

Trap saw something in her eyes and heard something in her voice that reminded him of a part of himself from another time.

"Is one of the guys in the Jeep the plastic surgeon that worked on your face?" There was no response, which given the question, was a response.

"Wait here. I'll be right back."

Trap turned off the car and pocketed the key. He thought about reaching underneath the seat for his gun, but two things stopped him. One of these whores would tip them off, and he would not get within 20 yards. The other thought was that it would be more fun to take them out without a gun. Besides, he needed the workout.

Trap walked over to the Jeep just as the occupants got out of their vehicle. Gineen had seen this act before. She held up her hands in a motion that said, "I did not have anything to do with this." The smaller of the two men smiled at her and motioned back that it was alright. The bigger man positioned himself in front of his boss.

"You don't want none of this, chump. Just get back in the pretty car of yours and ..." He never finished the sentence. Trap hit him with a wicked punch that not only broke his nose, but also shattered the socket of his right eye. The hulking enforcer was unconscious before he hit the ground.

"You done made a big mistake, muthafucka." The pimp pulled a straight razor from his pocket and made a clumsy attempt at an attack. Trap caught his arm in mid-flight, straightened it out, and then dislocated his elbow with the heel of his left hand. He put him down with a broken jaw, turned on his heel, and walked back to a stunned group of street walkers who could attest that they have now seen everything.

"Get in."

Gineen Walker did not think twice.

Trap pulled into a nearby diner where they took a booth in the back. Dressed in her "working clothes," all eyes were on them. Gineen was impressed that her dinner companion could not have cared less.

Over a cheeseburger deluxe and a diet Coke (a girl has to watch her figure), Trap presented his business card and his deal.

"I need you to pick a guy up, take him to a hotel, and make sure that the blinds are up when you fuck him. There is 200 in it for you, and you can keep what you get off him. If anyone asks, he's been a regular with you for years. If I have to bring you in for a deposition, there's an extra 100 in it for your time."

Gineen eyed him cautiously while the thoughts flooded her mind. She had just seen him take down two of the most dangerous men she knew. What would he do to her if she said no. Then what if he is a cop? His card said private investigations, but anyone can get a card printed up. Even so, on their worst day, no cop dressed as badly as this guy. He brought her to a public place, fed her, and made her a deal that would be illegal in any jurisdiction. And the most important part is that he gave her 100 bucks up front. No cop does that.

"Make it 250 for the pick-up and the fuck, you buy the clothes and cover expenses, and you've got a deal."

Trap noticed that she cut the burger in half before she ate it, used a fork instead of her fingers to eat the fries, and wiped the corners of her mouth with a napkin. She reminded him of the girls he went to college with. The ones who would fuck him in private but refused to be seen with him in public. The public princesses and private whores. This woman was the exact opposite. For a reason that he could not explain, Trap saw a certain honesty in that. He was impressed that she did not jump at the first offer but tried to cut her own deal. Smart. Trap smiled.

"I'll do the extra 50, but you buy the clothes out of the 100 that you already have."

"What about expenses?" Gineen gave him a smile that would charm a snake.

"I'm sure you have gotten men to buy you drinks before. I doubt that you have lost your touch." Trap laid a 20 on the table, then slid out of the booth.

"Call me at the number on the card tomorrow afternoon. I will tell you who, where, and when." That was the last night she worked a corner. The job went well, the divorce went through, and Gineen Walker became a regular employee of Martin Security Associates.

Her child went from public school to private school. She went from food stamps to credit cards. And her wardrobe went from K-Mart and Payless, to Nordstroms and Nine West. Gineen had money in the bank, a new apartment, and a health plan instead of the emergency room. Any time Trap needed "help" with a matrimonial, she got one of her friends to do it. That was Trap's rule, not hers. Her job, aside from handling the paperwork, was to be open and willing whenever he called, which was often. That was the very least of her worries. She was only doing now what she had always done. The difference was that there was only one man involved, and she was being paid a hell of lot more for it. Gineen never knew life could be this good.

Trap was not inclined to settle down, but there was something about this woman that put a hook in him. Since that night in the diner, he could not get her out of his mind. She handled herself well on the case, but that was not it. Love was a feeling that he did not give a lot of thought to. Whether this was love or not was something that he did not even consider. Trap wanted her with him. He did not want her on the street. When he made love to her, he did not see a whore. Trap laid out the deal as they lay in bed.

"Work for me. Stay off the street."

Inside, Gineen could not believe her ears. This was the brass ring, the prize of all prizes, but what was the catch? Hookers hear all sorts of things when they are lying on their backs, doing what they do best. She didn't know this guy. He could be just another white guy freaked out at having sex with a black woman. But then again, he did not know her either. In Gineen's mind, that evened the score. What she did know and what she would never forget was that this was the man that avenged the scar on her face. The scar that was put there just for the hell of it. No one in her life had cared not nearly that much for her or about her.

"Why? Why not?" Gineen held herself in check.

"Define work."

Trap laughed. This woman was no dope. Maybe that is what he liked about her, among a few other things.

"Personal secretary and more of what you're doing now."

"I don't type." She ran her hand over his chest.

"You won't have to." He sucked her breast.

"Full medical?" She stroked his penis, sticking her tongue in his ear.

"Blue Cross." He put her on her back and spread her legs.

"Benefits?" She wrapped her legs around his waist.

"Here's one of them." He mounted her, giving her the full measure of him. Gineen moaned, "Um, I'll take it."

Gineen brought herself back to the present as she re-opened the door to the office while Trap washed his hands in the sink.

"It seems like our girl started to go out last night but freaked and ran back home. Take a look at Jim's report."

Trap dried his hands with a towel that had long ago lost its softness, turned, and looked in the direction of his secretary and lover.

"Really?" Trap hung the towel on the rack by the sink, then walked back to his desk.

"It's the first field report. We know that Priscilla has been after her current boss for some time now. It follows the M.O. of her other jobs. According to Jim's report, there was something different about last night. It might be something to work with. The report's more detailed." Gineen laughed inwardly. After being busted more than a few times, she was now almost a cop herself. Life sure is strange.

Trap read the report and frowned. Old lady Whittington told him to make something happen. Time was running out. Priscilla's other marks were mid-level corporate types with wives and mortgages they could not afford. It would have been easy to concoct something with them and then put Pricilla in the middle of it. This new guy did not seem to have too much to work with. This was going to be tough.

Trap was not above blackmail. That did not bother him. What did bother him was that after all of these years, a very profitable and relatively easy assignment was about to come to an end. He closed the file and threw it to a corner of his desk. Quickly, he calculated approximately how much he had made on this case alone and then thought about what he would need to make up that lost income. The end result did not please him.

"Tell Jim to drop Priscilla and stay on the mark. He's to find out whatever he can on this guy but keep his distance. Have him call me later." Trap's thoughts drifted off to lost revenue.

Gineen made the notes on her pad.

"Will there be anything else?" The look on her face indicated that anything meant "anything."

Trap read her look and thought for a minute. Determining that he had other more important matters to think about, he shook his head no. He made a point, though, of not looking at her big, pretty, rear end as she walked out of his office lest he be tempted to call her back.

CHAPTER ELEVEN

The Eyes were up at dawn. They had to be. They had to meet the beast and follow it from its lair. The Eyes had to make sure she was the right one. No one else would do. The Eyes were ready, but the time had to be right. There were only two more left to do. There was no time for mistakes.

Lt. Maxine Stout held her case review meetings in the conference room. She chose to defer from her predecessor, who held such sessions in either the locker room, the bathroom, or the nearest bar. She made it clear that she expected her officers to update her on the status of their pending cases. She reciprocated by updating them on changes in procedures and the political climate in the department. The hidden agenda behind the formality was to remind them who was in charge and how connected she is.

Seated at the head of the table, Max took copious notes and asked pointed questions. By now it was well known in the squad that she would not tolerate a detective who did not have a plan. Satisfied that what few investigative cases they had were all going in the right direction, Max turned to the newest addition to her staff.

"Blair, what's going on with your woman killer?"

One of the younger cops cracked, "You mean Jack the Ripper?" His quip was met with a stare from his boss that would have frozen a pool of water. No one laughed.

Blair did not have to sit in on these meetings, nor did she have to report the status of her investigation to Max. On this case, Blair reported to the Chief of Detectives for the New Jersey State police, not some County Cop who just happened to get lucky. But when you are chasing a serial killer and are faced with the possibility of having to go through a locked door to get him, the last thing you want on the minds of the officers backing you up is that you are not one of them. Blair filled the squad commander in on her theory, then admitted to having a problem.

"The Feds are stonewalling me. I'm have to go through another source. I should have some additional information by tomorrow."

Maxine saw an opening here.

"Good. I want to know more about this source. Fill me in when we get done here." Maxine closed her portfolio and went around the room. Making it a point of never leaving a stone unturned, Maxine made sure she asked each of the detectives that reported to her if they had anything on their minds. With unanimous negative responses, Lt. Stout pushed her chair back and rose to her feet.

"Good. We're adjourned."

Blair followed Max to her office and took a seat. Max closed the door, then sat behind her desk.

"By the way, Blair, the dinner thing is a standing invitation, in case you are wondering. I don't usually have any plans after work, so any day is fine with me. Now tell me about your source and your plan for dealing with the Feds?"

The manner in which Maxine blended the personal with the professional momentarily put Blair off balance. She made a note to concentrate on the professional.

"There's a guy that I have used in the past. He is pretty good at getting into secure sites. I want to have him check a couple of things for me."

"What will this cost me?" The legality of the method was not half as important as it's effect on the budget or its ability to produce results.

Blair smiled.

"Nothing." Max gave her a look of disbelief.

"Well, it won't cost the department anything. It will cost me about four dollars, but that will come out of the State budget. Don't worry about it."

Stout did not like her detectives being coy with her. The opening that she thought would be there closed very quickly which is what really pissed her off.

"Cut the crap. All snitches have a price. How much are you paying this guy or are you trading favors?"

Blair laughed out loud at that thought.

"You might say that. Listen, Max, I have known this guy a long time. We went to school together. Let's just say that when I need a favor, he helps me out and then I do a favor for him. It does not involve police work if that is what you are worried about. It's more of a personal matter."

Stout's mind was working fast.

"What if we need him to testify in court?" This was not going the way she thought it would.

Blair stood up. She had informed her of what she was doing, but she hardly needed to justify it.

"The information that I am after will not be part of the case against the killer. This is more of background information to develop the evidence. There will be no need to place this source on the stand."

Maxine felt desperation building inside of her and fought to control it.

"Okay, Blair. Just keep me informed on what it is that you are doing. I don't want any surprises in my jurisdiction." Blair nodded in assent.

"Oh, and don't wait too long on deciding when you want to stop working and have something to eat." Max put her feet up on her desk as she opened a case file to review. Blair left the office thinking that she just somehow managed to dodge a bullet.

Maxine's mind was on a case much more interesting and frustrating than the one in the file before her. Blair Collins filled her thoughts more than she cared to admit, even to herself. She was going out on a limb by openly chasing the young detective, but she felt the reward justified the risk. Maxine cast a glance at her office door.

"All things in time."

Blair did not give the dinner issue a second thought. There were other things to consider right now. She sent a text message to a number on her cell phone.

"Morristown Hilton, rm513, 8p tonite," and then began to read again the details of past homicides, even though she had committed them to memory.

Jack Case awoke from a restless sleep, just as tired as when he went to bed. The fact that he had to employ skills that he thought he would never have to use again bothered him. He scolded himself for not thinking of another way. But then he reminded himself that anything less probably would not have worked. But what was it that was really bothering him? Was it something deeper, more personal? Was it something that he did not want to admit to, not even to himself?

Case started his car, backed out of the parking lot, and decided to be honest with himself. Priscilla is attractive, intelligent, and confident. Throw in fearless and aggressive and you have a combination of traits that you don't see in most women. Case admitted to himself that he could see them together but to have her would have been on her terms, not his, "and I guess that is really the problem, isn't it?" He said the last part out loud as if to validate the legitimacy of the debate. He knew what his terms would have been. He could only guess at hers.

"Well, what's done is done." Case upshifted from fourth to fifth gear and continued his drive without another thought of the enigma named Priscilla.

Priscilla lay in bed, fully awake, watching the sun filter into her bedroom. Whatever sleep she got the night before was in spite of, and not because of, her fear. She had never been as scared before, and last night, the thought that she could be driven to that point unnerved her. Priscilla effortlessly brought her torso up to form a right angle with her hips, pivoted, and swung her legs over the side of the bed. But this is a new day and that is in the past. There has to be a way to deal with this.

The wall clock in the kitchen showed 7:30. Estrella glanced at the entrance to the kitchen, hoping that at any moment her friend would come down the stairs and the world would be right. The hand on the clock moved to 7:31 and Estrella remained alone in the kitchen.

Last night, she was frightened. She had seen her protector frightened. Last night, she had seen the person, who she believed to be a saint, walk right past her with a gun in her hand and drive off into the night. Estrella was so frozen with fear that whatever words she might have thought to say became stuck in her throat. Last night was not a night that she would soon forget. Estrella looked at the clock again and knew that something was wrong. Not knowing what she would find but knowing that whatever it was she would have to face it, Estrella climbed the stairs to Priscilla's bedroom, taking a deep breath before knocking on the door.

CHAPTER TWELVE

Blair stood to the side of the desk with her hands behind her back. Max scanned the report, made a face at some similarities, and then handed the document back to the detective.

"Okay, what was that?"

"That is an excerpt from a confidential report from a very high-level section of the Defense Department database. It appears that one of their human weapons went haywire in Europe not too long ago and slashed the throats of a number of women. Before they could catch up to him, they lost his trail. Did you notice the detail on the depth of the incisions?" Max nodded.

"Did you also notice the detail on the width of the incisions?' Max nodded again.

"Well, the width of the incisions is the same width as the incisions on the women that have been murdered. My guess is that our murders are being done with the same weapon." Blair expected the look of disdain.

"Before you think I am wasting your time, take another look at the specs on the cut and then compare them with the dimensions on various types of military and non-military cutlery. The width of the blade is not standard issue. Further on in the report, you will see that the width of the blade is not standard. It is a custom-made combat knife used by certain high-level special ops guys. My thought is that all of these murders are being done by the same man.

Max had seen paper thin leads turn out to be the difference between conviction and acquittal. That was not what was bothering her.

"Why didn't Defense just turn this over to the F.B.I. and have them follow up?"

"That would be an admission that they have a mad dog on the loose. They can't afford to have that leak out."

Max saw the play.

"So, they just let him go and let local enforcement do their work for them."

Blair finished the thought.

"And if a few citizens get killed in the meantime, well, so be it. Collateral damage. The price you pay for a superior weapons system."

"Nice work. It's something. Now what?"

"Well, I am working on getting a list on the members of this command. My thought is that some of them have been discharged. If we can match a man to an area where a murder occurred, maybe we will have something to work on."

"I like it. It makes sense. Are you using the same source?" Stout recalled the statement from the night before, and what bothered then, bothered her now.

"Yes."

"Blair, tell me again how all of this is only going to cost four dollars?" If you don't ask the question, you will never get the answer.

Blair put her portfolio under her arm, leveled a cold, hard stare at the woman behind the desk, and made her way to the door.

"Lieutenant, I graduated in the top ten percent of my class in law school and was one of the top five graduates of the academy. I know the rules of evidence, including what is admissible in court. Don't worry about how I am getting the information. It will never be a problem in this case."

Stout cared less for the tone than the answer but decided not to press it.

"Okay, well, just watch yourself and keep me posted." She cast a discerning eye towards the detective as Blair left her office.

"Come in." Estrella entered the room to find Priscilla putting the finishing touches on her make-up. She smiled at her housekeeper and friend.

"I'll be down in a minute, Este. Is everything okay?"

Estella breathed a sigh of relief and smiled back at her benefactor.

"Si, hermana, everything it is fine. Si, muy bueno. I will have the coffee ready for you."

"Este, put it in my travel cup. I'm running a little late, so I will drink it in the car. Okay?" Priscilla turned back to the mirror without waiting for an answer.

"Si, hermana." Estrella left the room, closed the door, and said a prayer of thanks.

Priscilla strode into the office, looking as though she did not have a care in the world. She met every gaze directly and greeted every frown with a smile. In her custom-made tan slacks, very expensive cashmere sweater, and equally expensive beige pumps, she made all of the other females in the office look like motherless orphans. That only made their mood dourer and Priscilla's more cheery.

After an hour, Priscilla approached Peggy Flynn.

"Say, Peggy, do you have any idea when Jack will be in? I would like to speak with him about something."

"If it is about the computer thing, I've already taken care of it." Peggy took a quick mental snapshot of Priscilla and vowed that she would look like that one day.

"No, it's not about that, but thank you for taking care of it. I would like to speak with him about something personal."

"Oh well, he will be out of town for a few days. I tell you what, when he calls in, I will mention to him that you want to speak with him. How's that?"

"Thanks, Peggy. Oh, by the way, you are really doing well. Keep it up." Priscilla gave Peggy a pat on the back before walking back to her desk. Inside, Peggy Flynn beamed.

Priscilla took the absence of Jack Case as a positive thing. This gave her more time to perfect her plan.

It had come to her in the shower. She never ran away from anything, and she was not about to run away now. She made up her mind to go right at him and pull out all the stops. She was going to tell him that she was not going to stop until she got what she wanted. She was going to tell him that his silly little parlor trick with the computer image did not work and that nothing he could do to her would work, so he just might as well give in (Priscilla was betting high that he would not). Even if he fired her, she would still come after him. There would be no getting rid of her. Everywhere he went, everywhere he turned, she would be there, waiting and watching. And then when he did give in, when he could not take seeing her anywhere and everywhere and decided to give her what she wanted (and she absolutely knew he would), she would refuse him. She would humiliate him in the same way that he humiliated her. Priscilla smiled at the thought of it. Soon, her smile turned into a laugh and then that laugh turned into a feeling of well-being that she had not experienced in quite some time.

Blair was just about to sign out for lunch when she received an e-mail from the patrol sergeant.

"We received a complaint about an unfamiliar vehicle with a single male occupant parked in front of 909 Quaker Street. The complainant is positive that the resident of the house was not home at the time and is not known to have visitors. The vehicle is a '97 Black Porsche, plate number UB729R, and is registered to a John Case. His home address is in the attached file from DMV. Given the female murders, I thought you might want to know about this."

Blair printed the information, sent a thank you reply to the sergeant, and then signed herself out for the rest of the day. She had a good few hours before she would meet her source for the rest of the information, so why not do some cop work and check out this lead.

Blair met the patrol officer who took the initial information at the corner of Quaker Street and Old Line Road.

"The woman who called it in is Ethel Peterson. Her house is 917 Quaker at the end of the street from the subject house. She told me…"

As he filled her in on the information he was given, Blair took in her surroundings. In a state that is known to have the highest property taxes in the country, this town was at the top of the top. Lawns were manicured down to the last blade of grass, the houses were huge, and there was not a soul to be seen. Blair found herself wondering just what kind of crimes were being committed in this perfect world and how long would it take for the people who committed them to get caught.

"…that's about it. We don't get much action around here. I just thought it was a boyfriend nosing around or something like that, but the woman who called it in seemed pretty adamant that the guy was stalking the house, so I thought I would pass it on. I hope I didn't take you away from something really important?"

Blair smiled at the young cop. He seemed like the type of officer that would eventually make it to the State force someday.

"No, not a problem. Hey, look, you never know where a lead will take you. Thanks for the information. Nice work."

Blair left her car at the corner and walked down to the house. It was a trick that her uncle taught her.

"A good cop always stays in touch with the street," he would say. Take a minute to walk, and you never know what you may hear or see. Blair heeded the advice and took note of the alarm sensors on the windows and the dead bolt locks on the doors. She noticed that very few had security lights at the sides of the houses and the trees seemed to obscure the lighting on the street. All in all, it would not be hard for someone to get to the rear of any of these houses unseen.

Blair rang the doorbell and had her business card ready. There was visible disappointment on the face of the older woman who answered.

"Mrs. Peterson?" The woman nodded.

"Blair Collins, New Jersey State Police. May I come in?"

The formidable woman with perfectly styled silver-grey hair did not budge.

"May I see your badge please?" Blair smiled and presented both her badge and police identification card.

"I guess it's okay. Please, come in." As Blair stepped though the door, Ethel Peterson closed it behind her and then took a moment to stare at Blair.

"Aren't you a little short to be a police officer?"

As she was clearly from a different age, Blair took no offense to the remark.

"I get that a lot. I just did make the minimum height requirement for the force, however, I can assure you that I am well trained to take care of myself. I would like to ask you a few questions about the car you reported the other day."

"The young man who took the report said a detective might be stopping by to follow up." She took another hard look at Blair and shook her head.

"Please, come this way."

The entry foyer was two stories high with a polished tile floor. To the left is the library with floor to ceiling bookshelves and a brightly polished hardwood floor. To the right is the living room. It, too, had polished hardwood flooring.

"Forgive my asking, Mrs. Peterson, but aren't you afraid of falling on these floors?" Blair had made a note to measure her steps in light of her own fear of falling.

"No, dear. All of my shoes have rubber soles and moderate heels. I am quite secure." The woman turned into the library whose picture window presented an unimpeded view of the entire north side of the street. The sheer lace curtain at the window made it difficult for anyone to see in. She took a seat in the chair by the window and motioned for Blair to take the chair across from her.

"Would you care for tea?"

In the fashion of a professional observer, Blair made a quick visual sweep of the room. It was not so much to notice what was in the room but more to notice anything that may have seemed out of place or did not belong there. Also, the condition of the room would say a lot about the person dispensing the information. Clutter in an older person might indicate someone who is confused or cannot keep track. Neatness would indicate clarity and attention to detail. Blair made a note to herself that the room was as neat as a pin.

"No thank you. Could you please tell me what you saw?" Blair had the field report of the officer who responded, so she did not see the need to take out her own notebook. Besides, it was her experience with older people that they will readily tell you what they know if you look them in the eye and listen to them rather than just record what you think they are saying.

"Well, I was sitting here having my afternoon tea when I saw the black car stop in front of number 909. We don't get many cars here in the middle of the afternoon, so I decided to keep an eye on it. What with that business with all the women getting killed and everything. Well, a man got out, went to the side of the house, and let himself in. He was inside for about ten minutes before he came out, got in his car, and left."

"Had you seen the man before?"

"No, never."

"Have you seen him again since that time?"

"No."

"Is there any reason why you did not call the police right away? It could have been a burglary or something more tragic?"

Ethel Peterson hung her head shamefully.

"Well, I guess I should have. And it was not until after he left that I thought of that myself. But he walked so confidently to the rear of the house that I thought he might have had an appointment."

"What changed your mind?"

"Well, if he was a tradesman, he would have arrived in a truck. If he were a salesman or some sort of professional, he would have went to the front door and not the rear. It was only after I thought about it that I found the whole thing strange."

"Do you know the resident of that house?"

The expression of the woman made it very clear that she had an extreme dislike for the resident of number 909.

"The owner of that house is that disgusting Whittington woman. Priscilla Whittington is her name." Ethel Peterson punctuated her statement with a nod of her head.

Blair made sure to keep her expression even.

"What is it that makes her disgusting?"

"Well, not only did she kill her husband, but she rides around here in that sports car of hers, making all sorts of racket. And then there are the stories of her and her men. Disgusting!"

"I'm sorry, but the information that I received stated that you were concerned because of the lack of male visitors to that house. Is that not correct?"

"Young lady, she does not bring them here. The longtime residents of this neighborhood would not stand for that sort of activity. She chases them hither and yon, causes them to lose their jobs, and wrecks their families. It is so sad."

"How do you know this?"

Ethel Peterson adopted a look of absolute certainty.

"I have a friend who I play golf with whose son used to work for a man whose manager lost his job because of her. While my friend's son no longer works there, he maintains associations with people who do. When the manager was fired, the poor man's wife left him and went home to her parents with the children. A terrible thing. All because of that woman."

Blair made her own assessment of how much of that story was fact and the rest the product of day time television.

"Mrs. Peterson, you mentioned that she killed her husband, was that recently?"

"No, it was some time ago. It was in all the papers, I'm surprised you do not recall it? There was a full investigation by the police. Well, in any event, she got off scot free, the little tramp."

Blair made a mental note to look into the Whittington case more out of curiosity than anything else.

"Mrs. Peterson, there is just one other thing. This is a pretty fair distance from number 909. How could you possibly see that far to make out the license plate number on the car?"

Ethel Peterson carefully took a look around the room, reached into a wicker basket by her chair, and pulled out a massive pair of Bausch & Lomb 5X30 binoculars.

"Most of the residents of our community here either work during the day or are out running errands or some such thing. With all the crime in the world, someone has to keep an eye out."

Blair could barely contain her laughter.

"Well, yes, I see. Thank you, Mrs. Peterson. You have been very helpful." As Blair rose from the seat, she slipped a little on the hardwood floors.

"Careful, dear. Perhaps you should look into some rubber soles for those shoes of yours?"

Blair smiled with a mixture of embarrassment and amusement.

"Yes, maybe I will consider them."

As Blair left the Peterson home, she took a look around at the houses in the immediate vicinity and wondered how many of the neighbors knew that Ethel Peterson was on duty protecting her interest and theirs. She satisfied herself with the thought that probably more of them knew than she would have guessed, and none of them liked it not one damn bit.

Blair walked back to her car, trying to figure all of the legitimate reasons why a man would be on this particular block in the middle of the afternoon. None came to mind. New neighbor? Peterson would have known. Salesman? In this neighborhood, they make appointments and Peterson's point about the front door was well taken. Mid-day lover? Nah, they would have met somewhere else. Visiting relative? Slim but possible. The fact that she could not come up with a plausible reason left her with only one option.

Blair rang the bell on number 909 for no other reason than to satisfy her curiosity. After all, she had been told that no one was home during the day. She was surprised when there was a response from behind the curtain.

"Who?"

"State Police." This time Blair showed her badge instead of a business card and switched her portfolio to her left hand, just in case she needed to draw her gun with her right.

When you are an illegal alien, the sight of a badge is far more frightening than reassuring. Not knowing what to do, the woman opened the door to about the width of her face.

"Si?"

Blair smiled to herself. This was one of those rare instances where her diminutive size worked to her advantage. Had she been a hulking white guy, there was no way this woman would have opened the door. Blair made a quick assessment and then took, what she considered to be, not too big a stretch.

"Buenos dias, senora. ¿Esta es la casa de senora Whittington?"

Hearing her native tongue seemed to put the woman at ease. Her body relaxed and her features softened.

"Si."

"¿Es la senora Whittington aqui?"

"No. Senora Whittington esta es trabajando."

Blair imagined Ethel Peterson watching this exchange with her binoculars, and it brought a smile to her face. The smile was infectious as the woman behind the door smiled back.

"Muy bien. Por favor, triagalo mi tarjeta a senora Whittington?" Blair handed her business card to the woman, who took a second to read it, then nod her head.

"¿Donde es el trabajo de senora Whittington?"

The woman studied Blair for a minute, looked at the card, and then looked back at Blair. "Uno momento." She returned with the telephone number written very badly on a piece of paper.

"Llamarle por la nombre."

"Gracias, senora. Muchas gracias." Blair stepped away from the door and continued down the street. She liked it when she did good cop stuff.

Blair sat in her car and recorded her activities, the time, who she spoke with, and the information that she had learned. She drove around the area just to get a feel for the neighborhood and to also see if there was a car matching the description. Cops do not believe in random acts. More times than not in a situation like this, there is a connection.

During her drive, Blair thought about checking out the owner of the car but ruled it out. There could be a simple explanation for this. Besides, a supposed tramp who is thought to have killed her husband and gotten away with it is far more interesting to talk to. Given that history, considering how much of it is true, there could be a plausible explanation to this or an even deeper crime to look into. Better to work from the inside out. Blair pulled over, took out her cell phone, and dialed the number written on the piece of paper.

"Operations." There was a crisp edge to the voice that seemed authoritative. Blair guessed that Whittington was a manager of some sort.

"Good afternoon, may I speak with Priscilla Whittington please?"

"Speaking."

"Blair Collins, New Jersey State Police. A report has been filed about a stranger seen in your neighborhood. I would like to meet with you to ask you a few routine questions as part of the investigation."

"Oh, yes. My housekeeper phoned and said that the police came by. I am assuming that was you?" Blair noticed that the woman's tone was relaxed. There was no hint of someone who may have had a brush with the law.

"Yes, I am the detective that has been assigned to your case."

"Well, I am normally at work during the day. If this will not take too long, you may come by my office."

"The questions are routine. I will not take too much of your time."

"Very well. I go to lunch at 12. That would be a good time. How is tomorrow?"

Blair took a look at her watch and decided that her meet tonight was more important than hearing how this woman gave her keys to her brother so that he could use her home to cheat on his wife.

"That's fine." Blair made a note of the address.

As far as cop stuff goes, this day had been somewhat productive. The good part was that it was not over yet. Blair noticed that there was a CVS drugstore on the way back to the highway. She smiled back at the wink that the female cashier gave her as she rung up the package of condoms and placed them in a bag with the receipt.

CHAPTER THIRTEEN

 Priscilla picked up the phone on the second ring, cradled the receiver between her head and her shoulder, and continued to process entries into the system while Estrella related the events of the recent past.

"It's okay, Estee. It was just that nosey Peterson woman at the end of the block complaining about my car again. Don't worry. I will be home in a couple of hours, and I will have a word with her. Don't worry. Everything will be alright."

Priscilla hung up the phone, but there was a nagging thought in the back of her mind. She did not like the police. After the death of William Whittington and the implications of her involvement in that event, her dislike turned to an emotion that bordered on hatred. One of the few things Priscilla learned in the free-range state where she was born and raised was that you took care of your own problems. With some degree of effort, Priscilla was finally able to block the thoughts of the police out of her mind.

Trap Martin ran the figures again to check for accuracy and then called his secretary into his office.

"I've got to start cutting expenses, so I had better begin now. Call Jim. Tell him that he is on call for the rest of the week. I will take over the surveillance on the Whittington case."

Gineen made a note on her pad.

"Then I guess I won't see you for the rest of the week?"

The statement made a sour mood just a bit tarter.

"No, probably not."

Gineen could see that her boss was in no mood to be teased or trifled with. She perched on his desk, took his large hand in hers, and kissed it lightly.

"Listen, if you get lonely out there, give me a call. I'll have one of the girls watch Devin and I will come and keep you company. Really, just call me. Okay?"

Trap looked back at the one person who, over the years, proved that she cared for him more than anyone he ever knew. He knew she meant what she said. He knew she would leave her son to come to him if he called. Trap knew that she would do anything that he asked of her, no questions asked. There was a part of him that liked that, and there was a part of him that did not.

Trap looked up at her and then went back to his figures.

"Thanks. I'll keep that in mind and check in with you later."

Gineen smiled, leaned over, and kissed him on the cheek and then left the office. She honestly did not know if he would call or not. But she did know that if he did call, she would be there, waiting.

Trap watched Gineen leave the office and fought an urge to ask her to come back. The words seemed to bounce off the walls.

"I guess I won't see you for the rest of the week?" Trap ripped the paper off the pad and threw it in the garbage. He cursed Priscilla. He cursed Victoria Whittington. And then he cursed himself and that sense of right and wrong that seemed to pick the worst of all times to get in his way.

• • • • •

It was just 8 P.M. when Blair pulled into the parking lot of the Morristown Hilton. The advantage that this hotel had over the others in the area is that there are a number of ways to get in and out of the building, and it is quite easy to get up to the rooms without being seen. Blair parked her car in between two massive SUV's and made her way to the eighth floor confident that she had not been seen. When she had reached the room, she knocked twice, paused, and then knocked three more times. Instinctively, she stood to the side of the door.

The door was opened, but there was no one visible behind it. Blair checked the hall and then slipped into the darkened room, making sure that she hung the DO NOT DISTURB sign on the outside and then locked and latched the door. Blair smiled and leaned back against the door as she watched the corpulent body of a balding man, not much older than herself, scurry back to his computer like a moth to a flame.

Blair secured her weapon in the safe in the closet, disrobed in front of the mirror by the door but kept her handcuffs out. The man who sat before his computer paid little attention to what was going on behind him. Before she proceeded to collect the information that she was there for and then reward her source for services rendered, Blair stopped to admire her transformation in the full-length mirror. She was no longer the petite cop with a law degree and a proper business suit. Standing in front of this mirror is a fierce woman who is not to be trifled with. With a degree of pride, Blair admitted to herself that she looked pretty intimidating with her hair pulled back, her black lingerie, and the black patent leather heels that she switched to when she parked her car. Admiring her well defined abdominals, Blair made an admission to herself.

"It's the abs. It has to be the abs."

The Eyes took a long time rolling the cigarette. It had to be just right. This was the best time. He was about to tame the beast. The beast had to be taught a lesson, and he was the only one who could do it. He was about to lick the paper when he saw her. His mouth watered. His facial muscles tightened. She was in his sight. He used the saliva to complete the perfect cigarette, but he would not smoke this one now. He would save it for later. It was time.

The Volvo started up, and as was her habit, she immediately dropped the car into gear and pulled off. She was running late and had to get home. She did not have a lot of time.

The Eyes knew the location of the lair. There was no need to follow the beast. He took a different route, parked, and then waited. It would not be long now.

As she pulled into the driveway, she noticed that the security light did not go on. It was the third time this month, and she made a note to call the electrician tomorrow to have it checked. As she got out of the car, she never saw him. Her scream was muffled by the gauze that was stuffed in her mouth. In the next second, she was unconscious. And in another second, she was gone.

Blair glanced at the clock beside the bed as she combed her hair in the mirror. Eleven o'clock. It would be a little past her bedtime by the time she got home, but it was worth it. She cast a critical look at the peacefully sleeping man in the bed behind her.

"The old boy was pretty good tonight." On the dresser in front of her were the printed pages of what was supposedly "Eyes Only" pentagon documents. The information that her source was able to get for her was worth more than 100 times the price of the protection. And as far as her part in the exchange is concerned, Blair had long ago chalked that up to the perks of the profession rather than the cost of doing business. She had needs on two levels, and mixing business with pleasure in this case, made perfect sense to her.

Blair scooped up the envelope, slipped into her shoulder holster, and then in a similar fashion, put on her suit jacket. She retrieved her service weapon from the room safe and was just about to leave the room, when she snapped her fingers and took out her key ring, making sure not to make too much noise. Fortunately, he was lying on his side, which made it easy for her to unlock her cuffs and free his wrists without disturbing him. Blair then left the room, making sure that she left the DO NOT DISTURB sign in place when she closed the door.

CHAPTER FOURTEEN

Maxine Stout entered the detective squad room and, instead of going directly to her office, took the long way around that brought her past Blair's desk. She really did not care if it seemed like she took more of an interest in her only female detective. To her way of thinking if the men under her command did not like it, that was their problem, not hers.

"What are you reading?"

Blair had become accustomed to her desk being the first stop her boss made when she came to work. Since there was nothing she could do about it, she just learned to live with it.

"Good morning. It's a two-year-old murder case. The victim is a guy by the name of Whittington. Pretty interesting stuff."

The expression on the Lieutenant's face went from passing interest to more than a little concerned. She dropped her pocketbook on the desk and took a seat.

"The Whittington case? Why would you be taking a look at that?"

Blair was surprised that she hit a nerve.

"Patrol called in a peeper yesterday, and I looked into it just to make sure that there was no connection with the women who have been killed. Well, the owner of the house that the guy was checking out is a woman by the name of Priscilla Whittington."

Blair filled in the details of the information that she obtained from Ethel Peterson.

"...so I decided to have a look at the case file more out of curiosity than anything else. Tell me something, Max, why was this thing shut down so fast? There are a couple of leads here that were never followed up."

Stout thought for a minute, looked around the squad room, and then rose from her seat. "Shut that thing off and come into my office, Blair."

Blair logged off the case file and followed the Detective Lieutenant into her office.

"Shut the door please and have a seat."

Instead of leaning back in her chair and putting her feet up on her desk, Stout sat down, leaned in from her seat, and folded her hands on her desk. Blair read the body language and put herself on alert. Whatever it is that she stumbled onto, Blair's gut told her she had better pay attention.

"Listen, there's juice and then there are those who squeeze the fruit to make the juice. In this state, the Whittington family owns the trees that make the fruit, they squeeze the fruit to make the juice, and then use that juice to wash their face in the morning. Do you get my drift?" Blair nodded her head.

"Listen, before I jump to any conclusions, tell me where you intend to go with this."

Blair instantly understood how this woman rose so fast through the ranks. She knew when to step on the gas and run over folks and when to slow down and read the curves in the road. Despite whatever personal issues she may have had with Max, Blair's professional opinion of her just went up several notches.

"Well, I made an appointment to meet with her and go over the peeper thing at lunch today. Nothing intense, just some routine questions. I don't think there is anything there as far as my cases are concerned."

"Why?"

"Well, it doesn't seem to fit. Broad day light, easily recognizable car, out in the open. I see my killer a lot differently."

Stout thought for a minute and then nodded her head in agreement.

"Okay, here it is. The Whittington case was ordered to be closed, and the order came from the highest level in the state. The head of the Whittington family is Victoria Whittington. She is as tough as nails and has helped elect so many politicians in this state that she can do just about as she pleases. Word has it that she asked that the case be shut down. She has had a private investigator looking into case for the past two years. Her angle was why should the taxpayers be burdened with a private matter? She made the commitment that once her man found out something, it would be turned over to the police. It would appear to be a win-win for everyone."

"Did this private eye ever turn up anything?"

"No. My personal thought is that he is milking this deal for all that it is worth, but I can't base that on anything."

"Do you know the guy?"

Max leaned back in her chair and crossed her legs.

"Nah. I've have heard of him. He was a low rent, matrimonial snooper until he hooked into this."

"Do you want me to back off?" Blair could read the footprints in the sand.

Stout did not think twice.

"No. If you made an appointment with her, you had better keep it. It is a legitimate investigation. To blow her off might be a mistake. Just do not push. Keep it simple. Get enough information to administratively close the case and then get out. If there is a problem, any problem at all, brief me on it right away. Is that clear?"

"Yeah, Max. I understand." Blair got up to leave and then paused at the door. She was just about to thank her commanding officer for listening to her side of the story when Russ Matson opened the door.

"Gee, I am sorry to interrupt you gals. Blair, it seems like the serial killer has struck again. Bakers County P.D. is on line two."

Max waved Russ into the room as she reached for the receiver of her phone. Blair helped herself to a pad and a pen. Russ Matson stepped further into the office, closed the door, and took a seat.

"This is Detective Lieutenant Stout. I have Detectives Collins and Matson in my office. I am putting you on speaker phone." Stout hit the button for the speaker-phone and then hung up the receiver. All three listened to the accounts of the discovery of the body, what appeared to be a particularly vicious sexual assault, and the situation at the crime scene. When the supervisor finished his report, Max advised him that Blair was on her way and hung up.

As the three detectives walked out of the office, Max took command.

"Okay, Blair, get down there. Put the Whittington thing on the back burner. Russ, you go with her. Give me a phone call after you have..."

"Well, it looks like the big bad wolf has struck again, and Little Red Riding Hood is about to go after him." The comments came from a newly minted detective who appeared to be speaking to no one in particular. He had made it clear to his male colleagues, on more than one occasion, that he did not like working with or for a woman. As soon as the words left his mouth, Maxine Stout was on him like a cat.

Despite her heels and the tapered skirt that she was wearing, Max hurdled a desk, grabbed the man by the lapels of his jacket, and jerked him out of his seat. She threw him against the wall, knocking a good bit of wind out of him. Then, without letting go of his jacket, she threw him against Blair's desk. In the manner that rookies are taught at the academy to secure a suspect against the hood of a car, Stout bent him over the desk, put her knee in his back, and with one hand, she pinned his arm behind him, and with the other hand, she grabbed his hair and forced him to look at a picture of one of the murdered victims.

"LOOK AT HER! LOOK AT HER! She was somebody's mother, wife, daughter, sister. She was somebody's friend. GO AHEAD! LOOK AT HER! She could have been your wife, your mother, your daughter, your sister. BUT NOW SHE IS DEAD! What are you doing about it? TELL ME! WHAT?!"

After about ten seconds of silence, Stout released the man. She stood back and made eye contact with every single man in the room.

"IF ANY OF YOU THINKS THIS IS A JOKE, IF ANY OF YOU THINKS THE WORK WE DO HERE IS FUNNY, I WILL ACCEPT

YOUR TRANSFER PAPERS AT THE END OF YOUR SHIFT! And as for you, you little piece of shit, you've got 30 days to impress me with some police work or you're history. Now get the fuck out of my sight."

The jokester detective took the shortest route to the door, knocking over a chair, a garbage can, and a cup of coffee in the process. Those that opted to stay in the room found a case file to stick their noses in or a phone call they had to make. To Blair's amazement, Stout regained her composure remarkably fast.

"You better get going, Blair. You're going to have to hurry to get there before the news media destroys the crime scene." Without another word, Maxine Stout returned to her office to document her version of the incident before she got the call that she knew would come from the Chief of Police.

CHAPTER FIFTEEN

The Eyes lay in bed, smoking the perfect cigarette. The hunt went well. She was the right one and he was satisfied. For now.

He blew a smoke ring in the air and held up a print of her face. Yeah, she was the right one. The Eyes put the photo down and turned to the mural on his wall. It was almost complete. He needed one more and then he would be done. The thought of it saddened him somewhat. But then he thought about the final hunt. After he had tamed all of the other beasts, then he would claim his prize. He took another drag from his perfect cigarette and felt his body harden as he relived the night before.

Blair winced at the thought of sitting in a car with Russ Matson for the hours ride into southern New Jersey. The man was hardly ever seen without a cigarette in his mouth. Blair's apprehension was somewhat relieved when Russ opened the window, flipped on the car's strobe, and floored the accelerator. At the speed that they traveled, the secondhand smoke that made its way to the passenger side of the car was minimal.

They made the hour's drive in just over 20 minutes and found a circus-like atmosphere when they arrived. There were seven police vehicles, two ambulances, and a heavy weapons truck, all with their strobes flashing. A local news van was parked nearby with a correspondent interviewing an officer. There was yellow tape everywhere and more people standing around talking than actually doing any work, police or otherwise. Blair was out of the car before it came to a full stop.

Blair flashed her badge to the first officer she met.

"Sergeant Miller?" The officer pointed and then lifted the tape for Blair and Russ to duck under.

The crime scene was an area just off of County Road 521. With woods on both sides of a winding road, no lights, soft ground, and not a house for several miles, it fit the pattern of the other locations where the bodies had been found. Before going any further, Blair remembered one of the tips from her uncle. She stopped, took a complete look around.

"Good grief. The only thing missing here is a marching band." Blair pulled on a pair of acetone gloves and was thankful that she grabbed her tennis shoes from her own car while Russ signed out the department vehicle.

Russ was about to light up another cigarette when he remembered he was at a crime scene. Reluctantly, he put the smokes back in his pocket.

"Don't be too hard on them, Blair. They don't get much action down here, so when something like this happens, everybody turns out. At least they had the good sense to keep the media out."

Blair nodded her head and let the comment pass. There still were more people tramping around the crime scene that she would have liked. Heavily armed SWAT officers with dogs were in the woods, uniformed officers were around the perimeter, and a team from the county coroner's office was taking photographs and making sketches. Off to the side, standing alone, was a tall, thin uniformed officer with Sergeants stripes on arms that were folded across his chest.

"I take it you're Collins and Matson. Which one of you is State?" Blair produced her State Police badge. While it was impressive to Blair that the man did not make an assumption that Russ was in charge, it did not go unnoticed that he did not offer to shake hands.

Miller pointed to an area off to his right.

"The body was found over there. Someone reported a body lying in the woods. One of my officers checked it out, found the victim, and called it in." The area that he pointed to had a thick grass bed but was pretty much out in the open. There were yellow stakes outlining the position of the body. It would not have been hard to find.

"We took photos and bagged the body. I told the coroner to hold off on the autopsy until he heard from you. There were no foot prints or tire tracks. The grass here is too thick. That's about all I got."

Russ Matson stood with his hands in his pockets.

"Any I.D. on the woman?"

"No. We're doing a three county missing persons check. I'll let you know if anything turns up."

"Sarge, what time…" Blair was cut short by a menacing look from the uniformed supervisor.

"All of the facts will be in the report and I will have it for you within the hour." Blair took offense to the officer's tone and made a face.

"Look, I don't like this type of thing happening in my county. It's quiet here, and it's my job to keep it that way. Whoever did this is some real sick bastard. I will tell you this only once; if I catch him before you do, there ain't gonna be no trial." Miller reached for his radio.

"All personnel. All personnel. States on the scene. Wrap it up and head back to base."

Blair was incredulous.

"Sarge, we may need some help here!"

"Listen, missy, the county's budget is stretched pretty thin and standing here with you ain't gonna help me catch the son of a bitch who did this. You will have access to our reports, and if you need anything, you can always give me a call. But as far as my guys are concerned, we're done here. Excuse me, I have work to do." Without another word, the man turned on his heel and left. In less than ten minutes, there was not a soul around.

There was an eerie kind of quiet after the last car left the scene. With the wind blowing through the trees, it was the kind of quiet that seemed to make a noise all its own. Death had been discovered here, but it seemed like all the component parts of nature were working in concert to blow away any trace. Soon the insects were heard and the birds were singing. Death had gone away.

Blair took out her own digital camera, took photos of the scene, and then began to make a rough sketch of the area. Russ Matson stood to the side of the area where the body had been outlined and looked to the road as if he were retracing a path. He then inspected the ground, working outward from the location of the body, and then suddenly stopped. He knelt down, put on his reading glasses, and closely inspected an area at his feet.

"Blair, come here please."

Blair came over to area where the older detective was kneeling, making sure to approach from behind him.

"I would say our boy is a smoker." Russ took out his pen.

"See this. This is loose tobacco, the kind they use in roll-your-owns."

Blair was impressed.

"How can you tell?"

"The leaf is longer and uneven. It's not much, but it's something."

Blair made a note of the find, took a photo, and then bagged the samples in a glassine envelope.

"Nice work, Russ. But does this mean that the killer or whoever dropped off the body stopped for a cigarette?"

The older man beamed. It had been a long time since he received any compliments.

"No, not necessarily. When you roll your own, you will always drop tobacco on yourself. If you smoke often enough, you will forget that it is there and it will fall off. It used to drive my wife nuts."

Blair turned back to the body outline.

"I don't think she was killed here. There is very little blood, and it is too wide open. My thought is that she was killed somewhere else and brought here to be found. The tip of the body in the woods tracks with the other murders."

Russ nodded his head.

"I agree. I would say that he came from the east. That way and then through the trees over there."

They traced the steps and found more tobacco leaves, which seemed to prove Matson's theory.

"How'd you figure that?"

"Well, if you are going to drop a body off, you do not want to cross the highway. So, he comes from that direction, pulls over, probably pops the hood and the trunk to make it look like a breakdown, and instead of the using the easier path over there, he sticks to the trees. If anyone passes, they will not see him. But if someone does and stops, he can ditch the body and lose them in the trees." Russ leaned against their car and lit another cigarette.

"How do you know he didn't just make a U-turn?"

Russ took a drag from his cigarette.

"We came from the west. That's where the highway is. That would be his exit route. If he came from that way, there is the possibility that another car might exit with him. He would not want to take that chance. Remember, this is not the first time he has done this."

"Nah. Our guy comes from the east, dumps the body, and then takes the quickest route away from the scene. In less than ten minutes, he is at the highway with the option of going north or south. Or he could have just continued straight on this road. In any event, he is well away from here in no time, and we have absolutely no way to know in which direction he went."

Blair reached inside the car and took out a local map.

"There is a small town east of here. That's probably where our victim came from." Blair made a note of the town and then folded the map.

"Let's head over to the coroner's office. I want to take a look at the body."

During the ride to the county hospital, Blair made notes of what they found and informed Lt. Stout of Russ's theories. She made a particular effort to mention that it was Russ's idea and that she agreed with him. When Blair handed him the phone, Russ smiled at the second compliment he received in one day.

"Thanks for the plug, Blair. Everyone in the office thinks that I'm washed up."

Blair continued to study her notes.

"Not everyone, Russ."

Russ slowed the car a bit. Blair sensed that there was something on his mind.

"What is it, Russ?"

"Can I ask you a personal question, Blair."

Blair closed her portfolio and gave the man her full attention.

"Sure."

"Well, you have a degree from a good college and a law degree from an even better one. How come a smart girl like you didn't go for the FBI instead of NJSP?"

Blair smiled. For some reason which she could not explain, no one ever asked her questions about why she ended up with the State Police. Russ was a cop alright. No obvious question would be left unanswered.

"The FBI was my first choice. When I applied, there was no problem until they did the background check. They dug up an old case where my father won a discrimination case against the FBI back in the 60's. And then they found another case where my father litigated and won a brutality case against the feds. That was enough to knock me off the list."

Russ Matson shook his head.

"That's a shame. You would have made a fine Fed. So, how'd you end up in Jersey?"

"New York didn't want me. They thought that I was too short, and since I already had a law degree, I would eventually end up in the D.A.'s office. Jersey was offering incentives, and when I convinced them that I did not want to go to the prosecutor's office, they agreed to start me at detective so that I would not have to do patrol. A lot of the guys didn't like it, but it worked out for me."

Russ dropped the corners of his mouth.

"I see."

A phone call to police headquarters told them that the coroner's office was located in the Baker County General Hospital.

"It's right off the highway. You can't miss it." With little effort, they found their way to the hospital. Russ parked the Crown Victoria in the spot marked "Official Business Only" and then they entered the hospital through the front entrance. The polite older woman at the information desk directed them to the rear of the building and told them that the coroner's office can be found in the basement. After a few wrong turns, they finally located the office next to the loading dock in the rear of the building. A map would not have helped.

Blair was annoyed.

"Couldn't she have just told us to go back outside and around to the back of the building?"

Russ laughed.

"Dorothy, this ain't Kansas." Always the gentleman, he opened the door and allowed the State Police Detective to enter the room before he did. Neither of them were surprised to find that no one was seated at the first desk, but they were surprised to hear the rap music coming from somewhere beyond.

"YO! BACK HERE!" They followed the sound of the music to the rear of the office. At the end of the hall, they stepped through a pair of swinging doors and into an old operating theatre that had been turned into an examination room. In the middle of the room was a metal table with a body on it. Around the perimeter of the room were cabinets and shelves with marked, and unmarked, beakers and jars. In the corner of the room was an office area with a desk, computer, and file cabinet. Over the desk, in between two bookshelf speakers, were several degrees and certificates, all bearing the same name.

The room was clean and appeared to be well organized, but it was obvious that it was dated. There was not a piece of equipment in the room that appeared to be current or up to date, with the exception of the C.D. player that obviously did not belong to the county.

The two detectives found a light skinned black man dancing to the beat of the latest Kanye West C.D. Blair would have guessed him to be in his mid-20's, although he looked much younger than that. He was dressed in green scrubs, but instead of an operating room cap, the young man wore a head wrap like the kind worn by inner city rappers and thugs. Over his Air Max sneakers were plastic bags. He held up one finger, waited for that particular part in the song to end, and then turned the C.D. player off.

"Hi, we're..." Blair began to reach for her badge when a wave of a hand froze her in place.

"Detectives Matson and Collins. Miller said you would be by. Your copy of his report is over there." The young doctor pointed to an envelope sitting on a counter on the left side of the room.

"This is your victim, and I would be Dr. Barton A. Turner. Everybody calls me B.A.T."

Blair shook hands with the young man while Russ waved as he went over to pick up the envelope.

"Blair Collins, State Police. That's Russ Matson. He's with Franklyn County P.D." Russ nodded from the counter. Victim examinations did not agree with him, and he was dying for a cigarette.

"Okay, doc, let's take a look."

Before the young doctor moved, Russ Matson spoke up from the side of the room.

"Hey, doc, how did you know we came into the office? With that thing on, I could barely hear myself think." Russ eyed the man suspiciously.

The young coroner broke into a wide grin and pointed to the corner of the ceiling. Hung in the corner was a small fixture with a red bulb similar to the kind that deaf people have in their apartments.

"I rigged it myself when they took away my help. I can't have people just running up on me."

Russ nodded in agreement and silently wondered just what else was rigged up in this office.

In a manner that seemed out of character to the man, instead of pulling back the sheet with a flourish, the young doctor took his time and rolled the sheet in measured folds, starting at the top and working down to the ankles. He was careful not to disturb any part of the body. Blair took note of that and was instantly relieved. What she saw was that he was not some butcher, fascinated with dead people. The incisions were clean and neat, and all of the wounds were cleaned, dressed, and neatly stitched. The mortician would not have a difficult time with the body. The young coroner took up his pad and began to recite his findings.

"The victim is a female, white, weighing 134 pounds, and is five foot, six inches in height. She has green eyes, blond hair, and a mole on the side of her neck. There are no other distinguishing marks on her body. The victim wore no jewelry, however, her ears are pierced.

"From my initial inspection, the cause of death appears to be a single knife wound to the throat. Trace elements of human semen, saliva, and assorted bruises were found indicating that the victim was sexually penetrated orally, anally, and vaginally. She was fully clothed at the time of discovery, however, she did not have on any panties and none were found at the crime scene."

During the reading of the report, Blair first studied the woman's face from several angles and then took several photos.

"Doctor, did you look underneath her fingernails?" Blair made sure to give the man his proper respect.

"No. I was told not to do anything intensive to the body until you guys had a look."

Blair looked at Russ, who appeared to be turning green.

"Okay, doctor. Thank you for waiting until we arrived. By the way, do me a favor and measure the width of the incision. It is very important." Blair handed the young man her business card as he nodded his agreement to her request.

"Please give me a call when you have finished your complete examination." Blair shook hands with the doctor and then joined Russ, who was already at the door. Before they left the office, the sounds of "Fade" returned and filled the space.

When they got to the car, Blair looked at the official photos taken at the crime scene and in the examination room while Russ enjoyed his cigarette and some fresh air. The condition of the body was identical to the others. The only difference being the face. Blair made it a point to look at each photo three and four times from different angles. There was something here that she was not getting, but she could not identify it.

"I'm sorry I wasn't much help in there, Blair. That is the one thing about the work we do that I will never get used to." Russ took a long drag and then turned to his partner for the day.

"You know, Blair, there is usually a connection with these nuts. From what we have seen so far, none of the clothing seems to match, the ages are different, the heights and weights are all over the place. There has to be something that is connecting all of these women to this one killer."

Blair started to ask the older detective to tell her something she did not already know, but she caught herself. Blair reminded herself that he is a short-timer and is only trying to help. The only reason why he is even here is because he was in the wrong place at the wrong time.

"Yeah, I know, Russ." Blair looked at her watch.

"Come on. If we hurry, I can still make that interview with the Whittington woman. Might as well kill two birds with one stone."

Russ nodded, stubbed out his smoke, and then slid into the driver's seat. He felt stupid. As he started the car, Russ chastised himself.

"Of course she would know that there must be a connection with all of these women. It was a dumb thing to say." As he flipped on the strobe and dropped the car into gear, he gave his bruised ego a reprieve.

"Well, at least she didn't bite my head off like one of those other guys might have." With the two compliments still fresh in his mind, Russ Matson exited the parking lot and was doing 90 miles per hour on the highway without giving anything else a second thought.

CHAPTER SIXTEEN

"Okay, Chief. I'll be right down." Lt. Maxine Stout gave the phone a hard stare after she hung it up. She had been expecting the call, so that was not what was bothering her. And it wasn't the man she reported to. She actually liked her boss, the Chief of Police. He was a fair man who gave her a shot when others might not have. What bothered her was that she had a punk in her command. And instead of dealing with her directly, he went to her boss. Maxine Stout made a promise to herself as she slipped into the jacket to her suit. "At some point in time, between now and the day he leaves her command, that sawed-off piece of shit is going to wish he had not done that."

Jack Case set the cruise control on 80 and then relived the recent past. One of his meetings went well. The other did not. That gave him plenty to think about. But before he got too deep into his thoughts, he decided to check in with Peggy Flynn and see what, if anything, is going on at the office.

"Hi, Peggy. Jack. Anything happening?"

"Hi, Boss. Nah. Everything is under control. Oh, Priscilla would like to speak with you when you come in. I told her I would give you the message when you called."

Jack made a face that was closer to disgust than curiosity.

"Did she say what she wanted to see me about?"

"No. She said it was personal." Peggy kept her tone even. She thought her boss was too nice a man to be running around unattached. On the rare occasion when she saw Priscilla and Jack Case together, she thought they matched up pretty good. If there was something going on between them, well, she was all for it.

"Okay. I'll be in around lunch time. I'll see her then." Jack hit "End Call" and then turned off the sound system in his car. Now he had something else to think about that he would rather not have.

Maxine Stout made sure that her posture was ram rod straight as she came down the stairs, turned the corner, and walked down the short corridor to the office of the Chief of Police. The kid she roughed up had a big mouth, and it was her best guess that the story was all over headquarters by now. Max did not need 17 years of investigative training to know that there was probably an over/under going on in the locker room as to how many days suspension she was going to get. That was fine with her. She could use the time off. Besides, if the truth be known, slamming that kid against the wall felt pretty damn good.

Max knocked twice, opened the office door, and then stepped through it. Before she closed it back, she gave another hard stare to the young detective from her command who was seated just outside the office. He returned her stare with the smile of someone who is used to getting his way. Maxine considered finishing the job that she started in the squad room but quickly dismissed that thought, stepped inside, and closed the office door.

Max was always stunned by how un-police-like this office looked. While there were the obligatory framed photos with the Chief shaking hands with this politician or that politician, the commendations and proclamations, there were also the framed works of art in equal number. The office had the look of a den rather than a command center. That look put her at ease as soon as she entered the room.

"Have a seat, Max." Max accepted the invitation and balanced her portfolio on her lap while the Chief of Police, a black man of average height and weight, in his early 60's, wiped his glasses with a tissue.

After sitting in on more meetings with this man than she could ever possibly remember, Max knew he had something difficult to say. Wiping his glasses before he spoke was a dead giveaway and everyone knew it.

She thought to herself, "The next thing he will do is fold his hands."

The older man put his eyeglasses back on and folded his hands in front of him on the desk.

"Max, I'll come right to the point. Some of the guys under your command have asked me to ask you not to put your feet on the desk when you are wearing a skirt or a dress. I know it's a different time now for women, but basically it makes the guys feel uncomfortable when they can look up the boss's dress and see her underwear." The Chief of Police thought for a moment.

"Quite frankly, Max, I agree with them. So, would you please refrain from doing that?"

Max felt like she was staring down the barrel of a gun that just misfired.

"Is that what you wanted to see me about, Chief?"

"Yes. Will you give me your word that you will work on that for me?"

Max could not imagine a time when she was more off balance. She began to nod her head like a bobble doll on the rear deck of an old Chevy.

"Yes, of course, sir. I will not put my feet on the desk when I am wearing a skirt or a dress. I am sorry that that the guys felt that they had to come to you and they could not come to me directly."

The Chief smiled a fatherly grin.

"Don't be too hard on them, Max. Perhaps I should not tell you this, but they have a lot of respect for you and they did not want you to take it the wrong way. It's a difficult subject. Sexual harassment being what it is. You've been to the classes. I am sure you understand."

There was more bobbling.

"Yes, sir, Chief. I do understand. Quite fully, sir." The Chief of Police rose from his seat and Max, taking the cue, rose with him.

"Is that it, sir?"

The Chief walked from behind his desk and then stopped.

"Well, there is one other minor issue." The older man balanced himself on the edge of his desk.

"I heard there was an incident in the squad room this morning." Max froze in her tracks and started to speak, but a wave of a hand cut her off.

"There is no need for an explanation. This morning, you gave my son the spanking that his mother and I should have given him a long time ago. When I assigned him to you, I told you to treat him just like every other officer under your command. I meant it then. I mean it now. As far as I am concerned, there is no record of that incident in any of my files down here."

Maxine Stout broke out into a huge grin that was infectious.

"Thanks for the support, Chief. Thank you very much."

The Chief took off his glasses and pulled his handkerchief from his back pocket.

"Not a problem, Max. Now send that punk kid of mine in here."

Max paused at the door, wiped the grin off her face before she opened it, and then motioned to the young detective.

"The Chief of Police would like to have a word with you."

Once she heard the door to the office close, the grin returned to Maxine's face. She took the stairs two at a time back to her office, closed her own door, and then let out one word.

"YES!"

Case tapped the brakes, disengaging the cruise control, and kept his speed even as he let the unmarked police cruiser pass him on the left. Like any other driver, an automatic tension took over his body at the sight of flashing lights in his rearview mirror. That tension did not subside until the lights, and the car that they were attached to, were well in front of him. Since he was close to his office, Case opted not to return to cruise control. He applied pressure to the throttle and returned the black Porsche to his normal driving speed of 80 miles per hour.

Habit, more than anything else, took over as Case eased his car over to the right and exited. The official exit for the town where his office was located was the next one up, but local knowledge had proven that there were fewer lights this way, thus making it a faster route. Case neatly turned into his personal space in the front row of the parking lot, a perk of his position and an off shoot of the fact that the bank owned the building. As he secured the car and walked to the building, Case took only minimal notice of the car that was just entering the parking lot after him.

Russ Matson turned off the strobe as he exited the highway. When you are out of your jurisdiction and there is no emergency, the unwritten rule is that strobes and screamers are not used. No cop wants to answer a complaint about another cop. Blair recited the address of the building and pointed to the appropriate driveway entrance.

Russ nosed the Crown Victoria into the space marked VISITOR. Before locking the car, he placed the POLICE – OFFICIAL BUSINESS placard on the dashboard. Blair shook her head.

"As if they could not tell from the four antennas on the roof of the car, the multi-colored lights on the dash and rear deck, and the CG on the license plate." She amused herself with that thought as she checked the address one more time.

Priscilla glanced at the clock and then smiled to herself. She was ready for him. The best thing about having a problem is having a plan to solve it. And there were two things about her plan that she liked. The first was that it was simple. She would go after Jack Case like she had never gone after anyone before. She would be relentless. There is nothing that she would not do, nothing she would not say, and nowhere she would not go. If he fired her, it would not matter. She did not need the money, nor did she the need to work. Getting fired would just give her more time to pursue him. Restraining orders, protection orders, and all the other legal stops for other people were just speed bumps to Priscilla. In her world, rules were made to be broken.

The second reason why she liked her plan is that all she had to do was be herself. This was her game and she was going to play to win. Everything else be damned.

Priscilla was just about to retire to the ladies room to freshen her make up when she spied the note by the phone. DETECTIVE COLLINS, 12-12:30. She cursed herself for forgetting about the interview with the police officer. Now this meant setting her plans back about a half hour. Priscilla sat back down and folded her arms across her chest. There was no need to look attractive for some feminist cop who has nothing else better to do than ask her stupid questions. This was something she would have rather done without.

Case entered the office through a side door, took the long way around the floor to his personal office, and was seated before anyone knew he was in the building. It was something that he worked on whenever he had the opportunity and had everything to do with him picking the office location that he currently has. He waited five minutes and then dialed Peggy's extension.

"I'm in. Tell Priscilla she can come in anytime this afternoon." After he hung up the phone, Case allowed himself one last thought on the subject.

"This ought to be interesting."

Russ held the door as Blair walked into the reception area. It was standard for the area and the function. Subdued, indirect lighting, neutral colors, and modest, contemporary art on the wall. The woman behind the desk was just as standard and just as functional. Blair presented her business card to the receptionist and made sure to smile when she asked for Priscilla. The young woman smiled back, invited them to sign the guest register, have a seat, and then she dialed Priscilla's extension.

Russ could not help but compare methods. In his day, a cop would show up, flash his badge, and imply to the gal behind the desk that if she did not move fast enough, she may end up in jail, too. Nowadays cops show business cards instead of badges and smile instead of sneer. Things sure have changed.

Priscilla met the two detectives in the reception area and showed them to a vacant room just off to the left of the receptionist desk that is used by Human Resources to interview job applicants. With an actor's talent, Priscilla hid her surprise that the female detective turned out to be black. Nothing in their brief phone conversation gave her away. Priscilla made a point of looking at the card again as they all took seats. While the guy was the perfect picture of every cop she had ever met in life, the woman was a completely different story. Priscilla never would have imagined someone so short, or that well dressed, to be a cop.

It hit Blair the moment the woman came through the door. Between the time they shook hands and then took seats around the table, images flashed at a rapid pace in her mind. Blair dismissed the agenda she had planned and went to a script that was just the bare essentials. Time was of the essence, and she had to get out of there.

"Tell me, Ms. Whittington…"

"Please, call me Priscilla."

"…how long have you lived at your current address?"

"Three years."

"Any problems with neighbors?"

"No."

"And it is just you and your housekeeper, is that correct?"

"Yes."

"Are you divorced, or widowed?"

"My husband died four years ago. I am sure you heard about it. It was…"

"Thank you, Ms. Whittington. I would suggest for the time being that you keep the curtains closed, alter your movements, and be alert to your surroundings. We will increase the patrols in your area as best we can. If there is a repeat of the incident, please call me right away. Thank you for your time." Blair punctuated her sentence by closing her folder and rising from her seat.

Priscilla was caught off guard by the abrupt ending. She expected a much more intense grilling.

"Yes. Yes, of course, I will call you at the first sign of trouble."

Blair smiled and was through the door in a flash. Not knowing what to make of the abbreviated interview, Russ Matson gave Priscilla his best fatherly smile, shook hands, and then caught up with his partner at the elevator.

"Would you mind telling me…"

Detective Blair Collins was a picture of concentration.

"Russ, please, just get me back to the station just as fast as you can. Don't say anything else, please just do it."

Not having a clue as to what was going on with this new age cop, Russ just nodded his head in agreement. He was a little annoyed that he could not have a smoke before they returned to the barn, but he chalked that up to dedication to duty.

Skip Hunter came into the reception area just as the meeting was breaking up. He paused at the desk, making no attempt to hide his review of the guest book and Priscilla's rear end.

"Who was that?" The receptionist showed him the business card that Blair did not take back. Skip studied the card and then replayed the image of Priscilla walking through the door.

The receptionist stopped chewing her gum and put on her most seductive look.

"So, Skip, when are you coming to happy hour again?" Her expression left no doubt that any time would not be soon enough.

Skip glanced at the card again and said the first day that came into his mind. "Thursday."

Christmas came early in this woman's world.

"Really? Wow, that'll be awesome. Gee."

Skip pocketed the card, thought for a minute, and then walked behind the desk.

"Listen, if they show up again, let me know." Reading the look of apprehension on the woman's face, Skip bent down, whispered in her ear, and then confirmed what was said with a nod of his head.

"I promise." The deal was sealed with a shot of the famous smile.

"Sure, Skip. No problem." For the next several minutes, not one phone message would be taken correctly.

Priscilla was again off balance. The cop was not what she expected. The questions were not what she expected. And the meeting did not last nearly as long as she thought it would, given her history and her experience with the law. Her mind jumped from questions to answers and then back to more questions. Was there more to this than she thought? Was she being investigated for a crime she might have committed? But what? She hadn't done anything wrong? Well, not lately anyway. Priscilla could not focus on the things that she wanted to do or needed to. Finally, as her efforts to retake control of her brain began to succeed, Priscilla received yet another blow to her equilibrium.

If there was one thing that did not sit well with Jack Case, it was waiting for something to happen. After going over the page for the third time, and not remembering a word that he read, Case got up from behind his desk and marched out to the floor.

Priscilla finally shook the thoughts of the police officers out of her head. Whatever reason they had for not wanting to speak with her was their problem. It certainly was not hers. With that thought clear in her mind, there was only one thing left to do. Priscilla stood up with the full intention of entering the office of Jack Case when, to her surprise, she found him standing right in front of her.

"You wanted to see me?"

For the second time in less than an hour, the Academy Award for best actress went to Priscilla Whittington. Her poise and posture hid the fact that she was caught off guard. It was her intention to take the fight to Case, not have him come to her. She was to be the aggressor, and he was to be put on the defensive.

"Yes. May we go to your office please?"

Case nodded, stepped aside, and allowed her to lead the way. Priscilla's mood instantly changed with that subtle act of chivalry.

"This is even better. It's like I am leading him to the slaughter house and the entire office is witnessing it. Everyone will see me take him in there. Everyone will remember this when they see me go after him. He will have to give in, and when he does, then I will have the last laugh."

Case kept his mind open.

"The best way to handle this is to go with the flow. You don't know what she has in mind, so don't try to guess." Case stepped in the office after Priscilla, closed the door, and then instead of sitting, balanced himself on the corner of his desk.

"Have a seat."

Priscilla stood with her body weight evenly balanced on designer heels with her arms folded across her chest. She became a formidable image of confidence. Priscilla made it a point to look Jack Case right in the eye.

"Thanks but no. I'll stand." Case nodded, shifted his weight to be more comfortable, and then relaxed.

"Listen, Jack, I'll get right to the point. When I want a man, I go after him. And when I go after him, I get him. Nothing has stopped me before.

Nothing will stop me now. I am coming after you. You might as well know that. You can make it easy on yourself and give in to me, but if you resist, I can tell you that there is nothing I won't do."

Case thought about smiling, then cancelled that idea.

"Are you threatening me?"

Hearing the response, Priscilla thought about what she just said and how she said it. She sheepishly smiled in a manner that she seldom used.

"I'm sorry, Jack. I did not mean for that to sound the way it did. I really doubt that you could be intimidated, especially by a woman."

Her body relaxed with the admission, and Priscilla decided to take a seat. Despite the fact that he was still sitting on his desk while she was seated in a chair, Case felt that they were still eye to eye.

"Just what is it that you want and why me?"

Priscilla balanced her elbows on the arms of the chair, steepled her fingers, and stared at Case for a long minute.

"Why you? You interest me, Jack. You interest me in a way that very few men ever have." Priscilla read his look and fought the insult that it implied.

"No, Jack, I am not attracted to you because you are a black man." His reaction to her comment confirmed that she was right.

"Quite frankly, that is the last reason why you would be interesting to me." Priscilla looked away and then came back to the present.

"And please do not think that thought will discourage me because it won't."

Case started to speak, but a well manicured hand rose to cut him off.

"And as to what it is I want, well, what I want to know about you is more than what you care to show in this office. I want to know the other side of you, the side that you will not let anyone else see. Then I want to show you my sides. Since I determined that you are interesting, I think you are entitled to that."

Priscilla rose from her seat, smoothed the wrinkles in her skirt, and took a step toward him. It did not go unnoticed to her that he did not flinch.

"I told you not so very long ago that life is too short. I refuse to live my life wondering, what if?"

Case studied her eyes.

"What exactly is the what if?"

Priscilla arched her left eyebrow.

"There are a lot of what if's in life, Mr. Case. Questions that have never been asked or answered. Take your pick."

Case took a deep breath. This was another session that has gone on long enough.

"Well, Priscilla, how you live your life and whatever it is that you believe in is your own affair. That I cannot control. What I can control is what goes on in my office and the conduct of my staff. I am paying you to work, not too flirt with me or anyone else. While I need you as a team member, I will not hesitate to fire you if you do not do your job, is that clear?"

"Now are you trying to threaten me?" Priscilla laughed in a light style that sounded good to Case.

"Listen, Jack, just for the record, I do not have to work. I don't need this job. If you fire me, for whatever reason, so what? It won't stop me."

"Well, in that case, why don't we have dinner? Tonight?" Case had to force himself to stop speaking because he did not know where the words were coming from.

Again, Priscilla hid her surprise. That was not the response that she anticipated. Score a hit for Mr. Case.

"Okay, Jack. Where should I meet you?"

Jack eased off the desk and walked around to his chair.

"Right here. We'll leave together." Jack sat down and felt like a stranger in his own body. "Is there anything else you would like to discuss?"

The wheels were spinning in Priscilla's head at a breakneck pace. Was this a con? Was she being set up? Who would be watching? Where would they go, and who was going to be there? It was a move that she had not expected, but then again, it was just the sort of thing that made him her target.

"No. That's all."

"Good. Then I will see you at five."

Case watched Priscilla walk out of his office and wondered just what he was walking into. Whenever it appeared that he was about to be trapped, his instincts always seemed to take over. And in more times than not, his instincts proved to be right. But this time, he had to admit he was not so sure that his instincts were right.

CHAPTER SEVENTEEN

Blair was out of the car before it came to a complete stop. With her portfolio secure under her arm, she looked like a female football player dodging tacklers as she rushed into the building. Those who saw her coming made sure to step out of her way lest they get run over. She hit the stairs in full stride, not giving a damn as to what she looked like. She had to get to her desk, and she had to get there RIGHT NOW!

During the ride in, the images would not stop. Over and over, from different angles, in different light, close up, and far away, she saw them. And she would keep on seeing them until she put it all together. It was there. She was close. There was absolutely no way she was wrong about this.

It seemed like hours had passed before Russ entered the squad room. According to his personal compass, Russ Matson felt that he was entitled to two cigarettes in exchange for driving at 100 miles per hour and basically scaring the shit out of himself. By the time he got up the stairs, Blair had every photo of every murder suspect spread out on the conference table. She commandeered a poster size easel and was standing with a pair of scissors staring at the photographs. When she saw Russ enter the room, she turned on him like a cat.

"RUSS! GET ME…" The startled look on the older man's face had just the right effect on the young female detective.

Blair put down the scissors and walked over to the man that had taught her in one day more than any other cop she had ever met.

"I'm sorry, Russ. I did not mean to yell at you."

Apologies, to this man, were as rare as compliments.

"That's okay, Blair. You're on to something, aren't you?" Russ's grandfatherly smile was offset by the look of concern in his eyes.

"Yes, and I need your help. Could you get me a photo of Priscilla Whittington, blow it up to about 12 by 14, and then ask Max to join us."

Storm clouds formed over Russ Matson's head.

"Yeah, well, I guess I could do that, but the problem is, Blair, I don't know where to look? She was never formerly booked for the case involving her husband, so we do not have anything on file." Matson began to fumble in his pocket.

"By the way, I have something…"

Blair crossed her arms and thought for a minute.

"Save it for now, please? I need to concentrate on this. Listen, try our files first anyway. There may be a surveillance photo or something else that we can use. If that doesn't work, then go to the society section of the New York, New Jersey, and Philly newspapers, going back a good few years. There has to be something there. The photo has to be a full-face shot, not a profile. And color would be better than black and white. When you find it, bring it over." Blair turned away without waiting for an answer.

Russ shuffled over to his cubicle, and in clear violation of department I.T. guidelines, opened his wallet and took out the sheet of paper on which he had written all of the passwords for his computer. He had to chuckle at the thought that he was actually using a computer to dig up clues. In his day, you pounded someone's head against the wall in the alley or behind the station house to find answers. But Russ told himself, This is the way of the future and Russ, old boy, until you hand in your tin, you had better get with the program."

Case caught sight of Skip Hunter making his usual entrance and prepared himself. There were some things in life that you just cannot avoid, and for Jack Case, Skip Hunter was one of them.

"The police were in to see her." Skip fished the business card out of his packet and presented it as Exhibit A.

Case took the card, read it once, and then handed it back.

"Who?"

"Priscilla. Oh, by the way, don't ever mention the name Nicole around her. She hates that name. Damn near bit my head off when I mentioned it."

Case stifled a laugh.

"Thanks. I'll keep that in mind."

When it was clear to Skip that of all the people in Jack Case's private office at that particular point in time, he was the only one interested in somebody else's private affair, he broke down and asked the question.

"What do you think the police wanted with her?"

"Beats me. Why don't you ask her?"

Skip shook his head.

"Can't. She told me to stay away from her."

"She told you to stay away from her, and you are going to accept that? Skip, you of all people should know that when a woman says stop, she means go. I'm a little disappointed in you, buddy. I really am." The lines were delivered with such dead pan cynicism that the unknowing might actually think Jack Case meant what he said.

Skip Hunter snapped his fingers, slapped his hands together, flashed the smile.

"Oh, I'm working on that, big guy. When I find out something, I will let you know." Skip performed another finger snap and slap and then left the office for parts unknown.

Case watched the young man as he made his way back across the floor.

"Damn! Almost got him."

Case glanced at the lower right-hand corner of the computer screen and then at his watch and then he laughed. It always amazed him that the device that everyone relies on these days for just about everything is always five minutes fast. He reset the time a dozen times, and within 24 hours, his personal computer went right back to being five minutes fast. So much for digital efficiency.

Case gathered up the papers on his desk, logged off the system, and was just about to rise out of his seat when she walked into his office. What he saw made him stop in mid-air and then slowly settle back into his seat.

One of the things about a woman that always fascinated Case was the way they could change their appearance with little or no effort. While the clothes were the same, the woman that stood in the doorway to his office did not appear to be the same woman that stood there just a few hours ago.

Case took in the sight before him. Her make-up was freshened, which was not surprising. But what was quite noticeable were the little things that were done to accent her face. A brighter shade of lipstick, the application of eye liner and mascara, and her eyebrows seemed darker. Then there was the trick with her blouse. She turned up the collar and opened another button to reveal just the right amount of cleavage. The effect was that her blouse seemed to frame her face and draw attention to her instead of away from her.

Priscilla was pleased with the reaction that she got. She was competing against a very worthy adversary. But this was her game and she was playing to win. That meant that nothing would be taken for granted, and she would use every trick she knew and any new ones she could think of to win.

Case relaxed his body, leaned back in his chair, and took in the sight.

"You needn't have gone through any trouble, but I appreciate it. You do look very nice." Case punctuated his comments with a smile to show that he was sincere in what he said.

"I'm glad you approve. On short notice, a girl has to make the most of what she has to work with." Priscilla smiled confidently and walked into the office.

Case nodded as he rose from his seat.

"I see. I was thinking about Antonio's. Is that alright with you?" Case walked towards her and took in her scent. It was light with a hint of spice. Just enough to get your attention.

"Nice scent."

"Thank you. I order it from a custom perfumery. You will not smell this scent anywhere or on anyone. That, I can assure you." Priscilla slipped her arm into his. She expected him to ease away, but he did not.

"I have never been there, but if that is a place that you like, then it is fine with me." As they walked to the elevator, Priscilla prayed that the maitre'd and the wait staff at Antonio's would not recognize her from last month.

It took Russ Matson almost two hours to come up with a photo, but he did and he was extremely proud of himself. In his day, being a detective meant kicking in a door, scouring a crime scene, or greasing the right palm for a clue. He never thought he would have to use those same skills to find a photograph of some society doll but he did. And to his utter amazement, he got what he went after.

It took him another half hour to figure out the photo package on the department software, but in time, Russ managed to download the digital photograph, crop it, and then enlarge it to the size that he wanted. Proudly, Russ Matson looked at the finished product the same way he looked at his five shot group that qualified him to carry a weapon at the academy.

"Here you go, Blair." Matson produced the 12 by 14 enlargement of an old photo taken from the files of the New York Times.

"You're lucky. The editor said they were scheduled to purge this set of files next month."

Blair stopped what she was doing, took the photo, but before she looked at it, she spoke to the older man.

"Hey, Russ, 'we' got lucky. I need you to help me with this case. Are you with me?"

Russ was taken aback. To the rest of the guys in the squad, he was the "old guy". The antique who had more stories than arrests. The guy who could not make it up the stairs without breathing hard. The word was you had better not depend on him because he could not see a thing without his glasses. And God only knows how he would do in a fight. He heard the talk in the locker room and at the bar after the shift was over. He saw the looks. You did not have to be a cop for almost 40 years to know what was behind it. They did not trust him.

Well, that was enough for him. If the guys did not trust you, then there was no use hanging around. He gave in to the majority and decided to turn the game over to the young. His plan was to slip out quietly. No fanfare. No parties. Just go. And now, he was being brought back in. The most unlikely person in his mind said she needed him. Blair is young, sharp, and has a law degree. She has everything on her side. But Blair said she needed him. Russ Matson felt a long-lost sense of pride. It awoke a part of his brain that made him feel alive again. Russ nodded his head and asked the question that he had no opportunity to ask in a very long time.

"Sure, Blair, what is it that you need me to do?"

Blair looked at the older man and felt relief. She was going into uncharted waters. In all of the serial crimes that she had read about, there had never been a theory like the one she was about to present. She needed someone who would look at what she came up with like a cop trying to solve a crime and not dismiss it out of hand simply because they had not seen it before, or even worse, because it came from her.

"Russ, right now I need you to tell me that I am not crazy."

Blair took another look at the photo and then placed it to the side of the table. She had laid all of the photos of the dead women from other murders in other states on the conference table. While Russ was searching for the Whittington photo, Blair had cut up the pictures and then put the pieces in the form of a montage. When she was done, the table top looked like a completed jig saw puzzle. Blair then scattered the pieces before Russ returned to the room.

"Okay, Russ, just bear with me on this. I have gone through this a couple of times, and I know that I am right. But that's not enough. I need to sell it to you and then I need to sell it to Max. So, all I ask is that you keep an open mind."

"Sell what to Max?" Neither one of them had noticed the Lieutenant approach.

"Blair has a theory about the serial murders. She was just about to present it to me." Russ beamed with a fatherly pride.

Maxine Stout balanced her weight evenly and then crossed her arms over her chest while leaning against the door frame.

"Okay, let's hear it,"

The night air felt good to both of them. To Case, it seemed to amplify her scent, giving him something else to think about. Something pleasant. Something new and different. For Priscilla, it was a release. It took away the confines of the office and allowed her to breathe. It meant freedom. She now had license to be whoever and whatever she wanted to be. Priscilla cast a sideways glance toward Case and then thought to herself, Who and what will I be tonight?"

Case led Priscilla to his car. There was no thought in his mind about asking who was going to drive. Although she would have preferred her 'Vette, with the top down of course, Priscilla uttered no comment as she slipped into the Porsche.

Blair was momentarily off balance. She wanted to test this out on Russ first before getting in the ring with the champ. Well, now there was no choice. She took a deep breath and went with her instincts.

"Here is what we know. All of these women were killed in the same fashion. None of them have a connection to the other. They are all of different ages, different weights and heights, and come from different parts of the county. They were all dressed in a different fashion when they were killed. There is nothing to tie these women together so far.

Now, what we also know is that there are eight points to the human face. Hair, forehead, eyes, nose mouth, ears, cheeks, and chin. I will not get cute with a game of 20 questions. Just watch for a moment and then let me know if it makes sense to you."

Case drove in the confident manner of a professional, fast but not reckless. Priscilla admired his smooth handling of the six-speed gear box and the precise way he turned the car. While the jazz music filled the inside of the car, the wind from the outside washed over her. She closed her eyes and allowed herself to get lost in the moment.

She was here with him. She finally got what she wanted. Or did she? She had been in his company before only to be dismissed. What would he do tonight? What would she do? Where would this end up? Priscilla felt the familiar rush begin to build in the pit of her stomach. With a practiced effort, she calmed herself.

"This night has only just begun. Best not to peak too early."

Case watched her out of the corner of his eye and was mildly impressed. There was not a hint of fear or uneasiness at the speed at which he drove. In fact, she seemed to be enjoying it. This told him something about this woman, and he filed it away for future reference.

Blair rearranged the puzzle pieces back into a montage.

"Well, what do you think?" Russ and Max were stunned. Between them they had almost 60 years of police experience, and yet they had never heard of such a thing, much less witness it with their own eyes.

Max studied the table, closed her eyes, and then waved her hand.

"Okay, Blair, do that again." With the confidence of a person who knows each and every piece of a puzzle by heart, Blair took one key facial component from each of the pictures on the table and made one partial portrait of Priscilla Whittington.

"Here is our connection."

Russ was incredulous.

"Max, if I did not see the woman with my own eyes, I would not believe this. But I have to tell you, that's her."

Max stood stock still, shifting her eyes from the puzzle Blair concocted to the enlarged picture of Priscilla Whittington.

"How did you come up with this?"

Blair could not help but beam with pride.

"In college, pre-law was my major, but I took Art History as a minor. It gave me an eye for detail."

Max Stout got closer to the montage.

"It's a long shot, Blair. But it is definitely a shot. Nice work. Very nice work."

From the pieces of the faces of the recent victims, Blair constructed the forehead, eyes, nose, and cheekbones of Priscilla Whittington. The only parts that were left were the hair, the mouth, and the chin. Blair stood to the side and let the others take in the image she produced.

"I would say that there is definitely a connection between whoever is committing the murders and the Whittington woman. Whether it is casual or something deeper, obviously we don't know just yet, but there must be some kind of a connection. There has to be."

Max nodded her head and walked around the table to look at the photos from different angles.

"Bring it together. What have we got so far?"

In her case file, Blair kept a summary sheet of important facts for just an occasion like this. Although she knew all of the facts by heart, she still referred to the list.

"All of the deaths are in the immediate area, they are all women, they were all killed with a knife, and it appears to be the same weapon in all deaths; there is evidence of loose tobacco at one of the murder sites, indicating that the killer may be a smoker; there is a connection with a prominent woman of means who has been implicated in the recent death of her husband."

"And there is one other thing." Both women looked at Russ with a mixture of curiosity and amazement.

"The license plate number and the description of the car in the peeper squeal belong to a Mr. John Case, who happens to be the manager of the department where Priscilla Whittington is employed. I'm sorry, Blair. I tried to tell you this before, but you were focused on the photos."

Blair made notes in her case file.

"That's okay, Russ. I should have known better. I'm sorry."

Max made her way back to the center of the table.

"Save the hug fest for later, Russ, how did you figure that part out?"

"Well, we passed a car matching the description of the peeper incident on the way to the Whittington interview. I caught part of the plate number as we passed by. Then on the way out of the building, the same car was parked in a space marked for the V.P. Operations. I took the full tag number, made a call, and found out that the Operations Vice President is a Mr. Jack Case. Then I ran the tag and confirmed that the owner of the car is a John Case. Here is his home address." Russ Matson tore off the page from his small notebook, handed it to Blair, and smiled to himself at the same time. He contributed to the team. He still had value. No one will ever be able to take this moment from him.

Max looked around the squad room and was thankful that they were the only ones there. "Okay, guys, this is starting to come together. Russ, bring that easel and pad over here please?"

Max drew a flow chart showing the victims on one side, connected to the murderer, and the name Whittington on the other side connected to Case, her dead husband, and the peeper. Between the words "Whittington" and "murderer" was an empty space with a question mark. The two detectives could see the wheels turning in their boss's head.

"Okay, Blair, it's your case, where do you want to go with it?"

"Thanks, Max. What I am thinking is that before we approach Priscilla Whittington, we should probably speak with the people who knew her the best. Get some background information and try to develop a profile we can work with. In the mean time, I am hoping to come up with some more information on the weapon used and who could possibly have such a knife."

Max was in step.

"As far as the first part is concerned, that would be her dead husband's family. I agree with you on that. Be careful on the second part. We do not want to tip our hand and have the feds come in and steal our case to protect one of their soldiers gone freak." Max froze in her place for what seemed like a very long time.

"Blair, you have to check in with your folks at State, right?" Blair nodded her head reluctantly.

"Tell them that you are still looking into some possible leads, but you do not have anything solid yet. I'm sorry, but I have to tell you that since they don't expect too much from you, they won't press you. We can use that to our advantage. If a problem comes up, I'll protect you."

Blair broke out in a wide grin.

"I'm okay with that."

"There is one other thing. The Whittington family has juice you guys could never dream of. If this is leaked out, we could have trouble. Blair, take a digital photo of what you have here, put it on a zip drive, and then purge the photo from the hard disc. I'll need that evidence when I speak to some folks in Trenton, and I do not want it lying around for somebody else to stumble upon. Russ, you mark the photos so that they can be easily re-constructed. Place them in an envelope and make sure the chain of custody is clear. Do not leave them here. We'll meet in my office tomorrow at nine sharp."

Max returned to her office, closed the door, and then fell back against it. The kid has a legitimate shot at cracking this case. One of the biggest cases in recent memory and one of her detectives is about to bust it wide open. Field commanders get ahead on the cases their troops solve. This is the way out that Max had been looking for. The Headquarters of the New Jersey State Police in Trenton was suddenly looking a lot closer, and for that, she could thank one Blair Collins.

CHAPTER EIGHTEEN

Everything about Antonio's had intimacy and seclusion in mind. Locally, it was known as a cheater's spot. The entrance to the parking lot looked more like an alley way than a drive way. The restaurant was actually part of an old and very large Victorian mansion that now housed a law firm and a couple of accountants in the upstairs portion of the building. The dining room is located downstairs and not visible from the street. There is only a small brass plaque that identifies the establishment, and even that is out of the way.

Case nosed the Porsche through the entrance to the parking lot and placed it perfectly in a spot well away from the rest of the cars. Priscilla looked at him warily.

"Worried about somebody hitting your baby?"

Case switched off the car and opened his door.

"Not really. It's going to get crowded in here in a little while. I just want to be able to get out."

Priscilla waited until he came around to her side of the car and opened her door for her. She made a neat pivot on her hips, keeping both of her legs together as she swung them out of the car. Then she stood straight up. The classy movement also did not go unnoticed. Case made a note of that as well.

If the maitre'd remembered Priscilla, it did not show on his face. He placed a check mark next to the name in the reservation book and ushered the couple to an intimate table in the far corner of the dining room. After helping Priscilla with her seat, he took their drink orders and disappeared.

The dining room reinforced the theme of intimacy and seclusion. With the exception of recessed lights in the ceiling and specific lights on the frames of the Venetian art work, candles provided much of the illumination in the restaurant. The colors on the walls and the upholstery of the furniture were a combination of muted reds and gold. Despite the absence of wall hangings and draperies, there was a subdued hush to the room.

Case leaned back in his chair and took in the surroundings. Despite the few other early diners, it seemed like they were the only ones in the room. The décor of the dining room accentuated Priscilla in a striking manner. The conservative European styling of the room and its furnishings highlighted the classic features of her face. It seemed an odd coincidence to Case that she just happened to be sitting underneath a spotlight.

As they entered the restaurant, Priscilla assessed the fine points of the room. When they arrived at their table, she made it a point to take the seat underneath the recessed spot light. Tonight, there would be no distractions. She was the only person he would have eyes for tonight. She toyed with the notion of pulling her chair closer to him, of undoing another button on her blouse, or employing a few other tricks that she had learned over the years, but she quickly dismissed that thought.

"There will be time enough for that later."

Case allowed himself to go back to his thoughts of a few months ago, when he imagined her standing in Red Square in Moscow and her striking grey hair falling on the collar of her black sable coat. With the up turned collar of her silk blouse taking the place of the mink coat, he could see that the image he had of her at that time was pretty accurate.

"I am surprised you have never been here before. The food is very good. I think you will enjoy it."

"I have heard about this place. Thank you for suggesting it. I have been eager to try it." Priscilla punctuated the lie with a smile, then sat back, crossed her legs, and relaxed.

The waiter for their table appeared with their drinks, recited the specials for the evening, and then suggested that they take a few minutes to relax with their drinks. Priscilla and Case nodded in agreement to the suggestion, clinked their classes, and enjoyed the taste of scotch and vodka respectively.

"So, Mr. Case, what made you give in so easily?"

Case met her eyes with his.

"I haven't given in to anything. I merely invited a staff member out to dinner."

"So, is that all I am? A staff member?" Priscilla laughed lightly.

"Come on, Jack, you've already broken a few corporate rules with me, and now you are breaking three or four more. Nobody takes that kind of risk for nothing."

Case smiled back at her.

"You're the one that said life was too short, remember? You threatened to stalk me, and I would like to know why."

"I told you why."

"Then I want to know more about you."

"Why?"

"Because I want to know more about the why."

Priscilla thought about what was just said.

"It makes sense. How much do you want to know?"

"Everything."

"From the beginning?"

"From the beginning."

Priscilla skipped the mundane details and went right to the items that were not in her personnel file. She is an only child and lost her parents in a car accident between the age of 13 and 14. Shortly after the accident, her hair turned completely grey. At first, she tried to dye it, but she was teased unmercifully at school, so she left it grey.

"You know, it's funny, when I decided to leave it grey, after a while I became the center of attention. None of the other girls had hair the color of mine. When the boys started commenting on how good my hair looked, some of those silly girls, the same ones who were teasing me, actually tried to dye their hair the same color as mine."

She was raised by an aunt and uncle on her father's side who had already raised children of their own. In some ways, they indulged her, and in other ways, they were way too strict. Priscilla admitted that she was a handful. She knew they could not keep up with her and took full advantage of that.

"It was that, plus the fact that my parents were gone. I did not know my aunt and uncle very well before my parents died. I felt that I was on my own, and no one could tell me what to do. It was a wonderful feeling."

Case took a sip of his scotch.

"So, you became this wild child."

"No. I was too smart for that. A wild child gets sent to boarding school. I was the sole recipient of the proceeds of two insurance policies, savings accounts, and stock portfolios of people who did fairly well in life. The court appointed executor made sure that the terms of my parents will were followed. My aunt and uncle could not touch the money for themselves. They were paid a stipend for my upkeep, but everything else was to be placed in a trust for me. When I graduated from high school, they made a very strong case for sending me away and taking that cost out of my inheritance. I stretched the envelope only as far as it benefited me while I was with them. At least until I was able to get away."

"That was college?"

"Yep. That was college."

During the telling of her upbringing, the waiter reappeared took their dinner orders and refreshed their drinks.

"Where'd you go to school?"

"I went to a small school in northern California. I took it easy during my first year, but after I learned the ropes, I did pretty much as I pleased.

"I found out quickly that in college, as an athlete, no matter what sport you chose, you had it made. So, I tried out for the swim team and made it. That gave me round the clock access to the pool, the locker room, and the field house. I got my pick of courses and instructors. I was a pretty good student, but for those subjects that I did not particularly care for or whenever I did not feel like working too hard, I found a way to get the grade I needed."

Case rolled his eyes as he took a bite of his meal.

"I can only imagine what was involved there."

Priscilla smiled and shook her head in a patronizing way.

"No, Jack, you cannot. I will simply say that a married, middle-age college professor who teaches the driest and most boring of subjects can turn into a crazed, sexual deviant when he has a young and willing college girl in his bed or his office or his car or the campus swimming pool at midnight. But it was fun and it was exciting and it was real. More real than the bullshit the same professor was teaching in his class during the day. And I gotta tell you, I loved every minute of it."

"Really?"

"Jack, have you ever dived head first off a ten-meter board?" Case shook his head.

"Well, the rush is feeling your body fall through space and knowing that if you do not hit the water just right, you could hurt yourself pretty bad. But once you feel that rush and know that you can do it and survive, you can't wait to get back up there and do it again. There is a rush like that in life, depending on how you live it. I felt that rush in more ways than one, and I can tell you that I loved it so much that I wanted more."

Case became silent. Most men would have challenged Priscilla's point with their own exploits. Case did not believe in competing with women. He saw no point in it. Priscilla's question took him back to a time in his life where he did feel a kind of rush. It is known as fear. And just as quickly as the thought came to mind, Case stopped it. To continue would dredge up memories that were best kept locked away.

Case was hardly surprised. He suspected as much, but Priscilla just confirmed it. She is an adrenaline junkie. The incidents in his office and in the conference room were still fresh in his memory. He had known men who took it to the limit and then a bit further. They were men who would wait until the last second to open their chutes just to beat the odds. Case never had much respect for men like that, but there was also a part of him that envied them. He was jealous of their daring and the way they bent the rules. In his mind, however, it was just a matter of time before the house won and they lost. Or at least that is what he told himself. Case had to admit though, he had never met a woman who pushed the envelope to the limit. And now that he has, Case had to ask himself, was he going to play it safe or would he try to beat the odds?

Case brought himself back to the present.

"So, you graduated and never looked back."

"Exactly. I had my history degree, an inheritance of almost two million dollars, and a pretty good sense of knowing just how to get whatever I wanted when I wanted it. I put my stuff in storage, packed a knapsack, and headed off to Paris. I decided that there is a world out there, I am going to see just about as much of it as I can, and Paris was as good a place as any to start."

"Tell me about Paris."

Priscilla wiped the corners of her mouth with her napkin and took a sip of water. She looked at him over the rim of her glass and tried to get a sense of where this all was going. He wanted her. She knew it. She knew it from the time, not so long ago, in his office. She knew it even before then when she would see him look at her when he thought no one was watching. But what she did not know was when he would take her or how he would take her. Would it be tonight, in the parking lot, or in her drive way? Would he be rough or gentle? Would it be tomorrow, with an invitation to have dinner at his place? What would she do? Would she let him have her or would she keep him at bay? When and how? Give in or tease? She did not know what he would do, and Priscilla did not know what she would do. It was that "unknowing" that gave her the feeling in the pit of her stomach that she was so addicted to.

"I'll tell you about Paris later. Now it's your turn."

"Studying the habits of your prey?"

"Oh, I think I have a pretty good idea as to who you are and where you came from, but I want to hear it from you." Priscilla thought for a moment before the look in her eyes and the tone of her voice changed.

"And Jack, be careful of who and what you make fun of." Case made a mental note of the fact that he hit a nerve.

The Eyes lay in bed and stared at the partially completed mural on the wall. Despite the dim light, he could see all of the details that are both there and not there. He wondered where she was and what was she doing? Who was she after now? Did he know she was after him? The Eyes laughed at the thought of it. Would she do to him what she did to me? Is she sitting with him now, over a drink, telling him about her past? Is she baiting him, begging him, to take her only to disappear and then reappear and then disappear again?

The Eyes took a slow drag from his hand-rolled cigarette and then blew a smoke ring in the air. He smiled as the ring circled the face on the mural and then disappeared.

"Stupid police. They will never figure it out, but I will know. This is my mark on the world. This, in return for the mark she left on me."

The Eyes took another drag from the crude smoke, then stubbed it out. There are three pieces to the puzzle that have to be found.

"Her hair, her chin, and her mouth." The Eyes closed and thought about her mouth. How it looked and how it felt. What she did with it and what he did to it. Then he unzipped his trousers, reached for the lotion that he kept by his bed, and let his mind wonder back in time to a place where he was sitting alone, having a drink and minding his own business.

To the people who were familiar with his work, he was known as The Eyes. He could not remember where he picked that name up or who had given it to him, but it stuck and he liked it. The Eyes. As an independent photographer working mostly in war zones, his eyes were his livelihood. He saw things in a manner and a perspective that most others did not see. He saw details and shades and tones and all of the textures that makes one photograph stand out from all of the others. The Eyes were good at what they saw and captured, but all that they saw and captured took a toll.

He began his career in Africa with the tribal wars. The Eyes then followed the conflicts from one hot spot to the next. Europe, Latin America, Asia. It did not matter. One civil war after another. Adults, children, animals. The butchering, torturing, murdering. It all began to meld together after a while. In order to tell the story, The Eyes had to get closer. He sacrificed everything to get closer. In time, he got so close that he became part of it.

The Eyes shunned human contact. He lived like an animal in the wild, learning to move without being seen and to see all that was around him. All fear was gone. He got the photos that no one else could get or would even attempt to get. His cameras told the stories that no one else could tell. But the process took all feeling out of him. In the end, The Eyes were just that. A pair of eyes. Nothing else.

He was in California and between assignments. The Eyes needed a place away from the crowd. He found it in a bar that was close enough to the hotel where he was staying, yet far enough away to not be convenient to the other hotel guests. What he had seen would turn the stomach of the most hardened individual. He did not want to answer some silly questions from some silly traveler who was looking to past the time. He thought he wanted to be alone. He told himself that he should be alone. Yet there was a part of him that did not want to believe it.

"Do you mind if I ask you a question?"

The Eyes reacted to the sound of her voice, soft and gentle. He was not used to that and the fact that he was not accustomed to any one speaking to him at all. Startled, The Eyes looked up and into the most beautiful face he had seen in a very long time. His hands hung in the air and the look on his face must have been quite strange, given what he was in the midst of doing.

"I'm sorry. Please finish what you are doing."

He licked the glued side of the crude hand-rolled cigarette, placed the entire cigarette in his mouth to moisten it, and then set it in the ashtray to be lit later. Not once did he take his eyes off of her.

Not bothering to wait for an invitation, the woman took a seat at his table.

"I was wondering, why do you do that?"

"Do what?" The question was sincere. The Eyes really had no idea what she was talking about.

Priscilla leaned forward, placing her elbows on the table and cradling her head in her hands.

"Hand roll your cigarettes. Is it that much cheaper? I have never seen that done before, and I am really interested to know why anyone would do that?"

The Eyes looked at the cigarette in the ashtray. No one had ever asked him about that before. In fact, he could not say the last time he even thought about it. But now here was this beautiful woman, who could probably have her pick of any one of the guys in this bar with no effort at all, asking him about something that he gave absolutely no thought to.

"I guess it started off as something different to do and then turned into a habit. Do you smoke?"

"Only occasionally." Priscilla took a sip of her drink, weighed the odds, and then went with her gut instincts.

"Do you mind if I try?"

The Eyes gave her the tin of tobacco and the package of rolling papers and watched her emulate his movements. Her fingers were slender and agile. After a couple of false starts, she got the hang of it. When she licked the glued end of the paper with her tongue, he was hooked. Two cigarettes and three drinks later, they were in the parking lot exploring each other's bodies. In less than an hour, they were in his bed putting to use the knowledge they had gained. In the morning, she was gone.

It had been a long time since anyone asked Case about himself. Still, his answer was immediate and matter of fact.

"My story is not that unusual or even interesting." Jack finished the last of his veal and wished there was more.

"Try me."

"Well, my life between from the day I was born until I graduated from high school was as eventful or uneventful as any other young man. I had a mother and father who I did not see very much of and a bunch of people who came and went in and out of my life. I chose to go into the military after I graduated from high school. It was the quickest way out of the mid-western town where I grew up. I did two tours of duty in the Middle East, worked for the government for a while, and now I am with the bank. That's it. The end."

Priscilla closed her knife and fork, pushed her plate away from the edge of the table, and crossed her legs.

"Come on, Jack. You can do better than that. What branch of the service were you in and what did you do?" Priscilla stared at him for a minute and then laughed.

"And please do not make up some story about being a cook. I would hardly believe such a thing about you."

Jack examined the bottom of his water glass. She was the first one to guess what he would say and head him off at the pass. He gave her credit for that.

"I was in the Marines, and I was a sniper."

"Did you always get your man?"

"Yes."

"Did you like it?"

"Like what? The war? No. No, I did not like the war at all."

"Then why the extra tour?"

"I was good at what I did, they needed me, and the pay was good."

Priscilla got the sense that she was close to a limit.

"Did you like the killing?"

"No."

"Then why did you do it?"

Case was sorry that he was not fast enough to think of another cover story, other than the truth.

"No sane person likes to kill people. I was a soldier, that was my assignment, and I followed my orders. Like I said, I completed my missions and thought that by doing that I was saving lives. That's all there is to it."

"What did you do for the government?"

"I cannot tell you that."

"I am not surprised. Do you want to know what I think?"

Case shook his head.

"No, but I have the feeling you are going to tell me anyway."

"You were a leader of men. You were in some super secret branch of the Pentagon, and you went on secret missions all over the world. And then the politics got to you and you got out."

As she spoke, the coffee and cordials were served. Case wondered if she was that good or was he just that much of an open book. Despite the pieces of her life that she shared with him, he felt that she knew more about him than he knew about her.

There were only a very select number of people who knew as much about him as he relayed to her tonight. Case felt like he had just exposed a vulnerable part of his body to an enemy who would use it against him. He did not like that. Not at all.

The Eyes woke up to find that an empty space inside of him had been created where she had been. It was a space that he did not know existed until he found her gone. In some ways, he knew it was too good to be true. He was lucky to have had just that little bit of her. But there was a part of him, the space that she created, filled, and left, that wanted her back.

Case was tired of denying what he knew to be true for no good reason.

"You are right. Sometimes I led a group of men and then sometimes I went alone. We went to where we were asked to go, did what it was we were ordered to do, and then returned to our command. Now please do not ask me anymore because I simply will not answer you." Now it was Case's turn to sit back and cross his legs.

Priscilla was undeterred. Her intuition told her that Jack Case was a dangerous man. Now it was confirmed. She could feel her heart beating inside her chest.

"How many confirmed kills did you have, Jack?"

The Eyes were in the shower when he heard the door to his room open. When he came out, she was standing there with a hand rolled cigarette. In the morning, she looked better than she did the night before.

"Get dressed."

"Why?"

"We're leaving. I have already taken care of your bill."

"Where are we going?"

She shrugged her shoulders.

"We'll know when we get there."

It did not take him long to get dressed, pack his clothes in the well-worn rucksack that was his form of luggage, and then take the passenger seat of her convertible. During the drive up the coast, she pulled over to one of the scenic look out areas by the side of the road, unzipped his pants, and buried her head in his lap.

It seemed to last forever. The bright sunshine, the cars whizzing by, the sensation of her mouth made it seem that much more decadent. The Eyes forgot about what he had seen, what it was his job to record, and what the world would think of the kind of person who did the work that he did. If the world thought of it at all. She took all that away and left him with a feeling that he thought he would never feel again.

They traveled up the coast of California to the boarder and then headed east. For the next three weeks life, for this man who had seen more death than any human should, had never been better. They wandered. A day here, two days there. Maybe only an hour someplace else. They rose with the sunrise or slept well into the afternoon. In time, the years of combat and conflict began to fade. The Eyes felt human again. He saw the things that war prevented him from seeing. He saw the sunset and the moon rise. He saw smiles and innocence and the beauty of a field of flowers. He saw the sun glint off her hair and the subtle change in color as she turned her head. The Eyes saw it all. They made love in public and in private. They walked and talked, laughed and joked, and treated the world like it was their private playground. And oddly enough, The Eyes never thought once about taking her picture.

Then one morning, The Eyes awoke and she was gone. He waited for her to come back. Hoped she would come back like she did before. But after three days, she did not return. She had taken him on the ride of his life and then she left. Without a word, she left. No good-bye, no argument, no note telling him it was fun. She just left.

When the clerk at the desk told him that the lady he was with paid for three extra days, and if he wanted to stay any longer he would have to pay, he knew she would not be coming back. The Eyes went back to the room that they had shared and packed his knapsack. She paid to keep him there. She knew he would wait there for her. She did that so he would not follow her. She gave herself three days to get away from him. She could be anywhere. He had no idea where to look. The Eyes stood in the middle of the room and re-lived the time they had spent together and the things that they had done. She gave him life. Then she took it from him. The more he thought about it, the angrier he got. To him, she was life. He wanted it back. To get it, he would have to find her. There was only one way that he knew to do that.

Case studied the coffee in his cup and then looked at her with cold, hard eyes. This had gone far enough. Priscilla reminded him of what he had been and what he was. A part of him wanted to confess, to tell it all, every last detail. But to do that would be to awaken a monster that had been dormant for a very long time. A voice told him that it would do him good. His gut told him that it would not. This was not the time. This was not the place. And she was not the person.

"Listen, tonight, you told me that I should be careful of what I make fun of. Now I will tell you, be careful of how deep you pry. When I worked for the government, I did things that I was not proud of, in places that most people in this country do not even know exist. I did the things that I did for far longer than I care to think about, and when I found I could not be effective any more, I quit. That is the extent to which I will admit my past to you. Do not ask me anything more."

Priscilla had seen more than one man pushed to the brink. In her youth, she had been foolish enough to push a man beyond his limit. When that hap-pened, she was lucky to have escaped with her life. She would not make that mistake with this man.

"Okay, Jack."

Case took a moment to de-arm himself and then signaled the waiter for the check.

The Eyes re-lived that moment by the side of the road often. He brought back to life the feelings that she had given him that day. She took him, and when he wanted to, he made her take more. He put his hands on her head and made her take him. When she wanted to stop, he would not let her. Not until every last drop was gone. Then, and only then, did he release her.

Using the dark night as a back drop and the tree lined street as cover, the black Porsche seemed to appear out of nowhere. Case smoothly brought the car to a stop in front of the house that he thought was really too big for just two women. Priscilla sat perfectly still in the car. Her heart was pounding, and the pit of her stomach was churning. This was it. The moment she had been waiting for. What would he do?

They had driven in silence. The night had started out light enough but seemed to be ending with a tension between them. It was the type of tension that was neither good nor bad, not the fault of any one person or any one thing but was definitely something that would not just go away on its own. It would have to be dealt with.

For a reason that Case could not explain, instead of going back to the office to pick up her car, he drove directly to her home instead. His mind was blank in the same manner as many years ago when he relied more on instinct than thought. Something inside of him told him that this is what is expected, this is what you want to do, there is a reward at the end of this and you need to take it. In most any other person, there is a counter point, another voice that will have some other message. Tonight, there was no such other voice. Tonight, Case was on his own.

When they arrived, Priscilla made no move to leave the car.

"Would you like to come inside?"

Case looked her for a long second.

"No thanks."

Priscilla opened the remaining buttons on her blouse and moved closer to him.

"I wasn't talking about the house."

Case held his position. Instinct had left, and another sense took over.

"Neither was I. Thanks, but no thanks."

Priscilla sat with her blouse open and her arm resting on the back of the seat, in sheer lingerie that made her breasts look more sensuous than if they were bare.

"Okay, Jack. Now you have seen the top and the bottom. When am I going to see the best parts of you?" Priscilla shifted in her seat.

"As I told you once before, there is a time and a place for everything. This is not the time, nor is it the place. Good night, Priscilla."

A cold, matter of fact expression came across her face.

"Wait a minute, Jack. You invite me to dinner, we spend a good part of the evening at an intimate little table trading details about our backgrounds that others around us do not even know, then you drive me directly to my house instead of back to the office so that I can pick up my car and now it's just 'Good night?'"

Jack fought hard to stifle a laugh as he stared at her. How many times in the past had she done this very same thing to some guy who was desperate for her? Teased him to the point of frustration and then left. And now, when the tables are turned, she is suddenly a victim? Truth really is stranger than fiction.

Case was about to get out of the car to open her door when Priscilla lunged at him. It was time for her to be the aggressor. If he was not going to take her, then she would take him. Once she got started, he could not resist her. No man can.

Case noticed her shift her feet and anticipated the move. Just as she leaped at him, he raised his right hand, wrapped it around her throat, and then squeezed, holding her at arms distance. At first, she smiled at the show of force, but then as he tightened his grip and the flow of air to her lungs was cut off, panic registered in her eyes. Like any human who is drowning, she fought to live. She scratched, kicked, and grabbed at anything that she could. It was no use. Life was ebbing from her body. Everything was going to black.

Case let her go just before she lost consciousness. Priscilla fell in the seat like a rag doll, gasping for air. He got out of the car, opened the passenger door, and stood back as Priscilla stumbled to her feet. Case drove away, leaving Priscilla to wonder just how close to death she had come and knowing that Jack Case could have killed her.

CHAPTER NINETEEN

Russ Matson ambled into the squad room and was hardly surprised to find Blair already there. He had seen this youthful enthusiasm more than once. He even had it once upon a time. It was more than just the thrill of the hunt. It was the thrill of knowing that you were smarter than some insane criminal mind. It was the thrill of knowing that you were on the brink of putting some monster behind bars for a very long time. It was the thrill that, in some way, you were going to save mankind from itself.

Russ had long ago lost that thrill.

"No matter what they did in the course of doing their jobs, mankind was going to do whatever it had to do or wanted to do, good or bad, and there was precious little a cop could do to stop it. With that bit of reassurance, Russ Matson made his way to the coffee room. What it took to save mankind from it elf would have to wait until after his first cup of coffee.

"Good morning, Blair. What have you got?" Russ made a note of the fact that there were more pictures spread out on the conference table, and there was a new map in place with pins in different parts of the country.

Blair just barely looked his way. She was concentrating on a new set of photos that appeared to be, from the hair styles and the clothes, older.

"Russ, this thing is getting scary. I am starting to get photos from the other killings in other parts of the country involving the same type of knife. Look at this." Blair took a set of photos of women killed in the same manner as the recent homicides. She then took parts of the images, created a portrait, and then stepped back without saying a word.

Had Russ Matson not had the years of experience in law enforcement that he had, he might have dropped his coffee cup.

"Blair, that's incredible. It's her all over again."

Blair slumped without looking into a chair that was right behind her.

"Yeah. Russ, we've got to get this guy. I don't know how, but we have got to get him."

Russ looked at the photos and shook his head.

"We'll get him, Blair. But I can tell you this, it will not be easy." Russ Matson said the only thing that was acceptable. In his mind, his experience was telling him that they were looking for a one in ten million needle in a haystack.

For the next hour, Blair and Russ poured over the cold case photos and the areas of the country where they had come from. The first set came from California. The case had been closed as unsolved. The State Patrol in Texas sent the second set. And again, the case was administratively closed. The third set was just coming in from Michigan. Before they had a chance to work out the puzzle of the faces, Max called them both into her office.

"Okay, I was on the phone with Trenton this morning. Going forward, I will be the contact with Trenton. I need you both to concentrate on the case." Both detectives nodded in agreement.

"We are clear to contact the Whittington's. This is how we will play it. Blair, you and I will interview Doris Whittington. That is about as good as we are going to get. No one speaks with her mother, so she will have to do. I'll set it up, and we will take my car.

"Russ, while we are out, see what you can dig up on that guy, Case. Draw up a request for a warrant and have it ready for me to sign in an hour. Trenton doesn't want any locals involved in this, so run it down to the state D.A.'s office, speak with A.D.A. Powell only. Show him what we have. When you have the warrant, come back here. We don't want to spook this guy, so we will need to distract him while you check his file at the bank. We can figure out how to do that this afternoon. Any questions?" Both detectives shook their heads.

"Good. Blair, I'll get you when our meet is set up. Russ, get started."

The detectives went their separate ways while their commander took a seat on the edge of her desk and dialed a number.

Priscilla awoke from a fitful sleep, made her way to the bathroom, and was shocked at the bruise on her neck. Last night was not a dream. She went for him, and he almost killed her. For a long time, Priscilla stared at the image in the mirror with the red bruise on her neck and tried to make the connection between the woman that she knew and the one who was looking back at her in the mirror. In frustration, she turned away. The woman that she knew would never have put herself in a position to almost have been killed. The woman who was looking back at her did.

Case sat up in the chair, still wearing the clothes from the night before. Beside the chair was an empty scotch bottle. He could have killed her. He almost did. For what? That was the part that scared him.

For what? Case looked at himself through his mind's eye.

"You know damn well for what. Priscilla is no different than she was."

She wanted him her way on her terms, on her time, in her way. And then once she had him, that would be it.

"I'll see you around. Maybe. If I am in the mood and in the neighborhood. And even then, I may speak to you or I may ignore you. Who knows? But you know what? It's all up to me now. You don't really count anymore." Case looked at the empty scotch bottle and the vision in his mind and made a face.

Case had been down that road before. How many years had it been? It didn't matter. He remembered it all like it was yesterday. Case had walked the hot coals, felt the pain, and smelled the stench of his burning flesh, only to see the prize that he thought was his, walk off with someone else. Case swore that he would not venture down that path again. But there he was last night, looking down that same road lined with the same coals with their warm, inviting glow. All he had to do was take the first step. Perhaps had she not lunged at him, he might have gone inside with her. Perhaps if she had waited, he might have changed his mind. Perhaps if she had tried another tact, he might have given in and then she might have won.

But she didn't do any of those things. So, she lost and he lost. He had her and could have had her, but he let her go. He thought the voice in the bottle would tell him what went wrong, but it could not.

The Eyes were up and out before sunrise. There were three more parts to the puzzle that had to be found. There was no time to lose.

CHAPTER TWENTY

"Okay, Blair, let's go." Blair Collins put the finishing touch on an e-mail message, slipped into her suit jacket, and picked up her brief-case. In their designer suits, pumps, and briefcases, the two women looked more like corporate attorneys or high-end Avon ladies than police de-tectives. Despite her shorter legs, Blair had no trouble keeping up with Max. She slid into the passenger side of the white BMW 325csi and let her body relax into the leather seat. Max cast a slight glance at her passenger, let a thought go in and out of her mind, then dropped the car into gear and made her way out of the lot.

Max used her red strobe to bypass most of the traffic between police head-quarters and the highway. Once she was on Interstate 287, she dispensed with the strobe, set the cruise control at 90 miles per hour, and then relaxed.

"Okay, here's the deal. The Whittington's, as I told you before, have got the juice and are as well connected as they come. They are old money, and they have more of that old money than the law should allow. Cops don't go where they live unless they are invited. That's why we're taking my car. One of the department cars would stand out like a sore thumb and that would not be a good thing.

We will be meeting with Doris at her office. She is the daughter of Victoria Whittington, an attorney and counsel to the Whittington Trust. I never met her, so I can't tell you anything about her. Let's just play it straight and see what happens. No badges when we go in. Present your business card, and don't sit until you are invited to sit. Since it is your case, you ask the questions. Keep it routine unless something jumps out. Check with me if you are unsure. I will let you know if you are on thin ice. We're not accusing anyone here. We're just looking for information. Any questions?"

Blair shook her head.

"No. But I am curious why a woman who married well and must have come into a pretty good estate is working as a clerk in a bank. Wouldn't a woman like that be doing volunteer work or hanging out with the idle rich? Something here does not add up."

Max dropped the corners of her mouth and cocked her head to the side.

"Good point. Maybe we can get a clue about that from Doris."

Blair put the information and her question to the back of her mind. It was good to get away from the pictures of women with their throats cut. Blair allowed herself to enjoy the ride of the sports sedan and the scenery of this elite part of New Jersey. She tried to imagine what the office would look like. Would it be some old, stuffy, wood paneled affair? Or would it be a glass enclosed, modern day fish bowl. Blair bet herself that it would be the former. For some reason, the name Whittington and the thought of anything contemporary just did not seem to go together.

Max exited to Interstate 78 at Basking Ridge and took the local road for next mile and a half to one of the many corporate complexes that seem to spring up out of nowhere in this state. Just as she turned the BMW into a visitors parking place, a restored Bentley passed behind them. Both detectives watched as a garage door at the side of the building opened and the car disappeared inside. Without a second thought, they collected their suit jackets and briefcases and ventured into the world of wealth beyond comprehension

The elevator stopped at the second floor and opened into the offices of the Whittington Trust. Plush carpeting muffled the sound of their footsteps as they approached the receptionist station to the right. The wall behind the station was wood paneled with the name of the firm prominently displayed in heavy brass letters.

To the left, there were the obligatory leather arm chairs and end tables. Included in the reading materials was a copy of the latest trust newsletter. Blair made a point of placing a copy in her briefcase. Directly in front of them was a conference room enclosed in smoked glass. Not a sound was heard. There were no other offices or workers visible.

Both women walked authoritatively towards the receptionist.

"Good afternoon. Maxine Stout and Blair Collins to see Doris Whittington, please."

The woman behind the desk was polished, efficient, and just attractive enough not to embarrass the firm. She rose from her seat and stepped from behind her workstation.

"Good afternoon. Ms. Whittington is expecting you. She asks that you make yourselves comfortable in the conference room. May I offer you water or a beverage?" As she spoke, she walked ahead of the police detectives and opened the door to the glass enclosed room.

Max accepted the offer of a glass of water while Blair declined. The receptionist produced a bottle of spring water from a refrigerator underneath a credenza, a coaster etched with the Whittington family crest, and a crystal glass, similarly etched. She opened the bottle, filled the glass half way, and then left the refreshments within reach on the conference table.

"Ms. Whittington will be with you shortly."

The far wall of the conference room was made entirely of tinted glass that went from floor to ceiling and looked out on the rear of the property. The scene was particularly peaceful with a small waterfall and brook in the middle of the landscape. Blair took a position at the window to get as close to the peacefulness of the landscape as she could. Max took a sip of her water and then joined the younger detective, but her thoughts were not on the view.

Max took a look around and envisioned herself in the room. It was filled with men and women of all shapes, sizes, and ages, locked in discussions about the fate of the organization and waiting for her to make a decision. She could hear the banter back and forth, voices rising, disgruntled sighs, and palms slapping the conference table. All the while, she would be standing there with her hands on her hips as she was doing now, looking out at the landscape and knowing that it all had to go through her. She had the power to make it happen or not make it happen. As she stood there, Maxine Stout felt the presumed power flow through her body. She liked the feeling.

Doris had had just about enough of the police. She found them to be rude, crude, and unsympathetic to her and her mother. She thought that she had seen the last of then when the investigation into her brother's death was administratively closed. Doris's first impulse was to cancel the meeting. But she knew how insistent cops could be.

"Better to get it over with now than have to deal with it later." When the receptionist informed her that her two o'clock appointment had arrived, she took her own sweet time putting down the proposal she was reading in order to meet her guests.

As the receptionist closed the main entry door to the conference room, a side door opened and Doris Whittington entered the room. Armed with a yellow legal pad in a burgundy portfolio bearing the Whittington family seal and dressed in a grey skirt, a white blouse, and a blue blazer with off black stockings and moderately heeled pumps, Doris looked every bit the corporate facilitator. That her blouse was open enough to expose a good portion of her breasts seemed slightly incongruous to the rest of her outfit.

The first image Doris saw were the heels. Then she worked her way up the shapely legs, past the slim fitting skirt, to the hands resting on a waist. She stopped briefly at the badge pinned to the waist band and then continued up to the silk blouse stretched tight across her breasts. Doris froze in her tracks and felt the nipples of her own breasts harden as she met the authoritative sneer of Maxine Stout.

Max became a predator. She had expected some mousey-looking, little nobody wearing an off the rack blue pin stripe suit and a bow blouse or cultured pearls, or both, that was straight out of "Little Women." This was something different. She took a deep breath that expanded her chest even more and made a note of the reaction of the woman that just entered the room. For a moment, she allowed her mind to change professions.

The images were a blur between the two women. They saw each other in reincarnations of their other lives, with common friends and acquaintances, in places known only to them and the members of their lifestyle. They saw each other in situations that only they would, or could, understand. The two women realized in that one short instant, they knew each other intimately, despite the fact that they had never met before this moment.

Blair looked from her commanding officer to the first live lead in her case, and she saw something tangible pass between the two women. The affect this "tangible something" would have on her case gave her cause for concern.

Doris regained her decorum smoothly.

"Good afternoon. I am Doris Whittington, Vice President and General Counsel to the Whittington Trust." Doris extended her hand to the only person she saw.

Max stared at the woman with hawk-like eyes and waited half a beat before stepping forward and taking the woman's hand. That pause sent just enough of a message. Doris received the message and made an effort to contain herself.

"Good afternoon. I am Lieutenant Maxine Stout, and this is Detective Blair Collins. Thank you for seeing us on very short notice." Max held the woman's hand in a powerful grip, and after what seemed like a longer than usual period of time, they disengaged. Blair waved from her place at the window.

Doris regrouped, although her face was still flushed.

"It is fortunate that I did not have any appointments this afternoon. Please have a seat." The two women exchanged business cards while maintaining eye contact. Blair produced a business card, but with no one interested in it, she simply laid it on the table.

Doris motioned to the chairs at the table. Before anyone could move, the door to the conference room opened. The receptionist stepped into the room, moved to the side, and allowed Victoria Whittington to enter with the hulking mass of Trap Martin dressed in a dingy beige suit, bringing up the rear.

Doris uttered a gasp.

"Mother!" Without hesitation, she re-fastened the two upper buttons on her blouse.

Victoria Whittington made her way to the head of the conference table, and not only took a seat, but took command of the room. She looked at each occupant of the room, including her daughter, and took their measure as if she were meeting them for the first time.

"Well, I think we can now all take our seats. Doris, please sit beside me here. I will have a glass of water please. Doris, please introduce me to our guests." A glass of water appeared in front of the elder Whittington as if by magic because no one had seen the receptionist move.

"Yes, of course, Mother. This is Lt. Maxine Stout of the Franklyn County Police Department. This is Detective Blair Collins of the New Jersey State Police. Officers, allow me to introduce Mrs. Victoria Whittington, Chairman of the Whittington Trust, and Mr. Trap Martin, President of Martin Security Associates, on permanent retainer to the Trust."

Doris turned to her mother and tried to recover.

"Mother, the purpose of the meeting today is…"

With both hands resting on her cane, Victoria Whittington froze the words in Doris's mouth with but a look.

"I am aware of the purpose of this meeting. What I would like to know is why was I not informed that this meeting was called, and why this meeting was not coordinated with my calendar?"

All of the occupants of the room whose last name was not Whittington gained instant insight into life as the child of Victoria Whittington. And all of those occupants felt an instant sympathy for the daughter of this strict and domineering woman.

Before Doris could speak, Max came to her rescue.

"Mrs. Whittington, I must take some responsibility for the urgency of this meeting. I mentioned to Ms. Whittington that we needed just a few minutes of her time and that the questions would be fairly routine. We just needed…"

Victoria took a sip of her water and only moved her eyes in Max's direction.

"Lieutenant, my daughter graduated third in her class at Yale Law School. She passed the New York State Bar examination without studying for it and is admitted to practice law in five states. I think she is quite capable of defending herself. Doris, I asked you a question. I would like an answer please."

Trap Martin smiled without moving his lips.

"Man, I bet ole Doris caught hell for coming in third." Trap intentionally took a seat away from the group at the far end of the table. The less attention he drew to himself, the better. Besides, he wanted to make his own assessment of the new talent in the game.

He quickly dismissed the boss. That dam was closed. As soon as she opened her mouth, he could see that she had issues with men. But the kid that was with her, now there was something to consider. True, she was short and light and looked like she was only about 16-years-old, but she was tight and cute and that was a combination that made sense in any man's book.

Doris had been down this road before. This was a fight she could not win.

"I am sorry, Mother. Due to the subject matter of this meeting, I should have consulted with you. In the manner that it was presented, I did not think there would be much discussed here that you did not already know. "

Victoria took another sip of water and made sure she did not look at anyone in particular. "Officers, were you prepared to disclose to my daughter that the murderous adulteress who happened to be instrumental in the death of my son is the subject of a serial killer in our midst?"

Doris's mouth flopped open in complete and utter surprise.

Blair could barely contain her shock. This was confidential information. No locals were supposed to know anything about what was recently developed. It is one thing to be told that someone has the power. It is quite another matter to witness it.

Max smiled knowingly, sat back, and crossed her legs.

"Mrs. Whittington, that is confidential information on a case that is under very active investigation. We cannot confirm or deny that statement at this time."

If Victoria Whittington's face could have become any colder, it just did.

"Young lady, anything that has to do with that murdering whore is my business and I will be informed of it. If not by you, then by your superiors. Have I made myself clear?"

A vein pulsed in Maxine's neck. No cop, male or female, will accept being told what to do by a civilian, no matter who they are. Max was just about to make a career threatening statement when the only man in the room moved in his seat.

"Mrs. Whittington, I do not think the police are trying to be difficult. I think they just do not have a sense of the history behind the situation. In the interest of efficiency, I would like to propose that we proceed with the meeting and that I brief the detectives with background information that might help their case later. I am sure that once they have an understanding of the situation, the flow of information will be easier." Trap started with Victoria and made eye contact with every female seated in front of him.

Victoria relaxed noticeably.

"Thank you, Mr. Martin. That is an excellent suggestion. Doris, please proceed with the meeting."

Doris glanced from Trap to her mother and then cast a look at the two detectives that were seated across the table from her. She did not like being upstaged by Trap Martin, but she had to admit, he diffused a potentially ugly situation.

"Thank you, Mother. Lieutenant?"

Max nodded toward Blair and then sat back in her seat. While the cheap gumshoe looked like he had just come from doing surveillance at a porno parlor, she had to admit that he cooled things off nicely.

"We feel that Priscilla Whittington might have some connection to the recent deaths of women in the area. What we would like to know is any information you can give us about her background, up to and including the death of her husband."

Doris made a note on her pad.

"The facts surrounding my brother's death are still painful for us. Mr. Martin has a full dossier on Priscilla. I am sure you will find that to be much more helpful than anything we could tell you here. I will see to it that you have a copy. Is there anything else?"

Blair sat up in her chair and leaned forward. Given what was just said, her next question was sure to set off more fireworks. But, well, that was just too bad. This was important, and the question had to be asked.

"Did Priscilla Whittington have any enemies or anyone who might have wanted to harm her?"

Trap laughed as he watched Doris's lips disappear.

"We are not aware of any associates, negative or positive, of Priscilla Whittington."

Blair made a note on her pad.

"After the death of Mr. Whittington, could you please tell us what Priscilla did, if anything?"

The attorney in Doris made an appearance.

"What exactly do you mean?"

"Did she go into seclusion? Did she travel? Did she visit anywhere particular? Was she immobile? Any little detail may be helpful."

Victoria drained her glass of water and turned her attention to the landscape outside of the office. It was clear that this line of questioning had very little interest to her.

Doris, on the other hand, was intrigued by the question and seemed to be going back in her mind to the recent past.

"Upon the death of my brother, Priscilla left the area shortly after the funeral. She said she had to get away from all of the media attention and the inquiries by the police. Once she was removed from the list of suspects, she took one of her cars and drove to California."

Max picked up on the question while Blair made notes.

"How long was she gone?"

"It was quite a while. Almost three months."

"Was she in contact with you or any members of the family while she was away?"

"No."

"What happened when she returned?"

Victoria's head turned away from the window and back to the group at the sound of the question. On her face was a look of hatred so intense that every person in the room held their breath.

"Officer, I will tell you exactly what happened. After the death of my son, that woman's belonging were removed from my son's house and placed in storage. Upon her return, she was given the location of the storage facility and told to find lodging elsewhere. The settlement of the estate was handled by attorney's retained expressly for that purpose. That cheap slut was banned from my home, and her membership in clubs affiliated with my family were terminated. That woman was told never to darken our door ever again. Never." Victoria held everyone's attention for a full beat before she turned back to the landscape, the waterfall, and the babbling brook.

Doris closed her portfolio with an audible snap.

"Now, will that be all, Lieutenant?" It was clear to those seated at the conference table that the meeting was now over.

"Yes. We do not have any further questions."

Doris took out a business card, made a note on the back, and then rose from her seat. "Good. I will have Mr. Martin send you a copy of his background file on Priscilla Whittington. Please take my card and feel free to call me should you have any further questions."

Max took a look at the back of the card and then slipped it into the pocket of her jacket as she rose from her chair.

"Thank you for your time and hospitality."

Trap flipped a business card to Blair.

"Call me when you have time to go over the file."

Blair picked up the card, flipped back one of her own, and wondered if the man was as sleazy as he looked.

"Thanks."

With the exception of Victoria Whittington, hands were shaken all around, and then Max and Blair made their way out of the room and the office.

The two detectives debriefed on the way back to the station. Both agreed that the next meeting needed to be with Trap Martin. Blair took a look at the business card of the president of Martin Security Associates and made a face.

"What kind of a name is Trap anyway? I feel like I should be wearing rubber gloves handling this business card. And speaking of which, didn't Doris realize that she had already given you a card when we came in?"

Max slapped the red light on the roof of the car and then sped up to 100 miles an hour. She was in a hurry to get back to the station.

"I guess her mother must have really spooked her. She looked like she had that kind of effect on people."

Blair glanced at the speedometer, took a look at her boss, and then checked the fit of her seatbelt.

"Yeah, I guess."

As she settled into the left lane, Max thought about the second business card that she was given by Doris Whittington. It was a train of thought that had absolutely nothing to do with the case they were investigating or the reason why they had been there. Written on the back of the card was a simple message.

"The Wayfarer Motel. Room 215. 6 P.M. tonight. I will be there!"

As Maxine Stout sped along the highway, she shook her head in amazement.

"It just doesn't get any better than this."

CHAPTER TWENTY-ONE

 Priscilla came to work late, stayed at her desk all day, and spoke to no one. She wore a scarf to hide the bruise on her neck, but no accessory could hide the bruise she felt inside.

This was supposed to be a game. It was her game. She created it. She wrote the rules. She selected the players. She kept the score, determined what was fair, and she alone decided when the game was over. That was up until last night. Last night, things changed. Suddenly it was not her game anymore. It was something else. The rules changed and the stakes changed. Last night, she was almost killed. Priscilla looked at the clock. It was well after five, and she was still at her desk.

Jack Case never left his office. He never opened his door once he went inside. He did not answer his phone. For the entire day, Jack Case did not do one thing related to his position as Operations Officer for Franklin Valley Savings & Loan. Jack Case spent the entire day staring out of the window, wondering how he could let a person take him to the point of almost ending a life, and what exactly was he going to do about it?

He recalled the first time with her, not so long ago, when he acted out of impulse. He took a chance and was rewarded. Did he think that was going to happen again? Jack scowled at his own ignorance. He should have known better. He should have known that she would stretch the envelope. He should not have invited her anywhere. But he did. And there is no way to undo what has happened.

At a quarter to six, Jack Case made the one and only decision he would make that day. He decided it was time to go home. He stepped outside of his office, saw the shadow of the only person left on the floor, and at that moment, the questions that had been haunting him all day were answered.

Priscilla looked at the clock on her desk. 5:45. She felt like her body weighed several tons. It was impossible for her to move. All of her co-workers were gone. She was the only one left on the floor. She knew it was time to go. But for a reason that she could not explain, Priscilla did not move.

It was 15 minutes before six when Max Stout pulled up to within 500 feet of the Wayfarer Motel. She turned off the engine, checked her watch again, and then sat back and waited. Max felt like she was back on the street in Newark. Back then it was her practice to always show up early for a meet. Some things never change. She felt the old adrenaline rush, the excitement of matching wits, and if it got to that, the excitement of matching physical skills with a worthy adversary. But she was not on the streets of Newark tonight, and she was not meeting some punk who should be behind bars. The adrenaline rush was real, but the nature of the excitement was much different.

Blair looked at the clock on the wall. 17:45 hours. She hated military time. It made the days seem like it was one endless loop. She made a face and dialed a number on her cell phone. There was a connection, but no answer on the other end.

"Why don't you ever say hello?"

"Because caller I.D. tells me that you're the one calling me." The voice was calm and condescending.

Blair cursed the logic behind the statement.

"Did you get my note?"

"Yes."

"Do you have the information?"

"Of course."

"Are you at the same location?"

"Where else would I be?"

"I'll be there shortly." Blair did not wait for a response. She ended the call and threw the phone on the desk in disgust.

It was understood between them that whenever she needed his assistance, Blair would call and then they would meet at a hotel. There was no need for them to know where either of them lived.

Tonight, Blair did not like his tone. He was acting like he was doing her a favor, like she needed him more than he needed her. After a moment's thought, it occurred to her that that was exactly what he wanted her to think. It was to get her on edge, to piss her off, to make her angry. Blair sent a mental message through the lifeless telephone to the person on the other end.

"Be careful what you ask for."

At six o'clock, Jack Case stopped at Priscilla's desk. Nothing was said. He just stood there. Priscilla looked up at him. She did not know what to make of him standing there. What would he do? What would he say? What did he want from her? She did not surrender, but the bravado was gone from her face.

Jack reached over and turned off the desk light. Priscilla stood, as if for the first time in her life, and allowed Jack to help her on with her coat. Jack and Priscilla looked at each other for a long time before Jack motioned to the door. Priscilla gave a small smile of acknowledgement and then moved in the direction of the elevator with Jack Case close behind her.

At exactly six o'clock, Max stood to the side and knocked on the door of room 215 of the Wayfarer Motel. It did not matter that her car was in plain sight. She changed the license plates before she arrived. If anyone ran the plate, they would get the name of a plumbing supply company that had long since gone out of business. The room was at the far end of a line of rooms on one level. The entrance to room 215 was not visible from the street or the office and appeared to be better maintained than the other rooms of the facility. The glass in the window seemed thicker than the other rooms. The draperies were heavier and of a different pattern and texture than the ones hanging in the other rooms.

While she was parked in front, Max did not see anyone go in or come out of the motel parking lot. She thought about it and figured that Doris would either have gotten there before she did, or there was a back way onto the hotel grounds that Max did not have time to find. Max shrugged it off as inconsequential. She was about to turn and leave when the door opened, apparently on its own.

The Eyes looked at the clock on the dashboard and decided to call it a day. He had been searching all day but was not able to find the prey he was looking for. He had seen several that would have made very worthwhile trophies, but that was not what he was looking for. He had a particular need for a particular type of animal, and not just any one would do. While rolling his last cigarette, The Eyes caught a glimpse of an advertisement about a three-in-one tool, and just like that, his problem was solved.

They drove in silence. He knew where he was going. She did not care. She snuggled next to him and placed her head on his shoulder. He pulled her close and placed his hand on her knee. When they arrived at his apartment, he helped her out of the car, unlocked the door, and stepped aside. This was her decision to make. He would not make it for her. She could enter or walk back to the car. Take the risk or back away from the edge. Priscilla looked at the threshold as if it were the edge of a cliff.

Max transferred the overnight bag she was carrying from her right hand to her left. Then she stepped through the door into the darkened room. If anyone made a move to grab her, with her right hand free, she would be in a better position to execute a move, put the freak on the deck, and then put her foot in the persons chest. The heels on the shoes that she wore were actually steel shanks, sharpened to a needle point just for that purpose. The door closed and Max breathed deeply. The scent that she took in told her that there was nothing to fear.

Blair knew she was being baited. The problem was that she did not like being baited. It made her angry and edgy. The meeting with the Whittington's was bad enough. Blair did not like the fact that an old woman could sit back, receive a phone call, and flaunt her influence as if no one else mattered. As if she, Blair Collins, did not matter.

There was an intelligent part of her that tried to fight against what she was feeling. But there was an emotional part of her that wanted to be angry and edgy. Blair was tired of being short, cute, and polite. A part of her wanted to take something out on somebody.

The Eyes leaned against the side of his vehicle, took long drags from his cigarette, and contemplated his change in plans. He looked at it from every angle. He considered the possible alternatives. When he was through, he was satisfied that this was the best possible way. The Eyes stubbed out the last of the smoke and then retreated to his lair. He had to prepare.

Priscilla stepped into the apartment and continued walking until she was in the middle of the room. She took off her coat and let it fall to the floor. She stepped out of her shoes and kicked them to the side. The she stood and watched him with her arms at her side.

Jack stopped at the door and watched her walk in without fear. There she was, standing in the middle of his space. Unafraid of what might happen but also not precipitating anything. Just waiting. The next move was up to him.

The door to the room closed at the same time that a lamp was lit. Max did not turn around. She scanned the area in front of her and was satisfied that there was no one in the immediate space that she could see. Max dropped her bag at her feet, snapped her fingers, and uttered a command.

"Heel, Puppy!" On command, a naked Doris Whittington stepped from behind the door, dropped to her knees at the heel of the police detective's shoe, and began to caress her leg.

Max smiled, bent down, and opened the overnight bag. She took out a dog collar, fastened it around the Doris's neck, and then snapped a leash in place. Max raised her skirt to above her waist and then pulled the leash so that Doris's head was just in front of her crotch. Max then spread her legs, jerked the leash, and closed her eyes as Doris began to satisfy her new master.

Max held the leash with her left hand, and with her right, pulled the head of her new pet further into her crotch. She let the feelings wash over her as she stroked the woman's hair. Max took the end of the leash and slapped Doris's flanks. With renewed energy, Doris went deeper and harder and faster. Max moaned and continued to stroke the woman's head.

After she had parked her car, Blair opened her small bag and took out the things that she would need. She changed her shoes, took the elevator to the fifth floor, and then walked down hall of the hotel with a purpose. Tonight, Blair had no use for codes. She knocked on the door once, and when it opened just a crack, she burst through it as if she were the point person on a raid. The short, fat computer nerd who opened the door was taken by surprise. He knew she would be a little edgy, and he wanted her that way, but he never expected this. Blair whipped her leg and up ended the man. It seemed as if at the same instant that he hit the floor, she was upon him. Blair rolled him over, put her handcuffs on his fat wrists, placed a thick black hood over his head, and then rolled him back over.

The two consenting adults had an arrangement that started during their college days. He would help her with internet research for her law courses, and she would coach him through the prerequisite classes that no computer nerd is ever interested in. Late night study led to other topics of interest and mutual satisfaction. The relationship ended at graduation and began anew when they met on the east coast by accident through mutual friends.

Blair stood up and made a point to take her time. She wanted his mind to start working. She wanted him to imagine what might possibly happen to him tonight. As she looked down on the helpless man who used a T-1 line like it was the key to his personal kingdom, Blair unbuttoned her blouse very slowly. She took a long time to unzip her skirt, kneeling close in order for him to hear it. She rubbed her shoes against his leg, digging her heel into his flesh to place an image in his mind. Blair took note of his reaction, smiled, and dug deeper. Stripped down to her lingerie, Blair recalled his tone during their phone call and wondered what he was thinking now. It did not matter. She uttered a gut-tural sound, ripped open a condom with her teeth, and then relieved herself of the image of being the cute little cop in the bow blouse that did what she was told. She had one thing on her mind as she dug her nails into his flesh.

"Tonight, this is more for me than it is for you."

The Eyes recalled the time, not so long ago, when they were together. There was something about her that he did not trust. Nothing this good and no woman this pretty comes to a guy like him this easy. During one of their overnight stops, while Priscilla was in the shower, he copied her name and address from her driver's license. At another point, he copied the license plate number of her car. He checked the registration to make sure that the car was hers and then cross referenced that with the name and the address on the driver's license. When she left him that day, he knew that it would only be temporary. He had all the information he needed to find her again.

Priscilla gave in willingly. This was not part of the game anymore. This was something else. Something different. Something new. It was not that she wasn't in control. She did not want to be in control. The game had changed. It was not her game anymore. It was his. They were playing by his rules now. Not hers.

Jack held her close. This is what he wanted. Just her. Lying bare before him. No pretense. No competition. No games. Just her. Just him. Nothing else. They made love with the intensity and passion of lovers who had nothing to lose. They held back nothing and gave everything. When it was over, they lay back spent and satisfied.

Doris and Max lay together with blankets and pillows strewn about the room, their hair slightly matted, bathed in sweat. The session had been rough and physical. Doris gently touched the marks and bruises of their style of love making while Max took off the clips and bracelets. Both were beyond satisfied.

Blair did not stop. His orgasm meant nothing to her. When he went flaccid, she raised the hood just enough to expose his mouth. When that no longer pleased her, she dug the heels of her shoes into his body to arouse him again. Once accomplished, she had her way with him again. She did whatever it would take to keep him erect. When she finally reached her own crescendo, she did not stop. It was only after she felt herself become dry and raw that she released him.

The Eyes imagined her on the wall with the rest of his trophies. He saw her face as he came for her. He would ask her if she remembered him and if she remembered the way it was. In his mind, he felt their pulse become one as he took her. Then he would mount her on the wall and complete the portrait.

It would be over then. The quest would have come to an end. But not before one last time. The Eyes reached for the lotion that he kept by his bed. There would be one last time.

Priscilla lay on her side with her eyes closed. She kept her breathing shallow, pretending to be asleep. The reality was that she was more awake now than she had ever been in her life. It was beyond what she could have ever imagined. The game that this started out to be was now a distant memory.

Jack sat up in bed and looked at the woman beside him. It had been a long time for him. He did not know what to expect of himself or her. As he looked at her, Jack felt that a part of him was now inside of her and that a part of her was inside of him. He allowed himself to believe that they had done something more than make love. A part of him felt that he would not be the same after tonight, and that same part of him suspected that neither would she.

Doris sat naked in the bed and sipped champagne as she watched Max get dressed. She envied her thin, muscular body and the confidence that seemed to come with it. She wondered what she would have done with a body like that. But Doris stopped the thoughts before they went any further. She heard her mother's voice in her head.

"You are a Whittington. Whatever bodies those little tramps have will never match the blood in your veins or the brains in your head." Doris quickly thought about all of her classmates who were either on drugs or alcohol or both, divorced for the second or third time, dependent on alimony, child support, and the gifts of strange men they would meet in even stranger places. Most were larger than her. Doris had to smile.

"The old bitch was right."

"When will I see you again?"

Max stopped combing her hair, looked at the woman in the mirror, smiled, and then returned to finishing her hairstyle.

"How do you know I want to see you?"

Doris did not go for the fake. She took another sip and pulled one leg up to her chest.

"Don't hand me that. You know it was good." Doris put the glass on the nightstand, pulled her other leg up to her chest, and wrapped her arms around her knees.

"You don't have to worry about where to meet. I own this motel personally. This room is never rented. We can come here anytime we want and stay as long as we want." Doris envisioned spending days at a time doing more of what they did tonight.

Max put her brush in her bag, clipped her badge to the side of her skirt, turned, and leaned against the dresser that was just a little better looking than normal motel furnishings. She took stock of the woman sitting in the bed across from her and wondered just how far she should go. It did not take Max too long to make up her mind.

Max reached into her bag, pulled out a silver case, crossed the room, and handed a business card to Doris. There was just a telephone number printed on the card. Nothing else.

"This one is on the house. In the future, it'll be $250 per hour, with a three-hour minimum. Call that number, identify yourself as Puppy, and request a date and time." Max looked around and smiled.

"We already know the place. You will get a return call within an hour. If I can make it, we're on. If I cannot make it, an alternative date and time will be offered.

"The first time you call, you will be given a number and deposit instructions. You are never to give that number out to anyone. You are never to give your name to anyone else to use. You are never to tell anyone of this arrangement. If you break any of these rules, someone will find you and that person will make you wish you had never met me. Is that clear?"

Doris looked at the card once, committed the number to memory, and tore the only evidence linking the two women into small, unintelligible pieces. She then put the pieces in her mouth and swallowed them. Doris stared back at Max.

"That is perfectly acceptable and not a problem."

Max began to fondle the woman's thick breast that bore the black and blue signs of rough sex. She gripped the pink nipple and squeezed.

"Does that hurt?"

Doris closed her eyes and let the pain wash over her once again.

"Yes."

Max smiled a wicked, sinister smile and squeezed a little harder.

"Good."

Max released the woman, picked up her bag, and left the room without looking back. When she was on the highway, Max pressed one number on her cell phone.

"We have a new client. Her name is Puppy. The rate is 250 an hour."

The tone of the voice on the other end was gender neutral and acerbic.

"Giving discounts, are we?"

"Don't worry. I get the feeling that we will make it up in volume." Max disconnected the call without another word. She hit the accelerator, and the BMW responded smoothly.

"Damn life is good!"

CHAPTER TWENTY-TWO

Blair drove to work with the sun coming up over the horizon. She looked at the envelope sitting beside her on the seat of her beat-up Toyota and gave only minimal thought as to how she came by this information. The only thing that mattered is that she had more evidence. The key thing is to protect it from the prying eyes of Victoria Whittington.

"Victoria Whittington." Blair said the name a few times in her head. Each time she said it, she became angry. Homicide investigations were supposed to be protected and confidential. How did that old bat get her information? Who did she know? What favors had she done to get that kind of access? What else is out there that she could possibly know? Blair put an end to the questions that were running through her mind just before she reached her exit. Whatever thoughts she had about Victoria Whittington would have to wait.

Jack Case awoke before Priscilla. As he studied her face, he was surprised by a transformation that took place during the night. Gone was the look of arrogance and defiance that seemed to be a large part of her. What replaced them was an air of peace and calm. Making a special effort not to wake her, he slipped out of bed, made his first stop, the bathroom, and his second stop, the kitchen. When she opened her eyes, he was standing before her with a cup of coffee in each hand.

Jack put his arm around Priscilla, and she gave in to his caress. She wanted to be a part of him. She wanted to stay right where she was forever. Priscilla felt alive in a way that she had never felt before. She had had her share of men. More than she could name. But none touched her like he did in the way that he did. With that thought, Priscilla began to laugh.

"What's so funny?"

"I feel like a silly school girl."

"Why is that funny?"

Priscilla placed her cup on the night table and faced him.

"Well, it's silly because when I was a school girl, I never felt like this."

Jack placed his cup on the table as well.

"I see." He took her face in his hands and kissed it gently. She returned the gesture. Then they lay together, enfolding their bodies and rekindling the fire from the night before.

Max strode into the squad room with the image of a new BMW 745 still in her mind. Her newest client would contribute greatly to that fund.

"Hell, if she behaves herself, I might just give ole Doris a ride in it."

She called out to her two detectives.

"Russ! Blair! My office."

The two detectives entered the office and could not have been more of a contrast of generations and styles. One was fresh faced, in a crisp suit, with a pad, pen, and a manila envelope tucked under her arm. The other was a rumpled mess. A worn suit, wrinkled shirt, and his tie hanging loosely around his neck. The only item he carried into the meeting was a cup of black coffee and holding the unlit cigarette in his mouth was a look of early morning exasperation.

Max let Blair and Russ get comfortable as she took a minute to hang up her jacket and her shoulder rig. While most cops never like to be without their guns, Max let it be known that she could just as easily do without it.

"Okay, guys, first things first. Blair, I need you to set up a meet with that snoop. Get everything you can on Priscilla. Russ, you go to the bank and find out what you can on Case. Be discreet. Only speak with the H.R. manager, and if she will go, take her out to lunch. If either of you come up with something that's hot, run with it. Just let me know what you are doing. Is that clear?"

Both detectives nodded in agreement.

"Good. What's in the envelope?"

Blair opened the envelope and started pulling out papers.

"Here is the DDS-61 form for Mr. Case. Here is the DDS-14 form for Mr. Case. And here is a summary of his military service from 1988 to 1998." Blair flipped the last piece of paper on her boss's desk and then sat back and crossed her legs.

Max scanned the documents quickly and then handed them to Russ.

"Is this more work from your secret source?" Blair kept her expression even.

"Okay, so what?"

Blair read from notes she made in her file.

"Well, we know that he was a Marine Corps sniper in Iraq. He served two tours and then was stationed at Quantico for a couple of years before discharge. His discharge summary does not indicate any forwarding address or contact info. My guess is that he got caught up in some government work."

Max started to put her feet up on her desk, looked at her skirt, then at Russ Matson and thought better of it.

"Again, I say, so what?"

Blair leaned forward to make a point.

"Well, it is a known fact that 'The Company" likes to use ex-service types with confirmed kills. We know that the murder weapon is a military type knife. Suppose we are dealing with someone who could not stop killing?"

Russ handed the papers back to Blair, coughed, and took a sip of his coffee.

"That's pretty thin, Blair. The corps does a pretty good psych evaluation on those guys before they sign them up for that job. And killing up close with a knife is way different from killing at long range with a rifle."

Blair looked at Russ with an expression of doubt. He returned it with a look of complete confidence.

"I was a sniper in Vietnam."

Both women looked at Russ Matson with new found respect.

"Russ, you never…"

Russ waved off any further discussion.

"It is not something that I care to discuss."

Blair and Max looked at each other and acceded to the man's wishes.

"Okay. I agree. It's thin. But at least it gives us a bench mark." Blair's eyes were pleading for someone to take her information seriously.

Russ picked up the DDS-61 discharge document again and took down a name and address.

"Well, it does give us the last commanding officer of Mr. Case and that is a start."

Max had heard enough.

"Russ, start with the bank. If you can't get anything, then go with the military angle. Blair, check with Russ when you get finished with the snoop. Okay, get started, both of you. Check back with me at mid-day."

Blair watched her partner shuffle back to his desk. She was having a hard time imagining him perched in a hiding place with a high-powered rifle, waiting to kill someone. There was a part of her that wanted to ask him about it. Yet there was another part of her that said, "You had better not go there." She acknowledged her common sense and left the man to his past.

Russ stopped at his desk and then retreated to the men's room. One sentence. That's all it took. One sentence. One thought. Just like the sniper motto, "One shot, one kill." Russ took the last stall, closed the door, placed his head in his hands, and then dealt with the images, the sounds, the smell, and the pain that he carried inside for a long time, from a far away place to this present day. One sentence. That's all it took.

Blair found the office of Martin Security Associates with no trouble at all. She parked in the back and made a note of the green Jaguar parked in the private spot. She shook her head at the sight.

"I would have never associated that guy with a car like that."

She by-passed the elevator and took the stairs to the second floor. Blair knocked once on the door at the end of the hall and let herself in.

One of the more interesting encounters in life is when two women who do not know each other meet for the first time. It does not matter in what capacity or the circumstances of the meeting. There is a period of sizing each other up. It may be brief or extended, but it will almost certainly happen. That encounter becomes more intense when both women are black. The intensity of the encounter goes off the meter when one is a cop and the other has a criminal record. Such was the intensity of the moment when Blair Collins stepped through the door of the office of Martin Security Associates.

Gineen Walker looked up from the issue of Essence that she was scanning at the sound of the door opening.

"This must be the cop that called this morning. Shit, she don't look like much. Good. She try to fuck with Trap, I'll cut her face." Gineen closed the magazine, slipped it in a drawer, and put on a smile.

"Good morning. May I help you?"

Blair paused and made sure she closed the door back.

"Looks like an ex-con, street walker to me. Probably got that scar in prison. This bitch better not give me any lip." Blair turned back to the woman seated behind the desk and returned her smile with one of her own.

"Yes, good morning. I am Detective Blair Collins. I called this morning to see Mr. Martin."

"Yes, of course. Please have a seat. I will let him know you are here." Gineen got up from behind the desk, knocked once on the door to the private inner office, and then stepped in.

Blair fought back a feeling of envy at the near perfect shape of the woman's ass.

"I bet she can't run a mile."

The door to the inner office opened, and Gineen stepped to the side.

"Mr. Martin will see you now." Blair entered the office and smiled a thank you to Gineen as the secretary closed the door.

Re-seated behind her desk, Gineen made a face and had one thought.

"Girl, you had better stop shopping in Brooks Brothers if you expect to get a man out here in the world." Gineen laughed at the thought of the short cop being directed to the little boy's section of Brooks Brothers and then turned her attention to the personal advice column of the magazine.

As she shook his hand, Blair tried to ignore the coffee stains on the light blue tie that Trap Martin wore.

"Thank you for seeing me on such short notice. I really appreciate it."

Trap looked right through her suit and saw Blair in just her bra and panties. He made a mental note of that image.

"Not a problem. There may come a time when I will need a favor from you." He punctuated the remark with a smile that said he meant what he said.

Blair had not thought of that and was momentarily stung.

"Well, yes, of course. By all means. At our meeting yesterday, you said I could take a look at the file you have on Priscilla Whittington?"

Trap pointed to a thick folder of papers and a smaller binder on a small table to his left. "The file is right over there. I had some parts of it copied for you. They're in the binder. You may have that. The rest is client data that I really cannot release without a court order. But I think you already know that." Trap leaned back in his chair and allowed the image of Blair in her underwear to reappear.

"Now, rather than have you sit here all day, let me hit the high points for you."

Russ Matson took a minute for one last drag on his cigarette before entering the building. He would have much preferred doing a scene canvass in the Ironbound section of Newark than having to face some yuppie corporate type, but you can't pick your assignments. At least not any more.

He decided to just show up cold rather than make an appointment. Russ was gambling on the fact that, without Blair with him, the receptionist would not remember him from his earlier visit. He was in luck. The regular receptionist was on a break. Russ used a cover story of wanting to apply for a mailroom job. Her relief dialed a number, spoke to someone in Human Resources, and then directed Russ to the floor below.

Russ presented his business card to the young woman that met him and mentioned that he was doing a background check on a perspective officer candidate and needed to discuss the candidate with the manager. The young woman ushered him into the office of the H.R. manager. Russ took in the huge office as he shook hands with the person who could be the poster child for the corporate women.

Tall, lean, with her hair pulled back from her face, she appeared to be doing five things at once. Behind her desk on a matching credenza were pictures of her husband, the kids, and the dog. Connected to their chargers were her cell phone and iPad. Her personal laptop with a photo of her kids as the screen saver was on one side of the desk. Her company laptop, open to an email, was on the other. Her desk phone had 32 buttons, with all of the speed dial connections identified with a name. Her degrees and awards took up an entire wall. Russ took in this environment and it began to make him physically sick.

Russ tried to explain the nature of his visit. He was cut off in mid-sentence.

"Listen, I am late for a meeting as it is. I know that whatever information you need is important to you, but I just do not have the time right now." The woman stood up and began to collect the tools of her trade.

"Maggie!" The H.R. manager snatched the cell phone from the charger and threw it in her bag.

"Maggie!" Next, the iPad went into her briefcase. She unplugged her personal laptop and shoved that into her briefcase as well.

"Mag…" Before the word left her mouth, Maggie appeared at her door.

Every department in every company of any size has a Maggie. She is the oldest member of the department in terms of age, has been there the longest, knows everyone in all of the other departments, and is neither seen nor heard. Computers were designed on her efficiency, corporations have profited handsomely on her work ethic, and she has been passed over for promotion more times than even she can remember. On the day that she leaves, no less than three people will have to take over her duties.

"Listen, Mags, I'm late. Log me off the system, give this guy what he needs, and then sit in on the benefits meeting for me this afternoon. Pick me up on my cell if you need me. I will be out for the rest of the day." With that, the new-age manager slipped into her tailored suit jacket, grabbed her Burberry raincoat from behind the door, and left in a whirlwind. Five seconds later, she blew back in, picked up her briefcase, and then blew back out. Russ and Maggie both looked at each other and then looked at the door, almost expecting her to come running back in for something else.

"Nice boss you got there. She reminds me of the woman that I work for." Russ stood with his hands in his pockets, feeling like he just got caught in a stiff wind.

Maggie walked behind the woman's desk, moving with the calm and speed of someone who has worked for the same company for 28 years and knows where all the bodies were buried.

"She ain't so bad. I've worked for worse." After reading the e-mail message that was left open on the screen, but before she went through the motions of logging off the system, Maggie extended her hand.

"Maggie Benson."

The calm of Maggie Benson put Russ at ease. He found his body relaxing.

"Russ Matson." The two senior professionals shook hands as equals. Using the skills of a smoker and an experienced police detective, Russ offered an invitation.

"Smoke?"

Maggie's accepted the offer with a smile.

"Thank you. I've been dying for one all day."

Outside, gray clouds began to move in. The temperature dipped and the day took on a raw feel. With no other smokers present, they had the corner of the building to themselves. Russ draped his suit jacket around the woman's shoulders to protect her from the chill in the air.

"Thank you. I should have brought my sweater." While he lit her cigarette, she gave him a long, hard look.

"Is there something wrong?"

Maggie shook her head in a way that made her hair move. Russ found it very attractive. "No. I was just thinking that men do not do that anymore. The jacket thing. I have been out here with guys who would watch me freeze rather than offer me their jacket. Thank you for being a gentleman."

Russ was taken aback. It seemed like the natural thing to do. To have it appreciated and to be thanked for it, surprised him.

"You're welcome."

Maggie took a long drag and pulled the jacket closer around her shoulders.

"You married, Russ?"

Matson shook his head.

"Nah. Two-time loser. I do not see a ring, so I take it you're not either."

"Nope. Had a couple of false starts but never made it out of the gate."

They both took in the cold air and companionship with the habit that they knew was bad for them but that they enjoyed all too much.

"What do you need from H.R., Russ?"

"You got a guy by the name of Case, John Case, who works in Operations. I need to take a look at his file."

"Why?" Maggie blew the smoke from her cigarette in the air. That simple question, followed by that simple act, registered with Russ that this woman was no dope. If he was to get anything he could use, he would have to come clean.

Russ handed her his business card and then flashed his badge.

"He's not wanted for anything. We believe there may be a connection between him and some activity that we are looking into." Russ paused for a minute as an idea struck him. "By the way, I would like to see the file on a Priscilla Whittington as well."

"Is she involved in this activity?" Maggie took one last drag from her smoke, stubbed it out in ashtray, and then gave Russ back his jacket.

"You take the cold well. Do you mind if I hold on to this?" When he shook his head, she slipped the business card in her pocket.

Russ took the jacket back and welcomed the warmth.

"A lot of years standing on street corners looking for trouble will do that to you." He stubbed his smoke and then held the door for her to step through.

"I didn't say he was involved. I said he may be connected with the activity. And yes, she may be connected as well."

"Thank you. Um, listen, you could look through the files on those two from now until the middle of next week, but they won't tell you much."

"Well then, how about I buy you an early lunch and you can fill in the blanks for me. I promise to have you back in time for your meeting. I would not want to see you get in trouble with your boss."

Maggie smiled a very warm and inviting smile.

"I was hoping you were from the old school. You're on for lunch only if you promise to fill in some blanks for me. That meeting is not an issue. It's tomorrow. And don't worry about Ms. 21st Century. Despite what you see, she got to where she is the old-fashioned way."

"On her back?"

Maggie nodded her head and Russ felt something stir within him.

"Yep. Right now, she is on her way to the Marriott to meet with the President of the bank, the head of the recruiting firm who has an exclusive contract with us, and the gal who handles our disability and managed care benefits. I am made to understand that the meeting will start out over drinks and lunch but will end in a top floor suite with at least two but probably all four of the participants."

Russ held the door to the elevator.

"Is there anything that happens here that you don't know?"

Maggie stepped into the lift and touched his chest.

"Very little."

CHAPTER TWENTY-THREE

The Eyes felt the anger building inside of him. He had arrived before dawn, using the path through the woods to avoid the busybody at the end of the street. From his vantage point, he could see three sides of the house and the entire length of the street. He was quite certain no one could see him. It was now late in the afternoon.

This was the part of the hunt that he most enjoyed. Stalk and then post. This was the time when he came to know the beast. It's habits and haunts. Where it liked to feed and sun itself and roam. This was the time when he felt its heartbeat. When he saw the world as the beast sees the world. He had his pictures, but they were not the same. You could not feel a heartbeat in a picture or see the true nature of the beast. For this you had to observe the beast in the wild, in a way that the beast could not observe you.

She is supposed to be here. The address is correct. The Eyes thought about the possibility that she could be away on a trip. He quickly ruled that out. He wanted her to be here. It is late in the afternoon. She is supposed to be here. That she was not only made him angry.

The Eyes considered knocking on the door and asking for her. He quickly ruled that out. It is better not to rush. He was successful by being patient. He captured all of the other beasts by waiting and watching. Now he was after the leader of the herd. This will take time. The Eyes checked his surroundings, and without disturbing the leaves that hid him from view, crawled back to his car.

After a breakfast of leftover Chinese food, Jack called in and said he was at an off-site meeting. Priscilla took a sick day. They showered together and then took the rest of the day to explore one another.

"Is this what you were expecting?" Case kept his mind open. The question was honest.

For the second time in less than 24 hours, Priscilla felt unsure of herself.

"No. It is not what I was expecting." Priscilla shifted in her seat as she brought a coffee cup to her lips.

"I thought we would hook up at some point. Sort of a 'wham, bam, thank you ma'am' kind of thing and then I would move on. I can tell you quite honestly that is not what happened here. Not for me. And it wasn't just last night."

Case took a sip of his own coffee and became very aware of the bruise that he had put on her neck. He was ashamed of himself and felt like an animal.

"I'm sorry about that. I lost control of myself." Priscilla smiled and eased his pain a little.

"There is no need to apologize. I deserved it. I had no right to attack you like that. You were just defending yourself." Priscilla held his eyes in hers.

"You know, Jack, I am quite accustomed to having my way. You warned me not to pry. I should have listened to you."

Case dropped the corners of his mouth and nodded in acknowledgement.

"Okay. But you're here now. Isn't this what you wanted?"

Priscilla looked off into the middle distance and then came back.

"I thought it was. But now I am not so sure. There is one thing that I am sure of. I am not here on my terms. I am quite certain of that."

Case smiled at her.

"So, where do we go from here?"

Thoughts, words, ideas, images, pictures, and a host of things that he thought he should do or say were flooding through Case's mind. He wanted her to know that he wanted her to stay. He was not entirely sure why, but he did know that he did not want her to leave. Case wanted her to know that she touched a part of him that he thought did not exist anymore. The one thing that he did know was that he did not how to say these things.

"I won't think for both of us, Jack. And I won't be the only one doing the heavy lifting." Her look was even and stern.

Case played with the ends of his fingers.

"I didn't know that something was missing in my life until you came to work in my office. I didn't know I had found it until I found myself standing in front of your desk last night." Case stopped playing with his fingertips and looked Priscilla straight in the eye. "Don't leave. At least, not right away."

Priscilla's smile touched his inner core. Priscilla left her seat and placed herself in his lap. "Now that wasn't so hard, was it?"

An amber autumn glow filled the apartment. Priscilla sat with her back resting against his chest and Jack's arms around her shoulders. For the first time, in a very long time, Priscilla felt that there was nowhere else on earth she would rather be and there was no one else she would rather be with. Jack Case took something out of her and replaced it with something of his own. Priscilla smiled to herself. She was glad he did.

Jack tightened his grip on her and kissed the top of her head. He wanted her close, and he wanted her to know it. Jack replayed the day in his mind. The thoughts, the sounds, the feelings were all right. Jack agreed with himself in that what he said was true. He did not want to accept that there was something missing in his life. He made his work his life until he met her. Priscilla changed all of that.

"And now, what was he going to do?" Case pushed that thought out of his mind.

"The future will take of itself. The present is what matters now."

"Tell me about Paris."

Priscilla gently broke his hold and stretched like a cat. Instead of returning to the position between his legs, she turned and reclined on the bed, staring into his eyes.

"As I told you, I wanted to see the world. But I did not want to see it as some rich kid blowing off steam and money before she found the doctor or the lawyer who would keep her in some style she thought she deserved. I wanted to see the world from the bottom up.

I took out a $1,000, gave myself three months to see the world, and vowed that if the money ran out before I was ready to come home, I would do whatever I had to do to survive. Well, to make a long story short, that $1,000 ran out faster than even I imagined; it seemed like every time I heard about a job, I was one step behind someone else who got there first. Pretty soon I was going days without eating. I was bouncing from one flat to another, sleeping in the same bed with people that I did not know. The whole scene was getting pretty desperate. At one point I thought about walking the streets, but I liked sex too much to sell it. Besides the thought of getting beat up by some French pimp did not appeal to me.

One of the girls found out that there was a strip club opening and it was looking for dancers. There were a lot of girls who auditioned for jobs. I was one of the few that they hired. I had never been in a strip club, much less dance practically naked in front of a bunch of men. I was scared shitless." Priscilla's face lit up into a bright smile.

"But you know something, Jack? When I got on stage and saw all of those men looking at me, I felt a feeling that I will never forget. It was this incredible rush of excitement.

Well, again, to make a long story short, I did well. I started making enough money to support myself and repay friends who helped me when I was down. Before long, I got to know the regulars at the club, and they began to tip me well. There was this one guy in particular who bought me drinks and would always give me a bigger tip than the other guys for no reason at all. His name was Richard Stone. He would not tell me exactly where he was from, but he was American. He was a very handsome man, nicely dressed, and was just a little older than me. He was very polite. He never touched me inappropriately or propositioned me in any way. We spoke about all sorts of things. Politics, religion, the things we liked to do and the things we did not like to do. All of the things that no man talks about in a room full of half naked women.

The way he spent money, he appeared to be very well off. All of the girls in the club tried to get close to him, but for some reason, he would only sit with me. I will admit that I was attracted to him and looked forward to the times that he came into the club. I would have broken the rules and went out with him away from the club, but he never asked me. I don't know why.

One of the other dancers and I were invited to a very fancy reception by one of the regulars at the club. He said he just wanted to show up with two women on his arm and he would pay us well for the evening. He promised us that there was no sex involved, so we agreed to go. It sounded like fun. Well, as it turned out, it was a going away party for the guy from the club who I had become very friendly with.

Towards the end of the night, after more than a little champagne, I found myself in a corner, alone. He spotted me and came over. I asked him why he was going away. He said that he was being called back home. Apparently, his parents found out about all the time that he was spending in the club, and with me specifically, and thought it was time for him to come home. He told me that he did not want to go. That the original plan was for him to manage one of the family's plants in France and that is what he wanted to do. I got mad and told him that was bullshit. That he should stand up for himself and not do something he does not want to do. I told him that I loved him and that I was sorry that he was leaving, that I was sorry that we never made love, and that I was sorry that I would never see him again. I told him that I wanted him to stay in France with me. Well, I guess I was starting to make a scene because two of his friends came over and took me away. The next night, he came to the club and asked me to marry him. I said yes without another thought. We took his car that night and eloped to Germany. We got married the next day. His parents found out and tried to have the marriage annulled. They failed. With no other options for managing the plant, they relented and allowed Richard to stay in France.

We spent every free moment running around Europe. We did everything. We raced cars. We dove in the Mediterranean. We skied the Alps. It was a really good time.

For our anniversary, we took a weekend trip to Austria. There was a mountain there that he always wanted to ski. He had been drinking heavily the night before, and I told him he was in no shape to ski the mountain. He kissed me and told me not to worry. The next time I saw him, he was dead. The guide told me he lost control and could not stop in time. He went off a short cliff and broke his neck. Of course, his parents blamed me. They said I was a bad influence on Richard and was the reason he had died. The mountain guide was a witness to everything, so there was nothing they could accuse me of. The truth of the matter is that he left everything to me. As you can imagine, that did not sit well with his family. In order to avoid what was going to be a nasty situation, I thought about what Richard would have done if the position was reversed. I gave them half of what was left to me, signed a release absolving me of any rights to anything related to his family, and returned to the states.

Jack read the look in her eyes.

"You loved him."

"Yes. I loved him. I would not have married him if I didn't. But with the death of my parents and Richard's death, I learned a very…" Priscilla's expression changed from soft to determined, "…I was about to say valuable, but that is not the word. I learned a very painful lesson."

"Which is?" Jack had an idea as to what the lesson was but decided that he needed to hear her say it.

"Nothing is promised, and anything can be taken from you in an instant."

"So, how did you meet you second husband?"

Priscilla smiled, looked off into the middle distance, and then turned back to Case.

"I'm smiling, but I don't know why."

Case dropped the corners of his mouth.

"Maybe because fate is funny at the times that it shouldn't be."

Priscilla nodded in agreement.

"I think you're right about that, John Case."

"After Richard died, I found out that he did not have a will. It was something we never spoke about. I was told by his family's attorney that I was listed as the beneficiary on his insurance policy, and as his wife, I was entitled to all that he owned. Well, his family would not hear of that and threatened to fight me in court. For a lot of different reasons, I was not prepared to fight them, so we agreed to a cash settlement and my release of all rights. I was now a very rich young women in the City of Lights.

With Richard's death still fresh in my mind, I lived life to the fullest extent possible. I bought the best clothes, went to the best places, and did whatever the hell I wanted to with whoever I wanted to. I was determined to live life to the fullest with no regrets. Well, all of that led me to be invited to a very exclusive reception for some very exclusive people. That is where I met Mr. William Whittington. He was there alone and so was I. He was just divorced, and I was just widowed, so naturally after a few drinks, we found a room upstairs and made love. He drove me home that night and stayed. When he left to return to the United States, I came with him. It was not too long after that that we were married. The rest, as they say, is history.

Priscilla paused to let the past return to being the past.

"Okay, Jack, now it's your turn. Tell me about her."

The question was not unexpected, but it was still a subject that Jack Case did not want to talk about. But he had to admit to himself that he started this, so he might as well ante up.

"As a young man, I was pretty boring. I took no risks. I did whatever it was I was supposed to do, when I was supposed to do it. The town in the Midwest where I grew up had limited options. You either went to the state college, got a job in the post office, or went into the military. I chose the Marines. I was a pretty good athlete, so after basic training, I applied to Scout-Sniper School. I was good at what I did and did two tours in Iraq. After my second tour, I had to decide if I was going to re-enlist for another five years or quit the service and see if I could do something else. It was at that point that I was recruited by a government agency to be an independent contractor. It was far more secret than that. I really cannot tell you anything about the organization or what we did, but if you can imagine it, we did it. All of it.

It is funny that you mentioned Germany because that is where I was stationed and that is where I met her. She worked at the American Embassy. Her name was Anika. I called her Nika. Her father was from Cameroon and her mother was Swedish. She was beautiful. What I loved most about her was her smile. She had this beautiful smile that made any space she was in, whether it was inside or outside, brighter. I think that was the thing about her that intrigued me the most. We began to talk, and soon, we were dating. She never asked me what I did, but I think she knew, or at least suspected who I worked for and what I did. After all, she worked in the embassy. We moved in together, which was against my operational profile. It was the first time I did anything out of line. I didn't care. I was in love. I was told to break it off, but I couldn't and wouldn't. We talked about getting married, where we would live, and raising a family. I began to think about what I would do when my contract with the government was up."

Priscilla made a face.

"I suspect that you were gone from home for long periods of time. She was okay with that?"

Case played with the ends of his fingers.

"Obviously, I could not tell her what I did. I told her that my work took me out of town for days at a time and that I could be called away on a moment's notice. More so to protect her than anything else, I could not tell her what it was I did. She said that I did not have to explain to her what I did, as long as what I told her was the truth. And then she smiled. What we had was a very nice life. We actually did spend quite a lot of time together, despite my work. We travelled around Europe, mostly by car, and we lived in a nice apartment in Berlin. We had an interesting group of friends. It was a very nice time in my life despite the work that I did. Of course, we got married. I was told that it would be frowned upon by my superiors, but I did not care about that. I had someone in a very high position speak up on my behalf and that helped. The organization that I worked for paid well, but after a time, the money was no substitute for the time away from Nika. We wanted to start a family and I wanted to live a normal life. When the time on my contract came to an end, I put in my papers and resigned from the organization. They tried to talk me out of it, but I refused to listen. I was through. Two weeks later, while crossing the street, my wife was hit by a truck and killed. A month after the funeral, I was approached by my control at the organization. I was asked if I would come back in now that I did not have a wife. It was right at that instant that I knew

Nika's death was no accident."

Case stopped talking for a very long while and looked back into a past that he had long kept hidden. Priscilla started to speak, but he placed his fingers to her lips. He had to make this leap on his own.

"She was life. I was death. I thought that what I did kept the world safe for her and people like her. In the end, not only did I fail to keep her safe, but my work, which until I met Nika was my life, is what got her killed. What I have told you, I have never told anyone. What I am about to tell you now is something that I am not proud of. If you and I are to go anywhere, are to be anything, then you must know this about me." Priscilla nodded her head and gave him her full attention.

"There are no secrets if you are in the secrets business. I went back in. I confirmed my suspicions. And then I killed the men who were responsible for the death of my wife. I stayed in until my contract was up and then I left the country. That's it.

Jack and Priscilla lay together in bed. For reasons that they both fully understood, they did not let each other go. They could not. They both felt, in their own way, that if they did, they would fall into some sort of black hole and not be able to get out. Together, as one, they were stronger and safer. Eventually, the exertion of confession got the better of them and they drifted off into a deep sleep.

Rather than re-visit more Chinese food, Priscilla volunteered to show her domestic side. Case watched her move about his kitchen. In her bare feet and dressed only in one of his sweatshirts, she looked more like the resident of the apartment than he did. He told her so.

Priscilla stirred the pot, added salt and pepper, stirred again, and then tasted.

"The way you have everything laid out is very logical. It really is easy to find everything." Priscilla went back to stirring the pot and wondered if she should admit that everything in this kitchen is right where she would have put it if it were her kitchen. She found that tidbit to be a little spooky, so she decided to keep it to herself.

"Taste." Priscilla held the spoon to his lips.

"More salt?"

Case licked his lips.

"No. It's fine the way it is. By the way, what is that? It smells great."

Priscilla returned to the pot and spoke over her shoulder.

"None of your business. It's a secret family recipe, and if I told you, I would have to kill you." She spoke without thinking and immediately regretted her choice of words.

"I'm sorry, Jack. I didn't mean to…"

Case walked up to her, kissed her tenderly, and smiled.

"Let's not tiptoe around each other, shall we? Life's too short."

Priscilla smiled back at the man she was falling in love with and wrapped her arms around his waist.

"Stealing my lines, are we?" She kissed him quickly and lightly.

"How are you at making salad?"

"The best."

Priscilla broke his hold and flipped a tomato at him.

"Good. Get busy. Dinner will be ready in a short while."

Blair sat in the window booth of the diner and watched the Ford Crown Victoria maneuver neatly into the parking space next to her beat-up Toyota. The contrast of the two vehicles rekindled thoughts of buying a new car. Blair made a note to herself to stop by a dealership next week and then she called the waitress over to order a cup of coffee for her partner and mentor.

As Russ Matson headed toward the building, Blair noticed that there seemed to be a little more pep in his step than she was accustomed to seeing. As he got closer, she noticed the remnants of a smile. Whatever happened at the bank must have gone far better than he expected.

"You seem to be in a pretty good mood. I take it things went well at the bank?" Blair opened the menu and began to peruse the burger selection.

"Dinner's on me. Take a look."

For the first time since they began working together, Blair saw Russ Matson blush.

"If you don't mind, Blair, I'll have to take a rain check on dinner." Matson took a sip of his coffee and tried to look nonchalant.

Blair was now intrigued. A peppy walk? A smile? And now blushing? A part of her wished she had been with him at the bank.

"Okay, Matson, what happened at that bank? Give."

Although it did not seem possible, Matson's face turned an even deeper shade of crimson. "Well, I actually have a date tonight. If you don't mind, Blair, can we make this quick. I told her I would pick her up at eight."

Blair closed the menu and felt her detective sense kick in.

"Sure, Russ. I am sure this will not take long. But tell me, does your date have anything to do with your trip to the bank?"

Mason burst into a huge grin.

"Okay. Okay. Her name is Maggie, and she works in the H.R. department at the bank. She gave me a lot of inside information on Case and the Whittington woman." Matson tried to smile and drink his coffee at the same time.

Blair nodded in approval and skepticism.

"That usually gets one lunch."

"She thinks I'm a gentleman. She's not married. And she is quite a gal. I like her, Blair."

The happiness coming from the older man was contagious. Blair felt his happiness and was happy for him.

Russ Matson's face suddenly took on a new seriousness.

"Hey, Blair, please keep this to yourself. You know I get enough ribbing from the guys as it is, and I really do not know how this will turn out."

Blair saw the fear in the man's eyes. She reached out and grabbed his hand.

"We're partners, aren't we?" She placed her index finger on her lips and gave him a wink. That was all the reassurance he needed.

The waitress reappeared and took Blair's burger order. Matson asked for a refill of his coffee and nothing more. The waitress left without giving either of them a second thought.

Matson checked the time on the clock by the register.

"Well, it seems as if you were right about our boy, Case. The president of the bank used to be a case officer for the C.I.A. He knew Case and offered him a job in Operations about eight years ago. When the head spot opened up, Case was promoted into it. That would confirm your theory that Case was a spook at some time."

Blair pumped her fist in the air.

"Damn, I like being right. Is there anything else?"

The waitress appeared again and filled Matson's cup. He thanked her with a smile that Blair had never seen before.

"Yeah. He's got a couple of beefs in his personnel folder from other managers who did not particularly like his attitude. Nothing serious, and for the most part, pretty subjective complaints. Other than that, he has been a model citizen. No credit problems, no excessive time off, no booze or woman problems. No real flags of any sort. Maggie says that he pretty much keeps to himself. He is not one to attend company functions unless he has to, and even with that, he comes late and leaves early. It is almost like he does not want to socialize with anyone. There is no next of kin references in his file either, which I found odd. I called it in to Max. She said to coordinate with you and then we can get together with her in the morning."

Blair nodded in agreement.

"Yeah, she told me the same thing when I spoke with her."

"There is one other thing. I went into the file on Whittington while I was there. I figured I might as well. It seems like our girl has been doing temp work for quite some time. She was hired as a temp and then went full time when one of the clerks turned up pregnant. She, too, has been a model citizen at the bank. One of the things that Maggie has heard about her is that Priscilla is pretty aggressive. Apparently, the temp agency has gotten complaints about her going after certain executives in the companies that she has worked at. They have warned her about it on a number of occasions. Maggie also told me that the scuttlebutt around the office is that Priscilla and Case are involved outside of the office. That's about it. What have you got?"

Blair opened her portfolio and scanned her notes.

"Well, the snoop hired by Victoria Whittington has had Priscilla under surveillance ever since the case was closed by the D.A.'s office. The directive was that if she broke just one law, it was to be reported and acted upon. The problem is that she did not break any laws, that is not any criminal laws.

Matson whistled.

"That must have cost a fortune."

Blair nodded in agreement.

"Yeah, but remember, these folks have it like that."

"Shortly after the criminal investigation into the murder of her husband was closed, Priscilla took off for the west coast. She picked up a guy in a bar, hung out with him for about three weeks, and then dumped him. She drove back east, bought a house, and then began doing temp work, mostly as a low-level clerk."

"Well, that tracks with what Maggie told me." Matson made a face.

"What I do not understand is, why she would do temp work?"

Blair did not miss a beat.

"Martin told me that she was married once before. That husband was well off when he died. She lost her parents when she was young, so there must have been some insurance money from that as well. Russ, think about it. If she already had money, was barred from the local social set by a mother-in-law that could not stand the ground she walked on, and is still a fairly young woman, where else is she going to have her fun? According to Martin, her game was to take a job, seduce someone in the office, and then either quit or get fired. She did not need the money. Her name is already mud. So, why not?"

Matson shook his head.

"It doesn't track. Why not pick up and start over someplace else?"

Blair looked off into the middle distance and then shook her head.

"Like where? Nah. She knows the area. She knows the people. And plus, what better way to stick it to the family that cut her off. Why leave?"

"You've got a point. I guess I am thinking about someone who cares about her reputation." Matson started to speak, stopped, and then decided to share his thought.

"Blair, do you think we might have some sort of black widow on our hands?"

Blair shook her head and laughed in a gentle manner.

"No, I don't think so. She's unluckier than anything else. If she was some sort of black widow, she would have married one of the executives that she has gone after by now.

"Someone once told me, 'Men are stupid, but women are crazy.' My guess is that this woman is some kind of thrill seeker. I would take a further guess that during her trip to the west coast, either the guy that she hooked up with or some other guy that she picked up along the way is the guy that we are after."

Matson looked into the bottom of his coffee cup and then back at his partner.

"Blair, you have been right more than you have been wrong, so I will not bet against you on this. How do you want to play this?"

The waitress appeared with the cheeseburger, a huge plate of fries, and enough lettuce and tomato to feed a family of rabbits for about a month. Blair immediately regretted ordering the meal.

"Well, you have a date tonight, so you had better get going. I will write it up and then we can go over it with Max in the morning."

Matson grinned from ear to ear.

"Thanks, Blair. I will see you in the squad room in the morning." Matson started to reach in his pocket for some money.

"I got this, Russ. Have fun tonight. I hope it goes well."

"Thanks, Blair." As Russ Matson left the diner on a cloud, Blair said a silent prayer that the woman he had fallen for would go easy on him.

CHAPTER TWENTY-FOUR

The two detectives walked into the office and found their boss with her feet on her desk, speaking into her cell phone. She waved them in, pointed to the chairs, and held up one index finger. Russ Matson remained standing and turned his back in deference to the view.

"Six-thirty at the usual place. That's fine." Max Stout snapped the cell phone closed, made a note in her pocket diary, and then swung her legs off the desk.

"It's okay, Russ. You can turn around now."

Russ Matson turned his head first and then took a seat beside his partner.

"Okay, guys, what else have you got?"

Blair handed over a case report form on the latest information to date.

"This pretty much lays it out. Russ and I thought we would meet with Priscilla to go over the west coast information. It tracks with the time frame of the first murder out there."

Max scanned the report quickly, keying on certain words and phrases.

"Okay, I am fine with that, only I would suggest that you take that snoop, Martin, with you. His people did the surveillance. If she tries to bullshit you, he can pull her up short. Any problems with that?" Blair and Russ shook their heads.

"Good. Keep me posted."

As Blair and Russ left the office, Max eyed the cell phone on her desk and turned her attention to her meeting later in the evening. There was something about Doris that was rubbing off on her. She was actually looking forward to seeing the woman. Max was well aware that this kind of feeling could be a two-edged sword in her secret lifestyle. She quickly pushed the feelings out of her mind. How she handled them would require more thought than she was prepared to give right now.

The Eyes were in place before dawn. Within a few hours, they were pleased to see the black Corvette exit the garage and head down the street. *She is back. The beast has returned to its lair.* The Eyes backed out of its hiding place, returned to its vehicle, and then took the local routes to the central office of Jersey National Bank.

"Detective Collins, this is Trap Martin returning your call."

Trap listened as Blair outlined what they wanted to do. He ordinarily would not have cooperated with a police investigation, but he saw this as billable hours on a case that was going nowhere, so why not? Free money is free money. Right?

Blair relaxed once Trap agreed to cooperate.

"Okay, here is what I suggest. There is a restaurant just down the street from the office complex where she works. The name of the place is Bogey's. You can't miss it. It is the only restaurant in the area. We can meet there. It will be less conspicuous than meeting her in her office. I will ask Priscilla to meet us there at six. Hopefully, she'll come."

Trap leaned back in his chair and thought about getting drunk at the expense of the state. "The restaurant is good idea. She'll come, just don't tell her that I am going to be there. That might spook her. Trust me on this. I'll meet you in the bar at 5:30."

Trap hung up and allowed himself a hearty laugh. A meeting with Priscilla after all of the time he had her under surveillance would be interesting. She had caught his guys a couple of times and tried to get a cease and desist order from the court. That was when she found out the full extent of the power of the Whittington family. Not only did she lose, but she was forced to pay their legal expenses as the case was deemed frivolous litigation. Trap knew he had dodged a bullet on that one and told his guys to be extra careful with that job.

The Eyes sat in his perch, licked the paper on a freshly rolled cigarette, and watched the beast from afar. It was lunch time. She had fed and was now walking around the parking lot. She had not changed much from the last time he had seen her. That was good. He anticipated how she would feel in his hands and the smell of her scent. The Eyes calmed themselves as they smoked and watched. The time would come soon.

Blair closed the door to the Crown Victoria and immediately turned to Russ.

"So, how did it go last night?"

Russ had to laugh to himself.

"Gee, Blair. We haven't even left the parking space yet."

"So what? I want details. Give!"

Russ stopped at the entrance to the parking lot and then eased the big car into traffic.

"We went to that place, Antonio's, just off of Route 22. I told her about my life. She told me about her life. I took her home and then I went home. The end."

"There's more to this story, Matson."

Russ thought as he drove. He was dying for a cigarette, but the new directive from the Chief forbid smoking in the cars anymore. Russ liked his young partner and honestly wanted to confide in her. He debated the issue with himself as he moved the car into the left lane. Unconsciously, one of his hands began to shake.

"Well, we talked for a long time in the restaurant and then she invited me in for coffee and we talked some more. I did not leave her house until after 12. It feels too good, Blair. I'm not used to this. This is only the first time I have gone out with this woman."

Blair looked at her partner and felt for him.

"Pull over." Russ looked at her like she was crazy.

"We're the police. We can do whatever we feel like. Pull over." Russ turned on the red and blue lights hidden behind the grill and on the deck behind the rear seat and pulled over onto the shoulder of the road.

"Good, now get out and have a smoke before you go insane."

Russ could not get out of the car fast enough. He fished out a cigarette and lit it in what appeared to be one motion. After the first two drags, he was noticeably relaxed.

"You know something, Blair? You're a good cop and a better friend. Thank you." He smiled a genuine smile at the young woman.

The fall air was made crisper by the traffic speeding by. Blair pulled her coat closer around her body as she stood next to her partner but upwind.

"Russ, don't be afraid of tomorrow. It may have been a while for you but, you know, it may have been a while for her, too."

Russ Matson nodded his head.

"Yeah, I thought about that. But the fact of the matter is that I am old. After this case, I am going to retire."

"Yeah, so what? Look, Russ, here it is, pure and simple. If she wasn't interested in you, do you think she would have gone out with you or invited you in to her house? Take life one day at a time and don't worry about it. If it doesn't work, then it doesn't work. But just give it a chance."

Russ looked at the young woman and was thankful for what she said. He ground out what remained of the smoke and nodded in agreement.

"Okay, Blair. I will. Come on. We're a little late."

Blair and Russ stopped at the entrance to the restaurant. The posters and pictures of Humphrey Bogart that covered every square inch of wall space told them that they were in the right place. They spotted Trap Martin seated at the bar in a hideously loud plaid jacket and striped tie. As Blair and Matson made their way to the table in the far corner of the room, Trap had his bar tab transferred to the table and joined them.

Blair approached the table, with Russ bringing up the rear.

"Trap Martin, this is my partner, Russ Matson." Russ extended his hand, but Trap chose to take a sip from his drink instead.

"You're late."

Russ glanced at his open palm and then took a seat across from the private detective. "Nice jacket and tie. Christmas gift, right?" His tone was pure sarcasm and not lost on either of the occupants of the table.

Blair spoke up quickly as she saw the private detective's eyes harden.

"Sorry, Trap. We had a call we had to take." The comment was enough to break the tension and remind Trap who he was dealing with.

"Priscilla should be here any minute. She is usually on time." Trap took the opportunity to openly ogle the female patrons of the place. Both Russ and Blair felt embarrassed sitting at the table with him.

When the waitress came over to the table, Blair ordered a diet soda. Russ waived off a beverage order and turned his attention to a poster of the Bogart movie, "To Have and To Have Not."

Blair turned her attention to Trap.

"Can I ask you a personal question?" The request seemed to catch Trap off guard.

"Yes. What is it?"

"Is there any significance to the name Trap? It is an odd first name, especially in this part of the country."

Trap took another sip of what appeared to be some type of whisky and savored the taste in his mouth for a long time.

"That is a personal question. Most folks who have known me a lot longer than you have never asked me about my name."

Blair was not deterred.

"Maybe they don't care to know. I do."

Trap thought to himself, "If this junior cop has the balls to ask me about my name, I guess I might as well tell her." Trap took another sip of his drink.

"My name at birth was Harold. I was named after my father, who happened to be married to someone else when I was born. My mother was his secretary. Well, Pop made it clear that he was not leaving his wife for my mother. He did send her money, but I am told that stopped around a year after I was born. Mom did not take that very well. She wanted him and she could not have him, she took it out on me. In her mind, as I was told on more than one occasion, it was because of me why he did not want her. As I got older and she saw that the beatings had no effect, she would lock me out of the house. When I became 16, I got back at her in the best way I knew how. I had my first name legally changed to Trap. For as long as she is alive, I will be the reminder in her life that the oldest trick in the world does not work."

Blair was stung by the story. It was not what she was expecting.

"I apologize if I brought up a bad memory. I am sorry. I had no idea."

Trap made a face and took another sip of his drink.

"That's okay. Don't worry about it." Even he did not know why he told this very personal story to someone that he did not know, but for some strange reason, he felt better for telling it.

Russ nodded in the direction of the door.

"Here's our girl."

The distinctive grey hair of Priscilla Whittington was visible from across the room. Blair rose from her seat to meet her.

"Thank you for agreeing to this meeting, Ms. Whittington. We are at that table over there."

Priscilla paused at the sight of Trap Martin, regained her composure, and then approached the table. Russ Matson rose from his seat and then looked distastefully at Trap as he remained seated.

"Well, Mr. Martin. I had no idea you would be attending this meeting. It is so nice to see you in the light." The expression on Priscilla's face could not have been anymore condescending.

Trap drained his glass and then held it up as a signal for another.

"As I told you in court, Priscilla, you never know where I will turn up, so you had better watch yourself."

For the second time this evening, Blair felt the need to step in and diffuse a confrontation. "Um, Ms. Whittington, this is my partner, Russ Matson." Russ shook hands with Priscilla and then held the chair as she sat down.

"Thank you." Priscilla turned to Blair.

"Detective, I know you have your professional standards, but as I requested when we first met, please call me Priscilla. 'Ms. Whittington sounds like you should be addressing Doris or Victoria, whom I will assume you have met since Mr. Martin is here."

Blair felt like she was walking into a trap but saw no other option.

"Yes, we have spoken to Victoria and Doris Whittington." Priscilla's response struck a chord with Blair.

"Why did you not assume your maiden name after the death of your husband?"

Priscilla's smile was more sinister than friendly.

"The Whittington name was a right that I earned. I was not about to give it up. Besides, ...," as she cast a glance in the direction of Trap Martin, "...it is the best way to get back at the family who has made a practice out of invading my private life." This time Priscilla looked directly at Trap.

"You may quote me on that."

The waitress arrived with Trap's drink and then took Priscilla's order of Absolut on the rocks. Russ asked for coffee while Blair passed, as her diet soda was less than half gone.

As the waitress moved away, Blair leaned into the table.

"Well, I will come right to the point. Priscilla, we asked you here to follow up on some additional information that may be important to a matter we are investigating."

"I take it this has nothing to do with the person who broke into my house?"

Blair looked at Russ before answering.

"Well, it might and then it might not. That's what we are here to find out."

Priscilla looked at her watch and decided that the fastest way out of here was to cooperate.

"How can I help you?"

"We know that you took a trip to California shortly after the death of your second husband, sometime in late June 2011. While you were there, did you spend any time with any one man in particular?"

Priscilla leaned back, balanced her elbows on the arms of the chair, and crossed her legs. Her face hardened in a manner similar to her former mother-in-law.

"I meet a lot of people during my travels, Detective. Before this goes any further, am I a suspect in this case of yours?"

"No. You are not a suspect."

"Then why come to me?"

Russ made eye contact with Blair and then spoke up.

"Um, Ms. Whittington, I'm sorry, Priscilla, we are investigating several leads in this case. The connection with you just happens to be one of them. It is quite remote, but nevertheless, it is something that we have to check out. Will you please help us?"

Perhaps it was the tone of Russ Matson's voice or the look on his face or both. Whatever it was struck a nerve with the woman and her features softened. Priscilla took a sip of her drink before answering.

"I spent some time with one guy in particular. I met him in a bar, and he seemed interesting."

Every nerve ending in Blair's body was on alert.

"What made him interesting?"

"Well, he had this look about him like someone who had backpacked around the world and had seen a more than a few things while doing it. His clothes were casual and very well worn, and he looked like he needed a haircut. Like I said, he was interesting in an odd sort of way."

"What was it about this person that you found odd?"

"He had this habit of hand-rolling his cigarettes. It seemed odd in this day and age, and I asked him about it. One thing led to another, and we ended up spending some time together."

Both detectives hid their reactions well. Russ Matson spoke up while Blair made a note. "What was one thing and what was the other?"

Priscilla studied the rim of her glass, cast an eye towards Trap Martin, and then spoke to Russ Matson.

"Detective, Mr. Martin may have an idea of who I am, and he may have told you what he thinks I am. He is entitled to his opinion, no matter how narrow it may be. However, I will trust that in your line of work, you will look at things with a more open mind. I was alone and trying to put the past behind me. This man, I believe his name was Jonathan, seemed interesting, as I said, and he, too, was trying to put his recent past behind him. As two adults, we consented to spend some time together with the hope that we could help each other get through a difficult period. Do I need to draw you a clearer picture than that?"

Trap Martin sat up in his chair and became alert and attentive.

"Well, I for one would like to hear how you fucked him. Or did he fuck you? Come on, Priscilla, let's have the details."

Russ was noticeably embarrassed. If he had been 20 years younger, he would have yanked the private detective out of his seat and thrown him against the wall. Instead he touched Blair's arm to indicate that he would take this line and then spoke up.

"There's no need to go into details, Priscilla. I think we understand what happened. Do you recall this man's last name?"

"No."

"How long were you two together?"

"Approximately three weeks. We drove up the coast from L.A. to San Francisco and then began to take the northern route east. We split up after three weeks."

"Why?"

"Detective, I am a spontaneous person. I start things on a whim, and I will end them just as quickly. As time passed, he began to get possessive, and I thought it best to end it. So, I did."

"How did you end it?"

"I woke up before he did one day and left. I made sure our accommodations had been paid for and there was money for him to travel with. I felt it was the right thing to do."

Blair decided to take up the questioning.

"Was there anyone else that you might have hooked up with during your trip back east?"

Priscilla finished her drink, and the look on her face indicated that she regretted that the glass was not larger.

"No. I am aware of how that story may sound and what you may think of me. However, I can tell you that I am only attracted to men who I find interesting, and not every man I meet is interesting." Priscilla punctuated the last portion of that sentence by looking directly at Trap Martin.

The waitress came over with menus and was waved off.

"Is there anything else you can tell us about Jonathan? Anything at all?"

It is the fantasy of most women to pick up a man, have casual sex with him, and then dump him by the side of the road. Blair felt that the woman in her wanted to know the answer to that question as much as the cop in her did.

"Well, as I said, he hand-rolled his cigarettes. He had tremendous dexterity with his fingers. When he gave a massage, he would touch parts of my body in a way that was pure magic. But his special talent was that he seemed to see everything. He would point out little details in a room or in a field that you or I would not see. He told me he worked as a free lance photographer and that he had just come back from covering the civil wars in Eastern Europe and Africa. He had also covered the Iraq war, and other places in the Middle East. It appeared that he had seen a lot of death and wanted to get away from it."

Russ concentrated hard to block out his own war experiences.

"What makes you say that?"

Priscilla appeared disturbed at the question.

"Well, at night, he would have dreams. I would not call them nightmares because he did not appear to be frightened, and he did not wake up screaming. No, he would just mumble in his sleep."

Trap did not try to hide his boredom and amused himself by winking at a group of young women standing off to the side. In his mind, what he was hearing was pure bullshit.

Blair felt like she was pulling teeth, but she knew every detail was important.

"What did he say?"

Priscilla shrugged her shoulders.

"It was stuff like, 'Stop that! Let her go. That's enough.' Stuff like that."

"Did you ever ask him about it?"

"No. It was none of my business."

"Do you think you helped him?"

"I do not know."

"Did he help you?"

"No. No, he did not help me."

Before Blair could follow up that last sentence, Trap clapped his hands and rocked back in his chair. For a minute, the entire room stopped talking and looked at their table.

"For crying out loud! This is making me sick. Help you? Help me? Help who? You had one thing in mind, honey, and when you got tired of that, you left him high and dry and split. Isn't that your usual style? It's a wonder you didn't kill him, too."

Priscilla reached for a glass of water on the table, but Russ was faster and placed his own hand on top of the glass.

"It's would not be worth it. Please, calm down."

Priscilla looked from Blair to Russ and then back to Blair.

"Detectives. if you have nothing further, I must go." Without waiting for an answer, Priscilla rose from her seat.

"I do not have a problem cooperating with your investigation, but I will not attend another meeting if Trap Martin is present. Is that clear?"

Both Blair and Russ stood. Trap remained seated and turned his attention back to the group of women at the bar. Russ held out his hand.

"Thank you for meeting with us this evening. By the way, we have some information at the station that I think you should see. I know this is an imposition, but could you come by the office first thing in the morning. It is really quite important." Russ handed her another business card.

As before, the look on the man's face and the tone of his voice were more soothing than threatening.

"Will it take long?"

"We will not keep you long at all."

Priscilla nodded in the direction of the private detective.

"Will he be there?"

Both Russ and Blair shook their heads.

"No."

Priscilla was now sorry that she agreed to assist in their investigation. She did not want to be involved with anything even remotely connected with Trap Martin. Reluctantly, she nodded her head in assent.

"Okay. Look for me about nine." Without waiting for an answer, she turned and left.

Trap stood up and puffed out his chest.

"Well, I can now bill two hours on this case. Thanks, guys."

As the last words left the private detective's mouth, Russ Matson made a neat pivot on his left foot, and using the space on his right hand between his thumb and forefinger, he hit Trap in the throat just below the larynx. With the wind temporarily knocked out of him, Trap Martin slumped back into his seat. Russ Matson cast one look at the gasping mass dressed in a cheap suit and walked away.

Hearing the commotion and seeing only half of the patrons left at the table, the waitress rushed over with the bill. While it was not that much, she certainly did not want to get stuck with it should the police arrive and start hauling people away.

Blair picked up her portfolio and purse and then pointed to a still gasping Trap Martin. "He just billed two hours on this meeting. He can afford to pay for drinks."

Blair caught up to Russ as he was lighting a cigarette.

"Nice move in there. Hey, it looks like we hit pay dirt." Blair was beaming.

Russ blew his first drag into the air and then cast a disapproving look at the restaurant. "He's lucky I didn't shoot him." Russ took another drag from his smoke and then tossed it away.

"I hate guys like that. Let's get out of here before he comes out and I really do have to shoot him."

Russ backed the Crown Victoria sedan out of the parking space and then neatly merged with the rest of the traffic on the street.

"Blair, I hope you don't mind my asking Priscilla to come down and take a look at what we have."

"I was not expecting that. Don't you think it's a little early for that?"

Russ Matson shook his head.

"Nah. I've got a bad feeling here, Blair."

"Tell me about it."

Russ cradled his head in the palm of his hand as he settled into a cruising speed.

"Our girl picks up this burned-out war guy, who's already seen more than his fair share of shit, gives him a free ride in more ways than one for three weeks, and then dumps him one day without warning. He gets pissed off and starts killing women across the country in bunches that make up a composite of the woman who dumped him. Now he shows up here. Do you see where this is going?"

Blair looked at her partner with a hard stare.

"Priscilla is the next target."

"It looks that way to me. We need to break it to her in a way so that she will believe it and she will help us. If we just tell her, she will either not believe it or we may spook her." Russ did not like what he was implying, but he is a cop. And some crimes make cops do things they do not like to do.

"You want to use her as bait." Blair stared out of the window as the faces of all of the victims of this sick killer flashed by along the highway.

"I do not know if I can go along with that, Russ. This could get dangerous."

"I thought about that, Blair. But what happens if we just tell her that she may be the target of a serial killer and she decides to split for a long vacation? She's gone, then he's gone, and what have we got. We might have saved one person, but what about the others he will go after? I wish there was another way, and I will be glad to listen if you have one, but I cannot think of one."

Blair was silent for a long time. What Russ said made a lot of sense. There was only one solution to this. They had better not make any mistakes.

"Okay, Russ. I can't argue against what you have said. We can't screw up on this, though. We just can't."

"I know, Blair. I know."

CHAPTER TWENTY-FIVE

The Eyes watched as the car came around the corner a bit faster than usual. She was late. The beast should have returned to her lair long before now. Where was she before now, and what had she been doing that would make her late coming home. It was important. He had to know.

Priscilla was angry. She was angry at that sleaze bag Martin, and she was angry at herself. She knows all of his tricks, and yet, she still lets him get under her skin. Why?

Priscilla hit the opener from a half a block away and then skidded to a stop just inches from the rear wall of the garage. She slammed the door to the garage and then threw her purse at the desk in the kitchen. Without a word of greeting to her friend and housekeeper, Priscilla went straight to the bar in her den and poured herself a drink that was twice the size of the one she already had. In one continuous motion, it was gone.

Estrella watched Priscilla blow through the kitchen and knew immediately who and what the problem was. She turned off the stove, wiped her hand on the kitchen towel that was draped over her shoulder, and then went to her friend before she drank herself into a stupor.

"You see Trap Martin again, no?"

Priscilla looked at Estrella before she reached for the bottle of Vodka again.

"Estee, if I were a man, tonight, I would have ripped his balls from between his legs and shoved them down his throat."

Estrella looked at her with an honest innocence.

"Hermana, they teeny, tiny, little slippery huevos, no? How you hold on to them to do that?"

The two women looked at each other for a long minute and then burst into uncontrollable laughter. One woman created a space with her thumb and index finger, and the other would create a smaller space in return. Priscilla nearly dropped the bottle of liquor as she collapsed onto the sofa. After five minutes, both women had tears running from their eyes.

Priscilla hugged her friend.

"Estee, you are the best." She gave the woman a kiss and then collected herself.

"I really needed that."

Estrella felt very proud of herself. She had saved the woman that she would give her own life for, from herself. After a few minutes, when the laughter subsided, Estrella again allowed her face to become serious.

"Hermana, tell me something?"

Priscilla casually turned toward Estrella.

"Yes?"

"What would you do with his little beecho?"

Priscilla's face formed a malicious grin.

"I would cut it off, put it between two pieces of bread, and eat it like a sandwich." After a two count, another round of laughter began with both women sharing an imaginary meal of the private parts of Trap Martin.

The Eyes made their move as soon as the garage door closed. He did not worry about being seen. He practiced being invisible in places where his life depended on it. In this part of the world, no one would see him in broad daylight.

Silently, The Eyes made their way to the rear of the house. Even if you had been looking right at him, it would have taken a practiced eye to see his movement in the shadows. The Eyes eased up to the window. If it were someone else, or if it were another time, he would have used a small dental mirror to see into the house. But he was close. It had been a long time since he had been this close to her. He wanted to see her with his own eyes. He had to see her with his own eyes. It would be worth it to take the chance. There was something in the pit of his stomach that told him not to do it. But she was so close. He had to see the Beast. It had been far too long. The Eyes raised themselves to the corner of the window and looked in.

Priscilla clapped her hands at the sight of Estrella eating a sandwich made out of Trap Martin's penis. As she stood up and turned, Priscilla caught sight of a part of a head at the bottom corner of the window at the rear of the room. She let out a scream and then ran from the den into the kitchen. She opened the drawer to the desk, picked up her gun, which she now kept loaded, and ran back into the room.

Estrella became terrified.

"Hermana, what is it?"

Priscilla pointed to the window.

"Over there. I saw something. I'm sure of it."

"Should I call the police?"

Priscilla stood with her back to the wall and her pistol trained on the window.

"Yes. No! Wait. Bring me my purse." Estrella retrieved the bag from the kitchen in less than a minute.

"Here. Call this guy instead." Priscilla handed her housekeeper the business card of Russ Matson.

"Call the cell phone number. Hurry!"

The Eyes cursed his luck but did not panic. He knew she would be frozen in place for a good five minutes. That would be more than enough time for him to get away. He wanted to chance another look, but the reflection off one of the glass surfaces in the room showed him that she had a gun in her hand. If she panicked again and got off a shot, this place would be crawling with cops in no time. That would upset his plans. He could not have that.

Thinking that she might have already called the police, The Eyes withdrew a little more hastily than he normally would have. And in that haste, The Eyes made a costly mistake.

As Russ Matson sat across from Maggie in the restaurant, he felt like a young Marine on leave in a foreign country. Here he was on a date with a woman who wanted to be on a date with him. She was not looking at her watch every ten minutes or checking the voice mail on her phone. He did not have to think about paying her $200 at the end of their time together. He did not have to worry about a possible blackmail scam if she found out he was a cop. All he had to do was be himself. His young friend was right. It is better if he took it day by day.

Russ was just about to take a sip of his Old Fashioned when his cell phone vibrated loudly in his pocket. He cursed under his breath and mentioned that he was going to turn the damned thing off. Maggie shook her head.

"You're a cop. You had better take that."

Russ reluctantly nodded and opened the phone.

"Matson." The voice was so loud, Russ had to hold the phone away from his ear.

"Okay. I'm on my way." Russ ended the call and then turned back to his date.

"Maggie, I…"

Maggie closed her menu and signaled for the waiter to come over with the check.

"Listen, I've dated cops before. This is what happens when you go out with a cop. But here's a deal for you. I'll cover the drinks if you promise to come over after you're done."

Russ looked at her hesitantly.

"It could be late, Maggie."

Maggie fished around in her pocket book and then pulled out a key.

"I don't care. Here, this is so you don't have to ring the bell and I don't have to get up. The bedroom is on the second floor. I'll be up, so don't worry about making too much noise. Just do me one favor?"

"What's that?" The question was superfluous. He would have done anything for her.

"Take your shoes off before you come upstairs. Now go. I'll catch a cab."

Russ impulsively bent down and gave the woman who had just stolen his heart a long passionate kiss in the middle of a very crowded restaurant. Maggie was stunned, flattered, and amazed. No man had ever done that to her before. Russ Matson smiled at her, turned, and left, oblivious to everyone in the room but her.

Outside, Russ called in the job to central dispatch as he pulled out of the parking lot. He told them to make it a Code Three response (no lights, no siren) and that he was on his way. He then hit the speed dial on his phone and told his partner about the call.

"The housekeeper called it in. I've got a code three responding. I can be there in about 15 minutes. How about you? Okay, I'll meet you there." Russ ended the call, let GPS figure out the shortest route to Priscilla's house, and then let his mind wander to white carpets and a sleeping beauty waiting for him at the top of the stairs.

Russ Matson's tan Ford Taurus arrived at the home of Priscilla Whittington in just under 13 minutes. He reached into the glove compartment, took out his service .38, and clipped the holster to his belt. Before he could get out of his car, Blair pulled up in front of him. Already present were two marked cruisers from the town police force. Neither of the cars had their strobes flashing. Both Blair and Russ breathed a sigh of relief.

A rather young-looking sergeant approached them. He looked from Blair to Russ and back to Blair and appeared not to know what to do. It was only after Blair pulled out her badge and hung it on a chain around her neck that he seemed to relax. Blair did not take offense. Dressed in a jogging suit and sneakers, she looked like a juvenile coming home from basketball practice. It was not until both men looked at her head that she remembered that she still had her head band on.

"Sorry. I was just in from a run when you called, Russ. Sarge, do you have someone at the back?"

The young officer instantly recognized the state police badge and gave Blair her proper respect.

"Yes, ma'am. I've got one man at each corner. I told them not to go any further, just in case there is any evidence back there."

Russ smiled at the young man.

"Good job, Sergeant. Did you speak to anyone inside?"

"Yes, sir. I rang the bell, let the occupants of the house know that we were out here, and then I waited for you to arrive. They did not seem to be in any trouble, and since it was a Code Three job, I figured I would just wait out here and watch the front."

Russ took a look around the block and was happy to see that nothing seemed out of the ordinary.

"Nice work, Sergeant. What is your name?"

"Jenks, sir. Robert Jenks."

"I'll have a word with your Lieutenant, Jenks. You handled this well." It seemed like the young officer stood a little taller with the compliment.

"We will try not to tie you guys up too long." Russ took one more look around as Blair made her way to the door.

As Priscilla opened the door, the distinct sound of a Porsche exhaust drew the attention of everyone in front of the house. Jack Case seemed to get out of the car before it came to a stop. The young sergeant started to approach Case but stopped at the sound of Russ Matson's voice, who recognized Case from photos in his personnel file at the bank.

"It's okay, Sergeant. You can let him through." The sergeant stepped to the side, and Case continued to the front door.

Without acknowledging the two officers, Case directed his attention to Priscilla.

"Are you okay?"

"Yes, Jack. I'm a little rattled, but I am okay. Detectives, this is my manager, Jack Case. Please, won't you all come inside?"

Russ brought up the rear as they all stepped through the door. Inside, the house had a warm and comfortable feel to it. There was a scent in the air that was a pleasing mixture of food cooking and perfume that seemed too relaxing. Priscilla began to lead the way to the den when she was stopped by Russ.

"Why don't you guys wait here for a minute?"

Russ nodded to Blair. They both took out their weapons and began a search of the first floor. Within five minutes, they returned to the foyer.

"Okay, the first floor appears to be secure. Wait for us in the den, we'll be back in a minute."

Priscilla, Estrella, and Jack Case watched as Russ led the way up the stairs as Blair followed close behind him. They split up at the top of the stairs, and after a short time, reappeared in the den. By that time, both officers had holstered their weapons.

There is a protocol for situations like this that is taught in the academy and reinforced on the street. If one officer seems to have made a connection with a victim, it is best to let that officer take the lead and gain trust. In a relaxed frame of mind, the victim may remember a detail that may make the difference between an arrest and a conviction. Blair recalled the meeting in the restaurant and how Priscilla seemed to favor Russ. She stepped to the side and let her partner take charge of the situation.

"Okay, Ms. Witt... excuse me, Priscilla. Please tell us what happened."

Priscilla recited the events, indicated where she was standing when she saw the face at the rear window.

"I did not get a good look at the person, he appeared to have on a hood of some sort, but it was definitely a man."

"How do you know that?"

"He had a moustache. I am sure of it."

"Do you have a permit for this?" Blair kept her tone even as she held up the pistol. She was happy to see that the serial numbers were evident and the safety was on.

Priscilla answered in a matter-of-fact tone as well.

"Yes. I have a permit for that one and the one in the top drawer of the night table in my bedroom." Both detectives noted that she did not make a move for the gun, which would indicate that she had nothing to hide, and therefore, was telling the truth.

Blair replaced the gun on the table at the end of the sofa.

"I'm sorry, but it is a routine question that we have to ask."

"There is no need to apologize, Detective. I understand." Blair suddenly felt like she had been one upped.

During the exchange, Jack Case walked to the window and looked out, making sure that he did not touch anything. The rear of the house bordered on semi-dense woods, thick enough to hide in, but sparse enough to move easily in and out of. Jack thought to himself that if someone knew what they were doing, at this hour of the night, they could come and go and you would never see them.

The Eyes looked back at the man that appeared to be looking right at him. The Eyes did not breathe, they did not move, they became one with the night. He was dressed in a dark green jumpsuit with the hood pulled up over his head. Since he had been seen, he covered his face with a dark green ski mask. The Eyes lay low to the ground in an area of shadows, even at night.

As the man in the window continued to scan the area behind the house, The Eyes laughed.

"He is probably looking for someone dressed in black. Only a rookie would do that." There are colors, even at night. The dark is not truly black, just as the light is not truly white. Experience. Life and death experience. The experience that comes from the difference between being competent and being the best taught him that blue or green at night is far more concealing than black will ever be.

The Eyes could have run. They could have gotten away. But why? They were just as safe where they were. Besides, The Eyes had to see her again. These interlopers would be gone soon and then he would be able to see her. The thought of it made him hard. He was close enough to take her now if he wanted to, but the time was not right. He just wanted to see her again. For now.

"So, do you see anything out there?" Jack turned only his head at the sound of Russ's voice.

"The woods are thick enough to hide in, but they will not prevent an escape. For all we know, he may still be out there watching us." Jack turned back to the forest and thought he saw something move.

Russ stood to the left of Jack Case and looked out of the window in the same general direction.

"I see what you mean. That's a good observation. Were you in the service?"

"Yes."

"What branch?" Russ sized the man up as he spoke with him. He was younger by about ten years and appeared to be in good physical condition. Russ guessed that he was an Iraqi vet.

"Marines."

"Iraq?" The one-word answers told Russ that there was a lot more to this guy and there appeared to be something he was hiding.

"Yes." Case did not like to be questioned. The cop did not seem like a bad guy, and he appeared to only be doing his job. Still, unless he was being suspected of something, Case did not like answering questions.

"Have you known her long?"

"No. She came to work for me a few months ago."

"It seems odd that she would call you at a time like this?"

"We happen to be personal friends."

"Were you friends before or after you hired her?"

"After. As a matter of fact, since you are so interested, we became friends just a few days ago." Jack heard the edge in his voice and regretted letting the cop push him to that point.

"Are you married, Jack?"

"No, Detective. I am not married." Jack resented the question, even though he understood why it was asked.

"And yes, she was with me last night. Is there anything else you would like to know?"

"No, not at the moment. Listen, I asked Priscilla to come down to the station tomorrow. We have some information that I feel is important for her to know. It might be a good idea if you came with her. My only request is that you not divulge what you see to anyone. Is that clear?"

"Yes."

"Good. I'll look for you tomorrow around nine." Russ turned back to the center of the room.

"Blair, why don't we have a look around outside?"

"Okay." The two detectives looked more like a father and his daughter as they walked out of the room.

Estrella sensed that this would be a good time to leave as well.

"Hermana, I will finish the dinner and make some coffee, okay?"

"That will be fine, Este." Priscilla was thankful for the time alone with Jack Case. She stood very still as he approached her, but when he came near, she held him as if he were a tree trunk in a windstorm.

"I'm glad you're here, Jack. I am really glad you are here." Priscilla buried her head in his chest.

Case wrapped his arms around her and held her close. There were no tears, and he did not expect any, but the way she held on to him seemed to say that she was tired of facing the world on her own. Case cast a look in the direction of the sofa and the gun on the table.

"I think you can pretty much protect yourself."

Priscilla picked her head up and laughed.

"Here's a secret for you. I have never fired that thing. Not once. I have been meaning to go to a range and practice with it, but I have just never gotten around to it." Priscilla pushed away from Case and picked up the pistol.

"You know, Jack, I really do not know if I could shoot someone. I really do not know."

Jack took the pistol from her, placed it on the end table, and then sat on the sofa with Priscilla. "Let me answer that question for you. In order to protect yourself and someone or something that is important to you, yes, you could shoot someone. I am sure of it."

"Jack, the police want me to come to the station tomorrow. I do not know what it is all about. Will you come with me? Please?"

Jack looked at this woman who, not a very long time ago, was the picture of confidence and self-reliance. Now she is asking for his help. He thought to himself how funny it is how things change and how quickly they change.

"The older cop mentioned that to me as well. Yes, I will go down there with you. But first, will you please tell me what this is all about?"

"I will tell you all that I know, but let's go into the kitchen. Sitting in this room bothers me."

The Eyes saw the old guy and the kid leave the room. Then he saw another male join with the beast. The Eyes became angry. She is his beast. Instinctively, he reached for his knife, but it was not strapped to his waist. It was not time, so he left it in his vehicle. It is a good thing. He might have decided to remove the male that was trying to join with his beast. At some time later, he will have to decide what to do about that male.

The Eyes heard the voices at the corner of the house. They were coming to the rear. It was time to go. While he was certain they could not see him, he did not want to press his luck. The Eyes backed away in a manner that disturbed very little of the surrounding bush and made no sound.

Russ Matson and Blair Collins were a case study in similarities and differences. Both had on skin tight latex examination gloves and plastic operating room boots over their shoes. Russ, however, had a huge twelve-volt search light that lit up a wide area, while Blair opted for a small, halogen flashlight that threw out a thin pencil beam.

The area in the rear was a grassy yard that ran the width of the house. It bordered on woods that separated the lots. The adjacent houses were separated by oversized driveways, so it was not unusual for someone to be completely unseen in the rear of one of these homes. Despite the light in the rear of the house, there were still areas of shadows. No lawn furniture or other outdoor equipment was evident.

Working systematically from left to right, they began to search the area at the rear of the house. Russ would cast the wide light in a semi-circular arc while Blair would concentrate on specifics. Just as they reached the middle area of the rear yard, Russ stopped in his tracks.

"Blair, take a look at this." Russ pulled on his reading glasses as his partner came over. He pointed his flash light at a perfect foot print in the dirt of the flower bed.

"This may give us something to work with."

Blair bent down and studied the print. It appeared to be fresh, but there was something there that immediately jumped out at her.

"Russ, do you see this.?" Blair focused her light on the footprint and pointed to the combination of numbers and letters in the middle of the print.

"'28CM. European shoes are sized in centimeters. Whoever is wearing this shoe is not American or bought the shoe overseas. We need to get a forensic team out here to get a cast of this print and light up the area."

Russ shook his head.

"That will mean giving Max a call. She is the only one who can authorize that at this time of night."

Blair pulled out her cell phone.

"Okay I'll call her. You can… wait a minute, weren't you supposed to be having dinner with Maggie tonight?"

Russ's grim expression turned even more dower.

"Yeah. I got the call over cocktails. She was real good about it. Not a word of complaint. She's a special one, Blair."

"Hey, listen, take off. This area is secure, and I'll keep one of the patrol guys on scene as a back-up. It will be hours before we are finished up here. There is no need for both of us to be standing around when at least one of us could be having some fun. Beat it, Matson."

"I can't do that, Blair. We're working this together. I can't run off and leave you like that. It would not be right." Another part of Russ Matson's mind was making an alternative argument.

Blair anticipated the answer and was ready with a counter proposal.

"Okay, Russ, I'll tell you what. When the forensic team gets here, then you take off. They will be making so much noise that no sicko in his right mind will hang around. My guess is that Mr. Manager will be spending the night anyway. Besides, ole Priscilla has as much fire power as you and I combined. There. Now I will not take no for an answer."

Russ admitted to himself that the woman made him an offer he would be hard pressed to refuse.

"Okay, Blair. Deal. As soon as the forensic team shows up, I'll take off. Thanks, partner."

Blair looked up at the older man who she had liked from the first time she had met him. "Listen, there will come a time when I will have a date, and buster, you will owe me big time." The two partners laughed at the joke and also felt the firmness of the bond between them.

CHAPTER TWENTY-SIX

Max Stout listened to the events of the prior evening and the theories of her detectives as she studied the photos of the foot print. She was impressed by the work that Blair and Russ were doing on this case, but it bothered her that they did not check with her first before inviting Priscilla and this guy that she is banging down to view the photos. Max did not like her detectives to be one step ahead of her.

"Listen, guys, you did nice work last night, but you should have checked with me first before bringing her in. I am not so sure I agree with your theory on that." Max regretted lying. She knew that if she was in their position, she would have done exactly the same thing.

Russ stepped up before Blair could open her mouth.

"Boss, it was my decision. I take full responsibility for bringing the woman and the man in. If you would like, I will call them up and tell them not to come in."

"Max, Russ and I did discuss it. I agree with him. There is no alternative here."

Max held up her hands.

"Whoa, calm down, guys. No one is getting reprimanded here. It is just a disagreement, that's all. Let's go with it and see what happens. Tell me about this snoop, Martin. What are you going to do about him?"

Blair and Russ noticeably relaxed. Russ nodded to Blair as it was her case and the decision would be hers.

"He pushed buttons, Max. It is clear that he and Priscilla hate each other, and it is not hard to see why. But I think we need to keep him involved. If for nothing else than to keep Priscilla legit."

Max turned to Russ.

"What do you think?"

"I don't like him, Max. I agree with Blair that we have to keep him involved, but I don't trust him."

Max looked at Blair and Russ and felt a sense of pride. She liked her detectives backing each other up. These two made a good pair. Once this case is done, it will be a shame to break them up.

"Okay, I'll follow your lead on this. After you're done with the meeting, let's re-convene on how we take this to the next level. Any questions?" Both detectives shook their heads.

Max stood up and made a final point as Blair and Russ headed for the door.

"By the way, that's a nice shirt and tie you got on there, Russ. Looks good."

With his hair askew and sheepish grin, Russ Matson looked like he was ten-years-old. "Thanks, Max. It was a gift. I just got around to wearing it." Russ bolted through the door before another question could be asked.

Back in the squad room, Blair could not help herself.

"A gift. That was a pretty slick answer. It is a nice shirt and tie, though. You look great in it."

Russ looked around to make sure none of the other cops were within earshot.

"I tell you, Blair, I'm the luckiest guy in the world. I get over to Maggie's, and she is still up. She asks me if I am hungry and if I want anything to eat. Then this morning, there's this shirt and tie sitting out for me. She tells me, 'You can't go to work in the same clothes you had on the day before.' Can you imagine that? Wow!"

Blair smiled and was thankful that her partner confided his happiness to her.

"You are a very lucky man. I am really happy for you, Russ."

Russ turned serious.

"Yeah, well, I am taking your advice. At my age, you cannot move too suddenly or else you will break something. One day at a time."

Blair nodded in assent.

"Good. Now let's get ready for our company."

Jack Case awoke and was momentarily disorientated by the scent of the sheets. The events of the prior evening instantly came back to him and he regained his balance. As he confirmed that he was alone in the bed, he laughed to himself. There was a time when a feather falling on a blanket of snow would have been enough to awaken him. He sat up in the bed just as Priscilla came in with two cups of coffee.

"Good morning. Milk, no sugar, right?" She sat on the edge of the bed and handed Jack one of the cups.

"That's right. How did you know that?" Jack took a sip and was thankful for the brew.

Priscilla smiled over the rim of her own cup.

"I told you before that I know a good few things about you." She let the remark hang in the air for a minute before confessing.

"Okay, the first day that I started, you and I were in the coffee room together. I saw how you fixed your coffee and made a note of it."

"I see." Jack took another sip from the cup and started to wonder what else this woman knew about him. He dismissed the thought quickly as it did not seem all that important. What was more important was who was this woman, why was someone prowling behind her house, and what did the police want to show them?

"Jack?"

"Yes?"

"I have a bad feeling about this meeting with the police today. I think it has something to do with me and a guy I used to know and people being killed."

Jack put his cup down and pulled the woman close.

"Listen, I am not going to bullshit you. If the police want to see you, then it is about something that is serious and probably harmful to someone. To run from it will only make it worse. We'll go over there, see what it is they have to show us, hear what they have to say, and then deal with it. Okay?"

Priscilla nodded her head slowly. Jack held her head in his hands and then kissed her lightly on the lips. Priscilla returned the kiss with more want and need than passion. Soon, they were making love in the manner of one lover giving strength to the other.

The Eyes returned to his post at dawn. The beast and the male were still inside. The Eyes felt the anger begin to rise within him. She was his beast. He knew now that he would have to fight the other male for her. That was the way. He had claimed her, and now another male was trying to take her away. The Eyes took out the rolling papers and his pouch of tobacco. He needed to calm his nerves.

After stopping for a change of clothes, Jack and Priscilla were greeted in the lobby of police headquarters by Blair, who escorted them upstairs to the detective squad room. Just as they entered the door, Jack stopped short.

"Just a minute, Detective. There is something I would like to say." Jack Case stood with his weight evenly distributed on both feet. He looked like he was about to defend himself.

"Priscilla told me that someone broke into her house a few days ago. I was the person who broke in. I was, um, playing a trick on Priscilla. If you want me to sign a statement to that effect, I will do so."

Priscilla punched Case in the arm.

"I knew it was you!"

"Since it appears that nothing was taken, that will not be necessary, Mr. Case, unless Ms. Whit..., Priscilla, wishes to file charges against you." Although the idea of Priscilla pressing charges against Case seemed ridiculous, Blair kept her demeanor serious. Breaking into someone's house was not a joke.

Priscilla quickly spoke up.

"I will not press charges, Detective." Then she turned to Case and smiled playfully.

"You and I will discuss this later."

Blair looked from Priscilla, to Case, and then back to Priscilla.

"That's fine. I will let the patrol sergeant know." Blair looked down at her feet for a second and figured this was the best time to say what she had to say.

"Listen, what we are about to show you may upset you. Detective Matson and I feel that it is in your best interest to share this information with you at this time. Your admission, Mr. Case, now makes this information even more vital. Step this way, please."

Blair led the way into an interrogation room. All of the photos of all of the slain women were displayed on the table. They were separated by the states in which they had been murdered. Russ Matson stood to the side and greeted the group as they entered the room.

Priscilla took a look at the photos and turned away in horror. It did not go unnoticed to either detective that Case did not turn away but in fact moved in for a closer look.

"As you know, there is a serial killer in this area. These are photos of other deaths that we feel are attributable to the suspect. We feel that the same person is responsible for the deaths of other women in other states."

Blair moved closer to the table.

"Now, I want to you to pay very close attention." Blair waited until Priscilla re-focused on the table, and then in a systematic fashion, used component parts from the grouping of photos of women from each state to form a composite photo of Priscilla Whittington. She intentionally did not touch the group of photos from New Jersey.

Priscilla was horrified.

"You mean to say…" She could not finish the sentence. The words were stuck in her throat. She finally turned away from the photos and buried her face in Jack's chest.

"Is there a place where we can sit down?" Jack led Priscilla out of the room as Russ ushered the pair to a table in the middle of the squad room.

"Detective Collins, are you absolutely certain about the connection here?" Jack kept his tone even and unintimidating. What this situation needed was logic and reason, not panic.

"Mr. Case, we are about as certain as we can be at this time. The time frame of the first murder is shortly after the time that Ms. Whittington separated from the man she had met in California. Separately, there is nothing linking the victims to each other. However, the composite is unmistakable. The weapon used is the same, as is the method of death. We have every reason to believe that this is the work of the same individual."

Jack looked from Blair to Russ and then took Priscilla's hand in his.

"Detective, you did not do a composite of the women from New Jersey. Why?"

Priscilla removed her hand from Jack's, sat up straight in her chair, and looked from one detective to the other.

"They did not do the composite because I am the next target. Isn't that right, detectives?"

Telling someone that they may be killed is never an easy thing. Asking that person to become a target is even harder. Blair squirmed in her seat for a second before answering.

"We hope not, but the evidence is very strong."

With only the slightest change in her facial expression, Priscilla became cold and intense. "Those women are dead because of me. If I were to run away, others would probably die. Isn't that correct?" Blair nodded her head in agreement.

"Then the only way to stop the deaths is to catch this guy, and the only way that is going to happen is through me. Am I right?"

Russ and Blair looked at each other, and then nodded in unison.

"Yes, Priscilla. We need your help."

Priscilla looked at Jack.

"You do not need to be a part of this, Jack. I can handle this on my own. I am okay now."

Jack looked back at Priscilla and did not move.

"Proceed, Detective. How can we help you?"

Russ was not surprised. Jack Case did not look like the type of man to run from trouble.

Blair leaned in to emphasize the points she was about to make.

"We need anything you can tell us about the man that you spent time with in California. Is there anything about this guy that you did not tell us the other night? Anything at all? Did he mention friends or family in the area or agents or editors that he may have gotten photo assignments from? Any detail, no matter how insignificant, may give us something to work with. Do not try to figure this out yourself. All we are looking for is details. If there is a connection to be made, we will make it." Blair was pleading with her eyes.

Priscilla went back in time. She closed her eyes, hunched over with her fingers interlaced in her lap, and concentrated on the days and nights that they spent together. When she had gone over the three weeks twice in her head, Priscilla threw up her hands in surrender.

"All I can remember is that he seemed more interested in what was around him at that present time. I recall asking him about his past, and he changed the subject almost all the time."

Blair was on the statement like a cat.

"What was the one time when he did not change the subject?"

"Well, he admitted that he was a fine arts major in college. In his senior year, he participated in a photo safari in Africa. Kenya was the country, I think. He told me that he loved the country. When he graduated, he went back. He spent a number of years living in various villages, taking wildlife pictures. From that, he began taking pictures of the various civil and tribal wars that were going on. He said there was more money in that type of work."

Blair let the information sink in and made some notes.

"Okay, listen, we need you to go about your normal routine. We will assign a patrol officer to escort you to and from work and to keep an eye on your home while you are there. We will ask you to carry a locator device, so that we can track your movements, and we will place a similar device in your car. We will also give you a portable voice transmitter so that we can hear any conversation you may be having with someone. The voice transmitter will be under your control. We want to catch a killer. We do not want to spy on your personal life."

Priscilla laughed.

"Detective, last night I told you that this man sees everything. Every little detail. He will see when things are not right. He will see when someone is somewhere they do not belong. With all due respect, I do not think your escort will be very useful in this instance."

Blair took a deep breath and pursed her lips together. She anticipated this. What she had in mind was against policy and procedure, but this was no ordinary case.

"Suppose we constructed a trap? Would you be willing to pose as bait?"

Russ could not believe what he just heard.

"Blair!"

"I'm sorry, Russ, but she is right. If he sees things like she says he does, our people would stand out like a sore thumb. It's the only chance we have to catch this guy."

Russ was adamant.

"No! Let's get a decoy. Someone from out of the county or maybe even from the NYPD. We've done that before."

Priscilla shook her head.

"That would not work. He would know it was not me." She looked at Jack apologetically. "We spent a lot of time together in those three weeks, and we did a lot of things. He told me things about myself that I did not even know. I'm sorry, a look alike decoy would not work. It will have to be me."

"May I offer a suggestion?" All eyes turned to Jack.

"Allow me to accompany Priscilla into whatever trap you are going to set."

Russ shook his head.

"This does not call for heroics, Mr. Case. Besides, your presence may blow the whole thing. He may not approach her if you are there. Besides, putting one civilian at risk is one too many. We absolutely cannot risk two."

Blair spoke up.

"I have to agree with my partner, Mr. Case. While we appreciate your help, we cannot allow you to become involved in this matter." When Blair finished speaking, she was sorry that they did not have this conversation privately with Priscilla.

Case anticipated that response and said nothing more.

Blair stood up. This had gone as far as it probably should go.

"Listen, it was just an idea. Thank you both for coming down. For the time being, Priscilla, I would suggest that you keep all your doors and windows locked and stay away from secluded places. Now that you have been warned, it will be harder for whoever this is to catch you off guard. You have the advantage now." Blair felt that she had to leave the woman with some hope.

In the group of people gathered in the room, Priscilla looked totally alone.

"Thank you, Detective. Will there be anything else?"

Blair looked from Priscilla to Russ, who was less than pleased.

"We will want you to sit with our sketch artist to prepare a composite photo of the man you spent time with in California. The artist will call you to schedule a time. That will be all for now." Blair watched Jack and Priscilla walk out the squad room and wished she was going with them. No sooner than the door closed, Russ Matson grabbed Blair by the arm and led her into the interrogation room.

Once in the room, he slammed the door and forced her into a seat.

"ARE YOU CRAZY?! To suggest something like that without authorization can get you suspended! My God, Blair, at least you could have discussed it with me before you said anything to them. We've got to talk to Max about this before it gets out. Jesus, girl, what were you thinking?"

Blair refused to stay seated. Don't scream at me! This was your idea, remember? You're the one that said the only way we are going to catch this guy is to use Priscilla as bait. You're right about one thing though. I should have discussed it with you first. It just seemed like that was the right time to bring it up. I'm sorry, Russ."

Russ looked at the young detective. It was impossible to stay angry with her. She wanted to catch whoever was doing this. He was sure of that. If he felt anything different, he would have reported her to their commanding officer and walked away from the entire matter.

"Listen, I know I mentioned it first, but you don't spring something like that without thinking it through. We..." Russ stopped, looked around the room, and then pulled out his package of cigarettes.

"I need a smoke. Let's get out of here." Blair looked at the man who she had come to admire with every day that they worked together. She did not know what to make of his suggestion.

Russ read the quizzical look on the face of his young partner. He put a finger to his ear and then pointed around the room.

"Listen, young lady. Here is a bit of advice for you. Think twice before you open your mouth." Blair smiled, nodded her head to indicate that she understood the room could be monitored, and went to retrieve the jacket to her suit.

Jack and Priscilla left the station in silence. They drove in silence, and when they reached her home, they sat in the car in silence for a very long time. When Priscilla turned her head to face Jack, it seemed as if that motion made a sound that was deafening.

"Jack. I do not think we should see each other. Things have gotten out of hand, and I am not sure that I would continue to enjoy your company. Please accept my resignation from the bank, effective immediately, and please do not try to contact me ever again."

Jack Case turned to face her with a look that was beyond casual.

"Okay. I will alert Human Resources and have them send your wages to your home. Is there anything else?"

She expected him to argue with her. She expected him to reject what she was saying and insist on defending her. Priscilla expected a lot of things, but the last thing she expected was the cold, impersonal, tone of his voice and the fact that he appeared not to care one bit whether she lived or died. She did not answer his question. Priscilla just slowly got out of the car, stood in front of her house, and watched as someone she thought she knew drove away.

CHAPTER TWENTY-SEVEN

 "Where have you two been? I've been looking for you." Max was standing in the middle of the squad room in black patent leather heels that made her look ten feet tall when Blair and Russ walked in. "My office. Right now."

"Okay, so how did it go with the Whittington woman?" Max Stout kicked off her shoes as soon as she entered her office and fought an urge to rub her feet, noting that it would not look good in front of the troops. She did stare at her new shoes and vowed never to wear them to work again.

Blair and Russ looked at each other and nodded in agreement to something that was unspoken.

"It went as well as could be expected. Priscilla was upset at the pictures, but she agreed to carry a tracker and let us wire her car." Blair kept her tone upbeat and casual.

Max was not buying it.

"Russ?"

"Really, Max, she did not like the fact that she may be a target, but we told her that we would do all that we could to protect her. She gave us a couple of points to look into and that was about it."

"What about Case?" Max glanced from one detective to the other. Something was not right here, but she could not put her finger on it.

"He wanted to play the hero bit, but Russ shot that down. I don't think we will have to worry about him."

Max's cell phone vibrated with an audible hum. She looked at the number, held up one finger, and then swiped right on the device.

"Hold on, please." Max turned to her detectives.

"Okay. Keep me informed on what is going on with this case. I don't want any surprises, is that clear?" Both detectives nodded in agreement and then left the office.

Max waited until they were well away from the office before she spoke into the phone.

"Hello." After she spoke, Max realized that there was an edge to her tone that was not intended.

The voice on the other end was hesitant.

"Are you mad that I called? I'm sorry. It's just that I wanted to talk to you."

Max sat down and took a deep breath before answering the question.

"No, I'm not mad. I was just dealing with some office stuff. Actually, I was going to call you later this afternoon."

"Why?" There was anticipation in the voice.

"The shoes you had made for me hurt my feet." Max stared at the shoes again, but this time the look on her face was different.

"I'm sorry. I will take them back and have them adjusted."

Max got up and closed the door to her office.

"Put your collar on."

There was the sound of a door closing on the other end of the line, then a drawer opening and a something being fastened. When the receiver was picked up, the voice was breathless.

"Yes?"

"My feet hurt. I need you to attend to them." Max turned her back to the door to her office.

"I would love to rub your feet. Hold on. I'll use the other line to transfer the funds."

"There will be no need for that." Max leaned back in her chair and stretched her legs out. She completed the picture with her image of the person on the other end of the line.

"I do not understand." There was doubt and fear in the voice.

"Don't you..."

"Do you have any appointments this afternoon?"

"Yes." All doubt was gone. Now there was real fear in the voice.

Max cradled the cell phone between her shoulder and her jaw and began to conjure familiar images and feelings in her mind.

"Cancel all of your appointments. Be at the room at three this afternoon."

"But what about...?"

Max closed her eyes.

"Do I have to say it again?"

"No. I'll be there." It is said that a smile can be heard over the phone.

Max ended the call without saying another word and went into a very private world. In this world, there was nothing to question. There was no one to suspect. Everything, motive, purpose, and intent were clear. Max was walking a fine line between the two worlds and she knew it.

Max was violating an agreement, and if her agent found out about it, there would be hell to pay.

After her first client, Max met with her agent and shook hands on the type of contract that will never see the inside of a courthouse but is just as binding, if not more so.

"Our agreement will be simple. You will get your clients from me. Any new clients have to be cleared through me. Everybody pays. There are no free rides. I will suggest a rate, but you can change it if you wish. After all, you are doing all of the work. I get 30 percent of what is made. Know this, we are both in this to make money. That's what this is all about. Neither you or I can afford a jealous lover. Cross me, go off on your own, and you will never get another client."

Max recalled the tone of the voice of her agent. It was business like and also somewhat threatening. At the time, Max dismissed the threat as something that needed to be said. Now, she was not so sure. There are just some things that money cannot buy. Max was now just starting to find that out. The

"Puppy" she just adopted was giving her something that she never had before with anyone. Max Stout looked at the phone and then the shoes that were only a part of very elaborate gift set and then replayed the voice from the other end of the line.

Max shook her head and said out loud, "There are just some things that money cannot buy."

Blair and Russ left Max's office, went to their respective cubicles, and began the work of looking busy. After about 15 minutes of feigning some meaningful activity, they chit-chatted about following up a lead in the southern part of the state and then signed out for the day.

They drew a department vehicle and drove in silence for 15 minutes to a diner on Route 22. They parked the car, walked ten feet away from it, and burst out laughing.

Blair was beside herself.

"That went exactly as you said it would. She said exactly what you said she would say! How did you know?"

Russ was having trouble lighting his cigarette and laughing at the same time. In the end, he stopped laughing long enough to light the smoke.

"Listen, kid, when you have been around as long as I have, you know what management will say before they say it. And it doesn't matter if it is a man or a woman. Got it?"

Blair looked at her partner and was amazed. In the past 24 hours, she found that the kindly old man who she could not picture pulling his weapon, much less using it, turned out to be this cunning and devious detective who is still capable of physically taking down a suspect.

"Yes, Russ. I got it. Do you really think she had the car bugged?" Blair looked back at the Crown Victoria as if it might explode.

Russ took a long slow drag from his cigarette and then watched the smoke disappear.

"I had a commanding officer do that to me once. It could happen again. Why take chances?"

Blair saw the logic in the statement and did not argue.

"Got 'cha."

Russ took two quick drags from his cigarette and then ground it out with the sole of his shoe.

"Okay, let's go inside and talk about this trap of yours."

The two detectives stayed in the diner for over an hour. When they came out, Jack Case watched as the young female slid into a beat-up Toyota while the old guy took the unmarked police car. Jack held his position as he watched both cars leave the parking lot.

Jack had played a hunch and decided to wait for one of them to leave the station house. When they came out together, he knew he was on the right track. What he learned was that this stop was pre-arranged, which meant that they were up to something, and they were the only two who knew what that something was. If not, why would they come here to plot strategy?

Jack decided that there was no point in following either of them. Whatever it was that they were up to would certainly involve Priscilla. So, instead of running the risk of being spotted and arrested for interfering with a police investigation, Jack Case started his car and went to the one place that he figured they would not think to look for him.

The Eyes sat in his perch and watched the lair of the beast. From his position, he could see the rear of the house and the garage entrance on the side. The side of the house that he could not see did not have a window, so it did not matter. The Eyes gambled that no one would be coming to the door, so there was no need to watch the front of the house. Besides, if anyone did come to the house, the beast always took them into the family room, which he could clearly see from his perch. In a comfortable position, The Eyes pulled out his rolling papers and tobacco and treated himself to a cigarette.

When she returned home, Priscilla sat down with Estrella. There were tears in her eyes as she told her only friend about her meeting at the police station.

"Estee, a lot of people have died because of me. Maybe I could have prevented that, but right now, I cannot change that. I do not want you to be a victim. I could not stand that. So, listen to me. Tell me where you want to go.

Name the place. Anywhere in the world. Just tell me. I will send you there. When this is all over, I will send for you. I promise. I just can't lose you. You are the only friend I have."

Estrella looked back at the woman who she adored. In her mind's eye, she recalled the day several years ago that they met. It was a day that she will never forget for the rest of her life.

From the day she arrived on the small island just off the coast of Cancun, Mexico, the rich white woman with the beautiful grey hair was the talk of the chambermaid's locker room. Normally, rich "gringo" tourists drew no interest from these uneducated or undereducated women. But this woman was different. There was something about this woman that made all the other women want to be her. Some said it was her hair. Others said it was her body. But most all of them agreed that it was the way that she carried herself that made her stand out from all the other touristas that came to the resort.

Estrella Lopez was assigned to her room. On the first morning that she went to clean her room, Estrella found Priscilla having coffee on the balcony. She was impressed by the fact that the woman greeted her with a smile and said hello in her native tongue. For her part, Estrella returned the smile and then looked away. She had her duties to perform and secrets to hide.

On the third day, Priscilla stopped Estrella as she was about to leave the room.

"Wait. You cannot go through the rest of the day looking like that. Sit down." Estrella did as she was told, only out of the fear that not to do it would risk a complaint which would result in getting fired.

Priscilla opened her make-up case and took out brushes, powders, and lotions. She cleaned the woman's face and then began to apply the make-up to the bruise on her cheek. Like magic, it disappeared.

Priscilla stood behind the woman as they both looked at each other in the mirror.

"How long has he been beating you?"

Estrella smiled back at the first person to show her any kindness in a very long time. "Gracias, senora. I have to go." Estrella gave another weak smile to Priscilla and then quickly left the room.

The next day, it was a black eye. Estrella tried to hide it with sunglasses, but they were not big enough. Again, Priscilla would not let her leave the room. She applied her make-up to the wound and made it disappear. When Estrella tried to leave, Priscilla grabbed her arm to make her stay. Estrella winced in pain.

"Let me see."

Estrella hung her head and opened the top of her uniform. Bruises, both old and fresh, were evident on her arms and chest. On her back were welts. The sight of the abuse did not repulse Priscilla or upset her. It made her angry.

"Why does he do this to you?"

Estrella dressed and spoke with her head down.

"It is a small island. There is very little work. I have a job. He does not. He thinks I can get him a job here, but I cannot. He does not believe me, so…"

"Why do you stay with him?" As soon as she asked the question, Priscilla realized how dumb it was.

"Where can I go, senora, where he will not find me?" Estrella smiled a weak smile, put her sunglasses in her pocket, and then gave Priscilla a hug.

"Muchas gracias, senora."

In the privacy of the next room, Estrella fell to her knees and thanked God that someone would listen to her. She thanked God for sending the woman with the make-up to hide the shame that she had to bear. Estrella felt better in knowing that there was someone willing to help her and listen to her. Her world, at least for that one little moment, was not all bad.

During the two weeks that she was there, Priscilla taught Estrella how to apply make-up to hide the bruises on her face. The two women would meet in town to stroll and talk and share secrets in a way that only women can do. In that time, Estrella found herself referring to Priscilla as hermana. Priscilla had become the sister that she never had.

On the day before Priscilla was to leave, Estrella came to her room with regret. She knew that at this time tomorrow she would be gone. Priscilla would return to her world where men did not do such things and she would be left in hers. There was a part of Estrella that wished she had never met this woman.

Priscilla watched as Estrella cleaned the room. When the work was done, Priscilla walked over to her and handed her an envelope.

"Open it."

Estrella handed the envelope back.

"Hermana, you have been too kind to me. This is not necessary. Please, I cannot accept it."

Priscilla smiled and refused to take it back.

"Open it. It is not what you think it is."

Estrella looked at the envelope as if it were a bomb waiting to explode. Before she opened it, she wiped her hands on her uniform as if not to soil whatever was inside. Her hands trembled when she took out the passport, the travel visa, and the plane ticket to America.

"Hermana, I…" Estrella was at a loss for words.

Priscilla was stern as she placed her hand's on Estrella's shoulders.

"Listen, I leave tomorrow. You can either come to America with me or you can stay here with him. The choice is up to you. I will be at Calle San Martin at noon tomorrow." Priscilla took back the documents and then left Estrella to make the biggest decision in her life.

The next day, at exactly 12 o'clock, Estrella watched the black sedan come to a stop in front of her. She wore the only dress that she owned, and all of her belongings were neatly packed in a shopping bag. Priscilla opened the door to the car and welcomed her inside with a hug. She then directed the driver to take them to the nearest mall before going to the airport. There, Priscilla brought clothes, luggage, and the beginnings of a new life for Estrella.

Estrella came back to the present and looked defiantly at the woman before her. "Hermana, with all that you have done for me, how could you think I would leave you now? No, I am staying right here. If he comes for you, then he has to take me, too. There. That's it. No more talk." Estrella clasped the hands of her friend and employer and smiled at her. She started to walk away, stopped, and turned back.

"Hermana, perhaps later you show me how to work the pistolla?"

Priscilla smiled gamely and nodded in agreement.

"Yes, Estee, I will show you how to shoot the gun." Priscilla then smirked to herself. "But first, I have to learn how to shoot it myself."

CHAPTER TWENTY-EIGHT

It was late in the afternoon when Blair arrived at the offices of Martin Security Associates unannounced. She could not take the chance that anything would be leaked to Victoria Whittington that would then find its way back to Max. The last thing she needed at this stage was some administrative nonsense.

"Good afternoon. Is Mr. Martin in?" Blair produced a business card just in case the woman behind the desk did not remember her name.

There are some personality traits that you never lose. Gineen did not like cops who just show up. It usually meant that they were up to something, which usually did not mean anything good to Gineen. She looked at the card and then gave Blair an icy stare.

"I'll see if he can be interrupted." Gineen took her time putting her shoes on, rising from her seat, and then knocking once on the door to Trap's office before entering. Within five minutes, she reappeared.

"He will see you now."

"Thank you." Blair took no notice of the ice in the woman's voice. She had long since dismissed the woman as nothing more than hired help. At this point in time, she had much more important things to think of.

Trap Martin was at his rumpled best. Today, not even his hair was combed. He remained seated behind his desk, making no effort to rise or shake hands.

"Your partner owes me a re-match. You can tell him that I do not like being sucker punched. What do you want?" His distain was underscored by the look of absolute disgust on his face.

"Hey, look, as I remember the incident, you two were face to face. I don't think that counts as being 'sucker punched,' but that's just me. Listen, that's between you and him. You know where to find him. Deliver your own message."

Trap looked at the woman and saw her in a different light. She had an edge, and he had to give her credit for coming here by herself.

"Okay, so what is it that you want?"

Blair looked down, saw the stains on the chair, and decided to take a chance anyway and sit down.

"I need your help, Trap."

Russ returned the department car, picked up his own Ford Taurus, and then stopped at the liquor store for a bottle of Jacob's Creek Shiraz, Maggie's favorite wine. His next stop was the bakery for a chocolate fudge layer cake. Armed with the essentials for a very pleasant evening, Russ parked in front of Maggie's townhouse and used his key to let himself in.

Russ found her in the kitchen preparing a salad for dinner. He wrapped his arms around her and kissed her on the neck. Maggie put the knife down and let her body relax in his arms.

"You know, you could get arrested for breaking into a girl's house like that. I have half a mind to call the police." She closed her eyes and allowed certain feelings to wash over her.

"How are you going to call them when I have you in the Matson Death Grip?" Russ smiled. This was a game that they had played before.

Maggie turned to face the man that had the ability to make her forget any other man she ever knew. She draped her arms around his neck and looked him in the eye.

"Like this." Maggie kissed Russ passionately, leaving no doubt about her feelings of want, lust, and love. The smell of butter burning on the stove made them reluctantly disengage.

Maggie spied the packages and made a suspicious face as she reached for the pot and turned down the flame on the stove.

"Wine? Chocolate cake? Are we breaking up?"

Russ stopped in the midst of taking off his jacket and placed both hands on her shoulders. "Maggie, don't even joke about that. You're the best thing that has happened to me. I want you in my life forever."

The impact of the words on the woman was evident. Maggie hung her head, wrung her hands nervously, and then looked into his eyes for direction.

"Russ, no one has ever said anything like that to me before. Not ever. I don't know what to say."

Russ kissed her on the top of her head and went to the closet to hang up his jacket and secure his service weapon.

"Just tell me what's for supper, that's all."

During dinner, they caught up on each other's day. Maggie described her office drama and politics while Russ recounted his own very strange day. After the meal, Russ laid out the reason for the treats.

"Maggie, I am going to be on stakeout for a while. Blair has an idea as to how we can catch this creep. It's a long shot, but it just might work. The problem is that it will involve 24-hour surveillance. Here's the tricky part. The department doesn't know about it."

"What does that mean exactly, Russ?" The fear in her voice was matched by the fear in her eyes.

Russ took her hand and stared Maggie directly in the eye.

"I do not want to tell you too much about it. It is a plan that is not sanctioned by the department and could be considered illegal. The less you know about it, the better. The problem for us is that you will not see me for a while. I am sorry, but you will not even be able to call me."

Maggie hung her head. One of the things that she lived for was seeing him.

"How long will it last? Will you call me?"

"All I can tell you is that I think we are close to catching this guy. How long it will take is anyone's guess. But I will make you this promise. I will call you every day. Oh, and there is one other thing."

Russ rose from his seat, went to the closet, and retrieved an envelope from the pocket of his suit jacket.

"Here." He handed the envelope to Maggie and then helped himself to another glass of wine.

Not knowing what to expect, Maggie reached for her reading glasses. She opened the envelope, skimmed the travel documents, and paid close attention to the resort brochure.

"The tickets are open. We can use them anytime. I've already paid for our stay. All we have to do is set the date. Maggie, this case will be over soon. When it is, I want us to go to that place and have the time of our lives. What do you say?"

Maggie put the documents down, looked at Russ, and then got up from the table.

"I have something to show you." She gave him another look and then disappeared into the bedroom. Russ shook his head and wondered if he would ever figure out the mystery of women.

In a few minutes, Maggie stepped out of the bedroom. She was dressed in a sheer black negligee and high heeled mules with black feather pom-poms. She stood before him, not knowing what to expect.

"Do you like it, Russ? I mean, am I too old to wear this? I'm not too fat, am I? It's just that..." He did not let her ask another question. He pulled into his lap and let his kiss muffle what it was she intended to say.

"Does that answer your question? You look gorgeous."

Maggie beamed.

"Russ, I never had a reason to buy anything like this before, much less wear it. I was afraid that I would look ridiculous in it. But I wanted it for you, and well, for me, too. Do you really like it?"

Russ could not recall when a woman wore something just for him. He silently said a prayer that Blair's plan would work and they would nab the creep in short order. There was a life he wanted to live with this woman and time was passing.

"Maggie, I really like the outfit and the fact that you wore it for me. But now since I will not be around for a while, isn't there something we ought to be doing other than talking?"

Maggie stood up, held out her wrists, and put on her most seductive face.

"You caught me, officer. Take me in."

Blair opened the door to Trap's office, said goodnight to Gineen, and then walked confidently to her car. The hardest part of the plan was over, and now it is all about getting lucky. As Blair left the office, Gineen got up from behind her desk and went in.

"What was that all about?"

Trap watched Gineen walk across the room. He was always amazed that she could get a rise out of him at anytime and anywhere.

"They need my help."

"Doin' what?" Gineen walked right around the desk, hiked up her skirt, and straddled him.

Trap pulled her skirt up higher and then made an observation.

"Don't you ever wear underwear? That junior cop has a plan to catch that guy that's killing women. It sounds like it might work."

"Shit, Trap. I stopped wearin' panties when I was 14. So, you gonna help them?"

Trap slowly opened the buttons of her blouse and unhooked her bra. At the same time, Gineen ripped open his shirt, and in what seemed like one motion, unzipped his pants and exposed his penis.

"Yeah. There's a couple of bucks in it, and it could lead to some other stuff. There is just one problem. Hey! I like this shirt."

Gineen rose up slightly and then expertly let herself back down, taking Trap's very erect penis into her very wet vagina.

"I'll buy you another one. What kind of problem? Damn, you a big man."

Trap let the warmth of her flow into him.

"I won't be around for a while."

Gineen closed her eyes and began to move. She pulled Trap's head to her breasts while she scratched his back.

"Then I suppose I oughta make you miss me, shouldn't I? How's that feel, baby?"

The two women lay in bed and watched the fading sun. Doris's voice was soft and caring. "Are you okay?"

"I am better now than I was a couple of hours ago. Why?" Max stroked Doris's body with the leather crop.

Doris turned on her side, resting her head on Max's thigh.

"You seemed distant. Like a part of you was not here."

Max looked down on the top of the head of the first person who noticed more than the physical and cared enough to ask her about it. Even her agent never asked her how she felt. Max traced the welts on Doris's buttocks and then reached for her glass of champagne.

"No. It was not you. There is something going on in the office, and I cannot put my finger on it."

"Does it have to do with Priscilla?" Each time Max touched a welt, the sting would re-awaken a desire deep in Doris's body.

"Yes. Well, part of it does."

Doris rolled over onto her stomach.

"Well then, let me help you with that part of it." She buried her head in the lap of the police lieutenant and soon the two women crossed the line into another world.

Sometimes in life, it is better to be lucky than good. As Case dropped off Priscilla earlier in the day, he noticed that a woman exited from a house at the end of the block. She got into an airport limousine while the driver loaded the luggage into the trunk. Case waited until well after dark, and seeing no activity from inside of the house, picked the lock and broke in. Oddly enough, the house did not have a central station alarm system.

Without turning on the lights, Case quickly searched the house. There were only women's clothes in the master bedroom and no other types of clothes in the other bedrooms. It would appear that the woman Case spotted lived alone. Since she was headed to the airport, Case figured that she would be gone for more than a few days. Case smiled to himself. More lucky than good.

Lying on the floor of the second-floor bedroom, Case had a perfect view of not only the front and side of Priscilla's house, but also the woods to the rear. Using an infrared detector, Case panned the area. He picked up the heat signature of what appeared to be a body lying prone in the woods on the north side of the house.

Without taking his eyes off the area, Case turned off the detector, made a note of the location of the contact, and then reached for his binoculars. He studied every inch of the area of the infrared contact. He had to admit that the subject was good. He did not spot him until his third pass over the area.

Once you find it, the tell-tale sign seems to stick out like a puzzle piece in the wrong spot. Case followed the leaf patters until he found a shadow that was more rounded than any of the others. It turned out that it was the head of the contact resting against a leaf. Case did not see him before, so he must have just shifted his position when Case panned the area. More lucky than good.

Case disregarded the patrol car sitting in front of Priscilla's house. There was no way that officer could see anything other than the front door to the house. The contact in the woods would have to be the guy who spooked her the other night. So now there were only two things to think about. When was this guy going to make his move, and how was he going to stop him? Jack let the questions bounce off the walls as he made himself comfortable. It was going to be a long night.

CHAPTER TWENTY-NINE

The Eyes awoke feeling calmer than they had felt in a very long time. He looked at the mural and smiled. Today was the day. Today was the day he would complete his work. The male would try to challenge him for the beast, but that was okay. He would not win. He would vanquish the male and then the beast would be his.

He thought about it for a long time. The beast would be his. He would have her. He would own her. He would make her do all of the things she had done before, and maybe others. This time, though, she would not leave him. He would have his way with her. And then he would add her to the mural.

The thoughts made him erect. He welcomed the feeling. He imagined her joining with him, and he felt himself inside of her. What is a beast but something wild and free? That is what she is, and that is what he is. Now it is time for them to meet and mate again.

Max marched into the squad room with fire in her eyes.

"BLAIR! RUSS! MY OFFICE! RIGHT NOW!" The two detectives jumped up from their desks and followed in the wake of their commanding officer.

Once inside the office, Max dropped a copy of the Star Ledger on her desk and then faced the window. She was so angry, she could not look at the detectives. For if she did, and her assumptions were proven correct, all hell would break loose.

"Do either of you know anything about that?!"

Blair and Russ looked at the paper. They noticed that there was a small column on the front page with the headline, "Break in the case of the serial killer." Blair picked up the paper and started to read the article while Russ cleared his throat.

"I'm sorry, Max. I do not know anything about that. Blair, do you…?"

Blair held up one finger. After a few minutes, she shook her head.

"There is not a lot in this piece. It just states that the case is narrowed down to a few key suspects and that…"

"I did not ask you what it said. I can read, detective. I asked if you knew anything about it. Meaning just in case that is not clear to you, how did it get there in the first damn place?"

Blair held fast.

"No, Max. I do not know how it got there."

Max turned from the window to face her charges. She stood with her hands on her waist. The pose stretched her blouse across her breasts and made her look even more intimidating.

"You guys are up to something on this case. I know it. If I find out that this press leak is in any way connected to either one of you or both of you, so help me God, you will wish you never thought of whatever hair brained scheme you've got cooked up. Now get back to work."

Max Stout watched as the two detectives turned and left her office. Then she turned back to the window and let a smile form on her face. That article was the clue she was waiting for. Now she would bet 100 bucks that her two detectives were laying a trap for this pervert scumbag that they were chasing. She was certain of it. With the evidence that they collected, it would be the same thing she would do. Max picked up her phone and dialed the extension of the lieutenant in charge of the department garage.

Trap Martin backed the white van into the driveway of 917 Quaker Street. On his drive by the day before, he noticed that it looked like no one was home at this address. Trap checked with the local newspaper delivery service and confirmed that the resident of the house had her paper stopped for the next ten days. Trap made a note in his expense journal that the information had cost him 200 bucks, which was double what he actually paid. Without a receipt, he expected his bill to be cut by the accounting department at the Fund, so Trap felt no remorse in protecting himself.

Trap made a production out of taking a floor waxer out of the rear of the van and moving it to the back of the house. He then took out mops and buckets, and again, went to the rear of the house. On the third trip, Trap went into the rear of the van but never came out.

He positioned himself in front of the video monitors, audio recorders, and broadcast scanners that made up the surveillance equipment in the van. Using the joy stick, Trap moved the video camera hidden in the front grill of the van until he had a clear view of Priscilla's house. He would have the ability to zoom in on the front or the side of the house, as well as take still digital pictures of anything he deemed suspicious. Had it been a night job, he could have raised the black antenna pole with the long-range microphone attached to it and recorded ambient sounds from within the house. But for now, Trap sat back, opened the refrigerator, popped open a can of beer, and let himself earn $250 an hour, plus expenses.

Case awoke at the sound of doors slamming just below him. He kept his breathing even at the sight of the van in front of the house. Training will trump panic any day. Case lay still, listening for any signs of movement inside the house. Hearing no one inside, he looked out at the front of the house. He noticed the van with the name of the cleaning service and a man in overalls moving equipment to the rear of the house. Jack watched the man come and go and then checked the rear of the house. He found the equipment sitting on the rear patio with a tarp over it. The man who put it there had no intention of bringing the equipment inside the house. That left only one explanation.

The Eyes saw the front page of the paper as he filled his vehicle with gas. He was drawn to the article about the serial killer. Keeping his expression even, he studied the article more than read it. He read between the lines, behind the words, and into every possible meaning of what was written. After he had looked at the article from every conceivable angle, his purpose became even more clear.

Priscilla picked up the newspaper from her front step, scanned the front page, and stopped dead in her tracks. Terror paralyzed her for longer than she cared to be seen outside. Priscilla freed herself, and once inside, made sure both locks were engaged on all of the doors.

She sat down at the kitchen table and read the article as calmly as any worm would while dangling on the end of a hook.

"So, this is it. This is the plan. Flush him out with a phony article." Priscilla pretended to read the rest of the paper as she weighed her options.

"Do I stay and hope that the cavalry will come in and prevent me from getting my throat cut? Or do I run?" Priscilla suddenly recalled the photos of the victims and the manner in which they died. Even through closed eyes, she could not escape the horrifying scenes. She realized she only had one option. Priscilla went to her bedroom, opened the top drawer of her nightstand, and reached for the pistol that was lying there. Before she picked up the .38 caliber revolver, she froze.

"He was right, damn him. Jack said I had the ability to shoot someone to defend myself, and he was right."

Priscilla picked up the pistol, checked the cylinder, and then spent some time holding the gun in her hand. After she felt comfortable with the pistol, she placed it in her pants pocket.

"Thank you, Mr. Case, for at least having that much faith in me." Then Priscilla made a vow that wherever she went, she would be prepared to defend herself.

"Okay. Thanks. I owe you one." Max hung up the phone and gave a sideways glance in the direction of the squad room. There was one other angle that she had to check out just to be on the safe side. She was about to pick up the handset when her cell phone rang. Max checked the number, perched herself on the edge of her desk, and swiped right.

"I was just about to call you. I have to speak with your mother."

"That will be difficult. Mother had a stroke last night. We are in route to the hospital now. I was calling to let you know that I will be out of touch for a while."

Max stood up.

"How bad?"

Doris Whittington's voice was an odd mixture of calm and tension.

"It's hard to say. She has had strokes before, and every time we think we are going to lose her, she bounces back. I'll know more once they get the monitors on her."

Max walked over to her office door.

"What hospital are you going to?" She balanced the cell phone between her jaw and shoulder as she reached for her coat.

"Mercy Hospital in Warren."

Max slipped into her suit coat.

"I'll see you in a little while." She ended the call, put her service weapon in her briefcase, and then signed herself out for the day.

Russ Matson watched Max leave the office and then made a production out of looking for his cigarettes. Two minutes later, as he left the building, Blair went into one of the more secluded places in the building. The second-floor ladies bathroom. Within five minutes, modern satellite communications connected three cell phones.

"Trap, this is Blair. Russ? Are you on?" Blair kept the door to the stall open in order to keep an eye on who might be coming in.

"Yes, Blair. I'm on."

"You owe me a rematch, old man. I don't like being sucker punched."

"Knock it off, Trap. Are you on site?" Blair took command and put an edge on her voice. Her career was on the line here and there was no time for juvenile, macho bullshit.

"Yeah, I'm in position. She just came out to get the paper. It looks like she saw the article from the look on her face. There's no sign of your perp." Trap popped a Fig Newton in his mouth and washed it down with a swig from a can of Budweiser.

Blair was running through scenarios in her head.

"How about her boyfriend, Case? Any sign of him?"

"Nope." Trap could not have cared less.

"By the way, the clock starts at seven."

"Okay. Stay on it. I will relieve you at 12, and Russ will take over at six. If you see anything before then, don't make any moves. Give us a call immediately. Are we clear on that?"

"Don't get yourself all wet, sis. I know the drill." Trap took another pull from the beer can.

"Watch your mouth, kid." Russ saw himself taking a black jack to this punk's head.

"Fuck you, pop." Trap ended the call with the thought of breaking the old cop's nose.

Russ Matson put his phone back in his pocket and helped himself to another cigarette. He had seen too much to get riled by some kid feeling his oats. There were more important things to think about. Halfway through his smoke, Russ took out his phone and dialed Maggie's number at the office.

Max threw her briefcase in the trunk of her car and took off. She would not need a weapon where she was going. She punched in "Mercy Hospital, Warren, New Jersey" into the GPS system, slapped the red light on the roof, and backed out of the parking lot. By the time she got to the first traffic light, the directions to the hospital appeared on the screen.

If she had to, if someone put a gun to her head, Max could not explain how or why Doris Whittington became a priority in her life. Love and affection were not emotions that Max Stout was familiar or comfortable with. But right now, all she knew and all she felt was that she had to be there for Doris. Max let that thought hang in the air as her car sped toward Mercy Hospital.

"Be there for Doris." Max then asked herself the obvious question, "Who was ever been there for you?" It did not matter. Doris needs you, even though she would never say it. And you know that you want to be there for her, even if you have trouble admitting it to yourself. Those thoughts were the things that money cannot buy.

Just as Max was entering the highway, her cell phone rang. She checked the number and made a face. This was the last person she wanted to talk to. Max hit the "talk" button on the radio console as she merged into the middle lane.

"Yes?" Max did not try to hide the edge in her voice.

"We seem a little testy today. Are you okay?" The genderless voice reeked with half hearted concern.

Max checked her blind spot and then smoothly moved into the left lane.

"I've got something on my mind."

"Well, maybe this will ease your mind or anything else in your body that might be tense. I have a date for you." The genderless tone was pleasant enough.

"I can't take it right now." Max fought hard to concentrate on where she was going, and more importantly, why.

"This client will pay double the going rate, and they asked for you specifically. Tell me when you will be available."

Instead of waiting for the slow pokes to get out of her way, Max went around them. "Listen, I am in the middle of a few things and I do not know when I will be available. I just can't do it right now."

That was not the answer the genderless voice wanted to hear.

"No, you listen. There has never been a time in the past when you were not available, so I am not buying that. This is the third time you have turned down a date that I arranged for you. There is a pattern here, and I do not like it. I told you when we started I only deal with professionals. This is the first and last time I will say this. Turn me down again and we're done. Oh, and let me remind you of something, this world that we play in is a very, very small world. Not everyone can keep a secret. Sometimes things slip out. Whoever you are giving it away to had better be worth it." The genderless voice was gone and the silence that remained was deafening.

Max let her mind go blank as she cut off a tractor trailer, crossed two lanes of traffic, and accelerated onto Route 78 West. With the maneuver complete, Max recalled the last statement of her phone conversation.

"Whoever you are giving it away to had better be worth it." Max thought about what was just said. She thought about what was said before that and what was done before that and about all the others who did not give a damn about her as long as they were being satisfied. Max exited the highway as smoothly as she exited that train of thought.

"Who gives a fuck!"

The Eyes went back to his room. The land had changed a little bit. He would need other things for this hunt. The Eyes thought about the challenge and welcomed it. It was good that this one would be different. She deserved to be different.

Blair Collins signed herself out to the field shortly after 11 and left the squad room. When she was half way to her destination, she slipped into the restroom of a gas station and changed into white coveralls, white sneakers, and a white painters cap that she turned backwards. In her beat-up Toyota, she looked like a college student off to make a few bucks on the side. She stopped one more time at a pizzeria to pick up the final prop for her cover. Blair approached the van, knocked on the rear door, and appeared to be anyone's helper out to pick up lunch.

Trap opened the back door to the van and immediately went for the pizza box.

"You're early. How'd you know I was hungry?"

Blair took in the electronic wizardry and was impressed.

"Nice set up you have here. It must have cost a few bucks." Blair shook her head as she watched Trap wolf down the slice of pizza.

"Only the best for The Whittington Trust. Besides, this thing has already paid for itself after the first couple of jobs we used it on." Trap held up a finger as he reached for another slice of pizza.

"And by the way, the rate still stands. $250 an hour for me and $250 for the van."

Blair kept her laughter to herself as she wiped the corners of her mouth with a napkin. It will only be a matter of time before this guy spills something on himself. Seeing him around all of this electronic gear is like watching a bull in a china shop.

"Is there anything going on?" Blair took notice of the beer cans as she sipped on her Diet Coke.

"Look here." Trap pointed to a monitor with a grey screen. Using the mouse, he opened a file on the computer and then began a slide show on the monitor. Blair watched the uniformed officer in the patrol car go from reading the paper, to talking on his cell phone, to scanning the pages of the latest girlie magazine, to taking a quick five-minute nap. Trap hit the escape button and helped himself to another slice of pizza.

"I have always said being a town cop around here is like being on welfare."

Blair felt a pang of embarrassment.

"After seeing that, I cannot disagree with you. Do you mind if I borrow that disc?"

"Yeah. I do mind. I'm being paid to watch Ms. Hot-To-Trot. If I.A.D. wants to catch one of their guys goofing off, have them call me. I'll give them a good rate." Trap popped the tab on another can of beer and put the disc in the pocket of his coveralls.

Blair was struck by the comment and looked at Mr. Martin in a new light. Perhaps he wasn't as sleazy as he appeared to be. One cop not wanting to rat on another cop. Or maybe it was all about the money. Either way, a sleaze ball would have given her the disc or sold it to her. He did neither. That told her there was more to this guy than what he allows you to see.

"Trap, how'd you get hooked up with high rollers like the Whittington's?"

Trap Martin froze as he reached for his fourth slice of pizza. The question caught him off guard. Not even Gineen asked him that. He took a minute to study the young cop, dropped the slice back into the box, and leaned back on the stool in front of the console.

"I had a little surveillance business a few years ago. Nothing spectacular. Mostly workmen's comp insurance work and maybe the odd matrimonial. I had been on the county force but ran into a beef. The deal was if I quit, the parents of the punk who suffered brain damage would not sue. I held out for a P.I. ticket and a license to carry and got both. Doris Whittington needed some help with something. She called around and got my name. We met, I signed on, then one thing led to another and I was offered a staff job as head of security." Trap smiled to himself as he recalled his first visit to the Wayfarer Motel.

"It's a cozy set up actually. The firm is set up as a wholly owned subsidiary of the trust. Through their contacts, the Whittington's set me up with enough clients so that I turn a profit at the end of the year. In between, I am on call to Doris and her mother."

Blair drained her can of Diet Coke.

"And that includes keeping tabs on Priscilla in the hopes that you can pin her to the murder of her husband?"

Trap started to reach for a can of beer and then thought better of it.

"You're half right."

Max skidded into a handicapped parking space, left the red light on the roof of her car, placed her police placard on the dashboard, and then walked quickly into the hospital. With a little help from the security guard at the front door, she located the Intensive Care Unit without too much trouble. She stopped short when she saw Doris standing at the end of the hall, looking out of the window. Max had never seen anyone look more alone. Despite the nurses and the doctors and the announcements on the public address system, there she stood on an island by herself.

"Hi." Max was surprised at the sound of her own voice. It was hardly above a whisper.

Doris turned to Max. There was a smile and a warmth in her eyes that Max had not seen before in any human being.

"Max! Thank you for coming. I am glad you are here."

There are customs and protocols in all walks of life. There are greetings and ways of conveying messages that would go completely unnoticed to those who are not of any one particular culture. Doris turned back to the window and placed her hand on the sill. Max stood next to Doris and placed her hand over hers. With that small gesture, all the strength and comfort one human being could give passed to another.

"What do you mean, 'half right?'" The twist in the story spiked her appetite, and she reached for the last remaining slice of pizza.

Trap checked the monitors as he thought about what he would say next. Maybe it was what they were truly after that made everything else seem trivial, or maybe it was the innocence of this young cop, or maybe he was just getting tired of carrying around something that should have been put to bed long ago.

Whatever it was that helped Trap to finally decide to tell the truth about a lie that he was helping to perpetuate would suddenly have to wait. The cell phone in the pocket of the overalls vibrated.

"Just a sec."

A voice, although soft, shattered the thoughts of the two women.

"Excuse me, Ms. Whittington?"

"Yes, doctor?" The older man who seemed more than competent looked from Doris to Max and then back to Doris.

"Doctor, you may speak freely. This is a very dear friend of mine."

"We have called your mother's cardiologist, and he is on his way. However, I must advise you that the news is not good. It appears as though her heart is very weak, and she has some cerebral bleeding. With her advanced age, there is not much we can do. I am sorry."

Where most would have collapsed with news of that sort, Doris Whittington seemed to gain strength from it. Her back straightened, she held her head high, and clasped her hands in front of her.

"How much time, doctor?"

"Well, the tests are inconclusive, and there are other factors to be considered. I really would like to consult with Mrs. Whittington's personal cardiologist before I…"

Max did not have a position in this community, nor was she on the board of this hospital. Max opened her jacket to reveal the badge that was pinned to the waistband of her skirt.

"Just answer the fucking question, doc!"

The doctor first looked at Max with the resentment of someone being forced to do something against his will, then turned to Doris with new found compassion.

"In my estimations, she has less than 24 hours, Ms. Whittington. I am sorry."

As the doctor took his leave, Doris closed her eyes and listened to her mother's voice in the back of her head.

"Doris, you are a Whittington. Stand up straight. There will be no crying. We have prepared for this and you know what to do. Now see to it."

Doris turned to Max.

"There are a number of things that I have to do. I would like you to stay here with me, but I will understand if you have to go. But before I get tied up in the things I have to attend to, you had said that you wanted to ask my mother something. What is it that you wanted to ask her?"

Max suddenly felt aware of her own presence. The one question that she wanted to ask did not seem to matter. A part of her felt that she should not have come.

"You have a lot to deal with, Doris. It can wait."

Doris looked at Max with an honest look of love.

"When we are together like this, Max, in private, please call me by the name that you gave me the first time that we were together. It means a lot to me."

In the course of her very private career, Max gave a lot of names to a lot of people. But none of them ever said those words to her. She made the decision without thinking about it. She was through with her agent. She was through with her professional life. She had money in the bank and property and clothes, but all of that could not hold a candle to what she just got here without lifting a finger.

"Puppy, there was an article in the paper this morning about the series of murders that we think Priscilla may be connected with. Did your mother have anything to do with that?"

"No, Max. After dinner, mother went straight to her room. She spoke to no one but me for the remainder of the night."

Max gripped her friend's hand.

"Thanks. That is all I needed to know."

"Will you be leaving now?"

"No. I will stay with you for as long as you need me."

Doris took a deep breath. In order to share a burden, she had to unload another one. "Then there is something that you need to know about this case and this family. I will not have time to tell you later, and you might find it important, so I might as well tell you now."

CHAPTER THIRTY

"Thanks. I'll call you later." Trap ended the call and looked into the middle distance for a long minute.

"Well, it looks like things are going to be changing around here." Trap read the puzzled look on Blair's face and thought it made her look sexy. He fought an urge to pull her close.

"The old girl had a stroke last night. She is in the hospital and it does not look good. By the way, your boss is with my boss at the hospital." Trap pictured the two women in bed together with very little trouble at all.

Blair recalled the time when the two women first met and then dismissed the thought. There were more important things to think about.

"Trap, you were just about to tell me something about Priscilla."

"Oh, yeah. Well, to make a long story short, I know Priscilla did not kill her husband."

Blair was incredulous.

"Then why…?"

Trap looked at his watch, decided he was off the clock, and helped himself to another beer.

"Listen, when the rich want to believe something, and they are willing to pay you well to help them believe it, you help them believe it."

Blair let the logic of the statement rattle around in her head.

"Well then, who killed him?"

Trap took a swig from his beer can.

"I guess it will not make much difference now. With the old girl gone, it won't much matter if the story leaks out. Besides, if it does get out, I will know that it came from you and then I can blow the lid on your little bullshit entrapment scheme here."

Trap gave Blair the knowing look of a man sitting with all the aces. Blair conceded. "Okay, it's a deal. You have my word on it."

Trap Martin smiled and nodded his head. He thought about shaking hands, but the physical contact with this woman in his slightly drunken state might not end up very well. The side of him that was still sober reminded the drunken side of his brain that this woman carried a gun.

"Word got back to Doris that her brother, William, was gay. It's my guess that Priscilla didn't know this when she married the guy, but you would have to ask her about that.

William was pretty good about keeping his other life quiet, but he was starting to get careless. There were threats of blackmail and extortion. He had been seen in some places and was known to have been with some of the local talent. Doris needed confirmation. That's when she contacted me. I started working him and confirmed that he was hanging and banging with the boys. That did not take long since William was none too subtle. So, for shits and giggles, I started working his wife, Priscilla. She's a good-looking woman. I wanted to know what she was all about. I came to find out that while her husband was out doing the boys, Priscilla was doing his business partner. I made my report to Doris, who hid it from her mother. Doris confronted William with the evidence of both he and his wife's play time. She had me sit in on the meeting as a witness. Doris told him about the blackmail threats and that, as Counsel to the Trust, she had to do whatever she needed to do to protect the Trust. If need be, she was prepared to file an injunction barring him from using the family name in his business. His private life would then become a matter of public record. After that, she would be forced to report his activities to their mother. William went from pale to bright red. He knew that would lead to him being cut out of all of the benefits that came with the Whittington name, including his portion of a very healthy trust fund. Quite frankly, I think if I had not been there, ole William would have tried to beat the shit out of his sister. Me, personally, I would have put 20 on Doris.

"Well, that night, William went looking for his wife. He found Priscilla and his business partner in the conference room doing the nasty. He busted in on them, pulled out a gun, and began to struggle with his partner. When the gun went off, his partner lay dead. William then put the gun to his head and killed himself."

"That's incredible. Why would he kill himself?"

Trap laughed in the same manner that a knowing parent would laugh at an innocent child. "Sweetheart, you really do need to get out more. William was sweet on his partner but was rebuffed on countless occasions. When he heard that the man he wanted was porking his wife and had been for quite some time, he meant to take out his competition. That would be Priscilla, in case you're having trouble keeping up with me. He did not figure that his business partner would try to defend her and end up dying for her. After William killed himself and before the police got there, I swept his house and found his journal. The man kept very good notes."

Blair held the can of soda in mid-air and looked back into the past.

"So that's why Priscilla was so distraught?"

"Yep. Paraffin tests, finger prints, and autopsy reports confirmed that William killed his partner and then himself. There was no evidence to link Priscilla to the deaths of the two men. Victoria used her political connections to have the evidenced suppressed to prevent a scandal. She then had some stories planted to suggest that Priscilla was involved in the death of her son. Initially, it was to protect the family name, but then Victoria actually began to believe her own lie. It then became my full-time job to find some dirt on Priscilla so that she could be put away."

Blair shook her head.

"I still don't understand why you went after Priscilla the way that you did and said the things that you said to her. If you knew she was innocent, why do you ride her like you do?"

Trap gave Blair a sideways glance.

"Ride her? Now there's a statement." The muscles in Trap's face hardened as he gritted his teeth in disgust.

"Listen, I've known a thousand 'Priscilla's.' I am around them every day. Ride her?" Trap pursed his lips and spit in the direction of Priscilla's house.

"You know what that rich bitch in there represents? She is all of the women who have looked down on a guy like me. She is all of the women who wanted me to fuck them in the middle of the night but would not even look at me in the middle of the day. That rich bitch is like all of the other rich bitches that I have known in my life who think that men are nothing more than toys for their amusement or a means for their support."

Trap paused and then leaned in towards Blair to stress his point.

"I'll tell you something else. My secretary is also my lady. She used to sell her body on the street before she met me. That's right. Anytime, anywhere, to anyone, as long as the price was right. When I offered her a job and took her off the street, she accepted me the way I am. Without hesitation. No questions asked. As far as I am concerned, she is more of a lady and more of an honest woman than the crazy bitch inside that house. Does that answer your question?"

Blair turned her head, stared off into the middle distance, and thought about what she was just told. She was suddenly propelled back to her college days and the times where she hooked up with a boy for the night only to dispose of him the next day. She did not think twice about it, after all, they both got what they wanted. Or so she thought. Now she was hearing the story from another perspective, one that she had never considered before. Blair wondered, of all the guys she took advantage of, how many of them felt like Trap. Her shoulders trembled slightly as she felt a chill go down her spine.

Trap's sober side became alert.

"Snap out of it, sis. We've got movement."

Max listened intently to every word. It never ceased to amaze her how the world of the rich contained so many more facets than the world of the poor.

"So that is why there was no ongoing investigation or referral to a cold case squad?"

Doris looked at her friend and lover and was thankful for the chance to relieve herself of this burden.

"Yes. For a while, I tried to talk my mother out of this foolish witch hunt, but she would not hear of it. She was obsessed with the thought that Priscilla had something to do with my brother's death."

"What would you have done if Trap was able to produce something?"

Doris smiled.

"Actually, I was hoping that he would have been able to produce something. Anything." Max's puzzled look reinforced Doris's need to smile.

"I knew the truth. I knew anything that she could be arrested for in connection with my brother's death would be circumstantial. If Priscilla had been arrested for this crime, secretly I was prepared to hire the best criminal attorney to defend her. Max, it would have been the first time in my life that I would have gone against the wishes of my mother, and I was so looking forward to that."

Max looked at Doris and wondered what it must have been like to be trapped in your own body. To be a prisoner, not because of any crime you committed or political stand that you took, but to be a prisoner simply because you were born.

Max took Doris's hand in hers.

"I have to tell you that there may be a chance that this information may come out. Cases like these are complex, and I cannot control…"

Doris looked her friend and lover in the eye.

"It's okay, Max. I understand." Doris bit her lower lip.

"Max? Do you think…"

Max looked around and then made a motion in the direction of the ladies room.

"Come on."

Case saw the movement along the fence that separated Priscilla's property from that of her neighbors to the rear. The figure was moving along the opposite side of the fence in the neighbor's back yard. Case looked ahead and saw the entrance point. There was a tree at the end of the fence run. It would be a simple matter to use the limbs to swing up and over the fence. Ten feet from the landing point was the back door to Priscilla's house. Case sprung to his feet and made a move to the door.

Blair fixed her eyes on the screen. At first, she could not see anything but then she noticed the movement of the plants and bushes on the other side of the fence. Blair hit the speed dial on her cell phone and instantly was connected to Russ Matson.

"Our boy's in play. Get over here, but do not come into the block. I don't want to spook him. No, there is no sign of the boyfriend yet, but I have a feeling he's close. I'll see you in a few minutes." Blair ended the call and returned her attention to the monitor.

Trap and Blair continued to watch the screen when they saw movement inside of the police cruiser stationed in front of the Whittington home. Within a minute, the vehicle came to life, made a neat U-turn, and left the block.

Blair was furious.

"Where the hell is he going?!"

Trap looked at his watch and dropped the corners of his mouth.

"It's lunch time. He's gotta meet the boys." Blair was incredulous.

Trap took off the clumsy overalls and threw them into a corner of the van. He reached for his nine-millimeter pistol, worked the slide to chamber a round, and then gave Blair a cynical look.

"Okay, sis, now what's your plan?"

Through the slats in the fence, The Eyes took in the area in front of the lair of the beast. It was as it should be and as it was every time he had been there. Peaceful. The white van had not been there before, but it was just some guy waxing floors in the house across the street. Nothing to worry about. The Eyes knew that the male was close, but that was okay. He was prepared for that. Soon, the beast would be his. Soon, he would have her.

Russ Matson threw out his coffee with one hand and started his car with the other. Thirty-five years on the force told him that this case was not going to drag on too long. He patted himself on the back for being right. With his game face on, he dropped the Crown Victoria into gear and took off. He would go in, Code Three. No lights, no siren. There was no need to announce that the cavalry was coming.

Suddenly, Priscilla felt like she was living in a fish bowl. She paced back and forth between the kitchen and the family room. She could not sit still. Eyes were everywhere. Threats were everywhere. She did not feel safe, even in her own house. She imagined herself pulling her gun out and shooting at something only to find out that it was not the person who was after her.

With the gun in her pocket, Priscilla felt like a fraud. Did she really have the guts to kill someone? Could she really take a life in order to save a life? There was a part of her that wanted Jack Case to be there. She knew that he had killed before. If it came to that, he would kill to protect her. Priscilla was certain of that. But there was a part of her that was glad that he was not. She was responsible for this horror. She created this monster. She needed to be the one to end it. Priscilla thought for a moment and then felt a knot form in her stomach.

"Or have it end with me."

Blair never took her eyes from the screen as she slipped out of her pair of coveralls. She did keep on the sneakers. They were much better to run in than the shoes that matched her suit.

Trap slipped the weapon into his custom-made shoulder rig and then leaned back in his seat. He knew damn well that this kid cop did not have a plan, and that was fine with him. He secretly figured that a serial murderer and rapist in this area would generate a lot of calls for security reviews and personal protection assignments. Trap saw his earning potential rise exponentially and that was good enough for him.

Case froze in place just before he opened the door. He let his mind work while the rest of his body went into neutral. If he ran out there, he would blow this thing wide open. The van had to be a surveillance vehicle. There was no other explanation for it. If the police were not charging in there, they must know something. Case backed away from the door while his mind continued to work all options.

The matronly woman at the sink did not seem to notice the two women as they entered the ladies restroom. Doris went immediately to a vacant stall while Max stopped at a mirror and pretended to fix her hair. Just as the matronly woman turned to leave, Max's cell phone rang, "Stout."

"The Crown Vic we assigned to Matson is on the move. It looks like he is heading toward the address you asked me to look out for."

"Thanks. There will be a bottle of scotch waiting for you at the end of your tour tomorrow." Max put her cellphone back in her purse and then turned toward the stall. Doris was rebuttoning her blouse as she came out.

"You have to go."

"Yes." Max did not want to leave her, but she knew she had to.

Doris gave a game smile.

"That's okay. There are a dozen things that I have to attend to myself. I was just hoping for a few minutes. That's all."

Max kissed the woman softly on the lips.

"I will be back as soon as this is done. I promise you that, Puppy."

Doris looked at the woman who she now knew she was deeply in love with. "Max?"

Detective Lieutenant Maxine Stout turned to face the only person to steal her heart. "Yes?"

"Please be careful."

In all her years of law enforcement, in all her years of life, despite all of the people she knew and brought pleasure to in one way or another or protected in one way or another, no one, not anyone, ever said those three words to her. Max Stout looked at the woman who she had not known for very long, but now knew she would never be without, and smiled.

"I will." She turned and hurried from the bathroom, feeling as though she was now cloaked in armor.

Blair wished that Russ Matson was there with her. He would know what to do. But this was her case and she had to come up with something, fast. Blair ran through what she knew about the case, where the victims were found, and what they looked like. She had all of the forensic information logged in her head, and she went through it as though she were a fifth grader going through flip cards.

"Do you need some help here, sis, or what?" Trap was getting impatient. Something was about to happen here and he wanted in. Being the detective that brought down a serial killer would be good for business. On the other hand, being the detective that sat by and did nothing would be disastrous.

Blair shot the private eye a menacing look.

"He is not going to kill her in the house. We know that he takes the victims someplace else before he kills them. And we do not know if he made us or not. I am guessing that he did not. So here is what we do. We wait. Right now, all we have is breaking and entering and possibly menacing. I am certain that he will come out with Priscilla. When that happens, we have kidnap. Matson should be here by the time that happens. We follow him from a distance, call in air support, and at the appropriate time, we take him down. All we need to do is catch him with the knife and the woman. Then we can wrap this thing up."

Trap shook his head and began to shut down his equipment.

"Sis, your plan is lame. You forgot one small item that just might come back to haunt you some dark and stormy night."

Blair locked eyes with Trap Martin and felt like she was looking at a cobra that was about to strike.

"There is a housekeeper in there that doesn't have anything to do with that crazy bitch, her hair brained idea of fun, or the lunatic that is running around slashing up women in the name of love. That housekeeper is an innocent by-stander who just may lose her life because you chose to do nothing. I'm sorry. I don't know the woman and probably would not like her if I did. But she doesn't deserve to die simply because we chose to sit around here and wait."

Blair felt powerless. He was right. She did forget about the housekeeper.

"What are you going to do?"

Trap took off his jacket, put back on the coveralls, and then made a move toward the door of the van.

"Watch and learn, sis. Watch and learn."

CHAPTER THIRTY-ONE

Max walked quickly through the hospital, her mind running through a check list of things to be done. By the time she reached her car, she was on auto-pilot. Max popped the trunk, took her weapon out of her brief case, and changed into flat shoes without any wasted motion. She started the car, punched in the address to the Whittington house, and then strapped on her weapon while she studied the route. With only the slightest look in her rearview mirror, Max Stout backed out of the parking space and then peeled rubber out of the parking lot. GPS told her it would take 15 minutes to reach her destination. She told GPS she would be there in ten.

Russ Matson had been doing this too long to get excited. There had been too many times in the past when he thought they had some creep only to have fate intervene and the bum gets away. Experience taught him that there was as much of a chance of this going right as there was of it going wrong. The only edge he had was to keep his wits about him and not let his emotions get the better of him. He thought about Maggie and noticed that his body relaxed at the very mention of her name.

The Eyes froze at the base of the tree. He held his breath and became one with everything around him. He listened. He smelled. He calmed his body and let his skin feel the breeze. Everything was as it should be. The time was right.

Blair fought back panic. In the close confines of the van, she would lose a physical encounter. She had to find some way to keep Trap in here until Russ was on site.

"Wait."

Trap gave the diminutive police officer a look of annoyance.

"What?"

"You can't go over there like that. Your shoes are wrong. You would get made in a second. Where's your hat and your mask? If you are sanding and waxing, you would be wearing those things. Do you have that kind of stuff around?"

Trap changed his expression to mild respect. He thought about it for a minute and had to admit that the little pair of panties had a point. He pulled out his handkerchief, tied it around his nose and mouth, and then pulled it down to give the effect that he had just taken it off. Trap did not have a hat in the van, but he determined that his hair was unkempt enough that it would not be an issue. He had to admit, though, that she was right about the shoes. While they were hardly polished, they were a dead giveaway.

Blair was proud of her quick mind. She was able to buy a few minutes for Russ to get on site. Once that was done, she would call Max, fill her in on the details, and then have her request the support that they needed. That they were operating outside of department policy was something she would deal with later. Success underscores the saying that it is easier to beg forgiveness than to ask for permission.

Trap looked around the van. He made a mental note to keep an old pair of boots on hand just for times like these. He spotted a bottle of white out and an idea popped into his head.

Case leaned against the wall and took stock of the situation. If he saw the movement, then whoever was in the van must have seen it, too. That would mean that reinforcements are on the way. That's good. Now, what is the one thing that could go wrong here? Case came to a quick conclusion. He opened the back door to the house, took a diagonal route out of sight of anyone, and made it to his car unseen.

Trap uncapped the bottle of correcting fluid, hesitated for a minute, and then began to sprinkle the fluid over his shoes. He liked these shoes, but he had to admit that they were probably as old as this stupid cop, and he was due for a new pair. In very little time, they looked like beat up work shoes.

"There. How's that?"

Blair nodded grudgingly as she put her coveralls back on.

"It might work." She had an idea about what Trap had in mind.

Trap accepted the compliment and noted the feeling that it gave him.

"Let's go." Blair turned her baseball cap backwards, slipped her revolver in the pocket of her coveralls, and followed the private detective out the rear of the van.

The Eyes were up and over the fence with ease and at the rear door to the house in less than ten seconds. He crouched low and took the Koomba stick from his belt. A West African weapon, the Koomba is a curved club with a ball at the end. It is made of hard wood. In some areas, a steel blade is inserted in the inner curve so that the club can also be used as a knife. In the hands of an experienced warrior, it can be a most dangerous weapon.

The Eyes caught the scent of the beast through the open window. He felt his body harden with anticipation. He fought back the urge. There would be time enough later. And this one, he would savor. This one would be the best.

Priscilla sat in the family room, her back to the open window, flipping channels mindlessly. She was usually the hunter, now she was being hunted. She did not want to be there. She wanted to run. She wanted to find this sick bastard herself and blow his brains out. She wanted to turn back time and not be who she was. Priscilla threw the remote control at the television as the tears flowed from her eyes. She held her head in her hands as her fear poured out of her.

From a distance, Trap and Blair did look like a workman and his young helper.

"Okay, sis, when we get to the door, I do the talking. If he has the knife, you have enough on him to get a conviction for the other crimes."

"Why are you doing this, Trap? You hate this woman."

"I've got a business to run, sis. My picture in the paper is worth 100 re-ferrals. You can't buy this kind of advertising. Hell, I might just give the State a discount on my bill if this thing plays out right."

Blair was just about to say something when a blood curdling scream broke the silence in this high-end ghost town. The two detectives drew their weapons and sprinted to the house. Trap spoke first.

"You take the back. I'm going in the front." Blair made her way to the side of the house, stopping at the corner to check her sight line.

Estrella Ortega had just come out of her room when she saw what looked like a man come through the kitchen door. He was hunched over, using his hands and feet to walk like the apes she had seen on television. He had hair all over his body and was dressed only in shorts. When he turned on her, she screamed again.

In what seemed like one step, The Eyes moved toward her and hit her with the ball end of the Koomba stick. Estrella fell unconscious at his feet.

Trap placed all of his weight behind the sole of his shoe. The door gave way far too easily in a house of this value. Trap gave a look of familiar disgust at the cheap construction and then caught a glimpse of a gun being pointed at him. He ducked just in time.

Priscilla heard the scream from the rear of the house and then heard the front door collapse. She pulled her own gun and made up her mind to shoot the first thing she saw. She fired at the man in her sights but never saw the man that came up behind her.

Again, the Koomba stick struck, only this time not as hard. Priscilla was stunned but still conscience as her gun fell from her hand.

"STOP! POLICE!" Blair took a combat stance in the doorway to the fam-ily room.

What the academy does not teach is that not everyone will stop when a police officer says stop. Blair hesitated when The Eyes scooped up Priscilla and then came at her with the Koomba stick. Before she could get off a shot, she was rendered unconscious with a vicious blow to the head.

Private investigators are not normally shot at. Trap checked for holes before he stuck his head up again. He aimed his weapon just in time to see the man they were after head through the door to the garage with Priscilla draped over his shoulder. Trap hesitated when he noticed the two women lying on the floor before he turned his attention to the garage.

The Eyes grabbed the keys to the Corvette from the hook on the wall, hit the door opener, and threw his prize into the passenger seat. The car came to life instantly. The Eyes backed the car out of the garage and then expertly went from reverse to second gear, burning rubber in the process.

The Crown Victoria and the BMW hit the block just as the Corvette came out of the garage. The near collision of the two cars gave the Corvette just the opening it needed to escape. Before the two police vehicles came to a stop, another black car seemed to come out of nowhere and give chase.

Max was out of her car first as Russ Matson turned his vehicle around. Trap filled her in from long distance as he rushed to Russ's car.

"You've got two down inside!" Trap jerked open the door to the unmarked police car. "Let's go, Pop."

CHAPTER THIRTY-TWO

With her weapon out, Max cleared the room. Satisfied that there was no threat, she dialed the confidential number for police dispatch, gave her name, rank, and shield number, called for back-up officers, an ambulance, and a helicopter to be deployed. Max then holstered her weapon and inspected the results of a good collar gone wrong.

The one thing that could have gone wrong did go wrong. Case took no pride in being right. He concentrated on the black Corvette and what he would have to do to prevent another murder.

Russ went Code One. Lights and siren. He had the two cars in view and was gaining ground fast. Lucky for them that at this time of the day, there was not much traffic out. Russ figured the guy in the black Porsche had to be Case. He wondered how long he had been on site and how he was connected to this mess. Most men would not have become involved.

Trap put on his seatbelt and started to speak. Russ Matson froze him with a quick look. "Whatever you've got to say, kid, save it. My partner is down and I am chasing a serial murderer. I really don't have time for you."

The comment hit Trap like a punch to the jaw. The old guy was right. Whatever it was that he had to say or wanted to say would wait.

The Eyes could not help himself. He took one hand off the wheel and felt her skin. It was as he remembered it. He reached inside Priscilla's blouse and touched her breast, recalling the naked image of it in his mind. With the

309

wind washing over him and his prize beside him, The Eyes became suddenly at peace. In time he would lose those who gave chase. In time she would be his again.

Case kept his mind blank. This was a time when you reacted, you did not think. He concentrated on the car in front of him and only slightly cared about the one behind him.

Max checked the pulse of both women. Convinced that the pulse rate was strong enough for their injuries not to be a concern, she turned her attention to more important matters. Max dialed a number on her cell phone as she pointed out the two women to the para-medics as they entered the house.

"Patch me into Car Five!" While waiting for the electronic connection, Max walked outside. Now would not be the time to lose a cell phone signal.

Russ Matson looked at the car radio for a full second before picking up the microphone.

"Car Five, go."

"Russ, this is Max. I've got a bird on the way. What's the situation?"

"The suspect is in a black Corvette with a hostage, traveling west bound. It looks like he is headed for 78. There is another black sports car following him, probably the guy from the office. I'm about a minute behind them in a silver C.V. I've got limited visual. The private dick is with me."

"Roger that, Russ. Stay on it. Once the helicopter is in position, we will plan an intercept."

"Max, how's Blair?"

"She's fine. Just a bump on the head, which is not as bad as what she will get from me when this is over. Max out."

The Eyes suddenly hung a sharp right turn, ran through a red light, and accelerated up the hill. Case missed a delivery truck by less than an inch as he stayed with the Corvette. Matson was not so lucky. He screeched to a halt and then pounded the wheel in disgust.

Trap took a look around.

"Back up, turn around, and then take the next left." Matson took the suggestion, and soon they were on a parallel route to the Corvette.

The speed of the car and the force of the wind were enough to bring Priscilla back to consciousness. She looked at the driver of her car and was horrified. His hair was long and matted. He had a full beard that was equally unkempt and matted. He wore no shirt and very short pants and every inch of his body was covered in hair. He was grotesque. How she could have possibly spent time with this monster was unthinkable to her.

Priscilla put her mind to work. She had to get him to stop the car. She had to get away. Priscilla glanced in the mirror on her side of the car. Case was right behind them. She felt herself relax. If Case was near, she had a chance.

There were many things that Priscilla had done in a car for fun but now this was different. Now her life depended on it. She had to think. Priscilla reached for the key to the ignition. He caught her hand and slapped her in what seemed like on motion. Priscilla fell back into the seat.

Priscilla felt her mind working.

"Okay, that did not work. Now what?" She thought back to their time together and the things that she did that he liked. Desperate, and despite her repulsion, Priscilla began to fondle the man that held her captive. She rubbed his arms and neck and then proceeded to go lower. What she did not count on was his response. Instead of being receptive, The Eyes pushed her away. There would be time enough for that later.

Max switched to the radio in one of the patrol cars that responded to the back up call. "Air One, do you have a visual?"

"Roger that, Lieutenant. A black Corvette at high speed with a black Porsche in pursuit."

"What about a silver C.V.?" Max stared into the middle distance, forming the image in her mind.

"We've got him on a parallel street not far behind."

"Nice work, Air One. Can you give me an intercept vector?"

The voice of the helicopter pilot was calm professionalism. He had witnessed many of these hot pursuits and seen more than one turn out not so good.

"Negative. Your suspect is coming up on the entrance to 287. Once he hits that highway, it will be hard to intercept without causing a major pile up."

"Roger that, Air One. Stay with him."

The parallel route turned out to be a short cut. Matson made up for lost time and hit the entrance to the freeway just as the other two vehicles did. As he reached for the radio mic, Russ nodded at the younger man in appreciation.

"Car Five, come in."

"Go ahead, Russ."

"I've got a close visual on both cars now. We are north bound on 287. Any ideas?"

Max concentrated on a map of the area.

"Stay close, Russ. I've got a bird up. We will try to figure out an intercept vector. Max out."

Russ relaxed with the news that a helicopter was monitoring this thing. Now all he had to do was stay close.

The Eyes heard the helicopter. He had anticipated this. He increased his speed to over 90 miles and hour and watched as the two cars behind him increased as well. He then jammed on his brakes, down shifted, and pulled on the hand brake while turning the wheel to his left, he then accelerated through the U-turn. The Corvette exited the space reserved for "Official Use Only" and entered the southbound lanes at only a slightly lower speed. Caught by surprise, both Case and Russ Matson sped past the turn.

The Eyes glanced in the rearview mirror, smiled, and then slid across three lanes of traffic. He exited at the next ramp and then slowed along the tree lined road.

"Air One to Lt. Stout. We lost your suspect."

"YOU WHAT?!"

If the pilot was fazed, his voice did not reveal it.

"He hung a U, then took the exit at Holly Road. There is heavy tree cover on that road for the next few miles. I can't see a thing from up here.

Max hit the dash board in disgust.

"Stay with it Air One. Russ, where are you?"

"Looking for the next U-turn. When we get it, we will head back to Holly Road."

"Okay, Stay on it."

Holly Road ran into another town. Max called the chief in that town, reported the activity, and asked them to stand by for assistance. She looked up just in time to see Blair and Priscilla's housekeeper being wheeled out on separate stretchers.

Max made her way over to the stretchers and motioned for them to stop the one bearing Blair.

"How's the head?" Max found her tone to be surprisingly soft.

"It hurts. I guess I screwed up, huh?"

"Yeah, you did. But we have an idea of where he is. I am pretty sure we will get him."

Blair tried to sit up.

"I want to stay here."

Max put a hand on her chest.

"Not possible. I need you checked out." Max nodded to the paramedic, who continued with the stretcher to the ambulance. Once the vehicle left, Max commandeered a hand unit, started her own car, and then left for the vicinity of Holly Road. There was nothing left to be done here.

CHAPTER THIRTY-THREE

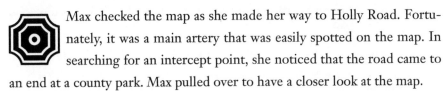Max checked the map as she made her way to Holly Road. Fortunately, it was a main artery that was easily spotted on the map. In searching for an intercept point, she noticed that the road came to an end at a county park. Max pulled over to have a closer look at the map.

Case allowed training that he had not used in a long time to kick in. Just as the Corvette sped past him, he made his own U-turn over the grass median and into the southbound lane just in time to see the Corvette exit at Holly Road.

Trap saw the Porsche cut across the median and turned to Russ Matson. Before he could say anything, Russ did the exact same thing. Crown Victoria's are not known for their handling. Due to the size and weight of the vehicle, the U-turn across the grass did not go as well. The vehicle became stuck in the median.

Trap slammed his hand on the dashboard.

"Goddamn it, Pop. Who taught you how to drive?"

"Fuck you, sonny. Get out and push." Russ dropped the car into reverse. With less weight, the vehicle rolled backwards. Russ then shifted into a low gear. With an assist from Trap, Russ brought the Crown Victoria back on solid ground. With Trap back in the passenger seat, they were back in the chase.

There is a fork at the end of the Holly Road exit. The Eyes went to the right, cut around a car waiting to merge into traffic, just missing an oncoming delivery truck. The Eyes up shifted and floored the accelerator. He had his beast. It was time to mate. He had to get her to the mating grounds. He had to have her. He pushed the car faster.

At the speed that they were travelling, Priscilla became acutely aware that any attempt to stop this car would only end up in them both being killed. Case was near. She knew that he would not let her die.

Case reached the Holly Road exit but not in time to see which way the Corvette went. He had two choices. Right or left? He went right.

Trap holstered his weapon and sat back in his seat. They had lost time in the chase and the helicopter had lost visual. Trap looked into the near future and saw his publicity fading from view, the money from his big payday flying out the window, and this grey-haired bitch lying on the ground with her throat cut. He waved at noting in the air and thought to himself, "This was too good to be true anyway."

Russ Matson reached the Holly Road and did not think twice. He turned right and prayed that he guessed correctly.

"Lt. Stout to Air One."

"Air One, go."

"The profile on our suspect is that he takes his victims into the woods. There is a park at the end of Holly Road. Go to that park, hover, and report if you see the subject vehicle."

"Roger that. Air One out."

Max then called the local police chief.

"Chief, I have a hot pursuit in the direction of the Holly Road park. The subject vehicle is a black Corvette, one male driver with a female passenger. The pursuit vehicles are a civilian black Porsche and a silver department Crown Vic. Set up an intercept at the entrance to the park. I am in route in a white BMW."

The voice on the other end of the line was worried.

"Um, this may take some time. Most of my boys are on their lunch break, but I will see who I can round up."

Max could not believe what she just heard. It was only extreme self-control that kept her from wasting time to curse out this washed out old coot. Instead she just hung up, jumped into her car, and headed in the direction of Holly Road Park.

Case weaved in and out of traffic. Soon, he had the Corvette in view. The phrase "more lucky than good" flashed in his mind and he smiled despite the chase that he was involved in. He had no idea what he would do once he caught up to the 'Vette, but he resigned himself to cross that bridge when he got to it.

The Eyes knew that the mating ground was not far away. As the thoughts of mating with the beast became alive in his mind, he looked in the rearview mirror and saw his male challenger coming up behind him. This was good. The Eyes touched the handle of his Koomba stick. He would use it to defeat the male. That would make the mating better. The thoughts of the combat, the victory, and then the mating excited him. He pushed the car even faster.

The entrance to Holly Road Park appeared just around the bend in the road. There was no gate, just a wide, open driveway into the parking area. What was present were parked cars, children running and playing, and adults looking to enjoy the park on a sunny afternoon. That a high-speed chase of a suspected serial killer was headed their way was not on anyone's mind.

"Air One to Lt. Stout."

"Go for Stout."

"We've got your vehicle headed toward the park at a high rate of speed. There are people in the park that might be at risk. What do you want us to do?"

Max rolled her eyes at the fact that she would have to tell the helicopter crew what to do, but she knew it was procedure for them to ask for directions.

"Use your P.A. to warn the civilians and then come down as low as you can get to stop the vehicle. I am in route and should be on site within 15 minutes."

"Roger that. Air One out."

Max knew that with the ordering of the State Police helicopter, her Chief would have been notified and monitoring the transmissions. There was no need to call this in. Still, she could not help but wonder what fate would be waiting for her when this was all over. The brass was in the dark about this operation. If there was extensive property damage, or worse yet, if a civilian was injured or killed, there would be hell to pay.

Max shook her head as she imagined the ultimate downside of all of this, but then she dropped the corners of her mouth and looked on the bright side. She had Doris. With that thought, the worst did not look so bad at all.

CHAPTER THIRTY-FOUR

The helicopter pilot was well trained in crowd control measures. To swoop down fast would result in a panic and a stampede which would cause more harm than good. Instead he made his decent slowly and spoke through the P.A. system in a conversational manner.

"Good morning, ladies and gentlemen. Please clear the parking area immediately. Please move to the picnic area. Thank you." He repeated the message three times as he watched the civilians run away from the parking lot.

In less than a minute, the Corvette sped uncontrollably into the parking area. Had the announcement not been made, it was a certainty that several men, women, and children would have been injured, if not killed. The helicopter pilot did not have time to pat himself on the back. He was searching for a spot to land and block the path of the car.

The Eyes thumped his chest and laughed as the other beasts ran from him. As well they should. He was mighty and about to claim his mate. He had no time for them. The giant bird above him did not worry him. He would avoid this threat and have his reward. With that, The Eyes weaved in and around the parked cars and made it to the far end of the parking lot. There was no way the helicopter could block his path without damaging several cars.

"Air One to Stout."

"Go for Stout."

"Your vehicle is at the north end of the parking lot. The woods are just beyond that. If he makes it in there, I'll lose him."

"Stay on station, Air One. Let me know when he is in the woods."

"Roger that. Air One out."

Max picked up the handset.

"Stout to Car Five."

"Car Five, go."

"Russ, he is at the north end of the parking lot of Holly Road Park. The woods are just beyond that. I don't care what you have to do but just get there. I am about ten minutes behind you."

"Roger that. Car Five out."

Trap sat up in his seat. He now saw the name of his firm in the newspapers and an upgrade to his office. He saw a vacation with Gineen at one of those high-end European resorts, and he would finally get a chance to be done with Doris and her "I Am Better Than You" attitude.

Trap smiled, took out his weapon, and said to himself, "There is a God."

Case followed the Corvette into the park. But instead of weaving in and around the parked cars, he anticipated where the 'Vette was headed and took the longer but faster route around the perimeter of the lot. Both cars skidded to a stop at the path leading into the woods.

Case opened the glove box of the Porsche and retrieved his .40 caliber Glock pistol. Despite the fact that it had been ten years since he held the gun, the custom grips felt natural in his hands. Case took a defensive position behind the Porsche and aimed his weapon at the driver of the Corvette.

The Eyes did not consider the male. He had reached the mating ground and would mate with the Beast. If the male challenged him, he would defeat him.

Before the car stopped, Priscilla unbuckled her seat belt. When the car stopped moving, she opened the passenger side door and jumped out. She saw Case and her only thought was to run to him as fast as she could. Her mistake was not looking to see where her captor was.

The Eyes grabbed his Koomba stick and hopped over the rear of the Corvette. He intercepted Priscilla as she tried to make her way around the rear of the vehicle. With his weapon in his right hand, The Eyes grabbed Priscilla, threw her over his left shoulder, and made his way into the woods on a dead run.

The sight of the grotesque human being carrying Priscilla was enough to make Case hold his fire. In his day, Case had been a deadly shot, but that was ten years ago. He could not take a chance of hitting Priscilla trying to bring this thing down. To his eye, the figure looked more like an animal than a human but that was of no consequence. Case stuck his pistol in his belt and took off after them.

Russ and Trap arrived at the park just in time to see Case in pursuit of the suspect and Priscilla. Always the cop first, Russ picked up the microphone. Trap looked at the older man with disgust and took off in pursuit.

"Car Five to Stout."

"Go for Stout."

"We have visual on the suspect and are in foot pursuit. He has the woman with him." Russ dropped the microphone without waiting for a response.

Max heard the static return to the line and knew that Russ was not waiting for any further orders, nor was he interested in anything she had to say. Max saw the entrance to the park just ahead and the helicopter hovering just above. Instead of going into the park, she pulled over onto the road shoulder and grabbed the handset.

"Stout to Air One."

"Go for Air One."

"I am beside the white beammer just outside of the park. Pick me up."

"Roger that." In less than a minute, Max was inside the helicopter and over the park.

The pilot handed Max a pair of binoculars, but she refused them.

"Just go in a straight line from where the path enters the woods. Let's see where that goes." The pilot nodded in agreement, and staying as low as possible, flew straight from where the path entered the woods.

Even with his burden, The Eyes were faster than his pursuers. He managed to put some distance between them in a very short span of time. He found the spot that he was looking for well into the woods. It was a plush, grassy clearing with shade provided by an old oak tree well off the path. It was perfect for the mating. He threw Priscilla to the ground and began to stomp and jump around her. He raised his Koomba stick over his head and grunted as if he were celebrating something. When she tried to run, The Eyes grabbed her by her hair and pulled her back to the ground.

Priscilla lay on the ground, frozen with a fear she had never known. Jumping and grunting around her was a monster that she had a hand in creating. That thought only heightened her fear. How could she have been responsible for this "thing." The word rang in her head and scared her even more. As she looked up, the strange weapon in his hand only made him more frightening. What would she do? How could she defend herself? Priscilla looked around but saw nothing that could help her. Vowing that she would not allow herself to be taken, she did the only thing she could do. Priscilla attacked.

Once the "Thing" got close to her, Priscilla leapt to her feet, screamed, and rammed her head into the torso of The Eyes. The unexpected attack took The Eyes by surprise. He was knocked off his feet and as he hit the ground, his Koomba stick flew out of his hands.

That was all the opening Priscilla needed. She regained her balance and took off in the direction from which they came. She had only one thought. Get to Jack.

Once they left the path, Jack Case had no idea where they were. This guy was fast and he was an expert at moving through the woods. There were none of the telltale signs that someone being chased would leave. Rather than proceed deeper in the wrong direction, Case stopped and listened for something, anything, that would reveal where they might be. Then he heard the scream.

"JACK!"

Russ Matson cursed the cigarettes that he smoked. He cursed the day, 50 years ago, that he started that habit, and he cursed the last cigarette that he smoked. Thirty yards into the chase, Russ had to stop and lean against a tree. His heart was pumping so fast, he thought that it was going to burst out of his shirt. He had no idea where he was or, worse yet, where his suspect was. Russ admonished himself.

"Chase? This isn't a chase. Hell, I can't even walk fast. What the fuck am I doing out here?"

Russ cursed himself anew for the last sentence. He was in pursuit of a serial killer who injured his partner and killed more than a dozen women. He's a cop and this is where he is supposed to be.

"Now pull yourself together and get after it." Russ Matson pushed himself away from the tree and took off in the direction of the scream.

Case arrived at the point in the woods where Priscilla broke through the brush. Had he not caught her by the waist, she would have ran right past him. Once she saw his face and felt his arms around her, Priscilla held onto Case with all of her strength. It was only the grunting and the thrashing of the brush that brought her back to reality. This was not over yet.

The Eyes found them. He found her, who would run away from him, and the male who would dare take his mate. Now it was time. He would defeat the male and have her.

Trap hated the woods. He hated insects. He hated trees and plants. And he hated the shit that always seemed to get in his eyes anytime he had to follow anyone into the woods. Many was the matrimonial case where the guy was too cheap to go to a motel and ended up in some secluded spot in the woods on a blanket with his dick out and some dumb bitch sucking it. More than once Trap accidently stepped on a branch, giving away his location and having some dude throw rocks at him. He hated the woods.

Now here he is, running through the woods, chasing some serial killer who happens to have in his possession the one woman on the face of the earth that he despises. Trap stopped for a minute to catch his breath and looked heavenward.

"You're a funny guy!" Then he heard the scream.

Case pushed Priscilla behind him and faced off against the hairy human in front of him with the strange weapon. Case pulled his gun, but before he could aim, his adversary swung the ball end of the weapon and knocked the gun from his hand. Case made a note that this "thing" was faster than he looked. This was not going to be easy.

The training that Case survived (you did not learn combat, you survived it) came back to him in a flash. He bent his knees, stayed on his toes and on balance, and watched his opponent's torso. That is the source of the power and is a dead giveaway as to where the strike will come from. Case remained still and only moved to keep his opponent in front of him.

The Eyes felt his mouth go dry, as they do before a kill. This male had his mate. He must be defeated. The Eyes showed the knife edge of his Koomba stick. He lunged at the male, swung, and missed. That was all that Case had to see.

The attack was crude and lacked training. Case prepared for the next attack. When it came, Case moved inside and hit his opponent in the area just above the solar plexus. Before he could recover, Case stepped to the side and hit him with a rabbit punch to the kidneys. Then Case grabbed his right arm, extended it, and then disarmed the man by dislocating his elbow. Finally, Case hit the man with the ball end of his own Koomba weapon, rendering him unconscious. Ten seconds later, Trap Martin burst through the brush with his weapon drawn.

"Damn! I really wanted to shoot that son of a bitch. Fuck, man, you took all the fun out of this!" Trap holstered his weapon and muttered to himself, "I ran all this way for nothing."

A good five minutes later, Russ Matson huffed and puffed his way to the rest of the group. He threw a pair of handcuffs to Trap.

"Do me a favor and cuff that piece of shit."

"Matson to Stout."

"Go for Stout."

"Lieutenant, we are about 500 yards into the woods. The suspect is injured and in custody. We're going to need a bus for him, but everyone else is okay."

"Who took him down?"

Russ looked at the group.

"The P.I. took him down. Did a nice job of it, too. He could have killed him, and it would have been justified, but he didn't."

"Okay. I'm on my way."

Trap looked at Russ and smiled.

"Okay, Pop. We're even. No need for a rematch."

Russ just nodded his head. He turned to Case.

"You okay?"

"Yeah. Thanks for not mentioning me. It would have been awkward."

"Yeah, I kind of figured that. Besides, the kid here could use the publicity."

Case nodded his head.

"Yeah." He then took Priscilla by the hand as he picked up his gun.

"Let's get out of here."

CHAPTER THIRTY-FIVE

Due to her concussion, Detective Blair Collins was out for a week on medical leave. When she walked into the squad room, she was met with a standing ovation. It is one thing to get a commendation from your commanding officer. It is quite another thing to receive a commendation from your peers. Ask any cop and they will tell you that the latter beats the shit out of the former. Blair smiled sheepishly, accepted congratulatory handshakes, and then sought refuge in the office of Lt. Max Stout.

"Max, where's Russ? I did not see him in the squad room."

Working a tough case and then achieving a good result brings partners close in a way most non-police types will never be able to understand. Max knew that the news she had to deliver would hit this young detective hard, but there was no other way to deliver it. Max rose from behind her desk and stood facing Blair.

"Blair, Russ is in the hospital. He has stage two lung cancer. It was discovered just after the chase into the woods. It is inoperable. He gave me these when I went to see him yesterday." Max opened her desk drawer and showed Blair Russ's service weapon and shield.

"He's not coming back."

Blair felt the tears forming in her eyes.

"Not even to say good-bye?"

"Nope. He will be getting out of the hospital tomorrow. He told me that when he gets out, he is leaving on a long vacation with a certain lady friend that he met not too long ago. He did not say when he would return." Max paused for a minute, pursed her lips, and then looked directly at the young detective.

"Russ said to tell you that you are a hell of a cop and a better friend than he could have ever imagined. It is the best thing that one cop can tell another. I hope you never forget that."

Blair pulled herself together and only concentrated on the last thing she was told.

"Thanks, Max. I won't forget it."

With the news about Russ and the last comment that was made, Blair felt like she was standing in a block of cement. She was at a loss as to where to go or what to do. Max walked past her to retrieve her coat and service weapon from behind the office door.

"Blair, listen, if you would like to put down roots and work for me instead of bouncing around the state, I am sure that Russ would be honored if you carried his badge. Think about it and get back to me before the end of the week. Now, if you will excuse me, I have a funeral to attend to." With that, Max stepped past her and out the door.

Blair returned to her cubicle and proceeded to take down all of the pictures of all of the deceased women that had become a part of her life. She was not sure if she would stay and work for Max or return to the State Police. But this case had taught her that life was better lived one day at a time. That she would remember.

THE END

CPSIA information can be obtained
at www.ICGtesting.com
Printed in the USA
BVHW041044191219
567196BV00011B/651/P

9 781644 268322